A. B. (Augustus Bozzi) Granville, Paulina Bozzi Granville

Autobiography of A.B. Granville

Being eighty-eight Years of the Life of a Physician - Vol. II

A. B. (Augustus Bozzi) Granville, Paulina Bozzi Granville

Autobiography of A.B. Granville
Being eighty-eight Years of the Life of a Physician - Vol. II

ISBN/EAN: 9783337111465

Printed in Europe, USA, Canada, Australia, Japan

Cover: Foto ©Raphael Reischuk / pixelio.de

More available books at **www.hansebooks.com**

A. B. GRANVILLE,

M.D., F.R.S.,—BEING

EIGHTY-EIGHT YEARS OF THE LIFE OF A PHYSICIAN

*WHO PRACTISED HIS PROFESSION IN
ITALY, GREECE, TURKEY, SPAIN, PORTUGAL, THE WEST
INDIES, RUSSIA, GERMANY, FRANCE, AND ENGLAND.*

EDITED,

WITH A BRIEF ACCOUNT OF THE LAST YEARS OF HIS LIFE,
BY HIS YOUNGEST DAUGHTER,

PAULINA B. GRANVILLE.

VOL. II.

HENRY S. KING & CO.
65 CORNHILL, & 12 PATERNOSTER ROW, LONDON.
1874.

CONTENTS.

CHAPTER I.

1814.

CHAPTER II.

1814—15.

CHAPTER III.

1815.

CHAPTER IV.

1815—16.

CHAPTER V.

1816.

CHAPTER VI.

1816—17.

CHAPTER VII.

1817.

CHAPTER VIII.

1817.

CHAPTER IX.

1817—18.

CHAPTER XV.

1824—28.

CHAPTER XVI.

1826—33.

CHAPTER XVII.

1826—55.

CHAPTER XVIII.

1827—35.

CHAPTER XIX.

1833—48.

CHAPTER XX.

1835—54.

CHAPTER XXI.

1838—48.

CHAPTER XXII.

1849.

CHAPTER XXIII.

AUTOBIOGRAPHY

OF

DR. A. B. GRANVILLE.

CHAPTER I.

1814.

Again in Paris—The Jardin des Plantes—Gay-Lussac's lectures on iodine—
Baron Cuvier—Relaxations of the capital—Baron Humboldt—Baron de
Staël—Comte de Méjean—How Prince Eugène was betrayed—Infamy
of General Pino—*Soirée* at Lady Westmoreland's—The Chamber of
Deputies—Monsieur Pinchon—Return to England.

TEN days after leaving Turin I found myself, on the 22nd
of August, in Paris, in the Hôtel de Saxe, Faubourg Saint-
Germain, which I was destined to revisit two or three years
later for some months, when my professional and scientific
pursuits would render it necessary that I should live in
what was then denominated the Pays Latin. Here I had
a very neat and well-furnished apartment, for which I paid
only forty francs a month. I mention this trifling circumstance to contrast it with what one is now obliged to pay
for house room.

My first care was to write a long letter to my wife, and
another to Mr. Hamilton, announcing my proximate return
to England. My brother-in-law, Monsieur de Lafolie,
came to see me, and I may say that a great part of the
time during my stay in Paris was spent with him and my
eldest sister Julia, his wife. They had a house in the Bois
de Vincennes, whence he used to come to Paris every

morning to attend at his office, as "Conservateur des Monuments Français," and to discharge the functions likewise of assistant-secretary to the Prefect de la Seine. I took advantage of his perfect knowledge of the city to go in his company to deliver the letters of introduction I had brought from Italy. A few of the visits which most interested me I repeated alone; among them were those to the laboratory of Chevreul, at the Jardin des Plantes. This chemist was then building up his well-gained reputation as a first-class analyst by his chemical researches for first principles, such as the astringent in vegetables, and *sur les corps gras*, the world being indebted to him for numerous useful applications of chemistry to the most important wants and requisites of life.

In the same vast scientific establishment of the Jardin des Plantes, I visited, during one of his brilliant lectures on iodine, Professor Gay-Lussac, who rose very soon to a well-deserved and high renown. He was kind enough to give me a small portion of that substance, just discovered, in a glass tube, which I was the first to exhibit at one of the meetings of the Royal Society in London, handing it over to Doctor Wollaston, who had heard of the discovery, but had never seen the violet vapour emitted by the substance when slightly heated.

I happened to meet an Italian physician, Doctor Pantóli, settled in Paris, who knew almost all the most eminent professors of the Ecole de Médecine and principal hospitals, and through him I was presently made personally known to Dubois, Dupuytren, and Pelletan, three first-rate surgeons.

To a man devoted to science, nothing can be more interesting than a visit to the Jardin des Plantes when you have the good fortune to be known to the professor or curators, gentlemen, every one of them, remarkable for their politeness in receiving strangers and treating their pupils. Such was my fortune with regard to Baron Cuvier, in whose gallery, all his own work, I spent several hours under his own eyes, and assisted by his ready and eloquent dissertations. I shall have to say much more of this most eminent naturalist in a later part of my history, and must dismiss him for the present, together with many of the *sommités* in the world of letters, science, and the fine arts with whom I became acquainted, and of whom I shall record the names and acquirements before I leave Paris.

I will not pretend to make my readers believe that I did nothing more while in this gay metropolis than attend to science and literature. No. I took also my full share of pleasure, accompanying my sister, alone or with her husband, to the opera or the Théâtre Français, where we enjoyed that naïve and exquisite real representation of human life on the stage which French actresses alone can so perfectly exhibit. As for the Opéra Comique, it is *caviare* to me, but the Italian Opera was fortunately open at the Académie Royale de Musique, Rue de Richelieu, and there I enjoyed often that famous quartet "Chi mai può la vita amar" in the "Così fan tutte."

Frenchmen are proverbially courteous and well bred; they are even punctilious in etiquette. I was not surprised, therefore, at receiving calls from many of the persons on whom I had left my letters of introduction. Among them I felt much pleased and honoured when on my servant announcing Monsieur le Baron de Humboldt, I beheld before me the great naturalist, traveller, and explorer, at whose residence in Paris I had left a letter of introduction from Lady Davy at Geneva. He impressed me at once as a person of very agreeable manners, with a most amiable mode of address, and great facility of expressing his wonderfully copious and learned opinions on many subjects familiar to himself and highly interesting to his hearers. He was above the middle height, with a well-shaped head, a square forehead, and a look which in any accomplished and handsome woman would be called *malin*, but in a philosopher like Humboldt would be more correctly considered as the scintillation of genius, with the additional pleasantness of its being invariably accompanied with a smile. It is unnecessary to say that he spoke French perfectly, and with less of the Germanic twang than the best-bred Prussians even are not free from, as was the case with the late Baron Goltz, for example, the great diplomatist.

Baron Humboldt kindly offered to introduce me to the principal French *savants*, with most of whom he was on friendly terms, and I may say companionship, as, for instance, with Arago and Gay-Lussac, but I stated that to most of them I was already personally known. While speaking of his travels in South America, I inquired of him in Spanish whether he had found the mountaineers on the Cordilleras speak the same language as the dwellers in the oak forests of Xalapa, or in the plateau of Caxamarca and in Cuba.

Referring to my own political explorations in Italy, and having had occasion in my replies to mention the name of my friend Sir Robert Wilson, and the part he had to act in that country, he assured me that often on conversing with the Emperor of Russia, he found that General Wilson had considerable influence with that sovereign, by whom he was much esteemed; so much so, he added, that " a note from him to Alexander, inveighing against the slave trade—that abominable disgrace of society, of which I have been a most distressed witness in South America—would have a great effect in the determination of the question soon to be brought before the public.

" With regard to your native country, my dear doctor, I sympathize with you. I have been in many parts of it, and I agree with you that it needs only a spark to set it all in flames. Should King Murat, as he is on his way now, under the pretence of uniting his troops with those of the allies, offer the command of them to his imperial brother-in-law, and conjointly proceed to combine their own with the armies of the father-in-law, who would then tell the Congress at Vienna what your Minister for Foreign Affairs, Lord Castlereagh, said at Chatillon, ' Messieurs, le Conseil est remis à une autre époque'? What then?" *

The next visitor I received was also from the north of Europe, a man of title, but of very different calibre, the young Baron de Staël. He came by desire' of his mother, who had given me a letter for him when I left Geneva, to inquire if he could in any way serve me, and I learned some intelligence of his mother's state of health. He was exceedingly courteous. He had never accompanied her in any of her journeys either in Italy or Germany, and did not see her until her return to Paris in the year of my interview with him. As a pupil of Auguste Schlegel, he could hardly help becoming a well-informed man of ability. His turn of mind was towards agriculture, which science he had cultivated assiduously; and he was also a strenuous opponent of the slave trade. We also know that he became in time the editor of both Necker's and his mother's works, a task which he accomplished just before his death at Coppet, in November, 1827, ten years after his mother's death. The baron offered to introduce me into a very fashionable house of that day, that of an Italian lady married to an English gentleman many years settled in Paris, and who was supposed to be an *amie intime* of Benevento. I thanked him, and excused myself.

On the following Monday (29th), after spending the Sunday with my sister and brother-in-law, I came into

---

* Singular coincidence with my own fantastical surmise mentioned in a letter to Mr. Hamilton, quoted in the first volume.

Paris, and accompanied by him I paid a visit to the Comte de Méjean, who for many years had filled the post of prime minister and chancellor to Prince Eugène, Vice-King of Italy. He had the good fortune to possess the best as well as the most comprehensive collection of the Aldine editions, from the very first specimen issued by the elder Aldus; a collection said to be unique and almost priceless. Of course we talked much of Italy, and I found him very communicative as well as a pleasing speaker. In his manner and dress he reminded me of the old aristocratic days. He seemed to be on most excellent terms with his former secretary, Monsieur de Lafolie, and we learned from him part of the intrigues that had preluded the recent history of the Italian revolution. He gave us a decree to read, drawn up by the viceroy when he learned that the Emperor Napoleon had abdicated. In his turn the viceroy abdicated likewise, but previously to that act he ordered a provisional government to be installed which should govern the country, without, however, altering the existing laws in any manner until the Electoral College should be assembled extraordinarily to provide for the exigencies of the state, and that in the mean time two deputies should be sent to the Allied Powers to demand the independence of the kingdom of Italy within the limits fixed by the Treaty of Lunéville. This decree of Prince Eugène, which had been placed in the hand of General Pino for publication, was never made public, but the general could not possibly pretend ignorance of it, as Count Alberto Lilla of the provisional government of Milan assured Count Méjean that it had been read at their board, and confided to Pino for promulgation. This general commander-in-chief of the Italian troops, who acted thus treacherously, had received from the viceroy a few days before the abdication the sum of fifty thousand francs, of which Count Méjean possesses the receipt in due form, and the obtaining of which sum was due to Count Méjean's personal intercession with the viceroy, who with the intercessor had taken pity on the embarrassed state of the general's finances.

So far as to the honesty and patriotism of the late heroic commander-in-chief of the Italian Army ; and now for the honesty, candour, and patriotism of the late president of the provisional government, Count Melzi, a nobleman not likely at all events to act traitorously from embarrassed circumstances. This nobleman pretended that he had endeavoured to influence the Electoral College to name the viceroy to the vacant throne after the abdication of his stepfather; but when accused of such an act by the Austrian authorities, he pretended and asserted that he never intended or wished it, and that he had acted by superior orders; whereas the real fact was, as attested by a letter in the possession of Count Méjean from Melzi, that he had solicited the viceroy's authorization *de faire cette démarche.*

Before I continue my narrative, let me stop to inquire of my English readers of the present day, after perusing all .I have set forth concerning the trials, sorrows, and grievances my fatherland has been subjected to by both French and allied powers for many years, after the destruction of all institutions and of a well-regulated society by the one party, paralleled in every respect by the extortions, imprisonments, exile, and persecution of men of letters, science, and philosophers of the other party—the facts now confirmed by the disclosures and authentic documents of Count Méjean—I would inquire whether they do not regret that, when their own government had before them in 1848 the opportunity of helping to bring about the present glorious reality of an Italian kingdom of twenty-five millions of souls (a kingdom whose friendship or the contrary will henceforth be a subject of serious diplomatic consideration) they, their said government, instead of lending a helping hand and sharing in the smallest degree in the glory of having accomplished such an act, preferred rather to turn a deaf ear to the counsellor who had whispered " courage" to Lord Palmerston to help Charles Albert, and hoped for persistency in aiding the bolder measures of Victor Emmanuel? *

On the day following the interesting conversation with the late prime minister of Vice-King Eugène just related, and after despatching some letters and writing my previous day's memoranda, I drove out to return the visit of Baron Humboldt, whom I fortunately found at home and in conversation with Mr. Clarkson, the strenuous advocate of the slaves, who inspired Wilberforce and other marked men by his own zeal in behalf of that persecuted race, in whose interest he had devoted half his fortune. Gay-Lussac entered soon after, and seemed to be very intimate with the baron. I was introduced, and we entered at once upon chemical subjects, I having mentioned to him my attendance at his lecture on iodine two days before. He then stated that since that lecture he had discovered a permanent iodic acid, which acid, according to a letter received from Sir Humphry Davy, dated Rome, February 16th, 1815, I am informed he considers to be a creation of Gay-Lussac's own imagination, as I believe Sir Humphry showed afterwards in a paper sent to the Royal Society.

Our whole party then adjourned to the Salle des Séances at the Institute adjoining the library, open to members and their friends. There was a meeting of the Section of Science going on, and there were present not a few illustrious *savants*, with some of whom I became acquainted.

* I really crave the forgiveness of my readers for this broad allusion to my own two published letters to Viscount Palmerston, " On the Italian Question," 1848. It was then in the power of the British government to bid the Italian kingdom rise and acknowledge its existence to the powerful diplomatic influence of England, rather than at last to bloody victories.

Business was conducted much as at the Royal Society in London. Among the visiting strangers I recognized Mr. König of the British Museum.

In the evening, after dinner at Véry's, I went home to dress, when the young Baron de Staël came to accompany me to Lady Westmoreland's, where I found assembled a number of distinguished guests. In the general company I was not a little surprised to meet Sör of Malaga, who was at that very instant accompanying on the instrument he so delightfully handled, one of the identical Spanish romances of the day, " Accuerdate bien mio," which we had so often tried together years before in his own country. We mutually rejoiced at this fortuitous *rencontre,* and recounted to one another some of our most recent adventures. Later in the evening I accompanied him to his lodgings.

There was another gentleman at Lady Westmoreland's with whom I was acquainted, and who, as Mr. King, was well known in London society under a very expressive sobriquet. I called on him in the Rue de la Paix, where I met Madame Grassini, who, with the free manner and without any ceremony, peculiarly her own, and also with the excuse of being a compatriote, imposed on me the commission of trying to recover for her " a large Indian shawl, worth eighty louis, which that giddy-headed maid of mine has forgotten in my apartment, No. 21, Argyle Street. It is of a chocolate colour, with large branches in the pattern." Of course I promised to do my best.

From her house, where I called next day, I drove to look at a new establishment, " Le Musée des Monuments Français." There I met my brother-in-law, the *conservateur.* It is really a superb establishment, open to visitors on Sundays and Thursdays, and to foreigners every day from 10 A.M. till 4 P.M.

I paid another visit to Baron Humboldt, where I again

met my friend Mr. König, the mineralogist. The baron was all courtesy, and most communicative. He showed us all his works in course of publication, as well as those yet in manuscript which he was preparing for the press. "This baron is really a most extraordinary man; he knows everything, and everything admirably." Such is the opinion I find inserted in my pocket-book, written at the moment.

As I was *en train* for business I presented myself at the Chamber of Deputies at the Palais Bourbon, to observe how the new Bourbonist deputies managed public matters. By sending in my card to one of the deputies with whom I was acquainted, I was soon admitted *under* the gallery of strangers, where I had a full opportunity of taking notice of the sitting, which happened to be rather an interesting one, as a rumour had gone abroad that there might be a change of ministry.

I dined, and went home for letters, and to dress for a *soirée* at Gérard's, the great popular painter of the day, whose full-length portraits of Napoleon in his imperial robes, and of his brother Joseph as King of Spain, similarly attired, have become universally known through some splendid engravings of considerable size. There were not many persons present: I saw Visconti of Milan, the antiquary, and Rovedino of London, who gave me news of the Italian Opera there. To Count and Countess San Antonio of London, who were among the guests, I made my bow. The count felt mortified that in Paris they did not consider him so great a nabob as he was thought to be in Hanover Square. A young French demoiselle, named Deschamps, who was about to come out at the Opéra Français, and the charming Signora Morandi, prima donna seria, were present. " A prima seria " like this at Gérard's, and the like of which there are many others in fashionable houses in Paris, constitutes a wide distinction between the Parisian and the London *beau monde*.

One gentleman I must mention more particularly, who was pointed out to me at Monsieur Gérard's, and that was Monsieur Pinchon, who had resided many years in the United States as French consul, and who had refused to lend or give any money to Jerome Bonaparte when in that country, in consequence of which refusal he had been recalled and much persecuted, until, by one of those whims which were so frequent in Napoleon, he was appointed Minister of Finance of the kingdom of Westphalia, governed by a sovereign to whom he had refused to lend money. Monsieur Pinchon was now Avocat au Conseil. In stature he was a short person with a sickly face and grey hair. He had just published a work against his royal master under the title of " L'Administration de B——," &c. What interested me more, was a short conversation I had with Madame Dubahors, who was in their company, well known as a writer of light articles in various Parisian journals, and who was gifted with much genius and judgment, but old, ugly, and a slovenly dresser. An exceedingly pretty English widow was with her, daughter of Dickinson the engraver, for some time settled in Paris. She was one of the most admired of the company, which was honoured towards the end by the presence of Baron Humboldt.

As I was nearing more and more the date for reaching my English home, I seemed to become more inclined to accept acts of politeness and courtesy from English people, especially old acquaintances. Thus I became inseparable the last two or three days from Captain Rae of the Marines, an old messmate of mine in the *Maidstone* frigate, with Colonel Pallen, and Lieutenant Ramsay of the Guards, whom I had not met for years, and I accepted gladly an invitation to breakfast with the Misses Cockerell, daughters of the architect, at whose house in London I had often visited with Mr. Hamilton, and whose son Robert distinguished himself in his father's profession, to all of whom in the present instance I tried to be of service by escorting them to different places in Paris, acting the part of a cicerone and thus preparing myself to use again the charming language that had become partly rusty.

The first use I made of that language had been to perform the duty of announcing my arrival in Paris to him who had enabled me to proceed to Italy in a semi-official capacity, giving him at the same time a brief "account current " of sums received and expended. Looking to the results, I do not think that any public auditor will decide that so modest a sum of the secret-service money of the Foreign Office as that I spent for services rendered in an important cause can be called in question. The government obtained reliable information, which should have been turned to good account, but was not. They were told that there existed every indication of the probable escape of Napoleon from Elba not long after Christmas, unless England and the other guardian powers looked sharp to prevent it. They did nothing of the sort, and Napoleon flew on the wings of his formidable eagle (a few weeks only after the day predicted) from steeple to steeple from Frejus, until it lighted on the central pavilion of the Tuileries ; veteran companions in arms and new insurrectionists, renegade marshals, and old faithful adherents following in the track of that wonderful triumphal flight.

The first of September, 1814, found me still in Paris, and I lingered a few days longer, seduced by a succession of invitations from *savants* and old English acquaintances, all eager to get some intelligence they could rely upon concerning " *La pauvre Italie*," as they called it. However, I decided at last to go by a new way to England, and willing to investigate every mode of travelling in France, I took my passage in a towing boat on the Seine to Rouen, whence I proceeded in the *coupé* of a vélocifère to Dieppe.

I found my snug little dwelling at Brompton very comfortable, albeit small and *mesquin* after having visited large edifices and dwelt in magnificent palaces in Italy and Paris. But none of those residences contained the treasures I found in my own snuggery—a good wife and two children, all in excellent health, and very happy to embrace me. Equally, and almost as warmly, was I welcomed at Mr. Hamilton's by himself and children. The latter I was glad to find had been put under a writing-master, and were having their elementary arithmetical knowledge cultivated. I think there is one advantage in caligraphy which has escaped attention, and which in my opinion serves as an encouragement to a free and more correct composition. Literary composition which flows freely from the pen is read and pleases the composer as he proceeds; he is encouraged thereby to go on, and expressions follow readily as he reads them. This satisfaction is lost, or is but stintingly vouchsafed, to the writer of a scrawl difficult to be deciphered even by the writer himself without taking extraordinary pains to understand what he has written. Therefore caligraphy is necessary, and also a source of self-gratification.

CHAPTER II.

I was again in London in September, 1814, after a lapse
of three months, at the same post I had filled with sedulous
attention at midsummer, full of vigour, and as eager as at
the first moment to pursue the work I had undertaken, and
fulfil the engagement into which I had entered with certain
wishes and projects concerning the fortunes of my native
land, all of which the lapse of a few weeks had sufficed to
efface from my mind; partly because of their accomplishment in some instances, and partly because of certain
expectations my new experiences had led me to form as to
their ultimate and entire success. During that same brief
space of time, more knowledge of men and circumstances
had accrued to me, and thus far, I may say, I sat down to
my old work a new man.

As my every day's morning occupation according to the
original arrangement left me a number of hours unem-
ployed—a condition my natural temperament could never
brook patiently—I set about to find how to apply to some
useful employment the many leisure hours at my disposal.
I certainly did not require any further medical instruction,
since the test of repeated examinations had declared me
worthy of a membership in the Royal College of Surgeons
of London, formerly the Worshipful Corporate Company of

Barber Surgeons. There was still the College of Physicians I should have to encounter if I wished to practise as a member or licentiate. I would scorn to offer myself as a candidate for public confidence in the capacity of a practising physician, except under the sanction of the ruling medical authorities of the kingdom. True, I possessed a diploma of M.D., but a foreign diploma alone did not entitle the possessor to practise in London; therefore I was perfectly aware of my obligation, and sorry to postpone the needful steps for obtaining the right until such time as I could easily spare the heavy fees demanded on the occasion. "*Expectamus et speramus*," I said to myself. In the mean time, let me apply myself to any pursuit that may turn out profitable both for honour and distinction, as well as for more ordinary worldly advantages. Accordingly, I undertook the lectureship on chemistry in the medical school of St. George's Hospital, held at the old Hunter's Museum in Great Windmill Street. I was succeeding Doctor Davy, agreeably to his brother's wishes as expressed to me at Geneva, and to his own still more earnestly imparted desires made known to me as I have already mentioned.

While in Paris I had received a letter from Sir Humphry Davy in Rome to his brother, in reference to this negotiation, wherein he alluded to a letter I had written to Lady Davy, in which I had occasion to refer to my transaction with her brother-in-law. In acknowledgment of this, she addressed me a courteous reply, which I produce, to show that our accidental meeting at Geneva was not soon erased from memory by the gifted and fair writer :—

"Rome. Nov. 6th, 1814.

" MY DEAR SIR,—Your letter from London to Sir Humphry, by some strange accident reached him two days before that you were so obliging as to write from Paris, which found me, and indeed reached me only yesterday. I have many acknowledgments to make for your recollecting the commission, and I am sure my English taste would have been satisfied by the elegance of your choice had the flowers arrived in time for my admiration. Still, I expect some friendly conveyance may forward them, and at all events your attention claims my thanks. I am not sure that I can renew my forgiveness for your shabby visit to Geneva, since the date of your letter shows me how easily you could have prolonged it.

" I avail myself of the permission you have given Sir Humphry, to enclose under your cover. The letter for my mother contains a paper of some importance. If you should be tempted to deliver it, instead of sending it by the twopenny post, it will procure her and Mr. Farquhar the pleasure of your acquaintance, which I am sure they will thank me for.

" I am glad to be again at rest, after nearly two months' journeying, which was, however, through exquisite scenery at a plenteous season, and with an almost invariable continuance of fine weather. Our winter here promises to be brilliant as to society and talkers, rather than dancers, which will suit a gouty lady best. English are come and coming by dozens, and some worthy to represent the superior advantages of our education and instruction, if, unluckily, their Italian may not weaken the effect of their conversation.

" I have occasional longings for the cleanliness, the carpets, the convenience, the comfort of dear England ; yet, windows open and a bright sun at this season weigh something in the other scale.

" Lucien Bonaparte's ball on Thursday was the best I can mention,—a princely house and full company were to be seen ; but also little gaiety. His seeking a Roman title, and his bearing his honour in striking liveries and forward pomp of manners, shock the Romans, and his vanity must damage what popularity he possessed before. His brother Louis is here likewise; but with modest and unassuming manners seeks no observation, and does not offend. I know not if sickness claimed sympathy, but I liked him far better than the prince and poet.

"I charge you with all that is most kind for Mrs. A. Hamilton,* whose skill and contrivances I wish I possessed, for then one of our numerous rooms here, now all comfortless, might be made supportable. Tell her I have learned to like comfort, but my genius never supplies substitutes where, as in Rome, the reality cannot be obtained.

"Yours sincerely,

"Jane Davy."

As Doctor Davy was no mean authority in chemistry and science generally, I thought it best to prepare my lectures carefully, and to deliver them from a written text instead of orally, as I could have wished to have done. But, before the end of the course, I insensibly got into the latter mode, which seemed so much to the taste of my audience, that at the second series I dismissed entirely the written process. Nor was it a matter of much difficulty for a teacher who, from the circumstances of the times, as regards modern chemistry, had chiefly to confine his instructions to the development of new subjects referable to recent discoveries, with which his foreign travels and intercommunication with foreign professors had made him familiar, such as Volta's pile, chlorine, sodium, hydrocyanic acid, &c.; all of which were perfectly new subjects to the majority of my English auditors.

* Daughter of Sir Walter Farquhar, and mother of the late Bishop of Salisbury : the two ladies were most intimate friends.

I did not, however, expect that in my endeavours to make my hearers familiar with the labours of Sir Humphry Davy concerning the real nature of chlorine, a subject so perfectly new, I should in my own person exhibit how it could produce the actual annihilation of one of the principal senses. I had prepared and carefully collected in the presence of my class, a considerable volume of chlorine gas in a globular glass vessel, intended to show the physical not less than its chemical properties, when the assistant on my right hand had occasion to pass something over to "George" (if any member of my class survives, he will quickly have in his mind's eye the bulky form of poor old George, a laboratory assistant equal in usefulness to Mr. Faraday's honest "Mr. Anderson"), whose fat hands were too clumsily shaped to keep fast hold of the proffered object. It fell into the glass recipient, breaking it, as a matter of course, and releasing the imprisoned gas, which went straight into the nostrils of the lecturer, who thereupon fell like a lump of lead to the ground, alarming not a little the whole class, which happened to be numerous. The first who rushed to my assistance, raised and placed me on a chair, windows were thrown open, cold water was poured on my head, liquid ammonia exposed under my nose, and a glass of brandy poured down my throat; the whole process ending in my recovery—but completely deprived of my sense of smell, which I have never recovered since. Some readers may feel disposed to exclaim, " So much the better for you, doctor, who will have to go through so many unsavoury matters." " True! but how much more shall I not miss the smell of the rose ! "

I shall only add another trifling physiological fact, from its curiosity, and also because I have never been able to explain it to my satisfaction. It was about ten years after the chlorine accident, and of the deprivation of my sense of smell, that driving with my wife towards Harrow, and while passing what were then fields celebrated for carpet beating, but now crowded with houses and streets, I became suddenly sensible of the delicious smell of new hay, which was in the process of being made that day. I pulled up my horse, and remained some time perfectly enchanted with delight (I don't exaggerate) at my recovered sense. We remained nearly an hour motionless, and I drove off towards Harrow, proposing to come back the same way at sunset, hoping to enjoy again the same delicious sensation. In this, however, I was disappointed, nor have I ever enjoyed it since.

As may be supposed, one of my first cares after I was again installed in my own little house in Brompton, was to pay my respects at Kensington Palace. His Royal Highness the Duke of Sussex was pleased to express the pleasure he felt at seeing me returned, and he at once entered into the subject of Italy's wrongs. Mr. Perry of the " Morning Chronicle " had from time to time informed the duke of what was going on in that country, and of the part I had taken in sending home communications for his periodical, which had in fact made the British press the particular organ devoted to the Italian cause, not only by inserting in its columns such articles as were communicated by myself, as for example those under the dates of the 11th and 20th of October, 1814, but also by the able leaders from the clever editor himself, inspired as he was no doubt occasionally from high quarters. The duke suggested a renewal of his literary and political *déjeuners*, an honour I accepted too readily, oblivious at the moment of the very serious engagements I had in hand elsewhere. Nevertheless, I was able to attend some of the meetings, at which the earnest manner of the Marquis of Buckingham, together with the energetic opinions of the royal duke, greatly

encouraged me in the political course I had adopted. Little
did I expect that a subject of paramount and extraordinary
nature would be brought under discussion at one of our
quiet meetings. This was no less than the arrival in
London of a deputation from the provisional government
at, Milan, composed of such persons eminent for birth,
wealth, station, and intelligence as Duke Serbelloni,
Colletti, and others, who came to make an offer of the
Italian crown to the illustrious duke, instructed at the same
time to waive all objections as to diversity of religion.
General Colletti having brought a letter to myself, de-
manding my patriotic assistance in the matter, I undertook
to inform the royal duke of the arrival of the deputation,
and ascertain whether and when it would suit his convenience to receive either the general alone, or the whole
deputation.

" Oh, the latter," was his prompt reply ; " it will afford
me much satisfaction to become acquainted with such distinguished Italians, whose patriotic views I highly approve,
as every Englishman would and should." Accordingly, the
deputation was presented to the duke on the following day
at noon.

Their proposal was so thoroughly unexpected, and considered as so improbable, that no intimation of the duke's
feelings on the subject could be expected, other than that
he should consult his friends and consider. In fact, His
Royal Highness did not appear to realize his projected
position in Italy.

General Colletti was an officer in the Neapolitan army,
who had come to Milan to offer his services to the provisional government, by whom they were deemed so important with regard to the organization and discipline of
the troops intended for the service of the new crown of
Italy, that they were at once accepted by the provisional

government, who appointed him Inspector-General of the Forces, with certain specific duties.

So far as my own political notions were concerned, I confess that, inasmuch as the proposed scheme had for its basis a monarchical and not a republican intention, I had no objection to it. However, financial difficulties intervened at the same time, respecting which the intended royal candidate was so decided, highly to his honour, that the whole scheme was abandoned, and my own more favourite one respecting a sovereign of Italian race remained as before the preferable one.

But at this conjuncture the intelligence of the flight of Napoleon from Elba came upon us like a sudden clap of thunder. Here, in Kensington Palace, the news startled the royal inmate not less than his noble visitors. The prognostication of the "political doctor," communicated to the "Monthly Chronicle," at the same time that it was forwarded in a letter to the ministers, who had considered the anticipations as idle dreams not likely to be realized, had actually taken place, and yet not one Power was found ready and prepared to adopt the best and only course proper to be followed in so great an emergency.

However, my principal care at the moment was of a more homely character, namely, that of upholding, as far as my individual exertion in the capacity of one of its lecturers could accomplish it, the character of the Windmill Street school, at the head of which we reckoned Mr. Brodie, certainly the most able as he was the most honest member of the association, for thus was the medical school in Windmill Street designated. After my second course, however, I had occasion to notice circumstances of such a nature as to induce me to relinquish all further connection with it, the more so as I expected to be obliged soon to return to Paris for a short time. Upon announcing to the Principal my

intention of relinquishing the lectureship, an offer was made
to Mr. Thomas Brande, who accepted and succeeded me in
the chemical chair.   But before the offer had been made to
him, Mr. Brodie called on me with a round-robin he had
received from the pupils of the school, protesting against
the change of the lecturer, and requesting the head of the
association to prevail on me to withdraw my resignation,
with many flattering expressions of attachment from the
pupils.   My answer was, that I was likely to be obliged to
absent myself for the summer months on business; and to
say the truth, I had reason to suspect the unsoundness of
the plan on which the school was conducted, as may be
gathered from the following letter to me from Sir Humphry
Davy's brother, some time after my resignation :—

                    " Head Quarters, Paris. Nov. 7th, 1815.

    " My dear Granville,—I expected long before this to
have had the pleasure of seeing you, and of communicating
viva voce ; but that pleasure is postponed for three weeks,
when I hope to leave Paris for London, to prepare for a long
expedition, of which perhaps you have already heard.   I
am about to engage in no less than a voyage to Ceylon, and
residence there of several years, in the double capacity of
staff medical officer with the prospect of rapid promotion,
and of physician to the Governor with the further prospect
(some of my friends tell me) of a rapid fortune.   But let
me defer my particular views till we meet and have nothing
more interesting to consider.

    " There is another subject that troubles my mind.   How
shall I express my indignation at the conduct of certain men
whom you emphatically but rather ironically call ' our
friends ? '   How is it possible that they can act in such a
clandestine manner, with their pretension to science and
philosophy and liberal sentiments ?   Philosophy, I suspect,

is with them a cant word; science a stepping-stone; liberal sentiments *vox et præterea nihil.* You are fortunate, in my opinion, in being out of the trammels of the set, and in having no more concern with the Windmill Street school party. The only one circumstance which consoles me for the trouble you have been at on my account, is the knowledge you have acquired by lecturing of your own powers, and the resolution you have formed of establishing a school of your own, where science will be taught, and scientific knowledge, I have no doubt, extended."

In a subsequent letter, still dated in November, he goes on to tell me—

" I saw Professor Brande to-day at the Royal Institution. The weather is cold, but we, to each other, colder. Newman [*] too, I have seen, and have learned that the old Windmill Street school is defunct; that Harrison has left England; and what surprises me not a little, he has left it with accounts unsettled! I am just from Paris, but I bring with me no news either political or scientific, except Ney's defection, and his impeachment of five or six of his brother general officers. What a villain! In a quarter of an hour I shall set out for Cornwall, to join my brother at Penzance, and shall remain there probably three weeks, and then return to London to prepare for my Ceylon expedition.

" Yours,

" J. DAVY."

Doctor Davy was right. I had delivered two courses of lectures on chemistry, for which the flight of the treasurer prevented my receiving any compensation; but the satisfaction of having done it with general approbation, and the conviction I had acquired that at all events I possessed the

---

* A very ingenious and scientific philosophical instrument maker, the best of his day.

ability of communicating my own knowledge, whatever it might be, to other people intelligibly and effectually, was a great satisfaction.

As I did not for many years after receive any letter from this clever and successful man of science, about to fly off to the extreme confines of southern Asia, I shall here insert two more letters received from him, both within a little more than a fortnight of one another, containing some interesting information.

"Paris. Nov. 1815.

"DEAR GRANVILLE,—I was wrong in stating that Paris was barren of scientific news. I have just learned that several curious facts have lately been ascertained. Cuvier, I have been told, has discovered that the ova of birds and mammalia, as to structure and development, are perfectly similar. Dulong has obtained a fourth oxide of lead,—the protoxide, which contains only half as much oxygen as litharge, and which when treated with acids is resolved into metallic lead and the deutoxide itself, being incapable of entering into saline combinations. The same ingenious chemist has observed a curious fact respecting the oxalate of lead. When this salt, perfectly dry, is gently heated, there is a rearrangement of the constituent parts, all the hydrogen of the acid unites with as much oxygen as the oxide of lead contains, water is formed and is evolved, and a new compound remains, in the examination of which he is at present engaged. What is curious is, that when the compound is more strongly heated it is decomposed, and converted into metallic lead and carbonic acid, which are the only products. Now the queries are, what is the nature of this combination? Is it a direct combination? Is it a direct compound of lead and carbonic acid, or of oxide of lead and carbonic oxide, or a ternary compound of lead, oxygen, and carbon?

"Perhaps you have heard of Gay-Lussac's paper on

prussic acid, published a fortnight ago in the 'Annales de Chimie.' As usual, it is elaborate and ingenious, and apparently brilliant, abounding in interesting results and happy analogies. As you will soon have the original, if you do not already possess it, I shall mention merely the leading features. The more important fact is the discovery of the basis of prussic acid, a permanently elastic fluid possessed of many singular properties; an acid by itself, and capable of forming acids by union with inflammable substances, and capable of uniting directly with metallic bodies. It is composed of azote, carbon, and though compounded (according to Gay-Lussac), analogous to simple substances, and to oxygen, chlorine, and iodine in the part it performs; hence he thinks that it deserves a simple appellation, and hence also, as it is the basis of Prussian blue, he calls it cyanogen; and prussic acid, the constituents of which are the substance cyanogen and hydrogen combined, he calls hydrocyanic acid; and he calls cyanuret of mercury a combination of cyanogen and metallic mercury. Such is the nomenclature he employs. Like his last dissertation, this is evidently written in haste, as if in dread of his results being anticipated, in consequence of which too many parts of this essay are extremely imperfect; especially the latter, in which he commences the investigation of the nature of prussian blue, but finishes his paper before his experiments have brought him to a certain conclusion.

" I hope to have the pleasure of seeing you in about three weeks, and of talking over the preceding and many other interesting subjects.

"My dear friend, yours respectfully,

"J. DAVY."

" Penzance. December 16th, 1815.

"MY DEAR GRANVILLE,—Your last letter afforded me great satisfaction. In whatever you attempt, you must succeed.

This is the prerogative of genius. I am sorry that I can give but little information respecting the objects of inquiry that my brother has recommended to your attention on your own account. This is of little consequence. You enter on a field hitherto almost entirely unexplored. I once made the attempt to form a combination of phosphorus and carbon, but without success, I need not inform you. Only one method I tried, and that was analogous to the process of Lampadius for procuring the sulphuret of carbon. I was but a young chemist, and perhaps it may be worth while to repeat them by following some other course. By exposing phosphorus on carburetted hydrogen, may not there be a probable means of forming the compound required? These are but crude ideas.

"I am very happy to hear that you are about to examine a collection of pulmonary concretions. The subject is interesting, and hitherto, I believe, little attended to. The result of my experience in the subject is scanty, but such as it is I must not withhold it. It is briefly this, that the few concretions I have analyzed, expectorated from the lungs, have been similar to bone in composition; at least in their most important ingredients—like bone, being composed chiefly of phosphate of lime and albumen, with a little carbonate of lime, but in what proportion I do not recollect. Instead of paying me for the galvanic battery, you will oblige me by paying Newman, that the money may be remitted as soon as possible to Professor Brande.

"In about three weeks I hope to have the pleasure of seeing you in London.

"My dear friend, yours respectfully,

"J. DAVY."

CHAPTER III.

Pistrucci the sculptor—His personal appearance—Strange story of a cameo—
Mr. Payne Knight imposed upon by Bonelli—Discovery of the de-
ception—Pistrucci succeeds Mr. Wyon at the Mint—Designs and
engraves the George and Dragon coin and the Waterloo medal—Canova
in Paris—Shuffling of Talleyrand—Restitution of works of art to Italy.

On leaving for Italy in 1814, I had let my house furnished
to the celebrated cameo engraver from Rome, Benedetto
Pistrucci, who was tempted to try his fortune in the British
metropolis. Italy had long ceased to give enough encouragement to real genius, either artists or authors, as we
have seen in the case of the ill-fated author of the "History
of America," and as was the case in the present instance of
the most eminent cameo sculptor in Europe. With this
gifted artist, the lasting friendship which subsisted to the
day of his death has been of too intimate a nature to admit
of my dismissing him with the bare mention of his name.

Pistrucci came to me as his fellow-countryman in a
strange land, looking for such support in his career from me
as my then position in London enabled me to give him.
He had his own great reputation to back him, and the aid
of my tried friend Mr. Hamilton, to whom I introduced
him, who at once took him by the hand and stood by him
like a staunch advocate and defender. Yes, defender,
against the many vexations an alien is exposed to in
England; for no sooner were the unrivalled merits of this
great artist divulged, than enemies or invidious rivals,

fellow-artists, started up to oppose him in all things, and by all possible or impossible methods.

Pistrucci was my junior by one year; a robust, hale man of a square form, though tall, and with a head of the true Roman type, so often seen in the busts of Roman emperors. His innate love of the arts interfered with his father's desire to impart to him a knowledge of the Latin language, which he deemed essential to a sculptor. "Why waste," asked Pistrucci, "so many years, or even months, in translating poets, historians, and philosophers from the Latin originals, when I can gather all the information they can afford me through the many translations in our own *bella lingua Romana?* I can employ the hours more usefully with my crayon or my scalpel."

Yet Pistrucci's imagination was fervid, full of bright ideas, and often approaching eloquent vivacity in speaking of objects dear to his taste. His general manner and behaviour were appropriate to the gravity and steadiness of his personal appearance. No human figure could be more striking than Benedetto Pistrucci in his morning costume as he entered his studio. I have seen strangers visiting it for the first time stand transfixed on the threshold as he came in to receive them and show his models and statues, looking up to him speechless as the most imposing specimen of his museum. Yet he had playful words and lively sentiments at times, which reminded one of pages in the life of his antitype, Benvenuto Cellini, whom he was fond of copying and ambitious to imitate. He was his equal in diction and in the manner of narrating his own adventures, as in describing his own work. He was naturally master of his own language, not unfrequently, however, mixing Roman provincialisms pronounced with the peculiar inflexions of voice and tone which reminded one both of the trans- and the cisteverene dialects. Unless suffering from some momentary

illness, of which his sedentary life and continuous confinement indoors had rendered him susceptible, he would be
playful and even humorous; many of his repartees indicating unmistakable signs of genuine wit.   With all this,
a *bonhomie* of character that made him an easy prey to
designing men desirous to make his talents and abilities the
handle for their own fortune.

Precisely such an attempt on the part of one of his
fellow-citizens of Rome was the cause which brought
Pistrucci to England.   I have had occasion to name the
person I refer to in a former transaction as a sort of picture
dealer who had succeeded in palming on a wealthy London
merchant a pretended original picture of Correggio.   The
occasion of Pistrucci's advent in the British capital was this.
When at Rome this same picture dealer, now turned into a
cameo merchant and dealer in gems, cast his eyes on Benedetto, and soon devised a plan for making him the means by
which to gain no trifling benefit in his trade.   He first presented himself to the artist as a well-to-do dealer in gems,
well acquainted with all the connoisseurs in London, in which
capital he urged the artist by all means to go and settle, as
the only place where his great merits would be properly
estimated.   In the mean time he would himself be the
willing harbinger of his fame if he would intrust to him
some choice specimen of his work to carry to England with
him.   He produced at the same time a small portion of a
hard oriental stone with a fractured end, and said, " Cut me
out of this stone the head of some mythological goddess, a
nymph, or some female head known in ancient times, but
do not put your name to it."

The commission was executed.   Cento scudi were paid
on the demand of the artist as the price of his work, on
which he cut his own private mark, as he used to do on all
his own works; and a head, to which the name of Flora

was given (from the circlet of flowers which surrounded it), was the result. The notion that his work might prove the means of bringing him to England, the land of promise for all foreign artists, served to stimulate the hand and genius of Pistrucci to excel himself in his performance. So Angiolo Bonelli (for he was the cameo, as he had been the picture dealer) set off for London, where it was not long before he parted with his Roman cameo to a wealthy purchaser who enjoyed the reputation of being the most knowing and keenest connoisseur of antiques in the country, and who, after some slight discussion as to the history of the fragmentary cameo, where it had been discovered, and also concerning its intrinsic value, willingly paid to Signor Bonelli fifteen hundred pounds!

The precious cameo, as a recent Roman discovery, became the subject of general conversation at all the meetings of antiquaries and learned societies, as well as among the higher circles. The London purchaser, Mr. Payne Knight, whose private collection of antiquities was well known, and who was an *habitué* at Sir Joseph Banks's Sunday *conversazioni*, was not a little flattered at being solicited by the numerous visitors to exhibit his precious antique, which he did, carefully ensconced in a modest plain morocco case, when every one, including myself, admitted the perfection of the gem, and agreed that no modern artist could ever hope to achieve so perfect a work. I well remember hearing of nothing else for many months but Mr. Payne Knight's Flora after its first appearance in private society, in which I probably had occasion to see it exhibited a hundred times.

At length the Roman *protégé* of Signor Bonelli (who by-the-by had contrived to delay by every means and subterfuge in his power the realization of the projected visit of Pistrucci and his settlement in London) reached that capital, came to me, was introduced to Mr. Hamilton, and by him pre-

sented to Sir Joseph Banks at one of his Sunday meetings.
He was made acquainted with the discovery of the antique
cameo, and a promise was made to him of an early opportunity
to examine it, at which Pistrucci seemed delighted and thankful. Mr. Payne Knight made his appearance by chance
that same evening, and at Sir Joseph's request produced his
fragmentary cameo, handing it to Signor Pistrucci, who
started as he opened the case, viewed it in every position
and in all lights, took from his waistcoat-pocket a lens,
turned the fractured end of the cameo towards and close to
the flame of a candle, directed his lens to the flowers of the
circlet, and quietly handing the cameo to its owner, said
deliberately, " Questa è opera mia ! " (That is my own
work !)

The general murmur that followed, not unmixed with
sarcastic exclamations, was put an end to by Mr. Knight
asking Pistrucci rather pettishly how he would prove the
assertion. " Easily," was the reply. I will repeat in
English what followed. "Look," he said, "between the
rose immediately over the left eyebrow and the leaf of
another rose adjoining, and you will find my private mark,
which I invariably put to all my works."

"And what is your private mark ? " " This," and he
made a design in pencil, consisting of only two lines.
Instantly everyone who had a lens directed his eye to
the spot indicated. Some could and some could not distinguish the lines. Sir Joseph did, and likewise his
secretary and librarian, the great botanist, Robert Brown,
and many more ; lastly, Mr. Knight himself, without the
least hesitation, after looking at the spot, admitted the
existence of the private symbol. Still he was incredulous,
and prepared to show how possible it was for Signor
Pistrucci to have been acquainted with the antique relic
when first discovered by Bonelli, to have examined it nar-

rowly, and having found out the particular mark, determined to appropriate to himself the authorship of the
fragment. Politeness, however, to a stranger forbade Mr.
Knight expressing a suspicion of such duplicity to Pistrucci,
and it was finally proposed and adopted that certain
persons, of whom Mr. Hamilton was one, should form a
committee of inquiry, for the further elucidation of the
facts. The report was in confirmation of Pistrucci's as-
severations, but he disdained to accept it as a complete
expurgation of his character, and at once declared he would
make another Flora as like as the nature of the stone (sup-
posing he could find one like) would allow, without looking
at the original or any species of model of it.

The proposition was accepted, and the work executed in
less than a fortnight. The similarity of the two Floras was
really so striking, that Mr. Knight was unwilling that his
own should pass into the hands of the person who held the
replica mounted in a case of the same form, lest there
should be no possibility of distinguishing the one from the
other. This *replica*, or second original, quite equal to the
first, was by Pistrucci presented to Mr. Hamilton, who insisted on the artist accepting one hundred guineas. Thus
ended this extraordinary transaction connected with the
fine arts between an eminent antiquary and an illustrious
artist, into the particulars of which I deemed it but just to
both parties to enter minutely, from the fact of my having
been almost daily in communication with Mr. Hamilton and
Pistrucci, and frequently meeting also Mr. Payne Knight,
and so assist in divulging the commencement as well as the
end of Signor Bonelli's *escroquerie* in cameos, as I had
done in another of his dealings in pictures.

In a very clever work on gems and cameos, illustrated
with exquisite representations of all such objects of art
(most of them being the works of Pistrucci), published by

a very learned medical *confrère* of mine, Dr. Billing, a
sketch of Pistrucci's biography is inserted, full of interest,
for the writer was well acquainted with the artist, at whose
house I often met him. To myself, however, appertained
the satisfaction of having attended professionally both the
great sculptor himself, his wife, his sons, and his two
youngest daughters (both inheriting their father's skill) as
long as the former lived, and until the latter removed
from England to Rome. I cannot conscientiously say that
my highly-gifted countryman met in this country all that
consideration and fortune which he had been led to expect,
and which his talents unquestionably deserved ; still, he
found such encouragement, support, as well as employment under government, as to render his life comfortable
and his intercourse with the great world friendly as well
as agreeable. Of his public works executed in England on
behalf of the British public, the great Waterloo Medal and
the St. George and the Dragon coin were the principal and
best known.

Being presented to the Master of the Mint, Mr. Wellesley
Pole, afterwards Lord Maryborough, and a cabinet minister
in 1816, Pistrucci suggested that beautiful design as a
better reverse than a coat of arms. He produced the said
design cut in jasper as a model, which he was directed to
execute in steel. The following year, Mr. Wyon, the chief
engraver of the Mint, died, and the post was offered to and
accepted by Pistrucci, with a salary of five hundred pounds
a year, and one of the houses within the walls of the Mint
appropriated to the officers of the establishment.

To such as were admitted to the privilege of entering his
sanctum, which he soon found the means of establishing on
a far grander scale than his predecessors, having with the
consent of the Master added premises to his own studio for
the working and display of larger works in sculpture, either

projected or executed, it is unnecessary to remind them how
industriously and indefatigably employed they used to find
his handsome and portly person in his working attire,
moving about from one department of his studio to another,
now with chisel and mallet in hand, working at the colossal
bust of Wellington in Carrara, and then quietly seated
before his lathe, with tiny and microscopic steel points
working out in steel, or on a hard oriental stone, the most
delicate lineaments of a lovely female countenance of his
own design as a cameo. Here in this *cœnaculum*, vast,
and of his own devising, would Benedetto Pistrucci be
working eighteen out of twenty-four hours, and my own
professional testimony may add, injuring all the time his
constitutional health, and damaging that still more precious
gift of God, his eye-sight, for the sake of which I have
more than once forbidden the use of his eyes, and consequently the prosecution of his works. During such painful
intervals, it was a real work of charity to him for some
chosen intimate to visit him and read out select passages
from Dante and Machiavelli, the one to remind him of the
sublime poetry of his native tongue, the other to nourish his
own innate love for terse language breathing a true affection
for a cherished fatherland.

Of the more important of the two works before mentioned, executed for this country by Pistrucci, namely, the
Waterloo Medal, I shall have to write more at length in a
subsequent part of these memoirs, for from one of those
strange combinations of circumstances which intervene at
times when nothing either existing or prospective indicates
the possible occurrence, I found myself involved in the
destination and application of a unique first copy in soft
metal, gilt, of this magnificent work of art; one certainly
unique in itself, and superior to the best efforts of the
ancient Roman cameo engravers, whether as regards genius

in the invention, size, and grandeur of work, or lastly, in the exquisite finish of its execution.

But I am now approaching the epoch in which objects of art of a far more transcendant importance were about to come under public notice, through the compulsory restitution on the part of conquered France, to Rome and other cities and provinces of emancipated Italy, of the several articles of statuary and painting forcibly removed from museums, galleries, churches, and private mansions in my native land, during the temporary domination of the French military for the last years which closed the eighteenth century.

By the end of August, 1815, British sentinels were placed throughout the galleries of the Louvre, in which nearly all the purloined treasures of art from Rome and other parts of Italy had been assembled for many years. Blücher, on the part of Germany, had directed similar measures for their own precious national objects. England was acting on behalf of the Pope and Italian princes and cities, as well as for some of the minor friendly powers.

Two agents from Florence arrived in Paris to reclaim both statues and pictures, and many antique manuscripts taken from that city twenty years before. One of those agents was the renowned painter Benvenuti, whose name I have already had occasion to commend in a previous part of my narrative. At the same time, later in August, a much more illustrious artist came also to Paris, Il Cavaliere Antonio Canova, on the part of the Pope, to claim the restitution of the objects that had been carried away from the public buildings and palaces of that metropolis of the Christian world. The Paris journals were desired to announce that Canova had come to execute a bust of the Emperor Alexander, it being intended to keep the real object of his mission a profound secret, a design in which the French authorities might have succeeded but for a humorous circumstance worth narrating.

Being myself at the time in Paris, and within a few days of my departure, I was walking early one morning on the Boulevard opposite the Hôtel du Ministre des Affaires Etrangères. Issuing from that house I beheld a gentleman clad in an embroidered court dress, with bag and sword, who had the appearance of a foreigner and an entire stranger, staring about as if looking for his carriage, and uncertain which way to proceed. I guessed him at once to be an Italian, and accosting him in his native tongue, I asked if a countryman could be of any service to him. Rather startled at the suddenness of my address, he simply replied that his carriage seemed to have left him; "No doubt," he added, "with the intention of returning in good time to convey me back to my residence after the audience I had come hither to attend at the office of Sua Eccellenza il Principe di Talleyrand, which audience it was expected would last long, but which terminated in a few minutes, the minister not allowing me a moment to explain the business of my mission, for which I sought a private audience." "And which is," I added, "to reclaim the objects of art violently abstracted from Rome and other parts of Italy, in virtue of certain articles of the Treaties of Paris and Vienna, and I have the honour of speaking to the celebrated Signor Canova." Having said which, I mentioned my own name, reminding him of a letter addressed to me not long before from Rome by his brother, l'Abbate Canova, with which our acquaintance had commenced.

The chevalier, finding that his carriage did not return, gladly accepted the proposal I made of taking a *fiacre*, and accompanying me at once to the residence of Mr. Under-Secretary Hamilton, then also in Paris, with the view of obtaining through him a better support for the *envoyé* of

His Holiness than the shifty Talleyrand had vouchsafed to him on the presentation of his credentials from the Vatican.

Of the two *quolibets* which the French journals of that day permitted themselves the liberty of perpetrating on the occasion, I verified only the first on inquiry as to their truth from Canova himself, who, it appeared, had on the day I met him coming out of the ministerial hotel of Talleyrand, been made the object of a disgraceful trick by that unscrupulous diplomatist. On presenting his credentials to that minister, Canova had desired to have an audience of the king. Talleyrand seeing the honest simplicity of the envoy, told him that he should receive the usual notice when to present himself at court; accordingly, on the day I had met him in his gala dress, Canova had received a ticket from the Lord Chamberlain, admitting him to see the king pass through the gallery to mass, thus shuffling off Canova as a private individual, instead of presenting him as a public *envoyé*.

Thus far I can vouch for the anecdote as verified to me by Canova himself, but not so as regards the additional particulars published, namely, that feeling indignant at the unworthy trick of the minister, and upbraiding him in becoming language of his own country for insulting His Holiness' ambassador, the brazenfaced Benevento replied: " Pardon, I mistook you for the Pope's *Emballeur* " (Packer). I repeat this *bon mot* of Talleyrand, which, luckily for the reputation of his wit, is contradicted.

In a volume of modest dimensions recently published, an account is given of Lord Palmerston's visit to Paris in 1815 and 1818, wherein it is hinted that his lordship had a hand in the restoration of the objects of art reclaimed from France. I am in a position to gainsay such an insinuation. That Lord Palmerston should have felt equally interested

with every enlightened Englishman in the restoration to
Italy of her stolen treasures, I admit to be possible ; but to
Lord Castlereagh alone, acting at the instigation of his
under-secretary, and on the personal solicitation of Canova
himself, belongs solely the glory of having achieved an act
of political justice which the wary Benevento had determined to thwart by every possible shuffling. Lord Palmerston,
moreover, a simple Secretary at War, would have had no
official influence or power while in Paris in 1815 as a mere
visitor, compared with the weight which attached to the
will and opinion of both the Secretary and Under-Secretary
of State for Foreign Affairs, for Lord Palmerston (to use an
expression of Ben of Israel in " Tancred "), " Only sat in
the queen's second chamber of council."

Mr. Hamilton was delighted to see and know Canova,
with whom a friendship commenced from that very moment
of the warmest kind, for the quiet, modest, and ingenious
character of each harmonized entirely with the talent of the
one and the learning of the other.

A day or two after our fortuitous meeting, I received the
following note from the famed sculptor :—" Stimatissimo
Signore,—Aurei bisogno estremo di conferire un momento
con lei, onde la prego indicarmi il quando io potrei trovarlo
in casa.   Io resto qui sino alle otto ; poi sarò dell' Am-
basciatore di Ecuador.   S' ella vi si trovasse tanto meglio
bavero, io paperò domani mattina per tempo da lei.   Mi
scusi e mi creda contutta l' estima suo amico, CANOVA."*
It seemed that some difficulty had arisen with respect to
. the officials at the French Foreign Office, where Canova

* " My very esteemed Friend,—I have a great wish to confer with you for a
moment, if you will kindly mention where I can find you.   I am here till
eight o'clock ; afterwards I shall proceed to the Ambassador of Ecuador.
Should you be there also, so much the better, else I shall call on you in the
morning early.   Excuse and believe me, with much ·esteem, your friend,
CANOVA."   This was dated, Paris, 2nd Sept. 1815, 6 o'clock, P.M.

had previously deposited his credentials for their preliminary inspection by Monsieur Talleyrand, preparatory to their being presented to the king; and that on applying to the *employés* for their restoration, he had received a long French official note, which, as being himself little conversant with the French language, he was desirous I should interpret for him, and suggest at the same time such a reply as might be deemed necessary according to the nature of the communication.

I waited on him early in the morning, as I had been prevented from attending the *soirée* of the *envoyé* from Ecuador. I read the note to him in Italian, and had no occasion to point out to him in particular the art of the writer, whose object was first to delay the operations of Canova, and next to cause him to fail altogether if possible. At his request I sketched out in pencil there and then a reply to Talleyrand, much in the style of his own jesuitical missive, and left it to Canova to have it copied and forwarded by a special messenger direct to the minister. The credentials came before the close of the day; after which everything with respect to Canova's business proceeded like a ship under prosperous gales, and his mission was crowned with complete success.

CHAPTER IV

Accident to Lord Castlereagh —Canova's account of the success of his mission —He comes to England—Contributions to literature—Guyton de Morveau—A philosopher seldom successful as a practising physician—Letter from Sir Humphry Davy—Sir Walter Farquhar—His great success, and death—Result of his advice.

In the " Morning Chronicle " of the 11th of September, 1815, in which journal, under various dates, a good portion of the notices of facts and letters herein recorded have appeared (they having been regularly communicated to that journal by myself), the following will be found :—

" Despatches were on Saturday received at the Foreign Office by Doctor Granville. This gentleman brings an account of an accident which has befallen Viscount Castlereagh. His lordship was walking in the Champs Elysées on Tuesday afternoon about five o'clock, when a led horse passing by threw out his legs and struck his lordship, *above* the knee fortunately. The contusion on one limb is reported as considerable by Dr. Granville, who left his lordship on Wednesday afternoon in good spirits, and thinks he is not likely to be confined by the effect of the accident more than a few days. The knee has escaped fracture, but was otherwise injured. Doctor Granville was desired on leaving Paris to inspect the injured limb, that he might be enabled to give an accurate account to his lordship's friends of the present state of the case on returning to England."

Before I left Paris I thought I would place my new friend in the hands of a stout-hearted Italian, a man of brain and

of great experience, who could be of service to his illustrious countryman in many things respecting which he
could hardly expect to obtain the desired aid from his more
ostensible patron, the Under-Secretary. Canova most thank-
fully accepted the proffered acquaintance of my friend Signor
Angeloni of Frusinate, whom I duly introduced to him
before I took my leave.

It was agreed with Canova that he should keep me informed of his proceedings as regards the restitution of the
statues and pictures he had come to claim; accordingly, on
the 31st of September, I had the satisfaction of receiving a
letter from him, of which I shall here insert a literal
translation :—

"Paris. 26th September, 1815.

"CARO SIGNORE,—By the courtesy of Signor Hamilton I
received your kind letter, together with the enclosed article
relative to the object of my mission, written in English by
yourself, as I am informed, with much energy and eloquence,
showing the spirit of a true-hearted Italian. I tender you
a thousand thanks, as I ought, and as far as I am able,
albeit a work of pure love and inclination finds its best
reward in the soul that inspired it. I abstain, therefore,
from enlarging on an argument which sheds light and glory
on itself without a word from myself.

"The more strictly to follow your advice and my own
wish, I sent off yesterday by an extra messenger your
original article to the Cardinal Secretary of State at Rome,
who will be most thankful for it I am certain, and will have
it translated in the 'Giornale di Roma.' The cause of the
Fine Arts is at length safe into port, and it is to the generous
and unremitted exertions of the British minister, Lord
Castlereagh, and Mr. Secretary Hamilton, that Rome will
be indebted for this triumph of the demand I came hither
to make in her name. What gratitude ought we not to

feel towards the magnanimous British nation! Fully does she deserve that the arts, in return for this generous act, should join hands to raise a perpetual monument to her name. But the best and most enduring memory will be engraved on the heart of every Italian, who on beholding the sacred objects torn from his country again restored to his land, will remember the nation that stood forth as her advocate for this restitution, and will call down upon her the blessings of Providence.

" Your very affectionate friend,

" ANTONIO CANOVA."

A week or two later, Canova tells me—" We are at last beginning in earnest to drag forth from this ' Vasta Caverna ' of stolen goods the precious objects of art taken from Rome. Among the many fine paintings we removed yester-day, I may single out that stupendous production, ' The Transfiguration ; ' also the ' Virgin of Foligno,' the ' Communion of St. Jerome.' Other choice paintings came away two days later, as well as other precious objects, such as the group of ' Cupid and Psyche,' ' The two Brutus,' and the very ancient bust of Ajax. Yesterday, again, the 'Dying Gladiator ' left his French dwelling, and the Torso. To-day, the two statues, unique in the world, ' The Apollo,' and the ' Laocoon,' were removed. To-morrow ' Mercury ' will quit the Louvre, between ' Flora ' of the capitol and the ' Venus.' The Muses will follow next, and so on to the close of this portentous procession."

In a later epistle, he tells me—" Your own dear Lombardy has been well cared for. All the precious and most valuable objects belonging to Lombardy and Piedmont have been recovered, and among them the famous Venetian horses. I am happy to be able to add, for I know how much you will rejoice at it, that even all our ancient MSS., medals, &c., will be included.

"Do not believe all the lies which the French papers are instructed to publish respecting the 'Venus de Medici.' She is still as she was before, *salva et incolumis.*

"A. C."

In a postscript to the last letter, Canova says—"I beg you to do me the favour to present my respects to His Royal Highness the Duke of Sussex, whom I remember well when he passed through Rome as Prince Augustus. Also thank him for the goodness he manifested towards me in wishing me to be presented to him at that time. Continue your friendship for me, and believe in the attachment and gratitude with which I remain your affectionate and sincere friend, "CANOVA."

Dismissing now my pleasing and gratifying reminiscence of the great artist, I will sum up the rest of my intercourse with him in a few lines. He was able at length to cross the dreaded Channel and come over to be almost stupefied at the sight of the vast Babylon of houses and other buildings that presented themselves in interminable masses of structures, among which one grand and magnificent building—Westminster Abbey—arrested his attention and called forth his admiration. But he used to say that the indefinite limits of the enormous metropolis, with its myriads of dwellers, formed of themselves the most striking monument that a city could present.

His friend Mr. Under-Secretary Hamilton, who had preceded Canova to England, lavished every species of courtesy and hospitality on him, and procured him an opportunity of visiting Windsor Castle, Queen Charlotte having happily expressed her desire to know him. I was commissioned to

escort him down in a royal carriage and four from London
to the castle, where I left him in the hands of the queen's
chamberlain.   Canova was delighted with the interview,
and in ecstasy at the grand old pile, through all the apartments of which he was conducted, ending with partaking of
some light refreshment, at which one or two of the princesses
were present, carrying on a conversation with their celebrated guest in his own language.   I in the mean time
sauntered about Windsor, and had some luncheon in the
apartments of the queen's lord chamberlain, with whom I
was well acquainted at the time.

Some days after this presentation Canova was solicited
by Mr. Hamilton to sit for his portrait to Sir Thomas
Lawrence, who was himself flattered at the opportunity of
knowing the illustrious artist, and to be the means of per-
petuating his lineaments, in which he was very successful,
as the portrait in possession of the Hamilton family testifies.
Finally, every object of his mission to France having been
satisfactorily completed, and his visit to the capital of
England and the most distinguished of her people being
concluded, Canova and his brother " l'Abbate," who had
joined him (*defunctus officii*) after accomplishing all his
work in Paris, departed from England, taking their way
homewards through Flanders and Germany, not caring to
pass through the heart of exasperated France.*

It was not long before the news of my return to England

* The following year, 1816, I was surprised and gratified by the arrival of a
most valuable proof of Canova's friendship, a portrait of Vesalius by Titian.
The painting, 3ft. 3in. high by 2ft. 7in. wide, was bought by Canova at Venice
in the early part of his life, while engaged in the study of the profession he had
at first selected, namely, that of a painter in oil colours.   Few portraits by
Titian exhibit the vigour and beauty of that inimitable master in a higher
degree than this likeness of his great contemporary and friend Vesalius, the
celebrated anatomist at Padua.   The picture possesses one great additional
value, there being an autograph inscription attached to the back of it, fastened
with seals of red wax, where it is still to be seen.

became known to the authorities of such public institutions as I had been personally connected with, and who were likely to have again use for my services. At the Royal Institution, a journal entitled " The Journal of Science and the Arts " was just about to be published, under the direction of Professor Brande, who requested me to assist him with some original communications. I complied by sending him for his first number an analytical paper on a new vegetable substance called Malambe bark, recently brought to Europe from South America, and carefully examined and analyzed by Vauquelin of Paris, member of the Institut of France.

A second paper I contributed soon afterwards, which I had read before the Geological Society of London, of which I was foreign secretary. The paper consisted of an exhaustive report on a curious memoir by Monsieur Methuon, on the manner in which earthy as well as metallic crystals are formed. I continued to supply the editor with contributions in each successive number of his journal. One of the most important contributions from my pen was an account of the life and writings of Baron Guyton de Morveau, the promoter of that complete revolution in the nomenclature in chemical science, which perhaps many judges of such matters may feel disposed to consider as the first and most effectual step towards that gigantic progress which theoretical chemistry has made since the commencement of the present century. With Baron de Morveau and his interesting wife I had been on habits of intimacy, and when death came to snatch him almost suddenly from us, I endeavoured to console the bereft widow by expressing the conviction that his surviving colleagues would do proper justice to his memory. But the baron's name had been found on the list of the regicides, and the Bourbonist *savants* of the day shrank from the task of commending the high scientific deeds of their revolutionary fellow member.

I timidly ventured to ask the disconsolate baroness whether she would confide to me the grateful task of putting before the world the works and scientific services of her husband through the English press. The offer was instantly accepted, and a collection of papers, diaries, and memoranda on many subjects was in a few days placed in my hands, by which I was enabled to draw up the biographical account of Baron de Morveau previously alluded to. It is flattering to the writer to report that the late eminent philosopher Doctor Thomas Young, having undertaken in a new edition of the Encyclopædia Britannica the article " Guyton de Morveau," at once declared that he could not follow a better guide than Dr. Granville's account in the " Journal of Science."

Another paper I contributed to the same journal was a translation of the Abbé Monticelli's description of the eruption of Vesuvius in December, 1813; besides a report from Vauquelin's experiments on the ergot of rye, a substance which I afterwards contributed in introducing as a valuable medical agent in obstetrical practice. Moreover, to each number of the same journal I used to forward monthly returns from the best scientific journals of the Continent. Willing also to assist two medical friends, Dr. Man Burrows and Dr. Anthony Todd Thomson, who had conjointly started a new medical journal under the name of the " Medical Repository," I communicated several articles to its pages, among which will be found one mentioning for the first time in medicine (1815) the name of prussic acid as a remedy. It was this subject that led me by degrees to the introduction of my own views and experience in the employment of the new and valuable medicine in a more extensive work a few years later (1819-20), which work served to stamp the character and promote the adoption of that remedy in the practice of medicine in England. To the same journal I contributed extracts from most of the foreign periodicals on medical subjects.

At this time I was in my snug little house at Brompton, my tenant and friend having recently removed to the Royal Mint. He had succeeded the elder Mr. Wyon as principal engraver of coins, notwithstanding a strong opposition on the part of the managers, who pretended that the appointment was invalid from the circumstance of Pistrucci being an alien, forgetting at the same time that of the last ten successive engravers to the Mint, more than two had been foreigners and unobjected to.

All these various and other occupations, however much they might add to my reputation for general knowledge, did not afford me the smallest chance of succeeding in the object I had in view, of settling in the metropolis as a practising physician. Far from it: I had lived long enough to find that a man of science who was a physician seldom succeeded in settling himself down profitably in practice if he insisted at the same time in maintaining the character of a *savant*. I can instance two striking examples of this truth, in the persons of Wollaston and Dr. Thomas Young, who seldom earned a physician's fee with their great reputation of men of science; and I can well remember also Mr. Owen, when in his capacity of a naturalist and professor at the Hunterian Museum in the College of Surgeons, in which he had succeeded his father-in-law, Mr. Clift, addressing to me a protest because I had stated in my "History of the Royal Society" that he might become illustrious and popular as a man of science in that post, but never would be employed as a practical surgeon, for which profession he had been educated. Every contemporary surgeon well knows Professor Owen for what he is, a most distinguished naturalist; but can they quote a single surgical operation he has been called in to perform?

Some of Mr. Hamilton's friends, and his own family and relatives indeed, I attended when occasion required, and in one or two instances the novelty and boldness of my practice (contrary to a long-adopted treatment by an ordinary London physician which had failed, whereas in my case the treatment had saved the patient) served to help me forward, but the prospect of being once reckoned as one of the well-known physicians in the metropolis was so little encouraging that I almost gave it up in despair. Occasions for keeping myself before the public as one connected with science occurred pretty frequently, and my position as a member of more than one learned society afforded me ample scope to maintain a certain position in the scientific world. Sir Humphry Davy, by kindly making me the means of communicating with the Royal Society, inspired me with the idea that, with some further exertion in behalf of general science, I might some day venture to aspire to the honour of the three mystical initials. Sir Humphry afforded me another opportunity of approaching the magic circle, by forwarding to my care a valuable memoir of his from abroad, which he destined for the Royal Society. As the letter refers to some other work of Sir Humphry, I shall transfer it to the present pages :—

"Rome. Feb. 10th, 1815.

"MY DEAR SIR,—Many thanks for your kind letter to Lady Davy, and many thanks for what you inform her you have been so good as to do for me in Thomson's journal. I had not the least idea that my theory I mentioned in a private letter on the volcano of Pietra Mala would be published, and my observations on that subject belong to a series of volcanic observations that are yet in progress. I send with this letter a third paper to the Royal Society. My two last were on the colours of the ancients, and on a new solid compound of iodine and oxygen, showing that Gay-Lussac's iodic acid is a creature of his own imagination. By his process nothing but a compound of sulphuric acid and oxyiodine can be obtained; and even this substance he cannot have procured pure, for it does not agree with his description.

" My third paper contains an account of the gas produced by the action of sulphuric acid on hyper-oxymuriate of potassa, which, though composed of four proportions of oxygen and one of chlorine, is not an acid.

" I return my thanks for your kindness to my brother. It will always give me great pleasure to hear from you. The bustle of setting out for Naples prevents me from writing at this moment a longer letter.

" I am, &c.,

" H. Davy."

It was on the 16th of May, after receiving this letter, that I became acquainted with a man eminent in his profession, whose good counsels at length set at rest all my doubts and fears, and who was the cause of my ultimately adopting that course which led to my final establishment in the metropolis in the position I have occupied as a physician for upwards of half a century. Sir Walter Farquhar, physician to the Prince Regent—and to the entire Red Book I might say, for a more prosperous or more popular practitioner did not exist in London—was induced to take special interest in the young aspirant in medicine, from the fact of a personal recommendation from his daughter, the wife of the Rev. Anthony Hamilton, incumbent of St. Martin's-in-the-Fields, and brother of my friend the Under-Secretary. Although Sir Walter had of late years relinquished the actual out-of-door practice on account of old age, he retained the more honorific branch of home or written consultations. When I became intimate with the family, as I did, I had the curiosity (very natural as well as excusable in one who was about to court the upper ten thousand) to count up the visiting cards left in the hall in the course of a few weeks, when Sir Walter's indisposition had been made known and his absence from Carlton House noticed. The cards and inscriptions in a visitor's book, which were meant for an inquiry after the baronet's health (among which a royal message from the Regent was daily conspicuous), showed that the sick man on his expected and hoped-for recovery would have to despatch many hundred "return thanks for kind inquiries."

How was such extensive popularity achieved among the most fastidious classes of high-born and highly-educated people, the like of whom foreigners fail to meet with in their own countries? Sir Walter Farquhar had not made himself known, as most London physicians try to do, by writing, or by zealously assisting in the management of public institutions, hospitals, or scientific academies. The whole of his attention was given to the consideration of the many difficulties that encumber the path of the practical physician in this country; in solving those difficulties, and in rendering their solution as bearable to the parties interested in them who happened to be the sufferers as it was satisfactory to the other parties whom Sir Walter's wisdom, prudence, tact, and irreproachable trustworthiness had relieved of a load of anxiety and apprehension; and all this carried on by Sir Walter in the quietest and most unassuming manner, a smiling, joyous, and faith-inspiring countenance, which alone must have greatly aided him in securing to himself an amount of popularity that accompanied him to the very last day of his life, which terminated at the age of eighty-five years on the 26th of March, 1819. He died with his head resting on my left shoulder as I sat in a chair near him, where I remained every day after watching him during the night, which I almost invariably passed in his house. In the morning I had to attend the consultations with his medical friends, Dr. Baillie, Sir Henry Halford, Sir William Knighton, Sir Gilbert Blane, Dr. Warren, and others. At these consultations I used to present a written report of the preceding night, mentioning the steps I had adopted in certain emergencies, especially in regard to either cupping or a small bleeding from the arm, which invariably afforded instantaneous relief from a sensation of suffocation and pain in the region of the heart, for Sir Walter was in fact dying from severe pneumonitis complicated with angina pectoris.

In the several private chats I had with him, he used to refer to these two maladies under the conviction that they had had their origin in a violent blow he accidentally received on his chest when a young surgeon of a cavalry regiment in garrison at Gibraltar.

In my eagerness to give a continuous and true account of Sir Walter Farquhar to the end of his successful career, I find I have leapt over nearly two years, from the time of my introduction to him down to the time of his death already alluded to. Those two years by his advice I had spent in Paris, following punctually the course he had pointed out to me with the intention of securing my success in London, instead of leaving it to chance. That advice was given to me at a private interview in May, 1816. By adopting it for a period of nineteen months, it brought me back to England qualified for my new duties at the commencement of 1818, in time to go through the various scenes in Conduit Street (the residence of Sir Walter) which I have already described, and in which I took a most earnest part from feelings of gratitude as well as of true affection.

The issue of that private interview with Sir Walter in 1816, as I have before said, changed the whole tenor of my life, established me permanently as one of the successful medical practitioners in London, gave me a character, helped me into the principal scientific bodies of the capital, made my name familiar to the public, brought applications from noble families to escort them as medical attendant in their foreign travels, and finally enabled me to transfer legitimately, and with my patients' good will, from their sachels to the custody of my own bankers—Messrs. Coutts & Co. during the first part, and next to the London and Westminster Bank during the second part of half a century—four score thousand pounds and upwards of English money; a pleasing contrast with the few hundred piastres given to a travelling physician in Greece, or with the amount of pay of a Turkish hekim-bashi.

THE meeting on the 16th of May had produced all these results, and more. It had taken place at Sir Walter's own suggestion, pressed by the anxiety of Mr. Hamilton to see me settled, and it consisted of the following dialogue, as put down almost verbatim on my return home :—

Loquitur, Sir Walter.—" My dear doctor, every one of your friends (and you will allow me to reckon myself as one of them) in England see with regret the great difficulty, if not the impossibility, of your settling as a stranger in this great city as one of its prosperous physicians. Few persons without a connection with one of the great hospitals, or the support of a leading medical man, can hope to establish for himself a practice at once honourable and profitable. Your progress would be so slow, and produce such scanty means of living, that in two or three years you would become discouraged, if not disgusted. Your experience has chiefly been in the surgical department of the navy. Naval surgeons, however respectable, cannot cope with the able and dexterous surgeons we have in every hospital. No one can hope to succeed as a pure surgeon in London, unless in connection with one of our great hospitals; and then only could you hope to obtain a large connection. When I came to London as a retired army surgeon, I saw

at once how useless it would be to contend with the great
dons of the day for a share of their practice, and I therefore
joined a respectable firm of what were then called apothecaries, at present styled general practitioners, and continued
thus until by an interposition from the highest quarters I
was admitted to pass my examination at the Royal College
of Physicians, and practised ever after as one of them. But
I had already had, in the inferior grade of the profession, as
I may say, the run of the town, which made me not only
well known, but also popular. You do not feel inclined to
try such a career, and indeed I am not sure whether you
would not have a swarm of hornets about you should you
make the attempt. You will say that this is a very discouraging and desperate prospect : so far I admit it is so.
But there is an opening for you, nevertheless ; one which
to a man of such various information, antecedent studies,
frequent intercourse with the higher classes in so many
courts, great energy as you can boast of, offers the greatest,
indeed I may say a unique chance of success. We want at
this moment in London a scientific physician-accoucheur.
The members of the profession who practise as such at
present, much as I respect them as men, are mere men midwives. I hold midwifery to be more than that ; and we miss
amongst them that degree of science and physiological knowledge which, combined with the dexterous use of manual
or mechanical aid, overcomes the many difficulties and
dangers of which we have had so many striking and
unfortunate examples in the last few years, since the
Smellies and the Hunters have passed away, and the
Sims and the Denmans have become aged. Now I am told
that in Paris there is a grand school of theoretical and
practical midwifery, in a vast establishment called La
Maternité. I know from good sources that the instruction
given by the professors attached to that establishment—

Dubois, Capuron, Marcus, Chaussier, and others—is not only of the ablest, but the most decidedly scientific, owing to the eminent and earnest character of the instructors, who are also able physicians. Go to Paris for a year, or a year and a half; give yourself up entirely to the acquirement of obstetrical skill and cognate sciences, including the knowledge of female complaints and the diseases of children, practically as well as theoretically. We will take care in this country to let people know in the mean while that you are gone for that purpose to Paris for a time; gone again to school, in fact, with the object of being made perfectly familiar with all the difficulties and resources of a profession which in its exercise entails a double responsibility on the practitioner who has two lives at the same moment in his charge, those of the mother and the child. A thorough acquisition of such art, coupled with the vast knowledge your education in medicine and experience in surgery have given you, will entitle you to consider yourself as *facile princeps* among the practitioners of that art in London, and to look with confidence for a complete success. Such is the advice I give you after much consideration as to what can be done in your behalf, as most kindly urged by all your friends in England, and by no one more so than by our common friend Mr. Hamilton, to whom I communicated my idea, which he thinks an admirable one, and towards ensuring the success of which he voluntarily will afford every assistance in his power. 'I am,' Mr. Hamilton said to me, ' the cause as it were of his coming to this country to seek employment in the profession he had fully mastered, and I feel bound to see that he be not disappointed.' "

My reply to Sir Walter was very brief, for I was deeply impressed with the truth of every syllable the venerable physician had addressed to me. " Say not another word, dear Sir Walter. I feel the justice and the whole importance of your advice, which I shall proceed at once to put into execution."

That promise I fulfilled in the course of the week, by ordering the same apartments I had before occupied in the Hôtel de Saxe, Rue du Colombier, to be prepared for myself, my wife, and now three little children. I should thus be within reach of the Ecole de Médecine, the Maternité, and the Hôpital des Enfants Malades ; in fact, I should be fixed in the Pays Latin.

Such readers as have followed me thus far must have thought it rather singular that during my many adventures, risks, escapes, and scrapes, I should never have given a hint, or the smallest fraction of a hint, as to the state of my own health. This reticence in the life of a physician is rather peculiar. Well, the answer is as short as it is satisfactory (to myself, at all events, and doubtless to many good-natured readers and friends). My health, with the exception of a tumble from my horse at Larissa, in Thessaly, which lamed me for a couple of days, the Theban fever at Athens, the plague at Stamboul, and the yellow fever at Port Royal, Jamaica—my health, I say, with those exceptions, has been of the best ! Even the loss of the sense of smell I look upon as a punishment (and not a malady), for not having taken care to engage a less careless assistant when I was about to embark on some delicate experiments. Therefore, under such circumstances one has a right to say, " As to my health, it has always been good, and I have nothing to complain of." But while on the point of being again displaced, and advised to move from one quarter to another far different, the story I had to tell was all the other way. Few people suffered more than I did at that moment. I was both dyspeptic and low ; to such a degree, indeed, as to disturb the whole nervous system to the extent of affecting the functions of the heart so seriously, that the professors of medicine, both in England and in France, who kindly offered their advice to a suffering brother, came to the conclusion that my cardiac functions were out of trim, and mayhap the organ itself out of gear. In fact, the good friends, two of them especially (great authorities in the line), had convinced themselves that the doctor of Michael's Place, Brompton, would die of a disease of the heart—a diagnosis and prognosis which the stiff-necked and brazen constitution of said doctor has protested against, and with success up to his eighty-eighth year! To say a good deal in a few words, I found myself in the following state at the period of breaking up my London establishment to proceed to Paris: a violent headache from early morn until after a full repast with *quantum suff.* of brandy and water or port wine. No appetite, and the most obstinate constipation; added to this a constant palpitation of the heart, with an occasional pain in that . region; nausea at times; the surface of the tongue like a dry, rough, yellow pasturage that requires mowing, and tormented with the blues all day. So ill was I, in fact, that the mere raising of my arm to give a knock at a door, or the doing of anything requiring a little exertion, would bring on a paroxysm of nervousness enough to alarm an old woman.

In such a state, then, and without the least exaggeration thus infirm, was I called upon to help to pack up and travel to Dover, cross·over to Calais, be dragged to our Paris hôtel, and get into a French bed in which in those days I ran the chance of being smothered in feathers and eaten up by B flats! Yet I went through it all. I knew I was sound; I did not believe there was anything seriously the matter with my heart, though at that identical moment palpitations were almost choking me. I persevered; did all that was needful; nay, more, I presented myself next morn-

AUTOBIOGRAPHY OF DR. GRANVILLE.
58

ing in the proper quarters, took out all the necessary
tickets for attending lectures and hospitals, struggled
through all the requisite exertions, patiently listening to
prosy as well as to eloquent lecturers, or affecting an im-
passibility of feelings at the bedside of hospital patients from
day to day, commencing at six o'clock in the morning (as is
the wont in Parisian hospitals), from week to week, and *de
mense in mensem*, during which time of excitement and
bustling fatigue, and I may add useful and successful employment, I continued to get better until I felt once more
quite well. Yes, perfectly well. All palpitations gone;
headache disappeared; digestion perfectly regular; appetite
moderate; tongue spotless, and the power of attending to
lectures, as well as to hospital patients, with now and then
some night watching at the bedside of some poor female at
the hour of danger. Now what is the secret of all this?
How does my medical knowledge explain this strange
valetudinarian puzzle? The progressive narrative of my
life during nineteen months passed in Paris will serve
not only to explain the puzzle, but also to supply some
practical and effectual notions to people suffering from
nervous dyspepsia, how to overcome it without the profuse
drugging on which authors on disease of the stomach published in England at the time in such abundance were in
the habit of insisting.

It is not my intention to give either a diary of, or to
enter minutely into, all my proceedings while in Paris; so
many were the objects of my pursuits, so serious the combinations that followed, and so important the results obtained,
that a separate volume alone could do justice to the subject.
Such a volume I had indeed prepared at the termination of
my residence, and all the materials collected for that object
remain yet in my possession, regretting, as I have never
ceased to do, the hasty resolution I adopted, at the sug-

gestion of timorous friends, of abandoning the idea of publishing a full " History of the State of Science in France during the Revolution." No one had ever thought of writing such a work, and mine would have been the sole authentic record of one of the most brilliant epochs of national genius, elicited by the absolute privation of all resources in devising means to supply every deficiency. The work I allude to was to be accompanied with copperplate designs of public scientific edifices, of establishments for the industrial as well as for the fine arts, museums, hospitals, and useful popular contrivances. As these designs became useless after my determination to suppress the MS., I found a suitable receptacle for them with the Institute of British Architects, which, with some other engraved illustrations of another work of mine, the members were pleased to accept. I hope that this little digression will be pardoned as a reminiscence of the exertions I had made to promote the true interests of science at a time when I was myself seeking at her hand, in one particular class of studies, as much benefit on my own account as I could obtain in return.

The following letter, addressed to my friend the Under-Secretary, will better show how my time and faculties were employed :—

'Paris. 5th August, 1816.

" Dear Mr. Hamilton,—We are at length settled and comfortable in this puzzling and perplexing metropolis; but not without some difficulties in regard to finding suitable and permanent apartments. In this I have succeeded, and I am satisfied both as regards price and the rest of it, the whole being within the limits of my means. My little Julia posted with me and my despatches all the way, and did not suffer in the least. Sir Charles Stuart received me very cordially, and mentioned immediately that there could be

no objection made by the police to my residence here.   M.
de Ragneval, for whom Baron de Montalembert had given
me a letter of introduction, promised to wait on Monsieur
de Cazes (the minister), which he did, and from him I
received the strongest assurances that I should not be
molested in the least.   The Duc de Chartres was also
very polite.   ' Je vous prends sous ma responsabilité pour
ce qui a rapport au gouvernement Français,' * he said, and
begged I might use his influence whenever likely to be of
service to me.   Both the duke and Ragneval inquired very
particularly respecting Alexander's sad accident, and how
he was going on.   Of course I was able to give them the
best as well as the latest information.   Mackenzie was
friendly, and promised to forward the object of my visit
here.   Newnham took my address: he may perhaps want
me shortly.   Mrs. Morier is likely to require my services.
Should I be fortunate enough to gain their confidence, my
future project will be rendered more encouraging.   I take
every pains at all events to deserve it.   Sir Walter, to
whom I write by this courier, was perfectly right in sending
me here for that object.   No place on earth offers such
multiplied opportunities for becoming both able and dexterous in a particular branch of the profession.   The private
instructions I receive daily, from two of the most eminent
professors of the Hospice de la Maternité, where I am a
constant visitor, would be sufficient, with common understanding, to make me, what I desire to be, an accomplished
practitioner.   To all the interesting cases that may occur to
them in their practice, I am to be called, either by day or by
night.   This gives me necessarily plenty of occupation, but
absque labore nullum lucrum. My instructors are Capuron,
well known for his capital elementary work on midwifery,

---

* I make myself responsible for you as far as the French government is
concerned.

and the other is M. Deveux, pupil and relative of the late eminent obstetrician Baudelocque, whose genius and originality of ideas he inherits. I like his theory much : a great part of it is new and highly plausible. With this I thought proper to combine a good deal of practical knowledge of the diseases of children and women, for which purpose I am in close attendance with the physicians of the Hôpital des Enfants. I do the same with regard to the Hôpital des Femmes. There are now under my daily inspection (for I have been named *élève interne*) two hundred and more different cases of female diseases connected with that branch of the profession I came hither to learn. Twelve months thus spent must, I should hope, qualify me for the position my friend in Conduit Street intends me to occupy in the metropolis. The remainder of my time I spend in attending a course of chemistry and mineralogy ; and another of medical police and jurisprudence at the Ecole de Médecine. I work an hour or two practically, three times a week, with Vauquelin in his laboratory, which happens to be just opposite to our hôtel ; and now and then Monsieur Barruel gives me an instructive private lesson on analysis. In the evening I occupy myself in visiting and taking down notes of all I have seen and learned in the course of the day.

         " Believe me, sincerely yours,

                      " A. B. G."

The acquisition of all this practical knowledge, however, was not the only object to which I would confine my attention or study while I enjoyed the good fortune of finding myself in this redundant focus of knowledge. There were several hours of the day yet unoccupied, and the temptation to devote some of them to other scientific pursuits around me were so numerous, and at the time so irresistible, that

I soon determined to draw up an additional programme of daily occupations.

Men of European reputation were lecturing at that unique establishment, dear to the memory of Buffon, the Jardin des Plantes. Here Cuvier was teaching zoology and comparative anatomy ; Desfontaines and Jussieu were developing the sciences of botany and vegetable physiology. To the celebrated crystallographer, the Abbé Haüy, was committed the teaching of mineralogy and the doctrine of the formations of crystals; while natural history acknowledged for its interpreters Geoffroy St. Hilaire, Daubenton, and Dolomieu. What men were there equal to these in any part of Europe ? All these eloquent lecturers did I, as a matter of course, attend, for none clashed with another. To all these lectures in public institutions, and to many others I have yet to mention, I was admitted and received as a foreign *savant*, member of the Royal Institution of Great Britain ; but above all as Foreign Secretary to the Geological Society of London, to which I had recently been elected, for the French have a great regard and attach much importance to the office holders in learned societies, and especially in the Geological Society of London, at that particular time much esteemed and valued in Paris; so much so, indeed, that those Frenchmen whom in my official capacity I had recommended as worthy of being elected foreign members of our Society, were unbounded in their acts of courtesy and thankfulness for the distinction.

I may state at once that the particular privilege thus spontaneously bestowed upon me, accompanied me in all the circumstances of my Parisian scientific and professional life.

My thirst for learning seemed to increase in proportion as I succeeded in certain departments, when I became eager to profit equally and succeed as well in others. Vauquelin,

Gay-Lussac, Thénard, a stupendous triumvirate of chemistry, were just then shedding immense lustre on the science they had made their own. One of them lectured at the Collége de France, another at the Jardin des Plantes, and the third at the Ecole de Médecine. Thither I repaired in turn at the proper hour, and brought away extensive notes of all the lectures. I will explain how, not by way of boasting, but simply to show what real zeal in a pupil can accomplish with the view of more fully comprehending and profiting by the instructions of his teachers.

I invariably attended each lecture a quarter or half an hour before its commencement, prepared with small quires of writing paper, pen behind the ear, and ink-horn suspended from a button-hole in my coat. As there was always a collection of objects, machines, and utensils, simple or complicated, on the table before the lecturer, I at once proceeded to delineate the same in their minutest details in ink-lines, which an acquaintance with descriptive geometry had made me familiar with. By the time the lecturer entered, my work was done, and as he proceeded in the description of his apparatus, which I had set down in writing, I was able to apply distinguishing letters of the alphabet, or Arabic numbers, to the various parts of the said apparatus. With regard to the text of the lecture itself, which was delivered of course in the purest and most fluent French, I translated it mentally, and wrote down actually in English full sentences and the import of every phrase or observation.

The professor at whose lectures I was the most zealous in seizing his words by such a method was Gay-Lussac, for, besides being a profound philosopher, he was a great and methodical experimenter, affording me full time for a successful accomplishment of my own part of the lectures, the results of which I look upon with some pride to this day, when I open the very thick volume of the different quires of

notes taken as described, and now bound together. The
same process I adopted at all the other lectures, though
I admit not quite so sedulously.

Next to chemistry, the knowledge I wished to revive in
me and improve while in Paris (the very ideal place for
such a knowledge) was practical anatomy, which, however,
as far as my specific object was concerned, I chose to confine to female anatomy. In the anatomical pavilion of the
Ecole de Médecine, or rather, I ought to say, "Hospice
de Perfectionnement;" Rue de l'Ordonnance, especially
adapted for the purpose,* and in a private room in the
Hôpital de la Pitié, complete scope was afforded me for all
I could desire in that branch of investigation; the result
being, that the knowledge I was very desirous to possess
I gained most completely. I also obtained interesting
anatomical preparations, which I was entitled to remove to
my own quarters when completed, as I had paid my
respective contributions in money to secure their possession.
Of these I made good use after communicating upon them
to the Royal Society, which communications that scientific
body deemed worthy of a place in their "Transactions."

I have thus passed in review the leading and principal
heads of human knowledge which I, an M.D. of thirteen
years' standing, a member of the Royal College of Surgeons
of England for half that number of years, came to seek and
obtain in the French metropolis. Yet time remained still
at my disposal, for say that the number of hours for work
in each day was eighteen, the lectures never lasted beyond
one hour, and anatomical investigations were not consecu-
tive, but only occasional, while my own attendance at
hospitals was limited to the few hours during which the

---

* The vicissitudes of this anatomical theatre are rather curious. It was
originally a convent; it became a manufactory of saltpetre, and ultimately the
head-quarters whence the cut-throats sallied forth on the ever-memorable 10th
of August, 1792, to execute their murderous work against the Tuileries.

attendant medical men were on duty. Now this surplus of
disengaged or leisure hours afforded opportunities for some
straggling courses on geology or mineralogy by Brogniart,
on mechanical philosophy by Biot or Beudant, or on
astronomy by Arago, toxicology by Orfila, and pure physiology by Magendie.

But there were two hours in every week which no literary
or scientific temptation, no matter from what quarter, could
seduce me to devote otherwise than I did. I allude to my
attendance at the meetings at the Royal Institute of France
(for that public body had descended from imperialism to
royalty without forfeiting, however, one iota of its importance, respectability, or renown). Yes; each Monday, at
2 P.M., saw me nailed to a seat among the limited
number of strangers admitted as visitors, which seat had
been by signal favour allotted to me, for I was not yet a
fellow of the Royal Society of London, which would have
secured mé a peculiar place within the inner circle. In that
private seat I never failed to appear, pencil and paper in
hand.

The arrangement of the *salle de réunion* is so admirably
planned, that the visitors from their loftier benches can take
a general as well as a special view of the members seated
before their own particular tables, and hear distinctly when
they address the choir, or *vice versâ*, or discuss academically
some important subject, or any of the members reads his
own special memoir or essay. The witnessing of all these
operations was immensely attractive for one who never
failed to take notes and give a full and faithful account to
one or other of the English journals of science.

Few people at all conversant with science are ignorant
that the Institute of France, which has become so famous,
is an institution established by the first Napoleon, who
borrowed the title from a public establishment in Italy, as

stated already in another part of these memoirs. The number of members, who are chosen by election (*scrutin*), to be approved by the sovereign, and invariably confirmed, is limited to persons who are publicly known to have distinguished themselves in some special branch of scientific knowledge. The system is one best calculated to secure the *crème de la crème* of the scientific world for the dignity of member of the institute; and not only that, but likewise to elect for each branch of scientific knowledge one whose name alone represents the science by cultivating which he has rendered himself famous, and thus eligible for membership. Thus, if we name Arago, or Delambre, we say astronomy; if Thénard's name or Gay-Lussac is spoken of, we understand that they are the lights of chemistry; and so of the rest. Now, in a cognate society in London, such is not the case. If we name a particular person to be a F.R.S., that does not suffice to acquaint the public for what particular reason he has so been honoured with those initials, the majority of the fellows being content with being considered as "lovers" or "patrons of science." As regards the Institute of France, on every Monday that I took my seat among the visitors, and I looked down on the different seats filled by the members, I sank the idea of the man, and only beheld in him the representative symbol of this or that other particular science. All have worked! Is that so in Burlington House? For a reply, let the tables I published in a work entitled "The Royal Society in the Nineteenth Century" be consulted. That work offended some people because it proclaimed undeniable truths. Nevertheless, it brought about the many salutary reforms it had suggested, and the name as well as the working of the English Royal Society since the publication of that volume has risen, to use a mercantile expression, fifty per cent. in the estimation of Europe. Compare the names of the fifteen fellows elected yearly at present, with those of the shoals of candidates proposed and elected before the appearance of the *hated* volume. Or place side by side ten or twenty of the last tomes of the Philosophical Transactions with an equal number of those previously published, and look at the importance of the subjects treated, the number and beauty of the illustrations, as well as of the paper and printing of the latter as compared with the former; and, above all, consider the various references by government to the society for counsel and help in scientific matters, and you will be able rightly to judge of the real worth of our present standing in the opinion of the scientific world.

CHAPTER VI.

Life in Paris—Cicerone to English visitors—M. Gérard—The English Geological Society—Cuvier's lectures on generation—The Darwinian theory—Contributions to English journals—Dr. John Davy in the East.

HAVING determined to remain in Paris steadily occupied with the principal objects of my mission, I set about arranging my domestic affairs in the manner best suited to my many engagements or occupations. It was therefore settled that my wife and children should live independent of me every day of the week except Sunday, which we invariably passed together. On other days I was to take both my breakfast and my dinner at a *restaurant*, as I left home too early for the little family to be ready at the former meal; as for the second, as I never could be sure at what time I might possibly return home, I was obliged to take my chance of such hours as suited my engagements, leaving the family at home to settle matters in the English way. We had a French *cuisinière* and an English servant, and the three children had an English nurse, whom I soon changed for a French *bonne*, for the sake of the language.

My own principal repast, when I had time for one, I partook of at one of two *restaurants* famous for the great attendance of medical students in the Pays Latin. Like them (for I fraternized with many of the best), I took tickets for dinners *à vingt-cinq sous*. My readers in 1871 will hardly believe it, but that sum procured me soup, two dishes of meat, and *les quatre mendiants* (almonds and raisins, figs,

and French plums). Half a bottle of *vin ordinaire* sometimes, but generally water, was my drink.

Besides the relatives of my sister's husband, we had a
number of charming Parisian families with whom we were
intimate, Mrs. Granville speaking French fluently. We
had invitations of course to Lady Elizabeth Stuart's *soirées*,
and now and then a dinner at the Embassy. As it was
known that I had come to Paris for a specific purpose, and
that in London I held a certain rank among the learned
societies, I received a not stinted amount of French civility,
for which I felt grateful, and which enabled me the better
to be of use in the character of a friendly cicerone to those
of my friends coming from England to lionize Paris. I
soon found myself in greater requisition than I had leisure
for. Still I tried to do my best, especially with regard to
studious and inquisitive physicians and surgeons, who would
have been lost without some one to guide them through
what they had come to learn. In this manner I was preparing for myself on my return to London a number of
fellow medical men, some grateful, others not quite so.

But there were also other applicants from England, of a
very different class, whom I was happy to assist, as I concluded that their countenance would be of service to me
after my re-settlement in the English metropolis. It was
thus I enjoyed the good fortune of becoming better acquainted with the nearest relatives of my friend the Under-
Secretary. Endowed all of them with that worldly knowledge and tact which good society demands, and in which
more than one of the four sisters excelled—while the brother,
the incumbent of St. Martin's-in-the-Fields, earned the
golden opinions of his parishioners and the respect of his
clerical superiors—they formed a striking group, set off in
the case of the sisters by the most refined manners, and in
that of the brother by the true bearing of a dignified clergy-

man. If I add, that in their intercourse with society they all exhibited that affability and graciousness of address which I have had occasion to mention when speaking of their elder brother, my friend, no one who has had the pleasure of their acquaintance will gainsay me.*

These relations of Mr. Hamilton I had the satisfaction of escorting to every part of Paris that afforded any opportunity either for mere admiration or for instruction, and no group of travellers eager for both or for either object enjoyed a better or fuller opportunity of indulging their wishes.

One of the private establishments we visited, which afforded me great personal gratification, was the atelier of the eminent and highly-popular painter Gérard, whose name one reads on so many large engraved views of the incidents in Napoleon's eventful life. In reply to a request from myself to be permitted to introduce Mr. Hamilton and his family to visit his atelier, and have the honour of making the great artist's acquaintance, the following reply came in his name written by his very intimate friend Baron Humboldt, by which the party gained the additional advantage of becoming personally acquainted with another illustrious character, and of learning from him his own as well as the world's opinion of the principal member of their party :—
' Je rends mille et mille grâces à M. de Granville pour son aimable souvenir. Il sait combien M. Gérard et nous aimons à recevoir ses ordres. Rien ne pouvait nous être plus honorable que la facilité de voir de près M. Hamilton, dont le nom était déjà si célèbre parmi nous, et qui réunit au degré le plus éminent la finesse des vues et l'élégance attique de l'élocution et des manières à l'élévation des sentiments. Monsieur Gérard s'unit à moi pour vous prier

---

* These gifted sisters travelled afterwards to Italy, and visited my eldest brother, the governor of the city and province of Bergamo, at whose residence he had the gratification of entertaining them.

d'agréer, monsieur, les expressions de la haute considération ; et de ma part pour vous, monsieur, celles de ma reconnaissance et de mon attachement inviolable.—HUMBOLDT. Paris. Octobre, 1817."*

This intimate daily association made the cicerone better acquainted with the members of Mr. Hamilton's party than he ever was in England. The natural result being, that the cicerone became afterwards the medical counsellor whenever any occasion occurred for his being called in, and I have the satisfaction of knowing that through the long period of our subsequent intercourse their countenance and support never failed me, but, on the contrary, proved instrumental in promoting my professional advancement. My next step in life will show this, when on my return to London our intimacy was renewed and continued ever after unbroken.

By a fortunate coincidence the visits of the great folk from London to Paris chimed in very nearly with the vacations of Parisian lectures, so that I had more time at my disposal. But much, or a good part of it, was required for another purpose which my position in Paris had entailed on me to a great extent, namely, to keep up a wider circle of correspondence with learned societies and academies, or with distinguished scientific men from Italy, Germany, Russia, Spain, and even France. It is well known how much my native land is endowed with public seats of learning. Every large city can boast of an institute or academy,

---

* "A thousand thanks to Mr. Granville for his kind remembrance. He knows how entirely M. Gérard and I are at his commands. Nothing could be more pleasing to us than to have the opportunity of a nearer acquaintance with Mr. Hamilton, whose name is already so celebrated amongst us, and who joins in a high degree delicacy of taste and attic elegance of diction and manners to the most elevated sentiments. M. Gérard unites with me in begging you to accept the expressions of our highest esteem, and on my own part that of my gratitude and sincere attachment.

and at all events of a certain number of men devoted to science, literature, and the fine arts and antiquities, with not a few universities.   Each of these publishes transactions, and undertakes to work out problems of public utility, by offering annual premiums and honorific distinctions to the successful competitors.   They naturally endeavour to keep up as much intercommunication with other cognate institutions, whether in their own country or in foreign lands. These public bodies are especially ambitious to be on good terms with those of England, as may be seen in the vast number of learned and scientific reports and memoirs received at our Royal Society from I hardly can tell how many Italian seats of learning.   Now a knowledge of the fact that a countryman of their own, Anglicized, had the good fortune to be connected with the institutions of the country, either as a simple member or as an official, caused numerous epistles to be addressed to me for some purpose or another, all of which demanded a certain degree of attention.   The task, however, was a pleasing one, and the number of friends made in the correspondents amply repaid the trouble.

The year before I came to reside in Paris I had been elected Foreign Secretary to the Geological Society, which had just emerged with a brilliant reputation into the scientific world.   I had succeeded a German gentleman practically conversant with and possessor of a splendid collection of mineralogical specimens, but not a literary man.   Finding the society without foreign intercourse, I pointed out to the committee what an advantage it would be to secure in many parts of Europe a connection with cognate societies; and I designated a certain number of names of men who were eminent geologists and mineralogists, who well deserved the honourable distinction of foreign members of our society. By a unanimous resolution it was left to me to address a sort of diploma, or nomination by letter, to a certain number of such distinguished individuals, a work I took in hand with great pleasure, and by the end of the London season of 1816 the Geological Society was in direct correspondence and association with every one of the most renowned scientific societies throughout Europe; all nations contributing some link of connection. I need not say how gladly the recipient parties welcomed and appreciated their nomination. But letters of acknowledgment were not the only produce of such a measure, for our society had further the benefit of receiving books as well as original memoirs, as I may instance in illustration Monticelli's description of the eruption of Vesuvius in 1822, which the Geological Society requested me to translate; or another memoir, on the formation of earthy and metallic crystals by M. Methuon, which Gillet de Laumont, a most practical geologist, valued justly, and a report of which I read before the Geological Society, and which was afterwards published in the English journals.

After the lapse of a few days a particular occasion suggested another letter to Mr. Hamilton, for I knew how much he liked to hear of scientific topics, a portion of which I give :—

"Paris. August 25th, 1816.

"MY DEAR SIR,—I must let you be a partaker of the great satisfaction I am at this time enjoying in attending closely a course of lectures at the Jardin des Plantes, to which I have been specially invited by the learned professor, and a seat reserved for me on the professors' side of the table, in order that I may not be annoyed by the very great crowd of attending listeners. The attraction of the professional curriculum in the theatre of the Jardin des Plantes received a fortnight ago an unexpected impulse, in the announcement that a course of lectures would be delivered on the laws that govern animal generation. It seemed as if

Fortune really intended me to be most thoroughly imbued with every essential part of the great subject I have come to Paris to master if possible.   Here was a chance offered me of studying and becoming conversant with the philosophy of that particular knowledge, the practical part of which, and its subdivisions, I was endeavouring to learn under the very best instructors.   And who was he who had undertaken to unravel to us the philosophy of the most mysterious of the phenomena of living nature?   No less a *savant* than the author of the great work in four volumes, just published, entitled ' Le Règne Animal distribué d'après son Organisation, pour servir de Base à l'Histoire Naturelle,' well known besides for many other former writings on subjects of natural history, comparative anatomy, and transcendent geology— in fine, Cuvier."

The course of lectures, two only of which were delivered in each week, I regularly attended, the distinguished professor having most considerately assigned to me a place within the inner section of the theatre, by the side of the lecturer, and presented me with an honorary *cachet*.   The proceedings were very impressive.   The lecturer informed us preliminarily that he intended to pass in review before us all the classes of animals of which their museum possessed specimen preparations, whether moist or dry, but nearly the whole of the preparations for the course happened to be of organs properly dissected and preserved in weak alcohol. These Cuvier undertook to expound to us by a process at once simple and most effectual, and his manner of obtaining the result was equally satisfactory.   He took up a glass vessel containing a particular specimen of the animal respecting which he was lecturing, and holding it in his left hand, proceeded to delineate on the large black board, with a bit of pointed chalk, the various parts of the animal known to be concerned directly or indirectly with the process through which the male and female of each species are known to reproduce themselves. This was most skilfully and ingeniously managed, and the process of dissection, as I might call it, was described as the lecturer proceeded in tracing the outlines of each part in clear and positively eloquent language, which could not fail to be intelligible to all, considering that the black board exhibited at the same time a finished and accurate drawing of the whole animal preparation. No two preparations resembled one another, yet they were all alike fit for the production of one and the same act; and for that act the same means were employed by Nature, whether in mammals or in insects. In fact, in no other branch of natural history does the studious observer discover more palpably evident signs of how rich Nature is in resources, in arrangement, and in the development of the laws which govern the act of animal reproduction, simple yet complicated, logically inevitable and a matter of necessity, yet mysterious.

Such a mental treat as this course of lectures afforded me I do not remember ever to have experienced in the course of my previous scholastic discipline. Could the Darwin of to-day have been present at this eloquent exposition of the real, positive, tangible, and uniform laws, and their equally uniform development in every species of the animal creation, as devised for the replication as well as perpetuation of the genera and species, and each variety of species through a diversified organization, yet enacting the same functions, he would not have ventured to deny that the evolution of the animal creation has been a work *d'emblée* (da veniam gallicismo), and not tentative and progressive, as he has suggested.

It is to be regretted that Cuvier's lectures on generation have never been published by him. When I run over the many pages of notes I took down, and when I study the deli-

ncations I copied from the large black board of the hundreds
of specimens of the organs, both male and female, by
which the reproduction of animals of every class or kind is
achieved, and I behold how very uniform in her means
Nature obtains a great variety of results, the conviction is
too strong to be resisted that the Darwinian doctrine must
be illusory and fallacious. Unfortunately the subject is
not one on which, in a work like the one I intend—to be
open to all classes of readers of both sexes—I can expatiate
more largely, still less to offer the vivid pictures which
the eloquent professor produced to illustrate and confirm
his arguments; otherwise no further discussion would be
required to convince the author of the "Origin of Species"
of his fundamental error.

An engagement had been entered into by me with the
editor of "The Journal of the Royal Institution," and also
of the "Medical Repository," to supply them from time to
time with matter for their respective periodicals. To the
first, called also "Journal of Science," I used to communicate all select scientific proceedings of the Royal Institute
or Royal Academy of Sciences, and also an account of all
the foreign journals. To the second-named editor, all the
proceedings of the principal medical bodies in Paris or
France in general, with a *résumé* of all the foreign medical
journals. The first of my contributions was communicated
to the Royal Institution, and then inserted in the "Journal
of Science," while the medical contributions for the "Medical Repository" were first of all read before the Medico-
Chirurgical Society, of which I was a member, and next
inserted in the "Medical Repository." It is not superfluous
that I should dwell on these facts, because on some of them
depend my means of exposing the plagiarism of some of my
writings, and they can be appealed to for evidence of the
priority of my communications to the world on the nature

of certain questions, or the value or novelty of particular remedies.

It will naturally be supposed that so much pen and brain work was likely sometimes to fail or run short, and the following epistle I received on one such occasion, from Thomas Brande, professor at the Royal Institution of Great Britain, will show how I was stirred up to exert myself :—

" London (no date).

" MY DEAR SIR,—I was not a little disappointed by your failing to send me the account of foreign journals, which I relied on as a leading article of this number of the Journal, and which is consequently short of its proper quantity. I delayed the printing till the last moment, and then received your very inadequate excuse ; and if the two young ladies you name had not been very pretty girls, I should have been yet more angry. Pray send me something very soon for No. 8. Give my regards to Gay-Lussac, and tell him that his friend never called upon me for the particulars of our gas apparatus ; so I shall take another opportunity of sending them.

" Murray told me he had answered your letter long ago. I trust to your making arrangements for the proceedings of the Institute. Barruel has forgotten me. I am just setting off for Worthing to see Sir Everard Home, who has been dangerously ill.

" Yours, &c.,
" W. T. BRANDE."

Another letter I had previously received from the same gentleman, dated 4th February, 1817 :—

" MY DEAR SIR,—Herewith you will receive the two first numbers of our journal, which I beg you will take the trouble to present to the Royal Academy of Sciences. With the 'Journal des Mines' I shall be happy to make an exchange. M. Barruel, to whom you gave a letter of introduction, has been a good deal with me, and I am much obliged by your making me acquainted with so sensible and diligent a chemist. He has greatly extended my information on the manufacture of sodium and potassium.

"You ask me who was present when I repeated Clarke's experiments, or rather, when I failed in doing so. Davy, Pepys, Wollaston, Marcet, Daniel, and a score of amateurs were in the laboratory at the time. Davy has made a curious experiment illustrating the combustion of gases without flame, of which you will hear soon. In regard to the next number of the Journal, I beg to observe that I shall continue the analysis of the foreign publications; and also insert the proceedings of the Academy, and hope you will send me the continuation of both those articles up to the 1st of March. You do not tell me how you liked the last number. Your review of Caventon on nomenclature will be very desirable; also Guyton de Morveau's life. If it should happen that we should have too much matter, which of the two articles will keep best for the ensuing number? The fact is, that we have been giving too much for the money, and must now retrench a little.

"I hear of an establishment in Paris for making sugar from starch, and then spirit from the same sugar. Is this so? If so, can you get me a notice of it? We want some little popular things for the Journal. I will take care to give notice of your intended work, which I am happy to hear of.

"To all your circle, *except Cuvier* (!), my best regards.

"Yours, &c.,

"W. T. BRANDE."

My other correspondent of the "Medical Repository" is equally earnest in securing a supply of information, and thankful for what he receives. Under date of the 3rd of

February, 1817, he says :—" I have this moment received your letter dated the 29th ult., with the valuable inclosure, which shall be read to-morrow evening at the Medico-Chirurgical Society. In the number of the Repository which accompanies this, you will find your two first letters, which I trust you will not think too much altered. It was necessary for the sake of consistency to omit several of the introductory passages relating to the Society, as they were not generally interesting. I am of opinion the letter begins as well as it now stands, and the whole appears of one character. The letter I have just received requires no alteration, and only a very few corrections of clerical errors.

" In answer to your inquiries, I have to inform you that Clarke gives a summer course of lectures. The College of Physicians takes no cognizance of physician accouchers, except when they take fees out of their particular line of practice, to which they conceive they should be confined. For your satisfaction I can tell you that a clever scientific physician in that line at present is a desideratum in this city. I mention Astley Cooper as my authority, and from whom I obtained my information.

" Yours, &c.,

"A. T. Thomson."

Those of my readers who followed me through the correspondence of Sir Humphry Davy's brother, of whose friendship I was not only proud, but gratefully pleased with, and whom we left as he was about to set off on a very distant expedition to fill an appointment, will not be sorry to peruse the first tidings I received from him, dated from his destination in Ceylon, which he had reached in safety. The letter, besides its intrinsic value, gave me the first reliable notice of the salubrity of the Mauritius I had obtained, by which I was enabled to give proper and safe advice not many months after to a distinguished patient of mine about to proceed to that colony with her husband as governor and their children :—

" Colombo. Sept. 14th, 1816.

"MY DEAR GRANVILLE,—Congratulate me on the conclusion of my long voyage, my safe arrival at this beautiful place, and the pleasant situation which I here enjoy. We were six months nearly at sea, and the only places we touched at were the Cape and the Isle de France. My time will only permit me to notice the geological features of each place, and a few particulars respecting the most prevailing diseases, subjects I believe in which you are particularly interested. The structure of Table Hill at the Cape, the most remarkable in the whole colony, is an epitome of the structure of the whole country in general. The hill, which is three thousand eight hundred and eighty two feet above the level of the sea, is composed of three different kinds of rocks, viz.: sandstone, granite, and killas, which present themselves to view and seem to be arranged in the order in which they are enumerated. The sandstone, constituting the summit, and indeed the principal part of the mountain, is siliceous, and in some places finely grained, in others extremely coarse and full of water-worn stones, and deserving the name of conglomerate. The granite, which occurs immediately beneath the sandstone, presents nothing remarkable in its appearance. Its composition, like that of most mountain masses of this rock, varies in different places ; here abounding in mica, there in quartz, elsewhere in feldspar and iron, and very apt to decompose. In one place, where a junction occurs of the granite and killas, the former rock penetrated by numerous veins of different dimensions into the latter, producing a curious and beautiful appearance. The killas, which forms the sea-shore, and which is the lowest of all, very much resembles the killas or clay slate of Cornwall, and I think decidedly belongs to the same formation.

"Let us now pass to the Mauritius. Two spots in every respect cannot be more strikingly different. At the Mauritius there is an infinite variety of scenery, and of the most beautiful description, but only one kind of rock, and this apparently of volcanic origin, abounding in augite and olivine, and very like the lava of Etna. Every circumstance I could collect respecting the adjoining islands seems to lead to the same conclusion—that they were produced by some violent convulsion of Nature, and that at no very remote period. The kind of rock seemed to show their igneous formation. The irregular form of the hills and the dry chasms in the rock and the steep narrow glens are favourable to the same idea, which is supported by the fact that in the middle of the island, and on the most elevated part of it, there is an unfathomable lake very like the crater of a volcano; and by another fact, that an active volcano, as you well know, still exists in the neighbouring Isle de Bourbon. That the antiquity of the Isle de France is not very great, I infer from two circumstances : from the detritus at the bases of the mountains being inconsiderable, notwithstanding the rock of which they are formed being apt to decompose ; and secondly, from the water of the lake in the interior being, as it is said, perfectly fresh, notwithstanding it has no outlet, and by rapid evaporation is constantly losing the water which it receives from the rocks surrounding it. I had almost forgotten to mention that basalt, distinctly columnar basalt, has been observed in small quantities in the interior of the country, which is an interesting circumstance to those who are satisfied of the Plutonic origin of the island.

"Now for another abrupt transition—from rocks to diseases. The diseases known at the Cape are few and of

rare occurrence, chiefly confined to rheumatism and hepatitis.
The former may be attributed to the vicissitudes of the
temperature, which are pretty considerable ; and the latter
to the average high temperature of the climate during nine
months of the year, and especially during the summer
season.   The great salubrity of the country, which from the
medical returns appears to surpass that of any other place,
may be referred to the nature of the soil, unusually dry,
sandy, and barren, and to the dryness and warmth of the
atmosphere, not to mention the plenty there is of all kinds
of provisions and their good quality and cheapness, which
insure an abundant supply of all the necessaries of life to
every description of persons.   The only inhabitants who do
not enjoy good health, to which the country and climate
entitle them, are the Dutch, and those in particular who
have been too much favoured by fortune, who have found
the means of collecting wealth but not the method of enjoying it, plunged in sensuality and gross intemperance.   Their
career is ultimately cut short by dropsy or apoplexy,
diseases the natural consequences of their debauchery.
The Isle de France is less healthy than the Cape, and
probably because the general temperature is higher, its
atmosphere less dry, and vegetation more rapid and
much more luxuriant.   Though not equal to the Cape,
this island has deservedly the reputation of a healthy
place.

"I have already alluded to the exciting causes of the
diseases of this island, and as these are few, so are the
prevailing complaints, which are almost limited to hepatitis or
remittent fever, the one sporadic and of daily occurrence,
the other endemic and seldom making its appearance.   Of
the nature of these diseases I have nothing new to remark.
The practice however pursued is rather novel in the
eastern world.   Calomel is falling into disrepute.   It is no

longer considered the panacea: recourse is had to more active measures, and particularly to the lancet, which in hepatitis is freely used till the active inflammation is subdued. The treatment of the remittent fever is regulated by the same principles. It is strictly antiphlogistic, and almost independent of mercury, and is much more successful than the old plan, which still keeps its ground in many parts of the East, to the great detriment of His Majesty's subjects. But more on this subject hereafter, when I write to you particularly respecting the diseases of Ceylon.

" At present I must say nothing of this island, for I have been here too short a time to collect any satisfactory or interesting information. If you indulge me with your correspondence, in return for the valuable information I expect to receive from you concerning everything that is most interesting to me in Europe, I shall occasionally communicate to you the observations I may make, not only on the diseases of the people, but on the people and country in general, and particularly in certain branches of natural history, to which I intend to devote all my leisure time. My situation at present is merely pleasant, not at all lucrative; my income being little more than £300 a year. I am attached to head-quarters, dwell in a house ready furnished belonging to the government, and adjoining the Governor's residence; live at the Governor's table as one of the family, and enjoy the best society the place affords; and further, I live in hope of speedy promotion.

" Adieu, my dear Granville. May I hope for the pleasure of hearing from you soon, I mean in about six months! Such, alas! is the meaning of the term in this distant and secluded place. Let me but have this pleasure, one of the greatest I can here enjoy, and you will greatly oblige your affectionate friend,

"J. DAVY.

"P.S.—Next week I intend going into Candy, one of the most interesting districts in the island. I shall remain there a fortnight or three weeks, to explore its mineral productions. I shall write to my brother on my return from Colombo."

CHAPTER VII.

1817.

DURING the time I was in Paris a considerable commotion was taking place in the great world, including even the court circle. Anne Louise, Baronne de Staël-Holstein, who had recently returned from an excursion into Italy, whither she had repaired in hopes of recovering from a serious illness, was reported to be getting seriously ill again. The venerable Doctor Portal, her friend, spoke doubtfully of her recovery. She had become very restless and irritable. Impatient when told to remain quiet, and still more so when she found that in disobeying orders Nature herself refused to obey her; that, in fact, her power of life was ebbing slowly yet surely. She fancied that foreign advice, without any previous consultation, would save her. She knew that Doctor Thomas Young, a man of congenial mind with her own, was in Paris, and she asked me (who had called upon her as a Geneva acquaintance) to send him to her. I did so, and he visited her as arranged, but declined to interfere with the treatment, which he thought should be a moral rather than a medical one. Her listlessness, her desire to move from place to place, he thought did not arise from physical causes.

"Call upon her yourself as a friend, and converse with her for half an hour, and you will agree with me." I did so, and chose the brightest hour of the day, that I might see her in that bright light, and watch well her eloquent physiognomy. After an interview and a conversation which on her part appeared *très-réfléchie*, I came away thinking I should never see her again, but still with an opinion differing from that of my London colleague, which was that Madame de Staël was afraid of dying. I, who had seen more of her, and had reflected as much as my very acute and learned colleague on Madame de Staël's writings, could not bring myself to believe that the eccentric behaviour she exhibited when near her death should be ascribed to the fear of it, but rather to a conviction of her mind, of long standing, that " human beings with great names and superior intellects should and would be exempt from the ordinary laws applicable to animated beings." She who had been idolized in three of the most intellectual and enlightened nations in the world—in Germany, in Italy, in France; she who had fought a mighty *duello* with the greatest and most colossal mind of her time, and triumphed, she would and ought not to perish, be extinguished like any ordinary creature, like one of her own servants. To such a fate she could not reconcile herself. She could not conceive such an ending possible. Fear could never have acted on such a soul as that of the authoress of " Corinne," " Delphine," of a work on the influence of the passions, and of the classic volume " Sur l'Allemagne." She was too stiff-necked a Calvinist to entertain any fear of the future, of which her co-religionists have formed no conception like the Roman Catholics. Their faith, truly, had composed a twin-future, a paradise, and beneath it a pandemonium of fire and flames. Fear such as haunt their death-bed could therefore not enter into her soul. But she revolted against the notion of being abruptly removed against her will from among the living, for whom she believed her presence and her genius must be matters of necessity.

The great Dr. Portal, whose intellect maintained itself intact in his ninety-fifth year, and who saw Madame de Staël in her last moments (for Dr. Young's and my own visits were tributes only of friendship and admiration), is entirely silent on her death. Dr. Young, a true philosopher, used to discuss with me this metaphysical phenomenon, yet while admitting the ingenuity of my conception, he insisted nevertheless on his own conviction, that the restless agitation evinced during the many days before her death—14th July, 1817—which led the patient to wish to be moved from one apartment to another, changing as often as there remained untried rooms, until at last the small garden at the back of the house was the only shelter left in which she fancied that grim death could not find her. These were the phantasms that disturbed the death-bed of the wonderful daughter of Necker.

On the 4th of September, 1817, I wrote a letter to Mr. Hamilton, begging him to forward an enclosure to Sir Joseph Banks, and to acquaint Sir Walter Farquhar that I had done my best in complying with his recommendation of Lord and Lady Ellenborough, who had arrived in Paris, and to whom I had been showing all the scientific and other establishments of note. Lord Ellenborough, who was much pleased with all the different places of public interest in the capital, now signified his wish to be present at some criminal trial in the superior courts of law, and also to examine one of the establishments for the treatment of the insane. I promised to procure a privileged admission into one of these institutions worthy of examination for an hereditary English legislator.

Lord Ellenborough had heard much of the Hôpital de Charenton, but as that was by some viewed as an almost private asylum, he would prefer to see an establishment of a more popular description. I at once suggested Bicêtre, or La Salpêtrière. His lordship was delighted at the idea, and on my part I was glad to have him to refer to when, by-and-by, I addressed to the Lord Chancellor my ideas on the nature of the laws which ought to regulate public as well as private asylums for the care and treatment of the insane in England.

La Salpêtrière was the establishment to which preference was given, and I set about procuring the necessary permission from the Minister of the Interior, Monsieur Lainé, in whose department all such medical institutions are placed, and by whom I had the honour of being known, as having accompanied there one of the professors of legal medicine who gave a few lectures on the spot upon medical jurisprudence. Without such an authority I should not have been permitted to introduce a stranger into the interior. Lord Ellenborough being aware that the subject of mental maladies was likely soon to come before the Upper House, was desirous of becoming practically cognizant of the system adopted in France in such matters. I therefore procured for him a collection of all the public documents, which in France are both numerous and minutely descriptive. Indeed, I had myself made such a collection on my own account. But for the moment the point needed was the visit to the hospice before named, the like of which we look for in vain out of France. Lord Campbell's account of Lord Ellenborough is imperfect as respects this visit of the Lord Chief Justice to Paris. He states that his lordship "went to Paris in 1817, in bad health," and adds nothing more, leaving on the reader the impression that Lord Ellenborough, like many more ailing persons who went to Paris for their health, continued there a certain time enjoying the *dolce far niente*. That this is an error on the part of the biographer, and that Lord Ellenborough while in Paris applied himself to the acquiring of information that might benefit him in his profession, even at his advanced age, and notwithstànding his own consummate knowledge, my narrative will show, while it will rectify the imperfect account given by the author of " The Lives of the Chief Justices of England."

The Hospice de la Salpétrière for women contains fifteen thousand dwellers, divided into eleven thousand insane, three hundred epileptics, and three thousand six hundred very old women, destitute of everything in the world. The insane are separated entirely, and distributed in distinct cells or chambers, erected in continuous and parallel lines in the centre of a vast area or square, in which are plantations of lime trees, gardens, and fountains, with dry, well-kept walks between the parallel ranges of cells, which are built all alike and symmetrically. At night it is usual for those who have no regular cell assigned to them to congregate in one of the dormitories, large and well aired. Almost all the patients who are not disabled either by persistent mania or extreme old age have every facility afforded to them to walk about at their leisure, an arrangement which in a fine clear day affords to a visitor permitted to enter within the portals a curious spectacle of hundreds of females walking about in all directions, as we see bees ramble about within a glass hive—up and down, forwards and backwards, crossways, stopping short, staring at one another, sometimes halting to gossip, at other times to look each other in the face and then burst out laughing, or give a shriek and part. Most of them are alone, some in couples, a few noisy, but the majority silent; and here and there a very serious and consequential person, looking as if she had all the most important and weighty matters of this world on her mind. All are uniformly dressed, exhibiting more or less coquetry or art in disposing a bit of ribbon or a stray piece of lace. Albeit not easily, yet we may distinguish in the throng of very ordinary and plebeian physiognomics the youngest from the more advanced in life; and even beauty may be detected conspicuous among the crowd.

Into this vast and bustling Vanity Fair, instinct with life, but bereft of reason, I had the privilege of introducing the Lord Chief Justice of England on the 1st of September, 1817, and never shall I forget the surprise he manifested, as he advanced a few steps within the gates, to find himself at once in the midst of a large number of apparently quiet, well-behaved females, some few of whom turned to us as we were conducted along by an assistant of Doctor Esquirol, one of the physicians, by whom he had been deputed to escort us until Pinel, the renowned head of the hospice, could join us.

Lord Ellenborough's imposing figure (for it was ever so, though divested of his chief justice robes) became soon more than an ordinary object of curiosity. Several of the patients came nearer to us, to stare and run off, either laughing or sulking. Many would touch his hands, most of them addressed him, to all of whom my lord showed himself kind and good-humoured, until one particularly good-looking young woman planted herself straight and rigid in front of him, while we were slowly walking along one of the avenues, followed perhaps by fifty other patients, some of whom were conversing with me, whose face was rather familiar to them. "Dis donc, Père Éternel," screamed the young woman, "m'as-tu apporté enfin le permis de mon mariage?" "On le prépare, m'amie," I interrupted quickly, to save my lord. "Mais c'est que chez nous on ne veux pas que je me marie à un Protestant; et moi, je le veux, je le veux," and away she trotted, singing out her refrain until she vanished. No further interruption took place : all the patients were good-humoured, and seemed hardly to require the vigilant eye of the attendant nurses I beheld mingled with the crowd, ready to suppress any ebullition of temper.

The manner of arranging the habitations of the patients enables the physicians to distribute the insane according to the character of their maladies. The cottages or cells in the central court, which is finely gravelled and planted with lime trees, with a fountain in the centre, are occupied by the intermittently insane. Adjoining are the cells of the melancholic who are clean in their habits and quiet. The next three courts form a section by themselves, which is enclosed both at the entrance and exit by a light iron railing and gate. Some of these are occupied by maniacs under treatment, and the others by the incurables. We saw in all three hundred and thirty-one cells, and we went over ten dormitories containing three hundred and twenty beds. In the first, forty-two beds for convalescents; in the second, ninety-eight beds for melancholic patients having fixed ideas and hallucinations; all the rest were occupied by every kind of insane clean and quiet person. There were three infirmaries; one of ten beds for surgical cases, another of forty beds for insane labouring under advanced suicidal mania. Lastly, one of six beds for extremely feeble patients requiring more immediate watching and greater care. Besides the new courts which divide the ranges of cells, there is a large garden planted with lime trees, the whole extent of which is entirely cultivated by the insane patients.

Lord Ellenborough's inquiries extended into all minutiæ, and he was very anxious to ascertain what particular system was adopted in the care and treatment of epileptic patients. Respecting the use of baths for the insane, and in particular the head-douche, which has been considered by professional people to be almost a panacea, we were informed that one of the physicians or a senior pupil is invariably present during its application, especially in the case of epileptic patients, through whose wards we were passing when one or two of the poor patients were actually writhing under a paroxysm of their dreadful malady. What struck Lord Ellenborough most, was the kind, incessant, and one might add, affectionate care paid to all the various classes of demented women.

There is a physician in chief, and three other physicians; one of them is especially charged with the treatment of epileptic patients: he has both indoor and outdoor pupils under him. The physicians visit the patients twice a day; and their morning visit is to be fully described and reported in a register kept for that purpose. When a new insane patient is brought in, the physician in waiting examines her, writes down all the particulars, and selects the cell she is to occupy. He fixes the time when the relations may visit the patient, to whom he alone has the power to give permission for that purpose. He fixes the day for her discharge when cured, and grants the requisite certificate. No stranger out of mere curiosity is permitted to have access to the patient; and whenever permission is considered necessary, the visitor must be accompanied by the doctor or his assistant, and by one of the officials of the hospital.

The entire management of the establishment is under the immediate authority of the medical staff; and when I state, for the information of English medical men, that in my time the two most celebrated writers on mental diseases,— Pinel * and Esquirol—were the physicians at the head of the Salpétrière, they may conclude with me that so important

* The first indication of this eminent man's abilities, before he burst on the scientific world with his great philosophical work on mental diseases, was a memoir in an obscure journal, in which he treated of what has been called "intermittent mania."

and interesting an establishment could not have been placed in better hands. So thought my noble and very learned companion, who thanked and congratulated most cordially the two eminent doctors who had just before joined us, and we both returned home pleased, though not a little tired with a four hours' visit.

Lord Ellenborough having expressed a great wish to possess some of the statistics which the physicians had quoted to us regarding the number of insane women treated in the establishment in the current year, I was able to procure them for him by the following morning, and from the most authentic source; for happening to be invited to dine with the Minister of the Interior, M. Lainé, that same evening, and having related to him the particulars of our visit to La Salpétrière in the morning, his excellency, in whose department were all the public hospitals, afforded me the means of obtaining the desired information.

Meeting Pinel two days afterwards, I informed him of the returns I had obtained at M. Lainé's office, and in reference to the causes of insanity, he observed that the malady very often baffles the most ingenious or subtle interpretation of the best and most experienced practitioner. "For example," he said, "until the last three years I could have shown you at Charenton a patient who was at one time a very popular, but who soon became an infamous, character by his writings: I allude to M. de Saade, the author of one of the most atrocious books which the licence of the press in Republican times in France could belch out in the midst of a dissolute population. He soon after became a confirmed and miserable maniac, often condemned to the cells for furious maniacs. He was a monster of libertinism; and nothing that ancient history or the records of more modern times have mentioned, can be compared with the atrocities of this wretched man, who, in a novel, the name of which I will not even mention, has left behind him the blackest traces of his infamy. He died three years ago in Charenton, despised by the good, and even more hated by the wicked whom he had seduced into vice."

What could have been the original or immediate cause of this raging mania in such a case? I asked the Lord Chief Justice a short time after if he could throw light on it. But my lord had other ideas in his head just then. He had a great wish, which he had communicated to me on his first arrival in Paris (a natural wish for one so highly placed in the law), to witness how criminal law was administered in France. He would much like to be present at a trial in a criminal court on some public or political subject that would remind him of the one he had lately presided over in the case of William Hone, the political libeller ; but it must be as a private, ordinary listener, and not in his more ostensible character, that he would request to be admitted. I mentioned to him that the admission to the court was free to the public, but that it would be necessary to apply to the proper quarter to secure a suitable place from which we should be able both to see and hear what was doing. This I undertook to execute, and by applying to the secretary of the President of the " Cour de Paris," the required accommodation was secured in a part of the court whence we might be able to withdraw without remarks, should the trial last longer than we cared to remain.

On the day I selected, two criminal trials were to take place, one of which (the second) was a political one, namely, the prosecution of a certain number of supposed conspirators against the Bourbon government, who were charged with being members of a secret society. We arrived at the termination of the first case. The next cause was

ushered in with pomp and solemnity. Gendarmes entered the court, escorting five prisoners, apparently of the
artisan class, who took their places in the part assigned to
defendants, and were ranged by an official appointed for
that purpose by the court, the members of which had
retired for a short time. A great deal of bustle and talking
pervaded the audience part, which was instantaneously
checked on the re-appearance of the three judges. The
trial then proceeded. Lord Ellenborough was particularly
attentive during the whole of these proceedings, which (he
whispered to me) were " too fussy, and not so simple as in
English law courts," a difference of action which he considered as detracting from the proper solemnity that ought
always to prevail in a criminal court of justice.

The present defendants were respectively asked their
age, and whether they admitted the correctness of their
names as read in the *acte d'instruction* and the date of the
arrest when assembled together in the same place at a
particular date—all which line of interrogation appeared
strange to my lord. However, he continued listening
patiently to what was going on, which seemed a very long
and tedious operation. Sometimes he would ask me to
explain to him more clearly words that had fallen from the
Bench, but in general he comprehended fully what was
going on, until we came to the cross-examination of one of
the prisoners, who was supposed to have been the ring-
leader of the gang. In defending him his advocate again
inquired what his age was. "Twenty-four," was the reply.
"You lie," interrupted one of the judges ; "you gave
another age to the judge, therefore you lie!"—"True,
true," added the Procureur-général.

The cross-examination went on for a short time longer,
when one of the prisoners, on some question being put to
him, gave such an outspoken reply as seemed to shock the

court. I could not well make out the real cause sufficiently to explain it to my friend, but the observation of the President (after silence had been obtained) was too much for the patience of the stern English Chief Justice—"Quelle autre chose pouvez-vous attendre d'un pareil coquin?" *

"No, no! doctor, I really can't stand this; pray get me away as quick as you can!" And profiting by the hubbub in court, we descended our three steps into the audience part, struggled through the crowd, found our way to the outward gate and into the carriage, and drove straight home, Lord Ellenborough expressing his wonder that such things could pass in a country which boasted of a Code Napoléon.

* "What else can you expect from such a rogue?"

CHAPTER VIII.

The Countess Rumford—Her soirées—Curious calculation—The Abbé Grégoire
—Anecdote of Laplace and Bonaparte—The Wellington Ball—Story of
Morrison of pill celebrity—The Prince Regent's burgundy—Letter from
Sir Joseph Banks—A note on Gout.

I HAD the good fortune of an introduction to the distinguished Countess Rumford, a lady who held in my time a
marked station in Parisian society on account of her antecedents, her *bel esprit*, and the graceful manner with which
she received two or three times a week at her house, in the
Rue d'Artois, a limited number of the *élite* of the learned
and scientific world, not unmixed often with some ot the
members of the upper ten thousand. My contemporary
visitors to Paris will admit the justness of my account when
applied to the Countess Rumford. Twice a widow, and of
what husbands! First Lavoisier, the founder of philosophical French chemistry, and one of the victims of the
republican guillotine. Secondly, Count Rumford, who turned
his United States republicanism into Bavarian aristocracy,
but who never ennobled himself more surely than when he
instituted the perennial premium at the Royal Society of
London for essays on light and heat, or when he founded
the Royal Institution of Great Britain. The later title of
Countess she bore with becoming modesty, but she was
not angry at being called by many of her countrymen
Madame Lavoisier.

A sort of magnetic sympathy, I may call it, attracted me
to her; the great difference in our respective ages having

much contributed to steady and maintain the sympathy which was soon established between us. She liked me because I had studied chemistry under the Lavoisian system ; she liked me still better because I could talk to her of that institution of which I had become a member two years before the death of her second husband, the founder. Her " petits dîners bourgeois," as she used to call them, some *tête-à-tête*, but oftener in company with one or two distinguished men, were for me an intellectual treat. Here it was I met Grégoire, the défroqué Évêque, so conspicuous in the revolutionary annals ; Roger-Collard, Châteaubriand, and the Prince de Beauveau, father and son, scions of the oldest Gallic *noblesse*, the latter of whom I had the pleasure of receiving under my own roof in Grafton Street some years later.

Madame de Rumford was one of the few Parisian ladies who tried to abolish the stupid French fashion of seating all the ladies round the room on fauteuils arranged in a line with the back to the wall, the gentlemen having to stand in front of those with whom they were acquainted and wished to address. In her inner *salon* the assembled guests, after having made their bow to the genial hostess, arranged themselves in groups or in pairs here and there or anywhere, whether on sofas or on chairs or standing. The conversation assumed the appearance of being general, and this is what constitutes the charm of a veritable *réunion, conversazione*, or *tertulia*, and ought to be so of an English " at home." Of course all the lady guests were not blue, or given to learned disquisitions, but a few sang and played delightfully without formality or pretension. The countess did not admire the reciting or declamation of poems : she thought it had too much the appearance of a school distribution of prizes. She deemed general and miscellaneous interchange of thought far preferable.

To one of these *soirées* Mr. Hamilton and his brother, the Rev. Anthony Hamilton, were asked, both happening to be in Paris at the time, but neither had been able to be present. The countess was very desirous of making their acquaintance. She therefore wrote me the following note :—

"Jeudi 17.

"J'espère, cher monsieur, que vous aurez offert mes regrets à M. Hamilton pour mardi dernier. Si la très-petite soirée que vous m'avez donné ne vous a point ennuyé, je serai charmée de vous recevoir demain, vendredi, à la même heure que mardi, et je désire que Messieurs Hamilton me procurent le plaisir de faire la connaissance de l'un d'eux, et de continuer celle de l'autre. La Fête du Duc de Wellington * vous laisse la liberté de votre première soirée. La beauté de l'assemblée ne sera que vers minuit. Je montrerai à M. Hamilton les paquets qu'il m'a promis de porter à Lady Davy. Bonjour.

"C^{esse.} DE RUMFORD."

This *soirée* turned out to be a very select one, and my two friends had an opportunity of making acquaintance with some of the leading members of Parisian society. The absorbing topic of conversation was one brought forward by the ex-Bishop Grégoire relative to the voyage of discovery just completed by the French corvette, the *Uranie*, commanded by Captain Freycinet, the particulars of which it was expected would be communicated to the Royal Academy of Sciences, alias the "Institut." The objects of natural history collected during the voyage in the South Seas were, observed M. Grégoire, not only numerous, but in many instances extraordinary. To this announcement I

---

* She alluded to a grand ball which the Duke of Wellington gave to the *beau monde* of every nation then in Paris.

was enabled to mention a parallel, one contained in a letter from Captain William Scoresby, with whom I had the honour of being acquainted, who during his voyage in the North Seas had discovered floating on the surface of still water, certain animalculæ consisting of a transparent substance of a lemon colour and of globular form, some appearing to have very little motion, while others were in constant action. The water had the appearance of being sprinkled over in parts with a mixture of flour and mustard. In a single drop of still water, taken promiscuously from the surface of the sea, about 26,450 of these animalculæ were calculated to be present from observations made with a powerful magnifying glass upon a single fraction of that drop. Now, reckoning sixty drops to a drachm of water, there would be in one gallon of the water a number exceeding by one-half the amount of the population of the whole globe. At this statement the company started. " But," said I, " there is in Captain Scoresby's account a still more curious statement concerning the progressive motion of these microscopical organized beings, which he found to be about an inch in three minutes. Now ornithologists tell us that the condor, or the great vulture of the Andes, could fly round the globe at the equator, assisted by a favourable gale, in about a week. These animalculæ could not, in still water, accomplish the same distance in less than 8,935 years."

The ex-Bishop Grégoire had been a friend of Lavoisier, and had taken a great part in the successive revolutionary governments that had ruled France. At the time I first met him we were carrying on warm discussions with Talleyrand respecting the restitution of the objects of Fine Art to Italy, and the bishop agreed that their proper home was the country from which they were taken, as being the only place worthy to possess them ; for, he added, " we in this country are not deserving of them. When I was in power in 1793, I was shocked, in common with the few remaining friends of public instruction, at the acts of devastation committed by our mobs and others against the monuments of science and the arts. I therefore moved in the Assemblée Constituante a decree of two years' imprisonment against any person found to injure or degrade, either through ignorance, barbarism, or wilfulness, any object connected with the Arts and Sciences, which decree was carried."

With the *ci-devant* bishop I had had a short intercourse by letter through a mutual friend, himself one of the leading characters in the early period of the great revolution. I allude to Citoyen Prieur,* a staunch and good republican. I forget at this moment what the "écrit" was to which the good bishop alludes, but here is the letter, written in a firm hand, distinct, and showing only a slight token of distraction (not surprising in an old man) in the omission of the first half of the word *souvenir* :—

"Paris. 29 Mai, 1815.

"MONSIEUR,—J'ai reçu avec reconnaissance, et lu avec un vif intérêt, l'écrit que M. Prieur m'a remis de votre part. Le *venir* de votre bienveillance en double le prix. A la première entrevue je vous sousmettrais quelques observations ; et agréez, monsieur, mes justes et sincères remercîments, que je me propose de vous réitérer incessamment de vive voix.

"GRÉGOIRE, Évêque."†

---

* Distinct from another Prieur de la Mâme. The present was member, with Canot, of that branch of the Comité du Salut Publique which had to provide the arms for the army and' superintend all objects of art and' instruction.

† "I received with gratitude and read with great interest the essay which M. Prieur gave me from you. The recollection of your courtesy enhances its value. At our first meeting I will submit to you some observations I have made, and beg you to accept my sincere thanks, which I trust soon to offer to you in person."

This remarkable character, better known under the name of " l'Abbé Grégoire," was considered a great metaphysician and a famous preacher. He was originally professor of moral philosophy, and has written many essays against the theists and " Les Esprits Forts." His conversation was pleasing and fluent, but I doubt very much whether his erudition was as profound as his loquacity was redundant.

At the countess's *soirée* to which I had introduced Mr. Hamilton, little more of importance was mooted, but as the Cent Jours had been referred to, which had only recently terminated, some one introduced the story of what had occurred to Bonaparte when First Consul as regards the Institut, of which he was a member, as contrasted with his conduct after his return from Elba. The object of such a reference appeared to me to have been merely a desire to expose the cringing disposition of the *savants* to the imperious First Consul in the person of the illustrious author of the " Mécanique Céleste." Bonaparte had been at college with Laplace, whom he liked and admired, and appointed Minister of Marine (a blunder soon to be rectified by dismissal). Being made First Consul for life, Bonaparte paid a visit to the Institut, and happened to arrive at the end of a discussion on a paper that had just been read, but of the nature and aim of which he was entirely ignorant. He nevertheless demanded " la parole " to speak on the subject, though unprepared, unfit, and uncalled. Every one affected a studied attention ; many laughed in their sleeves ; but there were members who saw whither Bonaparte was leading—the summit of power, which he would not be long in attaining. These thought that no time should be lost in trying to gain his good graces. Among such members Laplace was a foremost one. As little informed as Bonaparte himself on the subject-matter of the paper, he declared that the First Consul was perfectly right in what he ad-

francs for the hire of a splendidly furnished hotel for three days, and three thousand more for the hire of a suitable retinue of attendants, all dressed *en habit noir et bien blanchis*, together with about twenty-five thousand francs more for refreshments, besides handsome fees to the principal signori of the Italian Opera and of the Opéra Comique with their conductors—in fact, are you ready and willing to spend fifty thousand francs on a *fête qui fera époque*, as we Parisians say?"

"Quite ready," was the reply, "and delighted." Accordingly the announcement of the arrival of Monsieur and Madame Morrison was inserted in all the morning and evening papers, and a grand hotel, *entre cour et jardin*, belonging to a nobleman, and well known for its splendid furniture and choice collection of pictures, was hired in the Faubourg St.-Germain for three days, at the cost of five thousand francs. Two thousand francs additional were stipulated for the large retinue of clever and imposing servants in full evening dress, quite plain, as Mr. Morrison, in his character of a semi-United States man, could not have displayed liveries without an anachronism.

All the other preparations were made in proportion by the kind friend, and the cards sent out as arranged. Mr. and Mrs. Morrison knew very well that time must be given for people to accept invitations from a stranger, and that the intended guests would consult among themselves as to the propriety of accepting the invitation. He had therefore fixed on the evening of a distant day in the following week, and most assuredly the interval was a period of no little perplexity to most of the invited.

"But who is this Mr. Morrison?" asked a great lady of her own kind doctor, well known in the world. "Indeed, madame, I could not tell you, except that he is said to be a millionaire!" "Ma chère," inquired the husband of la

Marquise de D., "do you mean to go?" "Certainly," she replied; "the Duchesse de B. is going, and assures me everybody will be there!"

In another great family all hesitation was done away with by an assurance that at the English Embassy Mr. Morrison was considered as a most clever as well as an exceedingly wealthy merchant. And so everybody determined to accept. They replied accordingly, and sure enough never did the quiet and silent streets of the aristocratic *quartier* of Paris present such an unprecedented and tremendous mass of smart carriages as conveyed the *élite* of the *élite* of the high and fashionable society of Paris to the brilliant assembly of Mr. and Mrs. Morrison, both of whom did the honours of the evening admirably, especially the lady, who appeared perfectly qualified for her position, being both a handsome and a ladylike woman.

At one o'clock in the morning a magnificent supper was served, following a most delightful concert, in which the best and united talents of the Italian and French operas achieved great success. At dawn of day the company began to disperse, and as each guest stepped into his or her carriage, he or she received a splendid enamelled card, with an inscription in French, which the increasing daylight enabled the curious to read—"M. Morrison remercie, and begs to recommend the never-failing vegetable pills sold at the Hygeian Temple, City Road, London."

Incredulous readers of this droll story may refer for its truth to the Préfet de Police of the time, or to any survivors among the *employés* of the British Embassy in Paris in the month of June, 1817.

One very agreeable acquaintance I made about this time was Sir Charles Long, who, indeed, had joined the Ellenborough party in many of our explorations. Sir Charles honoured me with a visit, having a particular object in view on account of the Prince Regent, to whose court he was attached, and in which he enjoyed special favour. As a mineralogist, it had happened to me to make the acquaintance shortly before of Sir Abraham Hume, who had a choice collection of minerals. At his house I had met Sir Charles, who had married Sir Abraham's only daughter and heiress. Sir Charles being commissioned to execute in Paris a simple homely commission for Carlton House, was sent to me by Sir Abraham, and I felt too happy in the opportunity of being of essential service in enabling his son-in-law to accomplish his mission. It may raise a smile in such as peruse the following lines after having read this species of serious introduction, when I go on to say that Sir Charles, a man of the world and of talent, had come to Paris principally to secure the purchase of the captured emperor's precious collection of a certain exquisite burgundy, which gourmets who had frequently dined at the imperial table had extolled to the sky with so much pertinacity as to make the Prince of Wales very desirous to possess so delicious a wine. It was supposed by Sir Abraham that no person in Paris, taking an interest in English concerns, could better know how to help Sir Charles in his mission than the doctor. And so it turned out, for through the means of an Italian long connected with the *cuisine* of the late emperor, we were enabled to secure the whole quantity of the Clos de Vougeôt left, which was forthwith transferred to the cellars of Carlton House. I heard a long time after, from Lord St. Helens, that the Regent had expressed himself much pleased at the slender service I had rendered on the occasion; that he enjoyed the Clos de Vougeôt much, which had cost £10 per dozen; but that in a year or two the treacherous burgundy revolted at the *triste* and sad climate of Great

Britain, by becoming spoilt and good for nothing, as all
Burgundy wines will do.

I have mentioned this trivial fact because it procured me
a most agreeable connection with Sir Charles Long, who
some time after consented to be godfather to my fourth son
Walter, lately Consulting Architect to the Government of
India, and Architect to the Government of Bengal.*

In a short time Sir Charles Long became a peer, and
under the title of Lord Farnborough frequently invited me
to his delicious Tusculum at Bromley, near London. Here
I had on more than one occasion the satisfaction of looking
through a pane of purest white crystal—in a gilt frame
occupying the lower half of a wide window, so as to have
the semblance of a picture—at one of the most lovely
landscapes my eyes have ever beheld.

At the commencement of my voluntary duty as a reporter
of the proceedings of the Institute of France to our
journal of science published by Brande, which reports
formed not the least important portion of each number of
that journal, I knew almost all the members by name, and
many of them personally, with whom I used to converse
during the day meetings. Being desirous, however, to become more intimately acquainted with the most eminent of
those members, to a few only of whom I was well known,
I requested Baron Humboldt to introduce me to some I
named. It was settled in consequence that my object
should be carried out at the approaching annual assembling
of the classes of sciences at the Institute, which was to take

* [This son, Walter Long, was educated at St. Paul's School, and afterwards
received his professional education in Paris and London. He resided in India,
chiefly in Calcutta, for more than twelve years, where his services were
engaged for the purpose of designing and constructing the large public
buildings required by the government. Retiring from his profession on his
return to England in 1870, he only survived his father one year and ten
months, dying suddenly in the prime of life, of disease of the heart, January
10th, 1874, beloved, esteemed, and regretted by all who knew him.—Ed.]

place in the following week, but a day or two before I received the following note from the baron :—

"CHER MONSIEUR,—La séance de la classe des sciences de l'Institut a été transférée de lundi à mardi, à cause de la fête. Comme vous désirez être présenté à quelques savants illustres de cette capitale, je vous propose de passer chez moi, non à midi, mais vers les deux heures. Je vous prie d'agréer l'expression de ma haute considération.

"HUMBOLDT.

"Ce Mardi. Quai Malaquais, No. 3."*

With the personal acquaintance of those to whom the baron introduced me, and the few I knew intimately already, from having studied under them, I was enabled to enter more earnestly into the consideration of the actual scientific world and its doings in Paris, and of representing it accurately as well as correctly to the readers of the journal of the Royal Institution. Liberal, and even prodigal, as I had been for many months in my communications of scientific and literary news sent home, I did not meet in return with much alacrity on their part in keeping me *au fait* with what transpired in science in the United Kingdom. It was from the fountain-head of science itself, the venerable President of the Royal Society, Sir Joseph Banks (who had always permitted me to call him my friend), that I received the first glimpse of scientific and medical information in the following letter :—

"Soho Square. July 23rd, 1817.

"MY DEAR SIR,—In these times of vacation you will, I trust, be contented with the small proportion of novelty that presents itself. Science is, I trust, at work, but it works like a mole out of sight, and will not bring to light

* "The meeting of the science class at the Institute has been postponed from Monday to Tuesday, in consequence of the fête. As you are desirous of becoming acquainted with some of the most illustrious savants of this capital, I propose that you come to me, not at twelve, but about two o'clock."

its performances till the Society will meet again. I have, however, great pleasure in stating that our Astronomer Royal has, by an ingenious application of a fixed telescope, settled, I trust effectually, the question that was lately set afloat by Doctor Brinkley, who supposed that he had been able to observe a parallax in some of the larger of the fixed stars. This Mr. Pond considers as erroneous, for although his apparatus is far better contrived for observing minute differences than that of Doctor Brinkley, he is utterly unable to distinguish anything that can give suspicions even of any parallax being observable. He has given a set of observations on this head to the Royal Society, which will be continued till the paper must of necessity go to press, so that I consider the question is entirely settled, and the fact of no parallax reinstated in its ancient place.

" I have just taken a step in medicine that has given me great pleasure, after having for several years almost existed by means of the Eau d'Husson, which never failed to relieve me from the gout, although the returns were at one time not more than thirteen or fourteen days asunder. I have discharged my last attack on Sunday last by the use of the vinum colchi, as it is prepared at St. George's Hospital, which mode of preparation destroys the mischievous power of the colchicum, leaving it power to destroy the gout itself. The *rationale* of the process has been read at the Royal Society by Sir Everard Home, and will be included in the next volume of the Transactions. Eau d'Husson never failed to remove my gout; but this new medicine has acted with still greater energy, and with most perfect effect. I am better as I now write, better than I could write for some years, and I feel pleasure indescribable in the share I have had in placing in the hands of the medical faculty the certain means of relieving their patients from the most painful disease they had to encounter, as well as the most unprofitable. Let the gout be no longer called the *opprobrium medicorum.* Adieu,

> " My dear Sir,
>> " Very faithfully yours,
>>> " J. BANKS.*

" P.S.—Allow me to request the favour of you to forward the enclosed to Signor Capini at Milan."

Part of Sir Walter Farquhar's plan was that I should come to London to attend a course of lectures by Mr. Clarke, that I might learn the English peculiarities of the office of accoucheur where they differ from the French practice. I was just now at the end of all the courses of my Paris lectures, and therefore the time had come for me to cross over to complete the entire programme I had promised to follow with a view to secure a suitable as well as a reputable station in the capital.

---

* I recollect well the time when people suffering from gout used to fly to the French quack medicine, which, being a sedative, diminished the present pain at the expense of a more frequent repetition of the gouty attacks. Nor have I forgotten that the recommendation of a London general practitioner, who pretended to have ascertained that the basis of the Eau d'Husson was the seeds or the expressed juice of the autumnal meadow saffron, brought into vogue the infusion of that herb in sherry to mitigate the paroxysm of gout. Sir Everard Home, himself a great sufferer, was the first to adopt and eulogize colchicum. Next followed my excellent correspondent, who like his adviser, Sir Everard, Sir Gore Ouseley, Hugh Duke of Northumberland, and many more I could name (great partisans of the d'Husson, and afterwards of the colchicum), died worn out by the increased reiteration of their attacks and the imperfect manner each paroxysm was suspended by the remedy, so that both feet and hands had in all those instances become monstrosities. Good Sir Joseph only survived three years after his pæan over d'Husson and colchicum ! No ! gout is still the *opprobrium medicorum ;* and so are many other disorders.

CHAPTER IX.

1817—18.

UPON my arrival in London I disposed of my little house
at Brompton, which was still tenanted by my friend
Pistrucci, and purchased the remainder of the lease of a
house, No. 8, Savile Row, to commence on the 1st of
January, 1818, with liberty to put in furniture a few days
previously. Clarke's lectures, which occupied me about six
weeks, certainly placed the matter of my intended profession
in a different light from the French system as regards propriety and manner, respecting which, nevertheless, I soon
discovered that I could make further improvements. Still
Mr. Clarke did me good service, and Anglicized me to
perfection ; but I got nothing superior to what I had learned
where I had come from as regards judgment, dexterity,
delicacy of action, and firmness of nerves, and furthermore
as to the mode of getting out of unexpected difficulties.

The next step I had to take was to submit for three days
to a medical, anatomical, and physiological examination
before the president and censors of the Royal College of
Physicians, whose home was in an old edifice in the City.
The president was Doctor John Latham (I know not
whether the father or grandfather of the present excellent

physician of that name), and my friend Dr. Paris, whose assistant I had been years before at the Westminster Hospital, was one of the censors or examiners. The examination took place in the Latin language. I remember quite well having for companions two remarkable fellow candidates, namely, the surgeon who had received the last words and sigh of Nelson on board the *Victory*, and a Doctor Armstrong, author of a treatise on fever which had created quite a furore among the profession, and had secured an enormous practice to its author, for which latter reason he was pulled up by the censors and made to come before them for his licence. He was however rejected, not from malice, I am quite sure, not because he was almost entirely ignorant of the Latin language, but really and truly because, however successful he may have been in his practice, he appeared to be very deficient in his knowledge of anatomy and physiology. Doctor Paris told me some time after, that Doctor Armstrong had failed to answer almost every question as regards the internal organization and functions of the body, although they patiently waited a considerable time after every question. "At last," said Dr. Paris, "I thought of one of the simplest possible questions that should give him a chance to come off well, and so I asked 'Dic mihi, domine, ubi locatum est hepar?' 'In corpore, domine,' was the immediate reply! (Where is the liver placed? In the body, sir.) "Satis est," exclaimed the president, "you may retire, sir," and he was accordingly not admitted. Can it be true?* But Paris was a wag and a true Cantab of St. John's.

Nelson's surgeon, however, passed, and became a M.D.; and so did another naval surgeon at the same time, myself

* Of the fact of his rejection, however, there was no doubt, at which all the medical world stared.

to wit, who did not require a diploma of M.D., as I had presented on my first application for admission a diploma from my own alma mater with such signatures as made them all stare, being those of Scarpa, Rasori, Frank, Borda, Moscati, and Volta under the great sigillum of the Goddess of Liberty and the inscription of " Repubblica Italiana."

The next transaction of an equally satisfactory and flattering issue followed not many days after, namely, my attendance at the apartments of the Royal Society in Somerset House. Before leaving Paris this last time I had heard that my name had been suspended for ballot as a fellow, and that the certificate bore some weighty names. I was not aware of any enemies among the Fellows, many of whom I knew had worked hard for me. I knew also that I had the good opinion of the venerable president ; I therefore presented myself with little apprehension of the result of the ballot. Indeed, had I then seen, as I was permitted afterwards to see, the range of names subscribed to my certificate, I should not have entertained the smallest doubt of the success of the ballot. I may be excused, I hope, this bit of personal vanity if I exhibit the names of the friends who in my absence had arranged and brought to a successful issue a movement in my favour of which I was not aware till summoned for admission. Here is the copy of the " Certificate in favour of Augustus Bozzi Granville, M.D., Foreign Secretary of the Geological Society, Fellow of the Linnean Society, and Member of the Royal·College of Surgeons, well versed in many branches of Science," &c., &c. Signed Wm. Hamilton (Under Secretary of State for Foreign Affairs), William Daniel, W. H. Wollaston, J. McGregor, Wm. M. Leake, Thomas Young, M.D., Humphry Davy, Gilbert Blane, J. Solly, P. M. Marcet, M.D., Henry Holland, M.D., Wm. Blake—being twelve of the Fellows who not. only ruled but honoured the Society, and were justly deemed at that time the Principes Scientiarum. Alas! eleven of these out of the total number of my supporters have preceded me into another and a better world.

The issue of the ballot being known (for I insisted on being present as a visitor on the occasion) my name was called, and on my ascending the platform on which the president and the two secretaries sat, I was most courteously, and I am convinced most heartily, addressed by Sir Joseph Banks, who welcomed me among the fellows. Here again, as at the college in Warwick Lane, I paid my fifty pounds composition fee, and, loaded with professional honours, I retreated soon to recross the Channel and rejoin my family.

In the course of the last few weeks of the concluding year I took leave of my kind French friends, learned and others, for our domestic friends had gradually increased in number as we were almost considered as natives, so quickly had father, mother, and three small children acclimated themselves to Paris, its manners and language. I was rather surprised when the time came for bidding adieu to the acquaintances we had made during our sojourn in Paris of nineteen months, to find how large was the circle of such intimates as had interchanged domestic visits with us. My wife and I had been frequently invited to private parties as well as to dinners, which afforded us ample opportunities of becoming well acquainted with French domestic habits and ways of life, which, although differing from our own English habits, were still generally agreeable. We more than once spent our evenings with Monsieur and Madame Arago at the Observatoire, of which he was the director, which afforded us occasions for surveying parts of the heavens or of scrutinizing the surface of a full moon. My young wife had made herself agreeable to Madame Arago, with whom she was a favourite. "Comme elle est aimable, cette jolie petite Anglaise!" she used often to say.

The last time I dined at the Observatoire, I met Baron Humboldt, one of Arago's most intimate friends. The conversation was of course scientific, still lively, for both the baron and Arago were rather inclined to wit and humour. I however put in a word or two of serious conversation, by mentioning how much I had been delighted and instructed by the course of lectures given by Cuvier, and expressed regret that I did not possess a concise biography of the lecturer, which I could introduce into the account I might at some future period give of those admirable lectures to the English public. "Ne vous inquiétez pas pour cela, cher docteur; je serais charmé de vous fournir une partie de tous les renseignements biographiques de mon ancien ami Cuvier, qui est presqu'Allemand."[*]

Accordingly I received from him next day a short account, the translation of which I here insert:—"Baron Cuvier is a Protestant, born of respectable but obscure parents at Montbéliard, a town in the Electorate of Wurtemburg at the time. He obtained a place in the Court College of Stuttgart, where he acquired that stiff unbending manner which never left him; for being accustomed to a long queue, powder, and a cocked hat, it was difficult for him to change. Here, having terminated his first studies, he required to Tübingen, to prosecute the study of natural history; and it was at this university that his inclination directed him to the study of comparative anatomy, in which he had the advantage of the lectures of Professor Killmayer, a man than whom no one enjoys a higher reputation as an accurate observer and good anatomist, though he has pub-

---

[*] "Do not trouble about that, dear doctor; I shall be charmed to give you some biographical information concerning my old friend Cuvier, who is almost a German."

lished but few things. His MSS., which circulate through
the hands of his numerous and devoted pupils throughout
Germany, have served to spread his name. Killmayer had
worked on the molluscæ, for which purpose he made a
voyage to Holland and to the Italian coasts. Cuvier, by a
similarity of taste, followed greatly the bent of his master's
studies and researches, and he has since been put in possession of several memoirs on this interesting branch of natural
history, for which the Germans have raised an outcry
against him, adopting the words of a number of illiberal
persons in France, who accuse him of appropriating to himself researches not his own, but which accusation we are
inclined to consider as unfounded. He may perchance have
touched upon subjects in common with his old master, and
become enriched with new and accurate ideas without having
copied him. At the fall of the terrorist's reign, Tessier, an
agriculturist and a *savant* of mediocre merits, found him a
preceptor in the family of a ' cultivateur ' in Normandy,
where he had resided some time, making occasional
tours to the coast, whence he returned with new subjects of
inquiry. It was in this quality that he wrote his first essay
which made him known to the public, ' On the Larynx
of Animals.' Propositions were made to him to become one
of the assistants at the Jardin des Plantes, which place he
accepted, and immediately filled. Here finding that a connection with political men was perhaps the only mode of
getting on in the world, he turned a fierce republican—
wrote, spoke, and preached the favourite principles of the
day, and from that moment succeeded in coupling his
scientific with his political career," &c.—From Baron
Humboldt, Morin's Hotel, 19th November, 1816. Paris.

I preferred to cite this brief, able, though laconic, account
of the great naturalist of Wurtemburg from the pen of the
great *savant* and philosopher of Prussia as I received

it, the writer's sagacity and truth being guarantees of the reality of Cuvier's early career, which is after all what imports most to my readers as an indication of what Cuvier was to be. However, it is the case even with regard to a Cuvier to inquire, " Quel est le grand homme qui n'a pas sa - faiblesse ? "* and Cuvier's vanity was his. I will cite one or two examples. I cannot vouch for the veracity of both, as I certainly was not present when the interview between Cuvier and the Prince Regent took place, but I can for the second, as an eye and ear witness. When Cuvier visited this country, he was of course received with the greatest kindness and *empressement*. Much attention was paid to him by scientific men, and he was presented at Court. The prince, in his very affable manner, asked him if he had seen anything to interest him particularly in the way of public and private collections of scientific objects in London, and whether he were pleased with them. " Assuredly, your Royal Highness," answered the professor, " there is a great deal well worth seeing ; but it is a pity everything is not altogether in one and the same place as it is with us." " It is probably the ease with which you have formed a Louvre in France, that makes you think so, Monsieur le professeur," said the prince ; " but we do things differently in this country, and are none the worse for it." Here the great naturalist did not come out " best."

On another occasion when Cuvier was driving with an acquaintance to a dinner party in the country, the subject of conversation fell upon the English orators in parliament. " I have heard the best," observed Cuvier, " though I arrived but three days before the end of the session." " And who do you consider the cleverest—the one who made most impression on you ?" " Why, sir, I found Lord Grey's eloquence forcible, argumentative, terse, and to the point. Sir Samuel

* " What great man but has his weakness ?"

Romilly pleased me greatly: he has a fine presence, good action, and a pleasing voice. Of Sir Francis Burdett I hardly know what to say, but the man I think the most of, in every particular, is Canning," and he proceeded with a magnificent eulogium on Mr. Canning's eloquence ; then all at once he asked, " Did you ever hear me in the Chamber?" pulling up the corner of his shirt collar. "Never." " Tant pis " (so much the worse), was the reply.

As I had attended all the lectures necessary to qualify me to apply for admission as a doctor of medicine, and also as Docteur des Sciences, after proper examination, it was expected by the professors both of the Ecole de Médecine and at the Jardin des Plantes that I would avail myself of the privilege, and they hailed, as they told me, the occasion of receiving me as their colleague. But I respectfully declined to enter into more engagements with corporate bodies than I was already bound to in many ways and in more than one country. At the same time I expressed a wish to receive from each of my professors who should deem me worthy of it, a written declaration of the individual estimation they felt disposed to give me of my attainments and qualifications. Nearly all the professors and distinguished philosophers accordingly sent me attestations of their esteem and opinion during my career while in Paris ; and the history of the destiny of some of those, to me, precious documents, through the oblique morality of a late illustrious Lord Chancellor and philosopher, will appear singular when divulged in a future part of my present narrative.

It was arranged between my wife and me, that with our little daughter Julia I should proceed to London, to get our new house in Savile Row ready, and that mamma and the two younger children should soon follow, so as to be all reunited again in old England on a given day, the 1st of

January, 1818.   I had quite determined that, D.V., on the
night of the 31st December I would sleep under what I
might properly call my own roof, and wake to the light of
day on the 1st of January, 1818, which was to be, as the
Romans used to say to one another, "Annum novum
faustum felicem mihi"—the commencement of the great
venture, the attempt to settle in practice in the great
metropolis of England.

Again my connection with the Foreign Office and diplomacy enabled me to take charge of some important despatches
Sir Charles Stuart had to send home, not one of the King's
Messengers happening to be at hand.   The bags therefore
were intrusted to me, and with these, and my dear little
Julia, I set off from Paris on the night of the sixth of November, 1817.   It was with much pain I parted from my favourite
eldest sister, Madame de Lafolie, for I had noticed the very
uncertain state of her husband's health, suffering as he was
from disease of the heart; but I tried to comfort her with
assurances of my constant brotherly affection, and promises
to help her should she require aid and I possessed the
means of giving it—two coincidences which Providence
permitted to come to pass.

The crossing was prosperous.   At the Ship Inn at Dover,
my old shipmate, Mr. Wright, gave us some refreshment
while the chaise was being got ready, and we galloped off
soon after.   Arriving at the last turnpike at the dawn of
day of the 7th November, while the toll for the four horses
was being paid, the toll-keeper said, "I suppose you have
learned on the road the dreadful news?"   "What? the
Princess?" said I unconsciously.   "Yes!   Dead!   Died
last night in childbed."   "Too late!   too late!"   I
involuntarily exclaimed as we drove off.   "You need not
gallop," I called out to the postillions.   My little daughter,
who had been startled out of her sleep at the turnpike, now

inquired why it was too late, and appeared inclined to sob; but I soon quieted her by saying we should soon be home, and not too late.

The soliloquy, "Too late! too late!" was addressed to my own presumptuous spirit alone. In the course of the afternoon of the 6th of November, an evening paper had fallen under my notice at Dover, which I bought and took with me, and in which I found a paragraph giving an account of the dangerous state of Princess Charlotte, in consequence of some unforeseen difficulty that had arisen which baffled the skill of Sir Richard Croft, her attendant, and had rendered necessary further aid, but unfortunately aid sought from a practitioner, Dr. Sims, who no doubt was called in for his great seniority, and not from his adroitness in difficult cases. For how could such be expected from a man who had arrived at a patriarchal age? Here was a case calling for prompt manual dexterity, which the old physician had lost along with his youth and vigour, and for this reason (applicable equally to the former attendant, Sir Richard Croft) two most precious lives were left in jeopardy, looking in vain for help. Now, such cases were precisely those amidst which I had been practising for so many months; difficulties perilous always, but to be overcome by agile and bold interference. Repeated experience gives both those faculties to the practitioner, and such was the case with myself, who after all the difficulties I had confronted in the great lying-in hospital in Paris, felt that no case could ever present itself which I was not prepared for. That the case of the ill-fated princess was one of this nature, as I had conjectured, was afterwards asserted by Sir Richard Croft's medical assistant, Dr. Herbert, a young practitioner who was present (as I was informed) in the house, though not employed on the occasion. I had therefore, and in reality, been "too late!" Had I arrived (thus reasoned my presumptuous spirit), had I arrived one day sooner, Sir Walter Farquhar, as physician to the Prince Regent, would have recommended that a medical man fresh from a Paris lying-in hospital should be called in. The difficulty once over-come that threatened two lives, and these saved, the British crown might have descended on a different head. Never could it have been worn by one more fitted to fill the exalted station than the august lady who now wears that crown, only my own fate would have been different, for I should have filled the office which fell instead on a brother naval officer of mine, the late Sir James Clark, Bt.

" Pity you did not arrive sooner," was my first greeting from Sir Walter Farquhar as I entered his drawing-room, where his unmarried daughter, with Mr. Chilver, the apothecary, and Sir William Knighton, physician to the Prince Regent, were present and re-echoed the observation. But I found Sir Walter himself very far from the state of health which could satisfy an anxious, friendly, and keen-sighted pathologist. In fact, he was fast verging to that state which I described in these pages on my first introduc-tion to him, and the realization of which was now actually taking place. I at once offered my services, and to take my turn to attend upon him, whether by night or by day.

By the end of December my wife and children were to come from Paris to Savile Row. As usual with all English workpeople, when they say they have nearly done they are only on the eve of postponing the end. After a few days, seeing what the result would be, I was actually reduced to expel them and retake possession of the house furnished or unfurnished, for I had quite made up my mind, as I have already said, that the first day of the new year should see me in my own home.

During the interval between my arrival and that of my family from Paris, good luck offered me an unexpected opportunity of connecting myself with one of the first-class dispensaries in the west-end. In default of belonging to a general hospital, the position of physician accoucheur to a dispensary "for the delivery of married women at their own habitations" was considered by the profession as a very important one, as the contested election in which I found myself involved fully testified. Dr. Merriman, the physician who vacated the office after many years' gratuitous service, never imagined that any competitor would arise to oppose his own *protégé*, assistant, and pupil, Doctor Hugh Ley ; still less that a new man from abroad, unknown and a foreigner (for that was the point made most of against me), would thus venture to contest the election. Yet I did venture to contest it, and carried it by a majority of forty-five votes. On this occasion, all the English acquaintances I had made in Paris rallied round me and canvassed for me. Sir Joseph Banks, living and greatly esteemed in the very quarter of the town in which the dispensary was instituted, and of which he was a life governor, not only obtained a good number of single votes from the subscribers in the neighbourhood, but went himself to vote in person, the chairman going down to his carriage to receive his ten votes, as the gout prevented him from walking up stairs to the committee-room. The Ellenborough family had secured me the aid and advice, as well as the votes, of Sir Richard Birnie, the chief police magistrate, who in his turn got me the ten proxy votes of the Duke of York. Sir Walter Farquhar applied for the Prince Regent's (patron of the dispensary) twenty-five votes. Sir Charles Long and others, with some members of the Hamilton family, became life governors on the occasion, to enable them to give their personal votes in my favour. Still, the single votes of the dwellers round the neighbourhood and from the subscribers came pouring into the committee-room, as I

could see through the windows when they alighted from
their conveyances. At length the stroke of 4 P.M. arrived,
when Sir Richard Birnie from the chair declared the ballot
closed, and invited the two candidates to produce and
deposit on the table the respective proxy votes they had
collected. At that very moment a small packet was put
into my hand with the name of " Northumberland" signed
in the left angle of the packet. His grace was the president
of the institution, and his were twenty proxy votes. These
I added to my other packets, and the whole of them were
deposited before the chairman. The scrutineers, who had
retired into an adjoining room, soon returned with their
report. " Doctor Hugh Ley, 423 votes; Doctor Granville,
422." Sir Richard then proceeded to open the proxy
papers, and dictated to the secretary the numbers of votes
in each paper on either side, and these being afterwards
summed up by the secretary, and verified by the chairman
himself (in the presence of a large meeting of subscribers,
who filled the room), gave a majority of forty-five votes in
my favour, in consequence of which Sir Richard rose and
proclaimed me to be duly elected " Physician Accoucheur
to the Westminster General Dispensary." This result I set
down as a good omen for the future.

" Is this what you call being ready?" exclaimed my
good wife in mild but astonished accents when, arrived
with her two small children and their French nurse in
Savile Row, she surveyed all round the state of confusion I
was in, without a single article of furniture in its right place.
I wished to merit the reputation of a real man of business,
and was determined to be at my post on the first day of the
year; so after tea, and desiring the footman to see to the
resplendent lamp 1 had set up over the street door, that my
name in large letters on a brass plate, and the smaller one,
" night bell," might appear conspicuously (there was no gas

in those days), we retired for the night—to rest I can hardly call it.

It might have been about three or four o'clock in the morning, when a terrible rat-a-tat at the door and a strong pull at the " night bell " startled us all. " Here is the first case," I said laughingly to my wife, at the same time starting to my feet, for I had lain down with only my coat off. I threw up the window-sash and demanded, " Who is there ? " " Oh, sir," was the answer, " I wish you would come at once to my wife. Mr. Stone, her doctor, is out of town, and Mr. Clarke, who recommended him to us, at whose house I have just called, refuses to go out at night to any patient, and I fear there is no time to lose ; so pray do come, sir, for God's sake ! " " And where do you live, and what is your name?" " My name is Wagner, the hatter in Pall Mall, No. 15, and I voted for you at the Westminster Dispensary last week." " Enough ; I'll follow you immediately," I cried, as I closed the window.

I did so, arriving almost as soon as the man himself. I attended to the lady, and after remaining a certain time, was about to leave, with a promise to visit the patient again at noon, when I supposed that Mr. Stone would resume the charge of his patient. " No, no," said the lady in a subdued, feeble voice ; " I will never see Mr. Stone again, nor Mr. Clarke either, who sent him. The one goes away and leaves me, and the other, who has attended me before, refuses to get out of bed to come to me. I will never see them again. You must return." The husband thought she was right, and I acquiesced. " That is blunder number one," exclaimed Sir Walter Farquhar to me when I reported to him the story of the previous night. " You should have insisted on Stone being kept in charge of the patient, and made over to him whatever fee you received. I tell you, doctor, you must be careful not to commit yourself again in the same manner. Mr. Stone will from this moment hate you!" Sir Walter was right. 1 do not say that Stone hated me, but he certainly did not love me.

In spite of all the promising preludes to my practice, I confess to a degree of moral trepidation which I experienced at contemplating the vast field before me, over which I should have to tread cautiously and slowly (probably more slowly than I should quite like), considering what I was hoping and expecting to achieve in order to secure a permanent and sufficiently lucrative position in the great metropolis of the most renowned kingdom in Europe, the seat of learning, of wealth, popular liberty, and the best-adjusted government on earth. Of the large number of competitors I had to meet in the race I was well aware; nor was I ignorant of the great weight of their names and authority in society. I did not profess to confine myself to the obstetrical branch alone of the profession; but I aimed, as by right entitled, to concur with them in the more elevated branch of a consulting physician, thus by one single declaration ranging against me an overawing phalanx of hostile competitors. For, disguise it as we may, it is not the elevating of the science of medicine that is considered so much as the earning of money—the filthy lucre; and therefore to eject any one that might attempt to interfere becomes an act of necessity. There were, to begin with, Matthew Baillie (himself a host), Warren, Pemberton, Babington, Maton, Halford, Bright, Chambers, Blane, and in my own particular branch, Croft, Sims, Knighton, Clarke, Merriman, Ramsbotham, and a troop of minor celebrities. They were one and all known to me, as they were, in fact, to the whole population of London. But to them I was an unknown cipher. How could I expect any important business to fall to my lot? Yet the sequel of this narrative will show that I was wrong in my misgivings, and that my more sagacious counsellor in Conduit Street was right in his prognostic of my success. Mrs. Wagner of Pall Mall was only the commencement of a list of engagements, some in and some out of town, and each case improving in importance and respectability.

I had overheard in the course of this increasing connection, people, especially husbands and fathers, making remarks as to my age and youthful appearance. I was not descended from the consular family of the Barbati of Rome, and my cheeks were very smooth. I had, however, from the very commencement of my practice taken care to assume the garb of a much older person, by adopting the dress I saw Sir Henry Halford, Dr. Latham, and other popular physicians wear, at which the sprightly M.D.s of the present day would laugh indeed. Yet was that style not only in fashion then, but positively expected in a practising physician. So I donned a square-cut coat of black cloth, a single-breasted black cloth waistcoat, descending low down, showing off the well-starched frill of an irreproachable white shirt, smalls with knee buckles, black silk stockings, and buckles in shining black narrow pumps. I did not adopt the gold-headed cane as well, but wore powder and a broad-brimmed hat, which completed the dress. It certainly added age to my appearance, and I was not long in getting used to it, as I had done to the more theatrical transformation in the Levant, when I assumed the Turkish vestments; but oh! how different, with the bother of buttons and buckles in the present instance! Fortunately, the dons in physic whom I had taken for models soon swerved from the stiff practice, to become more modernized in their views, and I was not long in following their steps by adopting the more ordinary day garb of all gentlemen.

My fee-book, which I set up along with my medical diary, was commencing to display a not inconsiderable list

of showy names. The name of one flattered me greatly,
though, after all, in my manner of attending her I committed, as Sir Walter rather angrily observed to me, my
second blunder. Viscountess Melbourne, mother of the
afterwards renowned minister, had been in a very dangerous
state of health for some weeks, and was supposed to be
dying. Application used to be made daily to Sir Walter
for advice, he having been originally physician to the family.
Dr. Warren was in attendance, and I believe a Mr. Jackson,
a favourite apothecary of the day in the west-end. The complaint had been represented variously to Sir Walter, and, puzzled by the diverse accounts they brought him, he thought
that by sending me to see her I might give him a more intelligible report. Accordingly I walked to Melbourne House
in Whitehall, the family being prepared for my visit, which
occupied about half an hour. Putting in practice all the
means of investigation necessary to ascertain the nature of
a doubtful complaint, I discovered that the viscountess was
in fact dying of an unchecked inflammation of the spleen,
which was considerably enlarged, and exquisitely painful on
the gentlest pressure. All the rest of the organs appeared
normal, although there was present a considerable oppres-
sion in breathing, natural enough considering the nature of
the disorder. With all this there was present a continuous
fever, which had never abated. The pulse was very rapid,
and the radial artery round, full, and hard; tongue of course
dry and brown. I made other inquiries of her maid, as well
as of Lady Caroline Lamb, who had been present during
the examination, and who explained to me that the doctors
in attendance had never gone through the same inquiries.
I said nothing in answer, and very little when we returned
to the drawing-room. I stated that I considered Lady
Melbourne's life in danger, but thought not irremediably so,
especially after receiving from the ladies negative answers

to certain questions respecting the antecedent treatment. These answers were given more than once, and without equivocation.

It became clear to me, therefore, that no serious view had been taken of the disorder, and that consequently no energetic measúres had been adopted. It is possible also, that the medical attendants were awed by the age of the patient; although I had myself discovered no signs of decrepitude. Pressed by the family to state what I should have recommended or deemed requisite to do at first, I excused myself by observing that it would be needless now to consider that point. What was of importance was to determine on the measures proper to be adopted at once, which I stated, though with regard to internal medicine I would not venture to suggest any without a previous consultation with Dr. Warren, the attendant physician of the patient, but who had not seen her for some hours, and was not likely to call before his usual hour on the following morning. Lady Bessborough, who was present, at once suggested that I should go up to Brook Street to see Dr. Warren, and consult with him on the case. "My carriage," she added, "is at the door, and I shall be happy to accompany you, as you are not personally acquainted with Doctor Warren." I acceded immediately to the proposition, and we drove to Doctor Warren's house.

By a curious coincidence a stranger was ensconced on one of the seats in the front part of the large coach, but him I did not observe, it being a dark night and after ten o'clock, and the conversation between Lady Bessborough and myself went on concerning the case. The present Dr. Robert Lee of Savile Row was the person, and he may remember the fact. He occupied at that period of his life the post of domestic physician in the countess's family, having charge of a young son afflicted with epilepsy; and he had been

waiting in the carriage to return home with Lady Bessborough after her visit to her mother in Whitehall.

Upon sending up my card with a message to Dr. Warren,
we received a reply that he could not be disturbed, and
that he was indisposed; upon this Lady Bessborough
walked up stairs to him, and he agreed to accompany her
back to Melbourne House, where a consultation took place
after he had been in to see his patient, whom he reported
to be still in the same state as he had left her in the morning—neither better nor worse ; in fact, he said " her crisis
had not yet taken place." When I expressed my opinion
in a few words as to the nature of the complaint, and the
means which, after much pressure by the family, I had suggested—" a step," I added, " which I regret to have taken
without previously conferring with you "—his curt observation to me was, " Oh, there is no occasion for an apology, since
I disagree entirely with your diagnosis, and of course shall
not consent to the measures proposed." " In that case," I
said, " we need not prolong our interview ;" and making my
bow to the ladies and to Dr. Warren, I found my way to the
door, got into a hackney coach, and drove home.

Dr. Warren, I learned afterwards, made his observations
on the nature of our meeting, and wrote a letter there and
then to Sir Matthew Tierney to meet him at Melbourne
House the next morning at 12 o'clock, for a fresh consultation on Lady Melbourne's case, Sir Matthew having attended her conjointly with Dr. Warren. Of course at the
said consultation everything that Dr. Warren had said and
done was right, and whatever Dr. Granville had proposed
would be deemed to be wrong and of no avail. Dr. Warren
complained to Sir Walter Farquhar that he had sent a
stranger and a foreign physician to visit his patient, and I
got a good scolding for " blunder number two."

CHAPTER X.

Mrs. Siddons—Her *insomnia*—Practice at the Westminster General Dispensary
—Reform the midwives—Annual reports—Proceed to Cambray—Military quarrels—Return home—The Duc de Brancas—Death of Lord
Ellenborough—How to reconcile a large practice with absence from
London—Illness of Lady Ellenborough—A sojourn in Italy recommended—Pisa selected for the winter—Prepare for a trip as travelling
physician—A suburban medical oracle.

SHORTLY after the last professional incident a much more
gratifying one came to pass, not only because the case in
this instance terminated favourably, but because the patient
was one with whom to be brought in contact in the character
of physician and patient was in itself a distinguished honour.
I allude to the tragic muse of one of our national theatres,
the inimitable actress who, gifted with a splendid figure and
a most commanding presence, had become an idol in the
dramatic world. Received with the most cordial feelings
night after night on the stage, her every step, her every
action and emphatic diction called forth repeated acclama-
tions of praise with plaudits the most earnest not less than
the loudest. So surrounded, so popular, what must not
have been the temptations which a treacherous world would
be ready to throw in the way of their idol? But she resisted
them all, sustaining the still higher character of a model of
domestic excellency as a dignified matron in society remarkable (as a French biographer said of her) "pour la dignité
de sa vie privée." Need I name Mrs. Siddons after such
an introduction?

On the 2nd of May, 1818, a simple note with a few

lines from her, then residing on the south border of the
Regent's Park, signified her wish to consult me professionally, a summons which I most cheerfully attended.
Mrs. Siddons' indisposition was one of that protean class
of disorders which ordinary people call "nervous," and
for which medical science offers but little direct relief, except
as regards one of the prolific branches of the disorder in
question, namely, a deranged state of digestion, or a temporary disturbance in the regularity of the heart's action.
Any direct medication of the nerves themselves is not at-
tainable, for they are only affected symptomatically, and
symptoms cannot be cured, though the disease they represent can.   My attendance on this gifted patient lasted some
little time, but my visits, as in all cases of chronic indisposition, were not frequent, and our conversation turned
principally on the nature of the morbid feelings she had
experienced in the intervals, with the view of eliciting fresh
information respecting their origin, or of discovering fresh
reasons for becoming reconciled to them.

Fortunately disorders of this class are the exceptional, or I
might say from natural laws the exclusive, lot of the cultivated and easy classes of society, to whom alone medical
explanations can be addressed with any success calculated
to reconcile the patient to his fate.   It would be vain to
allege physiological explanations to a boor to account for
his "feeling nervous," for such an expression is become
almost vernacular in England.   I have many a time, when
treating patients differently placed in society, succeeded in
gradually rendering them amenable, and finally converting
some of them to my views, by simple, just, and plausible
explanations.   Such was the case in the present instance,
and so fully did Mrs. Siddons see the logic of my reasoning,
that at a somewhat later period of her life, when she had
become subject to that most distressing "insomnia," or

absence of sleep at night, which afflicts old age, she again desired my attendance, that she might have an opportunity of discussing with me the cognate questions of sleep and dreams, and the assimilation of the latter phenomenon to death. To the discussion of those points she herself lent the valuable aid of references to her own experience, and remarks on the impressions left on her mind by the exercise of her magic art when pushed to an excess of agonizing feeling. The dialogues that passed between us were of an interesting character. Mrs. Siddons, sitting erect at one end of the couch on which she had asked me to take a place, delivered her often acute and sagacious observations with all that dramatic dignity (even to the solemn intonation of her voice) which accompanied her to her last days and in the most ordinary transactions of life—a queen to the end.

In the exercise of my duties at the Westminster General Dispensary, which I regularly attended three days in the week at noon, I had occasion soon to find, with much regret, that the twenty midwives on the establishment were indifferently qualified either by medical instruction or domestic training to inspire much confidence. There were three or four of the number who had derived benefit from instruction by my predecessors, and had civilized themselves intuitively, and these women I encouraged in their work. It was their duty to visit such married women at their own habitations as were likely to require their services by-and-by, according to my instructions contained in a printed letter bearing my signature, which was directed to a particular midwife living nearest to the patient. The object of such preliminary visit was that the patient and attendant should confer together, and make suitable arrangements for the time when the attendance would be required, as well as for watching the patient for some days subsequently, administering such medicine to her provided by the dispensary as I might have

prescribed. The results of the case and attending circumstances were to be recorded in writing by the nurse, there
and then as they occurred, in certain columns of the printed
form inserted at the back and front of the letter. The sum
paid at the dispensary for her attendance would not be
allowed and paid by the treasurer unless the blank forms of
the report had been properly filled up. At every out-of-
the-way occurrence or difficulty it was strictly enjoined to
the attending widwife to summon me by a written message,
which I felt bound to attend in every case, so that I might
with justice say that my practice at this public institution
was a practice of difficulties only. All had got into confusion, and little or no order was observed before my appointment. I therefore set about altering the whole system,
and I printed a series of plain directions to be attended to,
including a strict injunction that the midwife herself should
always be decently dressed, should herself carefully administer the medicament supplied, and correctly and accurately
insert all the particulars in which my interference had not
been required. The penalty for omission or neglect was
forfeiture of the pay, or dismissal from the establishment after a third instance of irregularity. By such rigid
means, and with the aid of some of my cleverest pupils
(whom I was not long in collecting at the dispensary), I
succeeded in obtaining perfect regularity and accuracy of
proceedings, so as to supply me by the end of fourteen
months of my attendance with valuable materials for a
general report of my obstetrical practice during the year
1818, addressed to the President and Committee of the
Institution.*

The committee were much pleased at the introduction of

* My report as presented was soon afterwards published, and forms the first
considerable of the several medical works I committed to the press. It bore
the following title : " Report of the Practice of Midwifery at the Westminster
General Dispensary for 1818," by A. B. Granville, M.D., F.R.S.

this new feature in their medical institution, of which they approved, and for which they directed their secretary to convey to me the resolution, unanimously passed, that in "the introduction of so novel a feature in the department of the charity confided to my care, I had deserved the thanks of the subscribers and set an example to the other medical officers of this and other institutions." I do not give more importance to this resolution than it is meant to express, but as regards a portion of it I think I shall not be contradicted if I add, that previously to the example I set, the practice of reading and publishing a full report of the annual proceedings at a medical institution had not been adopted in a single instance; whereas since that precedent, most valuable productions of such reports of the hospital practice at benevolent medical institutions have from year to year appeared, to the credit of the medical men concerned and the medical profession in particular, for whose ultimate benefit the practice is calculated, as well as for the welfare of society in general.

The commendation of the committee soon bore its fruit, for I received in a short time from General Sir Lowry Cole, commanding the second division of the British army stationed at Cambray, as part of what was called the English army of occupation, an application for a medical man to attend Lady Frances, Sir Walter Farquhar having recommended me for the occasion. While preparing for this fresh expatriation, the post brought me a letter from the wife of General Sir John Lambert, in command of the Guards at Cambray, expressing her hope that, as I was to be in Cambray so near the period when she herself would require my services, I might make it convenient to extend my stay there, a request to which I acceded. Here were encouraging prospects of success for a medical man in the first year of his practice. When in addition I mention that during the short time I continued in town previously to my setting off for my Cambray engagement, I had been consulted by nearly fifty new patients, including persons of distinction and others belonging to the cultivated and easier classes of society, I think I shall be readily believed if I say that my spirits were unusually elated.

The special business which had called me to Cambray turned out happily, for not only were the principal parties particularly satisfied, but the result in both cases proved to me the commencement of a continuous series of engagements which extended my reputation to the male branch of the population, among whom I had the good fortune of making many excellent friends, whose friendship, countenance, and esteem I enjoyed ever after.

Cambray at that epoch presented in every respect an extraordinary mixture of daily scenes of virtue and vice, order and licentiousness, the dulness of military drills with the splendid display of grand parades, of many staid military households of exemplary conduct with the more general ostentation of fashionable life. The close neighbourhood of Valenciennes, a French military station, at which public gambling was permitted, and where the theatre was much frequented by young officers of the English contingent in Cambray, became the focus of almost daily disputes between the officers of the two armies. Bullies out of some of the French regiments, soured in their temper by the last great thrashing they had sustained, would provoke the youngest of the British officers, especially such as had just joined and whom they considered to belong to the Guards, to fight duels with the sword by purposely treading on their toes without the ordinary "Pardon, monsieur," when in the pit of the theatre gaping at the actresses. Englishmen are seldom in practice with the fleuret, which being a known fact, the French declined the choice of pistols. At length,

in an encounter a young officer of a Guards' regiment
having fallen, a peremptory order from head-quarters forbade English officers to visit Valenciennes, or to accept or
provoke a duel. I had become very intimate with the
Town Major, a Captain Gunthorpe, as thorough-bred and
as brave a soldier as ever honoured the British army. He
was none of your soft window-peering clubbists who have
not yet smelt powder, but a stern, square-built, and determined martinet. We rode together, and he lamented all
the frippery he saw about him, so little like a real soldier's
encampment, he used to say. He heard the scandalous
rumours without believing them, and yet was not able to
contradict them. He was quite exasperated by the fall of
one young officer, and but for the official prohibition would
himself have gone over, he said to me, not to tread on the
toes, but to pull the nose of the bully who had fought
almost all the duels, and who it turned out was no other
than a celebrated fencing-master belonging to, and brought
purposely from, another French regiment stationed elsewhere in France, for the purpose of satisfying French
vanity. Such a fellow was too contemptible to stand before
the point of an honourable officer's sword, but should be
chastised à la Gregson—*i.e.* receive a good thrashing.

I am spared the task of giving an account of the reviews,
especially of the grand one on the 24th of October, 1818,
in which the contingents of four foreign armies were present,
by a recent publication of slight dimensions, purporting to
be the travels of Viscount Palmerston in foreign lands.*
That identical review is there very ably and correctly
described, as far as I could see it by following the movements on a spirited charger, which ended by throwing me
at the last general discharge from the combined artillery,
luckily without much detriment. Viscount Palmerston,

* " Tours in France in 1814 and 1818," by Henry Viscount Palmerston.

whom I met at Sir Lowry Cole's head-quarters, I knew by
sight.   Little did I imagine then that our future social
relations would in a short time become of more consequence
to me, and of greater service to him.

Truth bids me avow, that when on a gloomy and foggy
day, the 6th of November, 1818, I returned to my quiet home
in Savile Row—from which I had been absent three months,
living in a world totally unsuited to my tastes, feelings, and
sense of propriety, although I had been treated with every
mark of kindness, courtesy, and even friendship, which I carefully studied to preserve—I felt as if I had awakened from a
long dream since the sunny day in August on which I had left
my English hearth.. A large foreign correspondence awaited
me at home.   Some of the most intimate of my Parisian
friends, members of the Institute, or professors at the Ecole
de Médecine, wondered that I should have left London
so soon after my installation in it, as they understood I had
done.   They were not aware of the reasons of my absence;
but as they looked to me to keep them informed as to what
transpired, whether in science or medicine, they felt disappointed at the total failure of their expectations during
my three months' absence and consequent silence.   Nor
were the few select ones among my social friends less disappointed.   My strict Cruscan correspondent, Angeloni,
sent forth his purest and well-balanced periods to revive
and keep alive my love for our native land and attachment
to its beautiful language.   Thiébaut de Bernaud, the erudite
librarian of the Mazarine library, continued his learned
epistles, written always in that copper-plate-like style of
handwriting which made their perusal a matter of positive
pleasure, irrespective of the materials and ingenious arguments which they embraced.

Another letter which awaited me was from Count
Lauraguais, Duc de Brancas, one of the favourites of

Louis XV. of France, who admired his wit and his great facility of writing verses—a dangerous gift, that drove him into exile for a considerable time in England, where he became a perfect Anglomane. He was eighty-nine when I first became acquainted with him in Paris, and our two families were soon intimate. He admired the children, and above all the manner in which they were brought up by "cette admirable mère," as the duke used to call my wife.

Our correspondence when I was not in France was chiefly on science, which the duke had cultivated, having been an "ancien membre dans la section de mécanique," in the old Académie des Sciences.*

On the evening of the 13th of December, 1818, died my recent companion in Paris, the Lord Chief Justice of England. Before and soon after my excursion to Cambray I had occasion to pay a professional visit to Lady Ellenborough. She was greatly concerned at the state of health in which Lord Ellenborough had come back from Paris the year before, but as he had returned to his labours as Chief Justice without complaining either of fatigue or of want of head energy, it was concluded that any little ailment he might complain of would pass off, as it had done on many other occasions. Such was the opinion of his medical attendant, a well-known apothecary living in Portman Square, who had more patients than half a dozen of the most popular physicians together could boast of. On this occasion, however, he was wrong, and Lady Ellenborough was left a widow, whom Lord Campbell has told us he recollected as a mature matron; "still a fine woman, with regular features, and roseate complexion;" to which

* To have been intimate in the year 1817 in Paris with a great nobleman aged ninety, a *bel esprit* of the time of Louis XV., whose good graces he had enjoyed for a time until infelicitously mixed up with his doggrel verses in the *tripot* of la Du Barry at the Petit Trianon, are historical facts deserving a foot-note in my autobiography of 1871.

his lordship adds, " when she first appeared she excited admiration almost unprecedented."

For a considerable time I had lost sight of the family, and my practice in the mean time, during the spring and early summer months, had become sufficiently extensive to satisfy all my modest aspirations. I had moreover enough occupation in preparing for the press the report already alluded to, of the result of practice during the year 1818 at the dispensary, besides publishing a small brochure on prussic acid.

I look back with some pride at the list of patients I find inscribed in my fee book, names of persons who consulted me in the first year of my practice, during what is called the London season—-April, May, and June. In the course of that period I attended upwards of one hundred and twenty new patients, all of them appertaining by birth, profession, standing, or rank, to the best of the cultivated classes of society. This fact has suggested the following reflections. The nature of my practice was of that description which permitted me to leave London at the close of what is called the season without any detriment of consequence to my worldly interests, for the plain reason that the patients themselves who were supposed to be of the class which supplied my own practice go abroad or into the country ; whereas the less wealthy classes of people, or those whose business or occupation require their presence, and who constitute in themselves a very respectable practice, worth the attention of any reputable physician who remains stationary, are sure to go to him whom they have known all their lives by name or experience. Such physicians are those who succeed in the end in having great levées at their morning consultations ; whereas the physician who has taken the court by storm, as we may say, by attracting to himself the pickings of the Red as well as of the Blue

Book, would find himself abandoned as soon as Parliament was up. *Experto crede.* Now a great many of these very patients who left me to proceed to watering-places I followed thither, to afford them the opportunity of securing the advice upon which they had been accustomed to rely, and I thus fulfilled two great objects—the patient was benefited, and my yearly practice was carried on continuously.

Since I set up as a safety beacon to invalids the delicious springs of Kissingen (now standing on its own solid and just claims) thirty years since, I have there spent the summer of each · year (with two or three exceptions), and have entered in a particular book the cases of all who consulted me; and I find that in 1868, the year of my relinquishing practice, the number of these volumes amounted to thirty-two—and very interesting many of the cases are, on account of the almost miraculous effect obtained in despaired-of chronic maladies.

I have been led to insert the preceding reflections because I have been repeatedly asked how I managed to leave London every year, as I have done, whether travelling as an attendant physician, or to reside for a certain number of months abroad. The considerations set down above will explain the matter and reply to the question. But, in my own special case, I owe it to myself to mention, that in adopting my plan of practice I was never moved by the desire of a *dolce far niente*, which my own poet Horace so feelingly describes—"Beatus ille qui procul negotiis," &c.; for if I travelled it was to write my experiences during my absence, whether in Russia, Germany, Italy, Spain, or the East; and if I remained stationary for a period in some favourite temple of health, it was with the object of affording advice to the many hundred patients from England whom my own works, or those from more able pens, had induced to repair thither for their cure. I was absent truly, but not idle. Can all absentee physicians from London during the summer allege as good reasons for their absence ? However, all this dissertation may be assumed or accepted as an excuse for a negotiation to absent myself again from England in the exercise of my profession and in the capacity of travelling physician.

During the early months of 1819, Lady Ellenborough, afflicted at the death of her husband and at the indisposition of a nephew and young niece—being herself, moreover, subject to occasional nervous attacks, which seemed to threaten some serious mischief in the chest, according to the opinion of her ordinary medical attendant, Mr. Pennington—was induced to call for a .consultation with other eminent physicians entirely new to her case, and without bias, so as to elicit an independent and suitable opinion with regard to the nature of the disease, its probable duration, and the best mode of treating it. As I was not one of those consulted, I omit to mention their names. After deliberate consideration it was decided that her ladyship should go to Italy for the space of two years, there to reside in some suitable part of the country, the selection of which the consulting physicians recommended should be referred to "Dr. Granville, as one who, besides being a native of the country, had visited every part of it more than once, and lived in many of the principal cities in turn."

Accordingly I was summoned on the 30th of July, and again on the 12th of August, 1819. I named Pisa for the ensuing winter; Florence and other parts of Tuscany for the next summer, including the baths of Lucca; and if sufficiently recovered and strong to be able to bear the fatigue of the journey, to spend the subsequent winter in the neighbourhood of Naples; after which, it was to be hoped that any prolongation of her exile from England would not be deemed necessary. My recommendations, and the outlines I chalked out for the journey, seemed to meet with the approbation of the family, and so it was decided that it should be carried into effect. I do not remember from whom, but a suggestion came that I should be requested to accompany them to Pisa, and that I should be free to guide the whole party in the long journey from one place to another, as in my opinion would be likely to suit Lady Ellenborough's state of health, and likely to rescue her, by changes of scenery, from depressed spirits and the inclination to morbid despondency that now and then prevailed. I asked for two days to consider the proposition, and to make such arrangements at home as should expose me and my patients to the smallest possible inconvenience from my absence.

The same expert pupil, now in practice, who had acted for me at the dispensary while I was absent at Cambray, was again appointed to act in my absence with the full consent of the president and committee of the institution, and I confided to Dr. Anthony Todd Thomson the more agreeable task of representing· me with such patients as would be likely to apply at Savile Row. Lady Ellenborough's eldest son, now Lord Ellenborough, took care to provide our passports from the Foreign Office and foreign ministers at the Court of St. James's, some of whom proffered letters of introduction. Lord Castlereagh also gave us his special passport and recommendation. On my part, knowing well that a black mark stood against my name in the books of the Austrian police, and being not oblivious of the Roman dictum, " Custos, custodi teipsum," I applied to Monsieur de Neumann, Secretary of Legation of the Austrian Embassy in London, to know whether I could rely upon being suffered to visit the Austro-Italian provinces in safety. The secretary's answer satisfied me on that point, and thus every arrangement for the expedition being declared ready, we prepared to start.

Three months was the period I had fixed for the execution of the whole project, including sufficient time for my return home after having safely deposited under proper medical superintendence my patient and her numerous family—and truly formidable was their number. A Swiss courier was selected by Lord Ellenborough, and everything arranged with him concerning the journey, subject to my control. He was sent to Savile Row for my inspection, and at the first view I could foresee that we should get into trouble with him before the end of the outward journey, as was unfortunately realized, for a greater rogue never existed. Depend upon it, there is some truth in old Lavater.

I must here go back a little to mention a charge I received at my second consultation in Lady Ellenborough's house; this was her young niece, Miss Towry, who had been attended from a very early age by one of those medical oracles who locate themselves in especial places to deliver oracular opinions in chronic disorders, or prescribe remedies to such people as choose to commit themselves to their care in full faith. London has never been without such miracle-working medical men, and if not found in London, in one of its surrounding villages. It was the case in the present instance. The young lady, a remarkably pretty person, with a fair and almost transparent complexion, the daughter of a brother of Lady Ellenborough, had been placed under a medical gentleman, well known as Doctor Scott of Bromley, a name and authority I heard almost every day referred to, whether in a medical or a surgical case, as the *ne plus ultra* of reliable success. He had treated the young lady for an exudation of a troublesome nature behind the ears, and had entirely checked the disease. The consultation was called for the purpose of my being made acquainted with Doctor Scott's opinion, to receive any information of the past, or any instruction he might wish to give for the future treatment of the complaint should it unfortunately return.

This part of the consultation accomplished, I inquired whether the friends of the young lady wished me to act as a consulting physician, free to express his opinion either of assent or dissent from Doctor Scott's views, or only as a depositor of the information he had imparted to me. The latter part of the alternative being the one agreed to, I observed that I accepted the duty of medical agent, but not its responsibility. To this declaration no objection was made, and so the consultation ended.

As a contrast between the speedier, cheaper, and less inconvenient mode of travelling of the present day and that of fifty years ago, I think it well to give a slight record of my travels in 1819, to be referred to by great grandchildren as a subject of amusement and surprise when perhaps the mention of post-horses may cause people to open their eyes in astonishment and send them to their dictionary to ascertain the meaning of the words.

We landed at Calais from the *King George*, freighted to convey us all, and two carriages, for sixteen guineas, on the 20th of August, 1819. The first thing to be done was to deposit 1300 francs for the two carriages, being one-third of their estimated value, at the Custom House, and we received two certificates to entitle us to claim back 935 francs. The next morning we started with thirteen horses, including the *bidet* for the courier, who rode in front in his gaudy blue and red jacket embroidered with gold, and leather shorts, with top boots well spurred. Each post of five miles cost thirty francs. At 10 A.M. we reached Gravelines, and in half an hour after were off to Dunkerque, where a good breakfast awaited us at the " Poste Royale." Over a hard sandy beach we trotted along, passed the Belgian Custom House, and on to Ostend, where we remained the night. The next morning, having missed the early direct boat to Ghent, but unwilling to be baffled in my dispositions of time and place, I directed that we should proceed to Bruges by the canal, and well examine that interesting city, one of the many objects of the extended journey being to instruct the young ladies, as well as to show them the different localities which offered some interest.

And now for a specimen of the contrast between boating on a canal fifty years ago and flying on a railway in 1870. The journey from Bruges to Ghent by the first mode of conveyance occupied nine hours. Now the same distance is accomplished in about forty-five minutes. We had dinner on deck, of two courses and a dessert, for which, including the passage fare, we paid five francs fifty cents, or about 4s. 7d. each. The freight of the two carriages was sixteen francs.

At Ghent the ladies were all much interested in the Béquinage, or Bage-huys, in which about 600 women, who can pay 230 florins (about £20) a year, find a comfortable retreat for life, with an apartment and board. A note to Monsieur Schamp, then one of the wealthiest proprietors in Ghent, procured us admission to visit his choice collection of paintings, some of which are *chefs-d'œuvre*, such as "La Grappe de Raisin" by Rubens; "The Fall of the Angels;" and the portraits of the first and second wife of the same master. M. Schamp possessed likewise many original and beautiful sketches by Rubens of some of his greater paintings, as well as several Vandykes of great beauty. On leaving we had great difficulty in procuring horses, and were obliged to content ourselves with a pair to each carriage, an almost impossible task, considering that one of the said carriages was an immense handsome family landau, purposely built to convey the whole of the young party.

Nevertheless our journey to Antwerp was performed in six hours. Our letter to Baron Vicke, the governor, brought him to us, and gave us facilities for seeing the specimens of Rubens's and Vandyke's pencils scattered about the town. Many of the best had just been recovered out of the hands of the rapacious French soldiers of 1799. I confess to having in former days been incredulous, or at all events unjust, as to the fame and genius of Rubens and other Flemish masters, blinded by my own native and supreme artists, until I beheld the masterpieces of that great artist, whose " Descent from the Cross " is the very triumph of art. Another sort of attraction led us to see the identical establishment whence issued those famous and much-prized editions of valuable classics, conducted by Moretus, father and son—and continued by a naturalized Frenchman, Plantin—in 1555. In this establishment of the great typographers we saw the celebrated polyglot Bible ordered to be printed by Philip II. of Spain. Portraits of those eminent printers by, or copied from, Rubens were hanging in two of the rooms of the house. The family, which was excessively rich, was about to become extinct in the person of the last Moretus, who was ill and decrepit. His nephew, a M. Depré, was to inherit the *atelier*, which was still as it existed three hundred years before.

From Antwerp to Brussels we were obliged to put up with sorry *voiturier* horses, no such thing as post-horses being known in the place. So entirely different is Brussels at present from what it was at the time of our visit, and the vast changes which have taken place in almost every quarter of the city—all great improvements—have been so numerous, that it would be useless to describe a city that has been entirely rejuvenated. Brussels was then a dull, uninteresting provincial town without any attraction; it is now an inspiriting, gay, clean, well-built, and well-administered capital, with many rich and well-born families occupying houses of the most elegant construction.

The 30th of August, 1819, proved a most melancholy day to us, and for my patient Lady Ellenborough a most distressing one. Her niece, Miss Towry, had attended with her cousins a grand ball given by the Governor of Brussels on the night of the 28th, at which she danced much, and especially fatigued herself by a prolonged waltz, a dance just come into fashion. At the conclusion of a long turn she slipped through the arms of her cavalier, who carried her to the nearest couch. She had become deadly pale and cold, and her breathing seemed to stop, the eyes to close as in sleep. Means were taken to rouse her, but not a word escaped her lips. As soon as possible she was conveyed to the hotel, where I had remained the whole evening. Finding no pulse at the wrist, I applied my ear to the left side of her chest, as I had seen Laennec do at the Hôpital Necker in Paris, but I could hear no indication of any distinct movement. I directed Dr. Doratt, the physician of the English embassy, to be sent for, to whom on his arrival I communicated my impression that some serious injury to the heart had taken place, occasioned probably by the prolonged waltzing. Neither of us could detect by the ear any vestige of movement in the heart; in fact, we anticipated a speedy death, despite every remedy science could suggest. In a few hours the sad scene closed, and she who had only three days before entered the city full of life and beauty passed away without a sigh, soon to be carried to the temporary God's acre of the English church, where she sleeps to this day.

The young lady was a ward in Chancery, with a large fortune she had inherited with an only brother on the death of their father. It was therefore necessary to make a professional report of the death and the attendant circumstances, so with the consent of Lady Ellenborough and a written permit from the police, after having requested Dr. Doratt's presence both as a medical assistant and witness, we proceeded in as private a manner as possible to the autopsy; the result being all that was necessary to satisfy us, and of course the Court of Chancery, as to the death having been caused by the rupture of the left auricle of the heart, with an engorgement of the corresponding ventricle. Our report was forwarded to Lord Ellenborough in London by his mother, for presentation to the proper quarter. The natural inference that would be drawn from our statement I did not suggest and add to it—firstly, because it did not concern the legal and formal part of the transaction; and secondly, because the condemnation of a medical man's treatment, however justifiable, could neither recall the patient nor be of service to the profession at large, who are perfectly aware that if you suddenly arrest spontaneous morbid discharges in young people, you run the risk of producing inward organic mischief. This is especially the case with regard to a discharge *pone aures*, as I had often mentioned when I explained to Lady Ellenborough why I had dissented from the oracle of Bromley on taking charge of his patient.

We left Brussels on the 31st of August, taking Waterloo on our way. The little inn where we breakfasted had been the scene of much misery after the battle. The daughter of the house, an intelligent girl, related the sad story of the hundreds of wounded and dying on that memorable day. Some of the officers had lodged in the house, and she spoke highly and with deep feeling of the courage, patience, and forbearance of the wounded. The first burst upon us of this truly magnificent battle-field and the classic ground to which belong so many heroic recollections, and which is in itself calculated to excite the most lively interest, riveted our attention, and from a small eminence in front of La Haye Sainte we traced, or fancied we could trace, distinctly the various phases of that great conflict.

More recent encounters between two of the same nations then engaged, show that greater battles may be fought in these days, in which thousands of combatants stand for the hundreds in the older conflict, and yet the conquerors have not excited the interest or acquired the glory that has made the name of Wellington immortal. How many hard-fought contests have the Prussian generals fought on Bohemian or French fields to dwarf the great Waterloo, and yet who remembers distinctly at the first asking the name of the conqueror? It is, as in many other human devices or actions, the more recent dwarf the older deeds and prowess; but in proportion as the present age is in advance of those gone by, does not the applause of man, or the glorification of the hero, keep pace in the same ratio! Wherefore?. A general suddenly called upon to encounter a whole world of armed soldiers, compels one hundred and twenty thousand men to lay down their arms and slink quietly away to their imprisonment, while their conqueror marches in hostile array to the investment of their capital; and yet Sédan is not considered a Waterloo, where the troops engaged on either side did not amount to more than ninety thousand!

The damp east winds of the Netherlands and Flanders coming fast upon us, I hurried through the remainder of my programme towards Cologne, the diverse views of the country around and before, as we advanced in the direction of the Rhine, exquisitely beautiful and fresh despite the slight tinge of gold upon the forests, cheered the spirits of the party, which had sunk very low after the grievous event with which our visit to Brussels had closed.

I have so fully detailed in other volumes the course we took from Cologne to Switzerland, that I consider it unnecessary to reindite former descriptions; I shall therefore limit myself to the merest outlines as we posted along the magnificent road on the left bank of the Rhine, a triumph of roadmaking, for which the Germans are indebted to Napoleon I. From Bonn the beauties of the Rhine commence, and develop themselves in a succession of panoramas, each of which forms a perfect picture, the ancient or ruined baronial castles that appear here and there on the eminences giving character to the whole.

The road is paved with broken basalt, and the indication of a volcanic origin is perceived everywhere; yet the industrious villager has raised the vine to the loftiest peak, has cultivated every small bit of a glen that offered any soil, making every yard of the latter to yield its yellow crops of corn to the spade, though it were hanging at an immense height and over a deep ravine. Prosperous as Nature looks, the villagers are poor! A wine country on the Rhine is a country of beggars. I showed the truth of such a fact in another publication of mine. It was so half a century ago, and I know not how much earlier than that date. It is so now.

Coblenz, Mayence, and Frankfort (where we stayed three days at the Hôtel d'Angleterre) were visited in succession, then on again to Strasburg and Berne, where deviations were made to Schaffhausen and the falls of the Rhine, and then to Lucerne to enjoy a full view of the five lakes and of the extended chain of the Bernese Alps. Perhaps a part of our Swiss excursion, the most pleasing and suitable for invalids, because unattended with fatigue, was an exploration of the Lake of Neufchâtel, its town of Yverdun and its pretty surroundings, including the Ile de St.-Pierre. That island presents itself well covered with vineyards, and the house on it in which Jean-Jacques Rousseau lived lies by the water-side. Lady Ellenborough, who had had one of her terrible attacks in the carriage the day before, and did not rise early to accompany us into the interior of the town, was persuaded, by way of a pleasant diversion, to go with us to a charming villa called "La Rochette," situated on an eminence behind the town, from which the chain of the Alps is seen to great advantage. The proprietor of the villa had erected an horizontal slate table on a fixed pedestal, on which had been traced divergent lines from a common centre, in which there was a small point with an eye-hole. Through this, and guided by the divergent lines, each bearing a suitable inscription, the more prominent mountains were easily distinguished and their respective denominations learned. On the same terrace an electro-meter, formed by a pendulum placed between two bells under a glass case, and connected at the point with a con-ductor placed at the summit of the house, served, by the agitation and tinkling it caused when the atmosphere is charged with electricity, to announce an approaching storm. The younger members of the party and myself adjourned to the Pestalozzi Institute, and at once I may confess that we were one and all sadly disappointed at the appearance of this far-famed establishment, and the method of education pursued in it. Much more disappointed were we at the sight of Pestalozzi himself, whose presence had nothing in it which was either commanding, striking, or interesting. He spoke the French language with difficulty, and could scarcely express his own sentiments. There was, however, an air of modesty in him, and of genuine self-conviction and earnestness, which, in spite of his *physique*, pleased us greatly. He endeavoured to explain to me his system, and when I mentioned to him that I had partly been educated at Milan in what was called Sistema di Pestalozzi, and likewise that when at Madrid, fourteen years before, I had witnessed his system in practice there, he replied that since that time it had undergone great improvements, and he assured me that very soon a work would appear in which the system and its *rationale* would be explained, showing at the same time that his principle had been completely misunderstood. He rejected emulation in educating children as mischievous, and endeavoured to make inventors instead of imitators. This system he carried into the study of languages, the Latin included. One of the leading features of Pestalozzi's method was that the pupil should be trained from the earliest period of his education to make minute observations. Thus they were not allowed to sit on a three-legged stool until they could describe its form and the materials of which it is made. Mr. Greaves, one of the professors teaching English to the boys, laid great stress on this part of the system, and assured me that the boys could tell us not only the shape and nature of the stool; but even the forest and the acre of land in which it had grown, together with the parentage of all the trees in the neighbourhood. "This may be all very well, Mr. Greaves," I observed to him, " but I suspect that it would never be required of the Speaker of the House of Commons to know (as a qualification) whether the chair on which he sat be of leather or prunella, except he found it too hard after a long and tedious debate."

A peep at Lausanne afforded us next the opportunity of beholding this sanatorium, as it was deemed half a century ago by brother physicians in England. The monuments in the cathedral show with what justice it was so called. Mrs. Stratford Canning sleeps here, awaiting a black and white marble monument which was being prepared for her at Florence. Gibbon's terrace, and the box in which his celebrated work was composed, was an object of great interest. From it the eloquent historian enjoyed a fine and perfect view of the lake. We passed Coppet, where strangers were not allowed to visit the tomb of the *spirituelle* daughter of Necker during the absence of the Baron de Staël. Alas! I heaved a sigh as I went by, and remembered her who had breathed her last in my presence only two years before in Paris.

At Geneva, by a mere chance, we fell in with Madame Patterson Bonaparte, much decayed in charms, and many old acquaintances of Lady Ellenborough joined our party. Admiral Durham, an old patient who resided at a short distance from Geneva, called on me. Doctors Marcet and Jurine were out of town. Pictet alone was in Geneva, and I spent some time with him in philosophical chat—such was my occupation while the family were preparing for departure.

With every possible despatch we did not succeed in starting before four o'clock on our way to the Alps. Our route was continued over Mont Cenis to Molaret, Susa, St. Giorgio, Rivoli, and on to Turin. My party were already feeling the benefit of inhaling the pure and warm air as we descended into the Lombard plains.

We cared not to linger long in Turin, attractive though the city be, but I was anxious that the ladies should have the enjoyment of seeing one of the greatest triumphs of pictorial art in existence, jealously preserved by the royal family, who owe it to the zeal of one of the domestics that the precious gem escaped the rapacious hands of the French in 1796. My wish could only be satisfied by the queen's consent and permission. Lady Ellenborough had been notified to the court, though formal presentation could hardly be accomplished in her state of double mourning; but we had the good fortune to meet her majesty, attended by the British Minister, in the garden at the queen's villa, six miles from the city, called La Vigna. The queen was accompanied by the two princesses, twin sisters, good-look-

ing and seventeen years of age, one of them about to be
married. A courteous recognition *sans cérémonie* led to
the desire of seeing the precious picture, and to the ready
accession to the chapel of the queen's private oratorio, in
which the head of a Madonna by Carlo Dolce was kept.
Words cannot express the delight experienced at the first
glance at the picture when the silk curtain was withdrawn.
Nothing can surpass the sweet expression of beauty and
humility here delicately painted by this very justly denominated "sweet limner," neither can ordinary speech
do it justice—the eyes of the Virgin appear to be slowly
raising their upper lids towards heaven, while the lips are
preparing to open and move as if to pronounce, " Ecce
ancilla domini ; fiat mihi secundum verbum tuum."

I had various calls to make in Turin, but I relinquished
all selfish objects to devote my attention to those of whom
I had taken charge, and the safety of whose lives required
that no delay should take place in Alpine regions when our
destination was the temperate climate of Tuscany. We
therefore quitted Turin at early morning and reached Milan
at night.

I felt no little pride the following day in showing the
most salient objects of my native city to my English friends,
and conducting them to the Palazzo delle Poste. We found
my father in his bureau, and Lady Ellenborough asked him
to dine with us the same day, as we had no intention to
make a long stay in Milan. It was an early dinner, according to the fashion of the place, and my father entertained
us with the news of the day. After dinner we all drove to
the Corso, the rendezvous of the *élite* of Milan, and Lady
Ellenborough and her daughters were struck by the sight
of the young cavaliers as they passed us on their English
horses, these equestrians reminding them in dress and appearance of those they had left in London, so close was the

resemblance in every particular (an Anglomania which always prevailed among the young Milanese seigneurs of birth). At breakfast on the following morning my father paid a visit to the ladies, and at the same time brought us a letter from the Governor of Como, my eldest brother, expressing his delight at the prospect of receiving us, and informing us that we should find a couple of gendarmes at the Post of Barlassina, half-way between Milan and Como, with a view to protect- the party from any possible attack from brigands on the road. He recommended us to apply for a similar escort out of Milan, which my father undertook to procure, the roads being infested by brigands since the introduction of the Austrian administration.

The meeting with my brother was most cordial, and his reception of the English ladies such as one would expect from an official accustomed to receive. We intended to remain only a few hours to see the lake, and after the *déjeuner* he had prepared for us, we proceeded by water first to the Villa Pliniana, and to that curious locality, " Onore di Bellano," and afterwards to the Villa d' Este, lately the residence of the Princess of Wales, " which," said my brother, " is visited by almost every English family that comes to this part of Italy." In the Villa d' Este we especially admired the Turkish boudoir.

In another hour we got our horses and were off to Lecco. Venice was reached in due time, but having passed over without a remark so much that interested us in the different places on our route, I shall add nothing respecting that city to what I have already stated at the commencement of these volumes. After leaving Venice we returned by way of Padua, Este, and Castelaro to Mantua. Here some objection was made to our admission, and we might have been kept some hours, perhaps the whole night, had I not insisted on being conducted to the commandant of the fortress, who after an explanatory interview of an hour gave orders for our admission, when the triple massive gates and drawbridges were opened and lowered for the introduction of our carriages into that dismal, dull, and pestiferous fortified city. It was not my intention to remain beyond a few hours, as we might all have been attacked with rheumatism, or worse, did we sleep a single night in Mantua, so I prevailed on the party to sit up with a fire fed with fagots until the hour of departure.

Leaving Mantua as soon as the gates were opened, we made our way to Modena and Bologna, where we slept. The tiring ascent over the Apennines after Pianoro proved rather a stimulant to my fellow travellers, and Lady Ellenborough admitted to me that she felt better already at the mere idea of being soon at her destination, and so we reached Pisa at last.

After checking the courier's posting account against my register kept day by day and summed up every night, I found that, exclusive of the tour in Switzerland, the general result of our journey from England was—distance travelled, 1495 miles. Cost of posting that distance, 9556 francs, equal to about £390.

Having settled my patients in a palazzo in the Lung Arno, I presented my friend Doctor Vacca, who was most courteously received, and to whose care I strongly recommended Lady Ellenborough's case, with the promise from him of some occasional written reports on the condition of the patients, for Miss Law was only just convalescent from a recent attack of rheumatism.

The season was advancing, and Lady Ellenborough, with that consideration for my personal convenience which she had all along shown through the journey, would not consent to my devoting any more time in showing them the beauties of the Italian Athens, whither we had gone for a few days, but impressed on me the necessity of reaching England before the winter set in, and so we parted with mutual regret. I was not long in reaching Paris in the light *calèche* which Lady Ellenborough had insisted on my taking for my journey back. She had confided to me some letters for Paris and England : one was addressed to Sir Charles, another to Lady Elizabeth Stuart, to each of whom I presented them, when Lady Elizabeth asked me to remain and dine *sans façon*, and early, as Sir Charles wished to attend the Chamber of Deputies. After perusing her letter, Lady Elizabeth observed to me that her correspondent wrote in terms which must be gratifying to me of the care I had taken of herself and her daughters.

Sir Charles had requested me to see him in his private office for a moment, where, after inquiring whether I intended soon to return to England, and learning from me that I proposed to start the next day, communicated to me the following :—" There is at this moment in agitation a sort of ministerial *coup d'état*, a change of ministers, and the adoption of a tighter *régime*, for which purpose the king intends to make important changes in the ministry, which will surprise the public not a little. The final determination is to be come to at a council which is fixed for four o'clock. I propose to be in waiting at the Ministère de l'Etranger at that hour, or in the House of Peers, and remain until the decision on the meditated change has been settled, which is, I understand, to include the removal from his post of the French ambassador at our court. I should be very desirous, indeed anxious, to inform our government of these changes before the French government communicate them to their London minister. There would be no chance of my being able to send news to Downing Street of this change in time for the packet from Calais, but I may send the communication by a private boat to cross over with the intelligence as fast as possible, striving to anticipate the arrival of any messenger the French government may despatch to their minister in London. Would you undertake this task, as I observe that the Foreign Office has more than once availed themselves of your services on such errands?"

"I should not have the slightest objection to undertake it," was my reply. "I can be ready at a few minutes' notice. I am still in my travelling dress, and could set off at once." Finally it was arranged that my baggage should be taken to a room at the Embassy, that I should eat my dinner at his house just as I was, await Sir Charles's return from the Chamber of Deputies, and taking charge of his official bag, set off for Calais with four horses to my *calèche*, which would be transferred directly from my hotel to the inner court of the Embassy. An office clerk in the mean time would procure me a special *visé* to my passport, and an order to supply the requisite number of horses as are granted to a government messenger.

All was done as defined. Sir Charles returned when Lady Elizabeth and I had finished our *tête-à-tête* dinner, having been in his private office to write his despatches, which he handed over to me in the drawing-room. Four horses that had just arrived were put to my *calèche*, when, making my bow to Lady Elizabeth, and with a hearty shake of the hand from Sir Charles, I ran down stairs, sprang into the carriage, and galloped down the Faubourg St.-Honoré in the direction of St.-Denis, and out of Paris *en route* for Calais, paying double tariff to my two post-boys, who belonged to the old set of men, *à longue queue* and heavy jack-boots, swearing not a little if they were stopped more than five minutes at each post.

It was not till after we had passed Abbeville that we were aware that our carriage was preceded by another, going faster and carrying off the first horses. This we ascertained was the French courier, bearing despatches to the French ambassador.

Arrived at Calais, I was informed that a French courier had gone in the packet-boat, which had been purposely detained for him by orders from Paris. However, on applying at the Consulate, Mr. Hamilton, the British consul, told me the Paris messenger had only that moment sheered off the pier, and gone with a brisk gale against him. "Let us hire a fishing-boat directly," I said to the consul; "one sail and four rowers; the wind is foul, but never mind, I must reach London before the French messenger. I shall be master of the course on the other side of the water as he has been on this, and we shall see who beats."

The fishing-boat was hired. "They ask eight guineas." "Give them ten," was my answer; but the bargain was made, and the boat brought up to the lee shore on the shingle outside the harbour. It was blowing hard, and rain was beginning to fall, while the waves came curling in with their foaming crests and spreading out with repeated roars on the beach. The boat was a large barge for four rowers, with one sail, and half decked, the usual ballast and a large loose tarpaulin. After shaking hands with Mr. Consul Hamilton, who bade me God speed, I jumped into the boat with my little leather bag, and at once laid me down, covering myself with the tarpaulin, my head under the shelter of the half-deck. A crowd of people helped to push the boat off through the surf, and presently we were in almost calm water under the lee of the shore of Calais. The gale was soon met, and then " Hold tight near the wind, and pull hard at the starboard oars." All this I heard, but not another word, for I fell fast asleep while seriously reflecting on the rash folly I was committing by exposing my life for no affair of mine.

However, we reached the shores of dear England, and I invited my rowers to the "Ship Inn" at Dover, where I recommended them to the care of my old shipmate, Mr. Wright, the innkeeper, and at the same time ordered the four fastest horses he had in his stables to be put to the lightest and soundest chaise he possessed, and come round at once, explaining to old Wright on what sort of errand I was bound. "Oh, I see it all," said the honest innkeeper; "you are racing with the Paris messenger. He came in before you, and is now eating his supper at the Hôtel de Paris. Won't you take some too?" "No, no; a glass of punch and a hunch of bread, and off as quickly as possible. I must be in town before the Frenchman!" "You'll do it, sir. Here's the chaise." "Now, boys, half a guinea each if you drive fresh."

As we passed in front of the other hotel we perceived that the bird was off already. At each post we found that we had gained something on our precursor. At Rochester he was driving out of one gate while we were driving in at the other. Before the next change we came in sight of the Frenchman. "One guinea each," I cried out to my wheel postilion, "if you pass him!" We did so, reached the next post. There four horses were out on the road. These we took: all fair in war! "On for your lives. A guinea to each if you keep up the same pace!" The chaise was actually quivering, and at times I fancied the body grazed the ground.

This last stratagem gave me plenty of time. I drove to St. James's Square, delivered my despatches, and begged for orders. It was now near daylight. A little note came down from Lord Castlereagh's bedroom, and a request that I would go and deliver it at the French Embassy in Portland Place. A few early risers, and such as had been out all night, came round the chaise and foaming horses.

The porter of the mansion answered the rattling knock, and received from me Lord Castlereagh's note, with directions that it should be sent up at once to the Marquis de la Tour Maubourg; then turning to the postboys I said, "Now drive quietly to my home, No. 8, Savile Row."

At the corner of Langham Place we encountered the galloping Frenchman. My boys hurrahed, rousing I dare say the neighbourhood. We reached Savile Row, to startle the maid who was just scouring the door steps. The boys got their guinea and were pleased: one never thinks of the poor beasts whipped almost to the beat of their last breath.

The evening papers of that day, and those of the following morning—November 21, 1819—detailed to the English public the nature and the importance of the measure proclaimed in the decree of Louis XVIII., of which I had been the bearer to this country : " Nous, Louis, etc., avons ordonné et ordonnons, etc. Baron Pasquier est nommé Ministre Secrétaire d'État au département des Affaires Étrangères ; le Marquis de la Tour Maubourg, ministre auprès du Roi d'Angleterre, est nommé Ministre Secrétaire d'État au ministère de la guerre ; Monsieur Roi, Ministre des Finances ; Mons. le Comte Decazes est nommé ministre au département de l'Intérieur et Président des Conseils des Ministres." The *ordonnance* was countersigned by the last-named minister, who had begun his career as Minister of Police in succession to the notorious Fouché. King Louis did not stop at this thorough upsetting of ministerial opponents, but went further a day or two after, by creating eight new peers with the right " de prendre séance à la Chambre des Pairs " at once, whether they can or not prove that right by *le majorat ou non ;* thus securing a majority in the upper chamber by one stroke of the pen. No doubt Sir Charles Stuart considered such a sudden and important reorganization of the French cabinet of immediate consequence, and one deserving to be made known to the British government, and it explains at the same time the sort of ambitious desire on the part of Lord Castlereagh to be the first to announce to the Marquis de la Tour Maubourg his elevation to an important post in the ministerial cabinet of his country.

Settled down snugly in Savile Row once more, I thought I should hear no more of my last rapid excursion, except perhaps to be blamed by friends for a foolish and imprudent undertaking on my part, in having exposed myself and family to considerable risk; but events turned out otherwise, as the following correspondence between the newly-raised President of the Conseil des Ministres in France and myself will show, and which I quote *totidem verbis* in the language in which it was written:—

"Monsieur le Comte,—Votre excellence voudra bien me pardonner la liberté que je prends de lui adresser la présente, qui nous est réciproquement importante. Mons. Hamilton, sous-secrétaire d'État pour les Affaires Étrangères, qui m'honore de son amitié, vient de me faire part du bruit qui paraît s'être répandu à mon égard à l'occasion des dépêches dont son excellence Sir Charles Stuart m'avait chargé le 20 du mois passé, me sachant sur le point de partir pour Londres au moment du changement du ministère en France. Par ce bruit on aurait pu faire croire à votre·excellence que j'avais été porteur à la même époque de lettres particulières compromettantes pour le Marquis de la Tour Maubourg, sur quoi votre excellence me permettra de l'éclairer de la manière la plus solennelle, comme j'ai l'honneur de faire par la présente, que ni à l'époque citée, ni jamais, ai-je été porteur de lettres, dépêches, ou communication quelconques pour le Marquis de Maubourg ou qui que ce soit de l'Ambassade de France, directement ou indirectement, et que par conséquent le dit bruit est dénué de tout fondement. Mon but en tâchant d'arriver avant le messager français était tout-à-fait particulier, n'ayant reçu aucun ordre spécial là-dessus. C'était celui de jouir du plaisir que je devais éprouver en remettant le premier entre les mains de notre ministère des dépêches que je croyais être de haute importance. Je dois cette déclaration franche à votre excellence, qui a bien voulu me témoigner de la bonté lors de mon séjour en France; et à moi-même, qui désire n'être du tout mêlé dans la politique si étrange à ma carrière.

" J'ai l'honneur, etc.,

" A. B. GRANVILLE, M.D., F.R.S.

" Londres. 28 Décembre, 1819."

His excellency was not quick, yet satisfactory, in replying :—

" Paris. Le 30 Janvier, 1820.

" C'est avec regret, monsieur, que j'ai vu par la lettre que vous m'avez fait l'honneur de m'écrire le 28 Décembre, que vous avez été péniblement affecté par un bruit qui se serait répandu à l'occasion · de votre dernier voyage de Paris à Londres, et qui aurait eu pour objet de laisser dans mon esprit une impression défavorable sur votre compte. Je dois à la franchise de la démarche que vous voulez bien faire auprès de moi dans cette circonstance, de vous rassurer sur les inquiétudes que vous m'exprimez, en vous priant de croire que je n'ai attaché aucune importance au bruit qui fait l'objet de votre lettre; mais qu'au contraire, je suis charmé d'y trouver une occasion de vous offrir le témoignage de mon estime et de la considération distinguée avec laquelle j'ai l'honneur d'être, monsieur, etc.

" DECAZES."

I may now terminate the report of this interesting professional excursion from home, by quoting the sentiments of grateful acknowledgment from the lady in whose family I had had the honour of spending the last three months. The remembrance of them has ever proved a source of satisfaction to me :—

" Pisa. November, 1819.

"I never wished for Fortune's gifts but upon occasions like the present, and although I feel no pecuniary offering can cancel the obligation I owe to you, yet I cannot help lamenting that it is not in my power, even in that form, to testify as I could wish my gratitude for the sacrifice you have made on our account. If my humble. testimony of your merit, and the high opinion I entertain of your professional skill, can at any time afford you gratification or service, pray call upon me ; and if my opinion has any weight in the scale of your excellent and valuable qualities, believe me sincere in the assurance that nothing will afford me greater pleasure than to express them whenever the opportunity offers. I cannot tell you what we all feel at the thought of losing you, or how anxious will all here be that your kind consideration of us should not in any respect have interfered with the flattering prospect of your professional career ; and I beg you to believe me, with very sincere regard,

" My dear Dr. Granville,

" Your very gratefully obliged,

" A. ELLENBOROUGH."

Shortly after my return home, Lord Ellenborough addressed to me a note which I may be permitted to reproduce in this place. It happily terminates a period in my laborious and eventful life—the character of which I have unreservedly and honestly (as I was bound) described from recorded facts, dates, and recollections—when I found myself in the enviable position of a permanent well-established English practitioner in a noble profession, valued more in

this than in any other country, a fit reward for much
labour, study, vigilant observation, and successful acts
which serve to stamp the character of a man who had all
to hope and look for from the enlightened classes among
whom he has passed over half a century since the date
herein last quoted.

"13, Park Place, St. James.

"Lord Ellenborough presents his compliments to Dr.
Granville, and will do himself the honour of calling upon
him at any hour he will have the goodness to appoint.
Lord Ellenborough is extremely anxious to have an opportunity of assuring Dr. Granville how deeply he feels his
kindness, and how grateful he must ever be to him for
the unexampled attention he has shown to Lady Ellenborough."

CHAPTER XII.

Government slow to settle accounts—The half-way house—Parliamentary com-
mittee on the quarantine laws—Edit the "Medical Intelligencer"—
Accept the editorship of the "London Medical and Physical Journal"—
Origin of the use of prussic acid in medicine—Its introduction into
England—Decline to act as interpreter on the trial of the Princess of
Wales—Establish a dispensary for sick children.

THE words of Horace were still ringing in my ears as I
was putting my right foot upon the unsteady plank of my
fisherman's boat—"Æs triplex circa pectus erat, qui
fragilem truci commisit pelago ratem primus: nec timuit
præcipitem Africum." Often during the rapid posting from
Dover to London, as the thought of the peril I had just
escaped from intruded in my mind, I shuddered as I had
never shuddered before when actually immersed in danger.
How imprudent, I reflected, to expose myself wilfully to the
imminent risk of being drowned while actually on my way
to rejoin a devoted wife awaiting impatiently my arrival, and
my young children expecting to embrace their returning
father! The contrast of this, the most serious part of my
incident of travel, with the trouble I had to undergo directly
after in order to recover the paltry amount I had disbursed
in incurring it, seemed truly ridiculous. For to refund the
eight guineas Mr. Consul Hamilton paid for the boat, I
gave him a bill on the ambassador. Two days after my
arrival in England, the bill was returned to me by Mr.
Hamilton, with a note from one of the secretaries of Sir

Charles Stuart, stating that I ought to charge the amount with my other expenses. Accordingly, I repaid Mr. Consul Hamilton's disbursement by my own cheque, and consented to wait to recoup myself at leisure from the government. So much correspondence, so many references, and so many days of waiting to recover my due, little enough in truth! This latter part of the transaction is but after all a trifling affair when compared to what occurred to me at another time, when H.M. schooner the *Millbrook* was shipwrecked, as was stated in a former part of these memoirs. On that occasion I lost, with almost everything else, my case of surgical instruments, with which every naval surgeon is compelled to provide himself at his own cost, amounting to between thirty-five and forty pounds. To recover that amount I had to make countless applications to the Admiralty and to the Transport Board, to obtain at length the insufficient sum of twenty-five pounds, and that only after many years had elapsed and I was no longer in the service : neither was I likely to obtain even that tardy and imperfect justice, I firmly believe, had not my good friend at the Foreign Office interposed in my behalf.

"In mezzo del cammino di nostra vita," sang Dante. He must have referred to the first half of a man's life, which serves him to prepare to live over the other half to come, and thus conclude the full period of his earthly career. Now my own position at this time differed from that. I too, I may say, had arrived at my half-way house, where I might seat myself, look quietly around me, and after reflecting on all I had gone through—whether for good or for woe, try—try to do what? Not what most people placed in such circumstances would try to do, namely, to study what should be the next move, or, perhaps, what one is in duty bound to do during the remaining half of his *cammino della vita*.

I was again taking my place in this great metropolis under different circumstances from those in which I first made my appearance, and I boldly assumed my place by the side of medical practitioners the best favoured by Fortune, the most patronized and felicitous, not presuming to equal them in professional worth and experience, but claiming to be placed on a par with them in the estimation of those families of note to whom I had yielded beneficial service, and whose gratitude for the past I had earned not less than their good-will for the future. Here is an example :—

"St. James Street. 11th May, 1819.

"MY DEAR SIR,—I have the honour of enclosing you a small memorial of my late beloved father, who expressed in May last, among other wishes, one to the following effect : 'I wish a ring to be presented to my friend Dr. Granville, as a token of my regard and my sense of his kind care and attention during my late illness.' I beg leave to add the expression of my own esteem and gratitude for your long and persevering attention to my lamented parent. Believe me always with great regard,

"My dear Sir,
"Yours most sincerely,
"TH. H. FARQUHAR."

But more flattering than the diamond ring was a subsequent present from Sir Thomas, with the following note :—

"I send herewith some medical books, of which I beg your acceptance. They are old editions, and I fear not valuable, but you will no doubt prize them as having been the property of my beloved and ever-lamented father, as a proof of the regard felt by him and by

"Yours sincerely,
"TH. H. FARQUHAR.

"St. James Street. May 19, 1820."

Many other equally flattering testimonials of approval, not a few of them enclosing tokens out of the ordinary usage, came from other quarters, and it became evident that my position in the metropolis was assuming a tangible character. I ascertained when in London that Lady Ellenborough had addressed a letter to the Duke of Clarence, recommending that on the approach of an important event in H.R.H.'s family I should be selected as the medical attendant of the duchess at a moment so significant to the interests of our country. Lady Ellenborough had quoted a letter from Lady Frances Cole, who spoke strongly on the subject from her own experience. I was favoured with a sight of the duke's prompt and considerate reply to Lady Ellenborough—"The Duchess of Clarence has already a medical attendant belonging to her household, in whom she confides." This was Doctor Halliday, doubtless a most respectable physician, but not an obstetrician in practice known to his brethren in London; the result of which was made known to the public in a repetition of the failure to change the line of succession to the throne of Great Britain.

Still, while I felt flattered at my success in the branch of the profession I had superadded to my other general qualifications as a physician, I did not wish to blend the two forms of practice so far as that I should be considered a mere accoucheur. This aim I kept uniformly in view, and with complete success; at the same time I felt it a duty to attend closely to the exercise of the obstetrical branch for my own sake, as well as for the sake of the public institution I had undertaken to administer.

Other occupations also engaged my attention as a matter of public interest. A mercantile association trading with the Levant had found the restrictions imposed by sanitary laws on their trade not only vexatious, but trenching on their profits. They induced a certain number of members of parliament to sympathize with them, and twice in the course of five years succeeded in obtaining the appointment of a select committee; the first time on the validity of the doctrine of contagion in plague, and the second time on the foreign trade of the country so far as it was affected by the existing regulations, or what are called quarantine laws. At each of these select committees I was examined, and I believe I may ascribe it in a great measure to the practical testimony I gave in both instances that the committee recorded in the Blue Book, "That they saw no reason to question the validity of the principle on which such regulations (*i.e.*, the quarantine laws) appear to have been adopted." The arguments I employed before the committee to obtain such a result were found to be irresistible. I implored the members not to propose any considerable relaxation on the existing quarantine regulations without due precaution, lest the other nations should include every English vessel in the quarantine restrictions, for fear of opening the door to contagious diseases. "Bear in mind," I said, "that in proportion as you relax your restrictions with regard to foul or clean bills of health from the Levant, or even from America, so will other European nations, particularly France, include you in their quarantine laws; so that were you to abrogate those laws entirely, all goods and vessels coming from English ports would be made to undergo quarantine to some extent, even in proceeding to Calais." The committee put to me this question: "Do you think that relaxation in this country would induce foreign countries to make more strict regulations respecting English vessels?" "There is little doubt of it. Let us look at the events that are passing before us. A bill is introduced under your sanction, abrogating all existing regulations on quarantine, and embodying more liberal and, as it is stated, less oppressive measures on the subject in a new act. The introduction

of this act gives rise to discussion in the British House of
Commons, during which principles are promulgated wholly
at variance with the doctrine sanctioned by a dear-bought,
experience by the highest authorities both dead and living,
professional as well as unprofessional, by the testimony of
many eye-witnesses, by the open declaration of many of the
highest medical tribunals in England, and lastly of a report
from a committee of that very House in which such heterodox
principles are now avowed and eloquently insisted upon.
Vessels coming from Alexandria are permitted to unload
their cargoes of cotton without performing quarantine, or
after performing only a short one, and now behold the consequence of all this. The board of health at Leghorn have
been deliberating on the propriety of subjecting all vessels
from Great Britain to quarantine (we are informed by
Lloyd's agents), in consequence of the dangerous changes
made in England in reducing the time formerly fixed for sur-
veillance ; and further, the magistrates at Genoa have
actually ordered that all ships coming from England with
or without any sort of goods should perform quarantine
fifteen days ; and if with Levant goods on board, that the
quarantine shall extend to forty days, the goods being at
the same time discharged and submitted to expurgation ;
and now, still more recently, in the third category of pro-
hibitory laws we have resolutions from Marseilles, Minorca,
Barcelona, Naples, and Palermo of the same restrictive
nature."

Public notice of all these foreign municipal regulations actually appeared in the public journals almost
simultaneously, as I predicted· on the very day after the
second reading of the Quarantine Relaxing Bill by a small
majority.

Now indeed was the realization of my distasteful warning
seen to come unawares upon us, and the commercial rela-

tions between this country and all other European nations were dislocated or broken. A revulsion of ideas among ministers, as well as in the Commons, became manifest, in the midst of which confusion and fright, came down with that irate yet scornful declaration of his, the prudent Canning, who bade the senseless non-contagionists look to themselves, and try their experiments *in corpore vili*.

I may now proceed with my narrative after such a disquisition, in which the reader no doubt will recognize the spirit of ambition that naturally animates the medical author who is conscious of having rendered service to his fellow-creatures. The length of time I had passed in Paris in reading and studying the various continental journals, whether medical or merely scientific, for the purpose of summarizing their contents, and in that state communicating them to societies in London, or to editors of certain English journals, had given me a certain facility, and at the same time a degree of pleasure and satisfaction in the doing it. No wonder, therefore, that I should readily accept a proposal made to me by a firm of medical booksellers, Messrs. Burgess and Hill, to edit a popular medico-scientific journal, the form and character of which I had myself suggested. Its object was mainly to be a monthly analytical index of the periodical literature of the day, of the transactions of medical and scientific societies, and, in fact, of all works, no matter from what country, connected with medical subjects. It was a small octavo, and in small type, so as to embrace much matter, and it was issued at a lower price than any other of the contemporary journals. Its title was " The Medical Intelligencer," and it appeared twice a week. It served as a stimulus for the establishment of another weekly journal which, under the title of the " Lancet," from the first commanded popularity, and next the esteem and approbation of the whole profession; while the same " Intelligencer " served to rouse the other, or second weekly contemporary, the "Gazette," from the torpor that was overcoming it.

Our little journal proved a success, and my ambition as its editor would have been quite satisfied to have continued it as originally devised, for at all events it possessed the merit of originality. But the booksellers were of a different opinion. Their aim was the establishment of a distinct rival to the "London Medical and Physical Journal;" and accordingly, when the second volume of the "Medical Intelligencer" was ushered into the world, in January, 1821, it had assumed the shape, size, type, and importance of the most favoured of the medical monthlies published in England. Two new and original features were introduced on assuming the enlarged form; viz., a department called the "Glance," in which I inserted all the medical, scientific, and literary chat or miscellaneous gossip I could gather from most worthy contributors; and secondly, another department or section, called the "Appellant," which offered to authors who considered themselves aggrieved by misrepresentation, partiality, unfair criticism, plagiarism, or any other moral injury, a channel for vindicating themselves or their doctrines, provided it were done in fair and condensed terms, a small charge being made for the insertion.

At about this period the resignation of the editorship of the "London Medical and Physical Journal" by Dr. Hutchinson having taken place, I accepted the offer of the same, deeming the post more consonant with the higher position I was acquiring in the profession. Accordingly I conducted that journal for two years, until the accumulating duties of a general and obstetrical practice, as well as of a lecturer, entirely precluded the possibility of my attending to so much extra mental labour. In the two years I edited this veteran journal it will be found that I left the mark of my eagerness and zeal for its advancement and improvement. I may point first to a more stringent and exhaustive process of critical reviewing adopted regarding a question which a work of Dr. Mackintosh had started in reference to the unfortunate epidemic of puerperal fever that proved so fatal in the winter of 1821-2 all over England, but more especially in the English and Scottish capitals; and next I claim having introduced into the journal at the end of every half-year a summary of what had transpired, either in works or doctrines, in the course of the preceding six months, in medical and scientific Europe.

I have recorded little or nothing of my renewed intercourse, while in Italy, with the few eminent professors or practical physicians surviving, with whom I had been in habits of intimacy or correspondence many years before, and yet to some of them I am indebted for the knowledge of that powerful medical agent which has been productive of great benefit to suffering humanity, and of no trifling advantage to myself, who introduced and made it known in England as an almost national remedy never again to be abandoned. Certain professors of materia medica, in the north of Italy, had found in the use of laurel water a remedy eminently calculated to allay excitement, or what Broussais called membranous irritation. I had been a witness to many acute paroxysms of irritative cough, accompanied with pain in the chest, which had given way to a few doses of laurel water, and I naturally became desirous of making myself master of the question, in order that I might introduce the subject to the consideration of my professional brethren in London.

The power of laurel water on the human frame had unfortunately been made sufficiently manifest by some cases of poisoning through its use. As the leaves of laurel had been found by analytical chemists to contain what Scheele, the Swedish chemist, had called prussic acid, it was inferred

that laurel water owed its peculiar property to that principle. Hence, as soon as Gay-Lussac had investigated this
substance, to which (after having made out its true chemical
nature) he gave the name of hydrocyanic acid, the medicinal
agent under the new name was adopted by the profession,
and under that denomination I introduced it for the first
time to the notice of my medical brethren in England.
Thus it stands at present duly registered in the medical
Pharmacopœia.

The foremost of the Italian profession who had studied,
and in their ordinary practice were in the habit of using
laurel water in my time, were Borda, Brera, Mangili,
Brugnatelli, my own preceptor, Dr. Rasori, and a few others.
But to Dr. Magendie in France and to myself in England
belongs the responsibility of employing the real hydrocyanic
acid in its intrinsic power, diluted with ten or twelve parts
of water, and in that condition administered in doses of a
few drops, according to the inveteracy of the disorder.

The publication of my essay on prussic acid in 1819,
which was followed almost immediately by a second and
enlarged edition, containing a complete history of the
remedy, and of the many remarkable recoveries it had
achieved in my own practice, and that of some well-known
professional men both in London and in the country, besides
increasing my general medical practice, involved me, *malgré
moi*, in a controversy with the very last person I should
have expected to be likely to show any appearance of ill-
will against me, either as an author, a chemist, or medical
journalist. The editor of an esteemed journal connected
with the Royal Institution,—to which we both belonged as
active members, and to whom I had supplied continuously
valuable materials and contributions,—openly attacked my
volume in general terms, simply because I demurred to the
preference he pretended to assign to the prussic acid pre-

pared under his own directions by the Society of Apothecaries, of which he was the chemist. It was admitted that the acid so prepared was discoloured, impure, and deposited a sediment in contrast with the acid prepared according to Professor Vauquelin's method by a pharmaceutical chemist named Garden, working under my direction in London. Fortunately the editorship of the "Medical Intelligencer" enabled me to demonstrate the complete fallacy of all Professor Brande's allegations and arguments, and at the same time the correctness of what I had advanced in my treatise on the remedy in question, which is now prepared uniformly according to the process I had recommended on Vauquelin's authority. It is doubly gratifying to me to be able to quote a letter from my best friend respecting the effect which my exposition of Dr. Brande's unaccountable, not to say ungrateful, proceedings in this instance of prussic acid appeared to have been received by the public :—

"Southampton. July 19th, 1821.

"MY DEAR GRANVILLE,—My thanks for the excellent account you give me of your proceedings, in spite of the opposition of Messrs. Brande and Co. You have certainly got the whip-hand in your Prussian warfare. But I should recommend much caution in your polemics, and remember that one enemy can do more harm than twenty friends can do good. I return herewith Mr. Ryder's letter, which I have not shown to Mr. F——; for though it is highly complimentary and satisfactory to you, it is evidently meant only for your eye. It is well to adopt at once a rule of not disclosing to any individual, however eager they may be in your cause, what has been confidentially communicated to you.

"Yours,

"W. HAMILTON."

But this identical remedy was destined to be the cause of more than one other remonstrance on my part, not against attacks upon me as the author of the mentioned treatise, nor for the purpose of refuting any severe criticism of that evoked, but simply to expose instances of plagiarism of my initiation of the remedy into medical practice; or again to show how deliberately some writers attributed to other authors the credit due to myself of having been the first to introduce that powerful remedy into the practice of medicine. Even as late as within the last year or two such a blunder was committed by the principal writer of a very estimable and useful work on materia medica, who assigns in direct words to another medical man " the first introduction of prussic acid in medicine in this country." In this instance, however, the writer has acknowledged his mistake privately to myself on the mis-statement being pointed out to him, and has promised to rectify it in a future edition. Indeed, the popularity which the remedy and the work which first made it known acquired in England, induced other medical men to assume the merit of having been the first to recommend it in certain complaints as a new remedy, although the identical recommendation had been distinctly and most emphatically urged by myself. The " Lancet," in vol. 35, for the year 1838-9, at page 113, exhibits the most flagrant example of plagiarism in regard to this very question that the history of practical medicine can offer. The treatise as published in 1820 contains a full and complete statement of one of the complaints for the cure of which I recommended the use of prussic acid, namely, that worrying and often dangerous complaint to children, the whooping-cough, and then proceeds to detail the number of cases of that description treated and cured by prussic acid, among which cases I signalize in an especial manner those of not fewer than four of my own children, and of a whole family of children of a particular friend of mine, all of whom had suffered simultaneously and recovered alike, besides quoting other cases, the names of each party even being given. Well! nineteen years after my publication, Dr. Hamilton Roe actually issued from the press, in all the pomp of a new discovery, a book or treatise with this title : "On a New or Specific Mode of treating Pertussis or Whooping-Cough by Prussic Acid," and it says not one word of that remedy having been first proposed and employed with complete success by myself in a work the existence of which is entirely ignored. In Christian charity I will ascribe the omission to forgetfulness, as otherwise one could scarcely conceive so glaring an attempt to strip another person and assume for oneself the credit of having recommended a new and particular treatment in a particular disorder under every circumstance identical.

Not long after the publication of the original treatise on prussic acid, my practice increased in a remarkable degree. It was evident that the true and most effectual mode of treating affections of the chest had not yet been found out, that the public were still waiting for a more successful treatment, and that one such being proposed under plausible auspices, its adoption would be prompt and extensive. Such generally is the march of any new heroic or extraordinary remedy on its first introduction, and it has proved so with regard to prussic acid, the value of which remedy continues in universal esteem until this day.

From all that precedes it will appear manifest that on resuming my post in the metropolis after my return from Paris I found plenty of work to do, and plenty of encouragement for doing it, but there had been other proposals made to me for work of a different class which it would be a distinction to decline. One morning, about the time when the town was in a state of commotion at an expected trial of an

exalted lady before the Lords, I received the following
note :—

"Foreign Office. Tuesday, half-past two.

"DEAR DR. GRANVILLE,—Could you call in upon me in
your drive for a moment before five o'clock to-day, or
(what perhaps would be more convenient) would you look
in upon me at my own house to-morrow morning, between
ten and eleven o'clock, for five minutes?

"Very sincerely yours,

"J. PLANTA."

The object of the interview was explained very briefly,
and it was as briefly responded to. The government was
embarrassed for the want of an interpreter to examine the
Milanese and Lombard witnesses to be brought over from
Como on the intended trial of the Princess of Wales. The
Italian interpreter they had at their disposal, the Marquis
Santini, a Neapolitan professor of Italian at Oxford, was quite
unable to comprehend or to make himself understood by
the common people that were coming over from Lombardy
to be examined. In my character of Milanese it was supposed that I could accomplish the task of interpreter on the
occasion, and the request was whether I would consent to
undertake that office. My reply to Mr. Planta was immediate, and in the negative, and I have every reason since to
rejoice that I adopted the course I did. My own friends,
and especially the one at the Foreign Office, expressed their
unqualified approbation.

One effect produced on my mind by success and approbation was an irresistible temptation to avail myself of the
opportunity offered to me of promoting the advancement of
my-favourite branch of the medical profession, for the improvement of which I was daily working. I have already
alluded to my introduction of the practice of publishing an

annual report on midwifery in the two lying-in institutions of which I had the direction. Next came the registration of all the cases admitted, showing their course and termination, thus forming an immense collection of facts which certain fortuitous circumstances very soon raised into public importance in a very interesting and notorious investigation before the House of Lords (a case known as the " Gardner Peerage ").

London was still deficient in one most essential branch of obstetrical experience, namely, in an institution or infirmary for the treatment of the diseases of children, which demand much knowledge, care, and attention, as well as a peculiar tact, discernment, and experience, in order to render the treatment successful. For a period of twenty-two months while in Paris I had attended, daily at first, and afterwards three times a week, the Hôpital des Enfants Malades, under the direction of a Dr. Jadelot, a very able physician, and probably the most endearing and paternal medical attendant one could desire for the care of young creatures under twelve years of age. The government in Paris made all suitable provision for their proper maintenance and treatment, and certainly no better accommodation could have been provided than I witnessed within the walls of the public edifice in which they were located.

" Why," I inquired of my well-to-do friends in London, and also of many medical men, " why do we not possess an analogous establishment in this great metropolis? " With my previous experience I knew that such a boon could not be claimed or expected from the British government by simply demonstrating the importance and absolute necessity of the required object. In this country private benevolence takes the place of government munificence. With such a conviction in my mind I addressed a private appeal to some of my wealthiest patients, who had by this time become pretty numerous, men with families, who I thought were more likely to sympathize with my scheme and be disposed to assist me in carrying it out. I was naturally anxious to set about my operations at once, and I adopted therefore at first the plan so well understood in this country, that of a dispensary, to which young children might be brought by their mothers for advice and medicine, or when unable, owing to the nature of the complaint, to attend, to be visited at their own habitations by either physician or surgeon, according to the nature of the case. To facilitate operations and multiply beneficial help, I proposed, and was allowed by the committee I had brought together, to establish three stations, each station attended by a suitable staff of medical officers and attendants, with the appointment of one or two respectable dispensing chemists residing near the station, so that the prescriptions of the medical officers might be properly dispensed on the application of the parents.

As in the category of medicines suitable for complaints of young children many are simple and applicable to many patients, the quantity given only being varied, I composed and printed a pharmacopœia *in usu nosocomii, ad morbos puerorum curandos*, in which the simplest formulæ for purgative, depurgative, alterative, strengthening, and febrifuge remedies were laid down, which the chemist was bound to keep prepared according to my printed formulæ, all of which were numbered so as to render the work of both the prescriber and the dispenser particularly easy. The required remedies thus indicated by number, and the dose to be administered mentioned, were all inserted on the back of the paper each patient's mother was furnished with on being admitted, on which paper the medical officer was expected in the first instance to briefly describe the case, and subsequently the progress of the complaint on every visit paid by or to the patient. Every mother on the termination of the case was bound to return the paper to the medical officer, with her name subscribed to a couple of lines with which she rendered thanks to the subscribers.

Nothing could work more satisfactorily, and speaking in a professional point of view I would infinitely prefer this system to that of a hospital, for no hired nurse can in a hospital-ward bestow the love and care a mother will give to a child in her own home. At the same time I confess that my aim at first had been to establish an indoor infirmary. But for such a pretentious scheme no funds could be secured, and when most of my own friends by whom I had been helped had seceded, or died, or left London, the funds even for the simplest and most inexpensive plan of a dispensary failed, and after fifteen years' incessant attendance I beheld with sorrow the closing of the institution. On my part I inherited the half-dozen ponderous registers of the medical and surgical practice of that period, among which very many extraordinary cases and instructive incidents of a medical nature were recorded. I owe it to the memory of many benevolent and humane persons to record these facts. From the commencement, as during the whole course of the fifteen years they stood by me as acting and directing committees of the institution, promoting subscriptions and donations by sermons, public dinners, or private applications to friends. Some of the members of the committee would visit the station in the locality in which they resided, Soho, Marylebone, or Lower Westminster, encouraging by their presence and kindness both patients and parents. Chief among such Samaritans it behoves me to name the Very Rev. E. Law, Bishop of Chester, of whose family I was the medical attendant; and also the Rev. Anthony Hamilton, the worthy brother of my old friend, who was constant and indefatigable in upholding the institution to the last, the committee of which often assembled under his own roof in the parochial library of St. Martin's, the Bishop of Chester generally taking the chair.   Beloved dead, Χαίρετε!

After an attendance of fifteen years at the principal station, I had the names of twenty-five thousand children on my own individual register, with the columns which contained the ultimate result of each case neatly filled up. A more important establishment of an analogous kind, I am happy to know, has succeeded my own.   I allude to the one in Great Ormond Street, in which sick children are admitted as in-patients, as well as many of them attended at their parents' homes.   I may therefore rejoice at the fact, that whereas on my first settling in great London, I found it entirely without any provision for the treatment of the diseases of children, there is at present such an institution, of which I may say our own infirmary may be considered as having been a stimulating model.

CHAPTER XIII.

1820—22.

An event in the history of the Royal Society—Sir Humphry Davy succeeds to the chair—Letter from Mr. Hamilton—John A. Ransome—A Persian satrap in London—A lady sculptor—Anecdote of Dr. Baillie—Great success of prussic acid—Saves the life of the Countess of Onslow—Rapid journey to Wilton House—Happy result.

IT was about the middle of 1820 that no trifling commotion was taking place in the scientific world in consequence of the vacancy in the chair of the Royal Society by the death of the venerable president, Sir Joseph Banks. At this election, the first that had occurred for a number of years, in consequence of the practice of annually re-electing the same person as president, the fellows split themselves into as many groups as there were candidates proposed to succeed to the vacant post. The first discussion entered upon was whether the chair should be filled, as hitherto, by a man eminent in some one branch of science, like Sir Joseph (who excelled in botanical science, besides having been a great navigator, the companion of Cook), or by a person illustrious for his birth, wealth, and love of science, of which he would be likely to become a patron. In the latter category of candidates was placed Lord Colchester, late Speaker of the House of Commons, and I forget who besides. In the former category, more than one really eminent scientific man had been nominated. Foremost stood Sir Humphry Davy, whose lofty reputation as a chemical discoverer received universal acknowledgment, when out of the two special alkaline bases of soda and potassa he eliminated by the power of voltaic electricity two new metals, sodium and potassium.

Some among the fellows considered Dr. Wollaston a proper and fit person to succeed to the chair. A committee of his friends was formed, in which one of the secretaries of the society took an active part, how far consistently with his character as an actual paid officer I do not pretend to decide. From him, however, I received the following canvassing note in behalf of the doctor :—

"No. 33, Great Portland Street. 21 June, 1820.

"Sir,—Dr. Wollaston's friends hope that he may be induced to offer himself as a candidate for the presidency of the Royal Society, in which case they beg to be favoured with your vote and interest. I have to add, that it is at the particular suggestion of Dr. Latham, who assists them on this occasion, that I have taken the liberty of addressing you.

"I have the honour to be.

"Your most obedient humble servant,

"J. F. W. Herschel.

"Dr. W.'s friends will be obliged by an early answer."

A rumour had also been spread that the Duke of Somerset would very likely be nominated as another candidate.

Sir Humphry Davy happened to be at Rome in that summer, his lady alone having returned to England on account of her health. I therefore took upon myself the duty of informing Sir Humphry of the different phases which the canvassing for the vacant chair was undergoing. One of my letters sufficed to put him in possession of all the information I could gather :—

"Savile Row. 17th August, 1820.

"My dear Sir,—It was only the day before yesterday that your friends became assured of the duke having no longer any pretension to contest the chair with you, and also that fair-play in another quarter was intended. But I was perfectly justified in calling your attention to the subject when I did so, because on the very evening before I wrote my letter to you, I received one requesting me to keep myself open, as another desirable candidate was likely to start. Since then I have seen two of the individuals whom I had originally canvassed for you (one of them Sir Gore Ouseley), who had then excused themselves from acceding to my request in consequence of a pre-engagement in favour of the Duke of Somerset. They both acknowledged that their candidate had withdrawn, and promised me their votes.

"Sure of success as you are, however, I still think that the plan of urging your friends (which I invariably do) to come and give their personal votes on the day of election is a desirable one to be followed. Sir Joseph's retention of office was carried by half a dozen votes each year; but a new president, and one with so many claims to the chair, should be seated in it by a majority of members all present to testify by their numbers the prevailing sentiments of esteem and respect for his talents throughout the society. One of the circumstances which led me to suppose that something mysterious was going on, was the nature of the answer I received from Mr. Newnham Collingwood, who is staying in Edinburgh, and whose vote in your favour I had applied for. His letter bore a very recent date, and gave as a reason for declining to act with my request, that he had the very day before been canvassed for Dr. Wollaston, to whom he thought his vote was due, because to him he owed his own election into the society. Of course this must be a mistake, and perhaps the distance at which Mr. Collingwood happens to be from the capital gave rise to it. I shall, however, keep on the *qui' vive* during your absence, and hold you acquainted with any circumstance which may come to my knowledge that may at all interest you. I am happy to inform you in the mean time that Lady Davy is decidedly improving in her health, and feels herself getting better daily.

"Believe me yours sincerely,

"A. B. GRANVILLE, M.D.

"To Sir Humphry Davy, Bt., Rome."

The ballot took place as usual on St. Andrew's day, when the election of Sir Humphry Davy was carried triumphantly.

Among many letters from abroad which afforded me real pleasure, was one from my constant friend, whose absence from London I had regretted much, and who was now appointed minister plenipotentiary to the court of Naples :—

"Southampton. July 15th, 1821.

"DEAR GRANVILLE,—I cannot be so near London without sending you a line to say that I hope to see you in the course of eight or nine days. I shall go up to town to the levée on the 25th, but as I shall be your neighbour at Mr. Planta's, in Burlington Street, I must beg of you not to lose your time in looking out for me before I call at your door ; and as I can guess at your hours of seeing company, I dare say I shall not fail in finding you at home. Our whole party are, as a body may say, in good health, Mrs. H. certainly the least stout of the seven travellers. She will, however, remain for a few months here and in the Isle of Wight, to pick up for body and mind, health, strength, and *embonpoint*. I am still as much wedded as ever to my vegetable diet, and hope to give sufficiently convincing proof that, if not for all your patients, it is at least advisable for me. I got your letter about Angeloni at Paris. He called once on me at a time I was very busy, and I never saw him afterwards. He had much better be quiet, and think himself in high luck to have got so well out of his scrape. I am delighted to hear your time is so well employed, and hope it will continue so for some years to come. My cousin, Mr. Ryder, is anxious that you should see his wife, but I do not know how he will bring it about.

"All here desire to be kindly remembered to you, and

"I am yours ever,

"WM. HAMILTON.

"Dr. Granville.

"Pray give me a line on the state of the natural sciences, and about the Royal Society in London, &c."

Now and then it was a great treat for me to keep up communication with friends whom brotherhood in a scientific society had rendered dear to me. One of these was the secretary of the Literary and Philanthropical Society of Manchester, who enjoyed, besides that of a scientific man, the reputation of being the most eminent surgeon of the Manchester Infirmary. John A. Ransome, like his chief, Dalton, belonged to the Society of Friends, and I loved much to be addressed by him, whether in words or by letters, in the *tutoyer* style, which, for an Italian like myself, awoke stronger feelings of intimate friendship and attachment than the more usual and formal style of address in English society. On the present occasion John Ransome fancied that I had taken a mortal offence at some neglect on his part to do a commission for me, and accordingly he expresses his wishes in his own style to effect a reconciliation :—

"ESTEEMED FRIEND,—If I did not believe thee willing to forgive those who have offended thee, I could not now have plucked up courage to address thee. There is left but one means of atonement, to acknowledge myself a transgressor, and to promise amendment. With this, wilt thou again restore me to thy list of friends? a name I have never relinquished, however unworthy, none having rejoiced more sincerely than I have done in viewing thy brilliant march upon the road of science, reaping plenteously the honour and rewards due to merit.

"After all, I wish this letter had been an offering less alloyed with selfish views. I blush when I think of the retort which is due, but having made the *amende honorable* in my power, I will cease apologizing, and state the cause of my intruding myself once more upon thy attention. Last November, or about that time, I sent, through the medium of Astley Cooper, Esq., a paper to the Royal Society, describing a peculiarity in the eye of the whale, which I believe had hitherto been overlooked by anatomists. It consists in two muscles running through the sclerotica, to be inserted into each side of the cornea, and adjusting it either for near or distant vision, or for adapting the focal powers of the eye to the different media of the air and water. This paper has, I believe, been read, and as I flattered myself that the discovery of these muscles will tend to establish the part of the eye which is adjusted for near or distant vision, I have felt disappointed in not finding it in the last volume of the ' Transactions.' I may, and I fear I do, fix more value on the subject than it deserves; but I am anxious just to learn whether the society deem it worthy of a place in their volume ; if not, I shall give it to the public in some other of the periodical scientific publications. They may rest assured that this is no creature of my own imagination. The muscles have been seen by Dr. Henry, Dr. Holme, and several professional men here, all of whom are perfectly satisfied as to their nature. Might I then trouble thee, at thy earliest convenience, to inquire the opinion of the council, and to favour me with a reply as short as my merit deserves, or as long as thy kindness will allow.

" I sent the preparation to A. Cooper, who I believe sent it to Sir Everard Home. Not knowing this gentleman, I could not muster up courage to address him. Since last year I have procured more eyes, which, if the present of one of them to the Royal Society would be acceptable, I should be very much pleased in offering it to them.

" Since thou hast left Manchester I have added much to my anatomical collection: a description of some *organis remora* which I have procured I should be glad to send to the society; but I feel discouraged, and almost tempted to think that my contributions are even so much below zero that I had better save pen, ink, and paper, and jog on as Nature intended, bleeding, blistering, and so forth.

" With every sentiment of esteem and respect, believe me truly thy small friend,

"J. A. RANSOME.

" Manchester. 12th December, 1820.
    " A. B. Granville, M.D., Savile Row."

I replied to this naïve and simple-minded writer at once, and promised to attend in my place at the next meeting of the Royal Society, make the necessary inquiries, and inform him of the result by the following post.

An occasion to visit and attend professionally a great Persian satrap, and an ambassador to boot, does not present itself so commonly to a London physician that I should omit to record the one which fell to my lot about this time, thanks to my intimate relation with Sir Gore Ouseley. Mirza Aboul Hassan Khan, envoy extraordinary from Persia to this court, was on a visit to England, when I was honoured with an invitation to meet his excellency at dinner, at Sir Gore's, in Bruton Street. Sir Gore Ouseley occupied the seat opposite the minister; Mr. James Morier, who had

resided in a diplomatic capacity in Persia, was on the
present occasion appointed interpreter, and he and Captain
Willcox, both of whom·I knew well, as having been once
my patients, with Colonel D'Arcy also, who had been five
years resident in Persia, were of the party. The present
was the ambassador's second visit to this country. He
had resided in London for a period of several months,
having landed at Plymouth on the 30th of November,
1809, after which residence he returned to Persia, accompanied by Sir Gore himself, who had been on that occasion
appointed English minister at the court of Persia, where
he resided for two years. On his first visit to London,
Mirza Aboul Hassan Khan was received by the king with
great pomp, the *cortége* being preceded by a corps of
lancers, followed by six of the state carriages, surrounded
by numerous detachments of the Royal Horse Guards; and
I was informed that when the ambassador entered the
presence chamber he carried his credentials in his hands in
an elegant gold casket, placed on an ornamental salver of
silver covered with crimson velvet. .

On his second visit, the one I am recording, Mirza Aboul
was received by the Prince Regent on his throne at Carlton
House in a style suited to his rank, and worthy of the
English court. Mirza was accompanied by Dill Arum
(heart's ease), a fair Circassian, who excited an immense
curiosity among the higher circle of ladies, who so pressed
their entreaties upon his excellency, that at last he graciously
permitted a certain number of great ladies to be introduced to her in the drawing-room of his excellency's
residence in Charles Street, Berkeley Square, to the very
complete satisfaction of the fair visitors and the full realization of their expectations.

Fortunately, the occasion for my professional interference
with the minister was of a trifling nature, but it afforded

me an opportunity I had not yet had since my return from
the Levant of showing my acquaintance with the Turkish
language, which Mirza was well acquainted with, and of
hearing myself once more addressed as hekim-bashi.

I must now mention another patient whom I was proud
in attending, on account of the distinguished place she
occupied in society as a sculptor in marble of considerable
merit. I allude to the daughter of Field-Marshal Henry
Seymour Conway, brother of the first Marquis of Hertford,
of whose health I had the care, and in whose studio I was
often admitted to pay my visits to her as the Honourable
Ann Seymour Damer, whose chiselled productions have
frequently been exhibited and admired at the Royal
Academy. She was born in 1748, and reminded me of
the fair *artiste* from whom I had taken lessons in painting
when a mere stripling ; nor was Mrs. Seymour Damer very
unlike La Signora Corneo of Milan, in manner, in talent, or
in kind disposition towards her attendant physician. I had
been introduced to her professionally by a relative of hers,
Sir Alexander Johnstone, and I frequently attended her at
Strawberry Hill, as well as at her London house in Upper
Brook Street.

Equally honoured did I feel at about the same time in
being called in consultation with Matthew Baillie, the great
physician and anatomist of the day, on the precarious state
of health of Bishop Tomline of Winchester, in whom I soon
learned to admire the acute and able biographer of the
great minister Pitt. Doctor Baillie and myself would sometimes fancy we beheld Pitt himself in looking at and hearing speak the man who had been both the preceptor and
the biographer of the most eminent statesman modern
England could justly boast of. I remember that at one of
our visits, Mrs. Tomline, who was by habit loquacious, after
hearing from Dr. Baillie the joint report of the result of

our consultation on the state of the bishop, commenced a voluble cross-examination of the worthy doctor in all and every topic referable to the case and its treatment, which I had left to my senior to explain. Doctor Baillie really behaved with admirable *sang froid* under the infliction of a string of unmeaning phrases and unnecessary questions, many of the answers to which she pressed the good doctor to write down for her. When he had come to the end of a second page, he rose and said :—" Now, dear madam, here you have every instruction and direction you can possibly require, and I must bid you a very good day." Shaking hands with me, he turned to the stairs, the bottom of which he had nearly reached, when Mrs. Tomline, rushing out of the drawing-room on to the landing, said, " Dear me, I have forgotten to ask a particular question after all," which she mentioned to me, " but the dear good man is so impatient." I cried out instantly at the top of my voice, looking down the well staircase—" Doctor Baillie, Doctor Baillie, Mrs. Tomline asks whether the bishop may eat oysters."   " Oh yes, yes, yes," was the reply that came up, " but not the shells."   I know that this repartee has been converted into a coarse joke, quite inconsistent with the humane feeling and good breeding for which Dr. Baillie was well known. But whatever degree of sarcasm the real reply as I heard it might be deemed to contain, I can vouch that it was so, and not otherwise uttered.

The publication of my treatise on the successful effects of prussic acid in arresting the progress of pulmonary affections threatening to merge into that state of organic destruction called consumption, had by this time made such an impression upon both patients and medical men, that I soon found myself embarrassed by difficulties arising from the distance at which some of the worst sufferers resided from the metropolis, who required personal as well as frequent attendance. A note from the Earl of Onslow, which I turn up amongst my cases, reminds me of an example of this kind of laborious practice, while it announces the favourable termination of the disease in hand. The Countess Onslow had been lying for several weeks at Clandon in the most distressing state of health, consequent on a neglected attack of pneumonia, which for many days had seriously threatened her life. Called to visit her at Clandon, I was able, after exploring the cavity of the chest with the stethoscope, to administer to her the hydrocyanic acid, which his lordship would not permit any other medical man to attempt. I perfectly remember his lordship's devotion and immense anxiety throughout the long attendance while my lady was confined to her bed ; and the pains he took to see that each day from the commencement of the attack, and three times a week subsequently until the case was completed, four of Newman's horses should be at Savile Row at six in the afternoon with my own britska, to convey me to Clandon for the night and bring me back the following morning. The distance of thirty miles was quickly accomplished, but the great depth and constant fall of snow during that severe winter sometimes retarded my arrival, which was always looked for with the very utmost anxiety by the patient, by whose bedside I used to pass a great part of the night. At last, after I had commenced to relax my attendance, the following cheering note came from his lordship :—

"Clandon.   Jan. 19th.

"My dear Sir,—I am enabled, thanks to Almighty God, to report most favourably of Lady Onslow, who I think is almost to be envied in the nest of down you contrived for her with an external temperature of 12°. Pray be good enough to let me know the name of your banker.

"Most truly yours,

"Onslow."

Much as I had reason to rejoice at the successful issue of this dangerous illness, which confirmed the opinion entertained of the efficacy of the new remedy, another medical case, differing entirely in its nature from the preceding, being connected with obstetrical practice and not with general medicine, afforded me even greater satisfaction, for in it I had positively been the hand which, guided by Providence, snatched a victim of ignorance from the immediate brink of the grave. Two simple remarks I will take the liberty of adding—viz., first, that the case I am here alluding to proved to the medical attendant one of those turns of fortune which suddenly, as it were, lifts a man from one station to a higher ; and next, that the difficulty of the case, its imminent danger, the manner in which that danger was averted, and the manifest advantage derived on the occasion from the possession of positive superior instruction over mere nominal repute in a profession, exemplifies most distinctly the truth, not less than the justice, of the observation I made when on learning the death of Princess Charlotte I exclaimed—" Too late, too late."

I had just finished my family dinner on the 7th of February, 1822, when a fierce pull at that night bell, which has always startled me with mingled feelings of hope and fear ever since I first admitted it at my door side, sounded two or three times in quick succession, and a servant soon appeared with a sealed packet, which he said a post-boy had delivered to him, calling it an express, and which was accompanied by an open circular from the Lord Lieutenant of Wiltshire, entreating all successive postmasters on the road to London to assist in hastening the transmission of the packet. The superscription outside the packet was— " Wilton House, half-past nine o'clock, A.M., February 7th, 1822." It was then a little more than six o'clock P.M. in Savile Row. The packet, therefore, had taken exactly nine hours to reach my house—a distance of about ninety-six miles. The road had been for several days covered with deep snow. I made this calculation at once, for I foresaw that I should have to go through the same operation as the express to get at the writer, should the present prove to be a summons to attend some patient, as indeed it turned out to be. This I discovered on opening the letter, which was signed by an eminent and well-known physician of Salisbury, Doctor Fowler, with whom I was acquainted. His communication was of so alarming a character, that even whilst reading it I cast off all hesitation, and then bade my servant fetch me a post-chaise and four from our near neighbour, Newman. The explicit manner in which the case was stated by Doctor Fowler, satisfied me that I should require nothing more than my head and manual dexterity. All I did was to put on some extra clothing, and taking my travelling reading lamp with me, within half an hour after his arrival the express boy from Wilton, who had brought me the summons, saw me turn out of Savile Row with four of Newman's greys to take the road he had just left. He had informed me that on arrival I should find four horses at every relay, for the Lord Lieutenant had given distinct orders to that effect, through himself, while on the road to London. I then read more attentively the despatch of my correspondent, which, after detailing the particulars of the case, went on to say :—" Lord Pembroke is very anxious that we should have your assistance, and you will therefore oblige us, and relieve him from much anxiety, by coming with all the haste possible. In case you should be so engaged as to render your coming impossible, his lordship will be obliged to you to beg Mr. Clarke, your neighbour, to come, if he can come immediately. If he cannot be had, Doctor Merriman, or Doctor Gooch. If no one of these gentlemen can come immediately, you will then have the goodness to send the person in whom you have most confidence.—I have the honour to be, Sir, your obedient humble servant, H. FOWLER." On the back of this was added :—"For God's sake come yourself if you possibly can.—PEMBROKE."

I arrived at Wilton House, by dint of hard driving through deep snow, an hour before daybreak, and was received with joy and open arms by the distracted husband, who at once introduced me into the drawing-room, in which I found all the medical talent that could be brought together from Salisbury and Devizes, with the ordinary accoucheur, and two other obstetrical practitioners besides, Doctor Fowler not being a practitioner himself in that line. They were all assembled, with various books lying open before them on an ottoman in the centre of the room, which I was told they had continuously consulted. Ice and vinegar had been repeatedly applied to the patient, yet the hæmorrhage had continued. On inquiring what further steps had been taken to remedy the evil, I was told that the fear of promoting more hæmorrhage deterred the three doctors present from attempting any operation.

I was well known to Lady Pembroke, and was told by her maid that she had often expressed a wish for me to see her. I was not, therefore, in the least afraid of producing any sudden unfavourable revulsion by my presence, so I at once requested leave to proceed to her room. On entering I was struck with the pale and sunken face of the patient, whose eyes were turned towards the door, and who, by raising her pallid hands a little, shook them as if to express her despair that anything could be possibly done to save her. "Take care of my poor Sidney, my dear little Sidney, that is all I wish ; take care of my dear Sidney." The young boy had just before been introduced to his mother at her own urgent request, and I promised to take great care of him, while at the same time I insisted that he should be removed.

My conscience approves the way in which I kept my promise, and the Right Honourable relict of Sidney Herbert fortunately survives to testify that I did my duty as his medical adviser during his lifetime.

Taking a seat by the side of my patient, I felt her pulse. It was scarcely perceptible. After a few minutes I desired to have ready in the adjoining chamber a bottle of brandy and another of sherry placed in iced water, also some vinegar equally iced, and once more seated myself by the bed-side. The next moment the cause of all the mischief was revealed, and soon I had done what was necessary, and a twin child lay in the apron of the astounded nurse. The patient had by this time become unconscious, or rather bewildered in her mind, talking or muttering in an under-tone all sorts of irrational and broken sentences, among which the dominant phrase was, "Take great care of little Sidney."

I now proceeded to make use of the iced styptic, adding some alum to the solution, until at the expiration of half an hour I had the satisfaction of knowing that the application was successful, and further of finding that the hæmorrhage, which was insensibly undermining the poor lady's existence when I first entered the room, had in less than an hour entirely ceased. Immediate danger was wholly removed, and the grateful intelligence communicated outside the chamber, with a positive injunction at the same time that no one, not even the husband, should enter the room. The patient being now made comfortable, I commenced my administration of the mixed wine and brandy in equal parts and in small quantities at a time. On the third administration the liquid, as I expected and desired, was rejected. This incident enabled me to continue my small doses after every vomiting, and in this plan I persevered until I obtained the two results I was eager for—a resuscitation of the pulse at the wrist, and a degree of exaltation in the head amounting almost to inebriety, denoting most satisfactorily the revival of life action. Lady Pembroke's life was safe, and I had the great satisfaction of imparting the comforting announcement to the distracted lord and his surroundings.

I may as well conclude the narrative of this most instructive case, by adding that I deemed it necessary to prolong my visit for three or four days, during which I had to guard against threatened excitement of the brain as well as against animal exhaustion from inanition. The problem was a delicate one, but its solution was not difficult. The first point was obtained by simple remedies; the second by means of suitable nourishment, some new fangled forms of which I introduced to the notice of Lady Pembroke's attendants. Some of these, prepared by myself in her presence, were never forgotten by the patient, who was somewhat like another patient of mine, Lord Palmerston, of whom Sir Henry Bulwer has left it recorded that he "never forgot certain delicious beverages prepared by Doctor Granville during a severe illness his lordship underwent in 1833." *

* See Sir Henry Bulwer's "Life of Viscount Palmerston."

CHAPTER XIV.

Gratifying results of the journey to Wilton House—Elected to a second medical institution—Ovariotomy performed for the first time in England—Contributions to science—An Egyptian mummy—State of obstetrical science in England—The Royal Institution in 1832—A chapter in the history of the Royal Society.

THAT I returned home thoroughly happy at the fortunate result of my visit to Wilton House need hardly be mentioned. I looked forward now with confidence to days of professional advancement and success as an inevitable result, which this narrow escape from death of a lady so exalted in rank and so well known in the highest society must produce. Nor was it long before events came to justify my anticipations. My only surprise was to understand how, in so brief a space of time after the event in question, I should be made conscious of the professional advantages which the divulgation of the story among the higher classes of society had so quickly given rise to. I could understand that the venerable and noble Count Simon Woronzow, for fifty years the representative of the great Catherine of Russia at the British Court, the father of Lady Pembroke, or his son, Count Michael, being such near connections, should both, without a day's delay, testify to me their own obligation and assure me of their future friendly countenance. The excellent wife of the last-named nobleman expressed herself even in warm terms on the fortunate escape of her sister-in-law ; and at a much later date, 11th May, when Count Simon himself came to town and again mixed in the world, the expression of his satisfaction at what had been done at Wilton House was accompanied by an invitation to dine with him in Welbeck Street, where I found under my plate a cheque for £150.

Grateful as I was for all these marks of approval, my *amour propre* as a beginner in my career was more flattered by the favourable impression produced in certain classes of patients, principally ladies, by the story of Lady Pembroke's escape from death. I look to my fee book of 1822–23. What a contrast with that of four years before, when, on the morning that ushered in the first day of 1818 my ostentatious lamp in Savile Row lighted the messenger who summoned me to my first fee for attendance on a respectable tradesman's wife! I need hardly remark in addition that the consideration vouchsafed to me by my professional brethren, arising from the facts just named, proved a source of greater satisfaction than all the preceding testimony of approval could afford.

Another good result of my suddenly increased estimation with the public as an accoucheur, was my appointment as physician to a second charity, called the "Benevolent Institution," which was presided over by Sir Richard Birnie, the chief magistrate at Bow Street, who regularly attended as chairman at all the meetings. The election was carried after a hard contest, for there was a yearly stipend of £100 attached to the appointment. From what I learned I believe there had never been on similar occasions of medical elections such an example of vituperative eloquence against "a poor foreigner," "an alien doctor," "a foreign courier," "a diplomatic spy," and heaven knows what besides, as on this occasion. My opponent had it all his own way in such eloquent display, even to the engaging of an eminent pleader, whose eloquence on the occasion was quite Demosthenian. The meetings took place in a carpet warehouse in Leicester

Square, once a royal residence, and now lately destroyed by fire. The good proprietor, Mr. Harris, who as a zealous governor of the Westminster General Dispensary knew my worth in the branch of the profession from which the elected was to be chosen, bore all the onslaught with perfect calmness, though not without replying to part of the learned advocate's invectives with that strong sense of wit which English educated tradesmen know so well how to employ in the defence of their own rights. Mr. Harris knew how the election would end, for he was living in the centre of almost all the subscribers to the institution, most of his own class besides the assistants. He knew Sir Richard Birnie had pledged himself to give me aid, some of which pledges he began to fulfil by handing in the Duke of York's proxy for twenty-five votes in my favour. The medical profession have had an opportunity of learning the use I made of this fresh addition of my means of collecting and regularly tabulating all useful information concerning the various phenomena of human reproduction among the industrial classes of the metropolis. If they look into the second volume of the transactions of the Obstetrical Society of London, they will find in it what the "Lancet," in reviewing that volume, has called " Dr. Granville's remarkable paper." That paper has been favourably referred to in more than one publication by eminent obstetricians and statisticians, both here and abroad.

The next important step I have to refer to in my medical career, is the having undertaken to repeat in England for the first time a daring operation performed by Professor Lizars in Edinburgh, consisting in removing a solid ovarian tumour weighing eight pounds from a patient. Ovariotomy, as the operation is called, has since been performed frequently in this country, and by no one more successfully than by Mr. Spencer Wells and a few others, all of whom have enjoyed an immense advantage over my own unassisted mode of performance, by the application in all their cases of chloroform during the operation, which, while it annuls pain in the patient, imparts courage to an almost undesirable degree of hardihood in the operator. Success in practice adds elasticity to the mental faculties of a medical man: he becomes every day more disposed to investigate truth, and devises means of improving medical knowledge by adding to what was known before.

I find that about this time I devoted my attention during a momentary lull from practice to the establishing of a new classification of remedial agents, published in a tabular form, pocket size, in order that each practitioner might carry one for ready reference. For the same reason I published a novel classification of diseases for children, based upon distinct physiological functions, giving to each disease a Latin or semi-Greek appellative, taken from the leading or most prominent symptom of the disease. I had an ulterior object in this, which was the expectation that my colleagues officiating at the different stations (three in number) of the Infirmary for Sick Children, would adopt the same denominative language in registering the cases that came under their care, and assigning a distinctive name to the disease represented in each case. I may mention some other more or less important investigations I entered into, for now was my season of vigour, during which work of either mind or body, or of both, is not only borne well but with positive pleasure. I published in the " Journal of Science " a better mode of analyzing vegetable bodies ; and, if I remember right, it was about this same period that I presented to the Royal Society my analytical preface on Labarraque's disinfecting liquids, the virtue of which, though dependent upon the presence of chlorine, and so far a plagiarism of Guyton de Morveau's disinfectants, was nevertheless acceptable as being presented in a more manageable form. This analytical paper was not honoured with insertion among the Transactions, but was published separately, and readily admitted in the philosophical journals of the day.

The Royal Society did not find any ground for setting aside and consigning to their sepulchral archives (where I was destined in the course of a few years to find it and shake off the long settled dust by a lively and fruitful ventilation) another paper which I had forwarded through Sir Everard Home, one of the vice-presidents, who had honoured me with his confidence and friendship. I had therefore in this instance the countenance of one who, besides being vested with authority, was by experience and practical study better able than other members of the council were to determine how far the subject of the memoir, and the manner in which it was treated, deserved the commendation of the Society. The paper I refer to was read April 16, 1818, and was published in the Transactions with all the honour of a copper-plate illustration. Another memoir of mine also communicated to the Royal Society, was read Jan. 13, 1830, and admitted with all the copper-plate engraved illustrations which the crayon of Bauer, and the burin of Bazire could produce. These were some of my scientific labours.

I am inclined to believe that the trite proverb of *l'appétit vient en mangeant* is equally applicable for the appetite of the mind for knowledge and inquiry, that it may get invigorated as much as the appetite of the stomach yearns for additional or more choice nutriment to sustain its strength. This I can assert on my own experience, that the more my mind worked to acquire fresh knowledge and assimilate it to itself, the more eager did I feel to discover, collect, and make my own, whatever other sources or objects of knowledge I could acquire. Such was the case with regard to the next object I seized upon as a fertile topic of investiga-

tion, on which, as a medical man, I might perchance be able
to throw a clearer light than could be done by a mere
literary or erudite or antiquarian investigator. I allude to
the interesting subject of Egyptian mummies, the character
of their race, and the peculiar process by which they were
fashioned and preserved.

A young baronet, Sir Archibald Edmonstone, just returned
in bad health from a long incursion into Egypt, applied to
me for advice, and at the same time commenced a conversation on the subject of Alexandria, which we had both of
us visited, branching off into an account of a visit he had
paid to the kings' tombs, where he had been able not only
to penetrate into the mummy pits, but, a rare privilege, had
purchased one of the best preserved specimens, judging
from the exterior case, which was perfect both in material
and painting. This he had brought home with him, and
kept in his house in Wimpole Street, where I went to see
it. I expressed my desire to examine the mummy after the
removal of its external covering, and explained to my
patient how deficient our knowledge was in regard to the
process of mummification by the old Egyptians, arising from
the fact that all the ancient naturalists and antiquaries who
had investigated the matter in England, had in no one
instance that I knew of found a specimen that consisted of
anything better than mere bitumen and hard brittle bones,
with little or no flesh. "Do you consider," inquired the
patient, "that a careful investigation of this mummy, which it
is evident from the exterior case is that of a female, might
be of advantage to science should it prove a well-preserved
one?" "Such is my conviction," was the answer. "Then
you shall have the inside, and I will reserve and retain for
myself the exterior case and its hieroglyphics."

The case was in Savile Row the next day. On that day
week my dining-room was open at one o'clock to some

scientific and other friends, to witness the examination of the mummy. During the week I had had the case carefully opened, which proved to be made of sycamore wood an inch thick,- whitewashed or plastered in its interior, with long ranges of hieroglyphic inscriptions painted in black characters. The body, enveloped in all its cloth wrappers, being taken out and deposited on a long table, was searched all over for papyri or amulets or any ornament, but nothing was discovered except a few segments of very slender glass tubing, tinted pale blue, and looking like enamel, and a few grains of wheat that looked as fresh as any grain of wheat of the last harvest. On the end of a white bandage extending across the waist were inscribed, in an inky pigment, certain characters, which Sir Gardiner Wilkinson, who was present, undertook to explain by-and-by. One or two of the characters had corroded and left a hole in the cloth. All the observations made during the examinations were carefully written down on the spot by one of my pupils, and served afterwards as materials for the composition of the extensive essay I read before the Royal Society, which is printed in the volume of the Transactions for the year 1825, where every important part of the essay is accompanied by a copper-plate illustration. I shall make no further observation on this matter, except to express in deliberate and explicit terms, firstly, that I claim in this laborious investigation to have demonstrated the fact of wax having been the ingredient which was successfully employed, not only to preserve the body from putrefaction, but also to keep the membranes as well as the ligaments in their supple condition, so that when the wax was discharged from them by the process of boiling in water, the soft parts came out with their natural structure, and in less than twenty-four hours underwent decomposition and putrefaction. To these facts antiquaries and such persons as are versed in the old Egyptian language, add the information that the Egyptian word corresponding to wax is "mum." Secondly, that by my measurements and other remarks, I have established the fact that the female Egyptian under examination belonged to the Caucasian, and not to the Negro or Mongolian race. Thirdly, that the distinction of human races is better established by the difference of the female pelvis than by the shape of the head, which is always in harmony with the dimensions and form of the female pelvis, the configuration of which in the pure Caucasian race differs in a very remarkable degree from that of a negro female, which I had ample means of verifying by specimens in my possession, as I stated in my essay published by the Royal Society. Fourthly, I have shown that the description given by Herodotus, of the manner in which mummies were prepared by the Egyptian priest, is not in every instance correct, inasmuch as in my own specimen, which is esteemed the most perfect yet found, there is no evidence of the lateral incision in the abdomen, as insisted upon by that writer.

The publication of this essay on mummies in the Transactions and other scientific journals led soon after to my being requested to deliver a lecture on the identical specimen. This I did with every requisite illustration by drawings, experiments, and the exhibition of all the parts of the mummy together, some of the wax obtained being manufactured into small tapers, which were lighted and burned during the lecture. This was delivered on one of the Friday evening meetings at the Royal Institution, and attracted general notice.

My investigation had led to the discovery of some inaccuracies set forth in a book then universally read, "The Epicurean," by Tom Moore, the poet, with whom I was well acquainted. I sent him a copy of my essay, calling attention to the facts, and immediately received the following reply, which may prove interesting to some of my readers :—

"DEAR SIR,—I beg you to accept my best thanks for the very interesting essay you have sent me. It seems to set the question with respect to the race of the ancient Egyptians completely at rest, and I take shame to myself for having been ignorant of so valuable a testimony to the opinion I was interested in upholding. . I regret, too, that your kind notice of my omission did not arrive a week or two sooner, for I should then have been able to avail myself of it for the fourth edition of my book, which, though not yet announced, is, I fear, printed off and beyond the reach of correction. Should the public, however, continue their present demand for the work, I may have an opportunity before the end of the year of expressing my opinion of your very valuable memoir. For your flattering opinion of my writings I cannot but feel deeply grateful, and am, dear sir, your faithful servant,

"THOMAS MOORE."

The presentation of a fresh mummy, which Sir John Malcolm had sent home as a present to the Royal Asiatic Society, of which I was also a member, gave occasion to a second lecture, which I delivered in the morning in the theatre of the Royal Institution.

A curious fact was elicited in the case of the female mummy first described, that on removing the several bandages from around the body, it was ascertained that not only each separate arm and leg, but each separate finger and toe was surrounded with appropriate bandages of linen of the same form and width as the ablest modern surgeon would employ; and when the entire mass of bandages was removed, they were found to weigh twenty-eight pounds !

Within the last few years the preparations of my original

mummy were purchased by the trustees of the British Museum, and placed in one of the glass cases in the Egyptian rooms of that establishment, though not displayed in the manner best adapted for the instruction or the amusement of the public. Some reasons for this anomalous mode of exhibiting these specimens were assigned to me by the very able and courteous curator of the department, which I doubt not are consistent with the rules and spirit of the place, though they failed to satisfy me. An additional ground of regret I experienced at this, as it may be called, suppression of the preparations of the original mummy is, that amongst them I had placed specimens of recent mummies prepared by myself with wax according to the Egyptian method, some legs and arms of still-born children, which from 1825 until the year in which I parted with the specimens—a period of nearly fifty years—had preserved intact their freshness, softness, complexion, and colour, although not enveloped by any bandage whatever. These specimens, like the rest, are shut up at present in a large case, a *museum clausum*, as some funny gentleman appertaining to the museum once said to me, in which the preparations may remain for an indefinite number of years without the means of ascertaining how far a practical illustration of the discovery of an ancient art propounded by a scientific man has turned out a reality or a myth.

When I look back to the work I spontaneously took upon myself to perform unsolicited by anyone, and to the nature of the work itself, I fear that I must confess that the motives that induced me to undertake it were akin to that spirit of restless impatience which the good preceptors in my college early divulged to my parents, when they sent me home for my holidays with a very gratifying encomium of my intellectual progress somewhat damaged by an explicit lament over the listlessness of my temperament and

my love of change. I was born to be a reformer! The
right of the oldest and best confirmed establishment that
evinced in my estimation any glaring error or abuse, any
shortcoming, in fact, made me uneasy, and instantly the
demon of revolt suggested the idea that it was my duty to
have redressed whatever was wrong. And now, for example, I could not practise midwifery long in the metropolis
without being struck by the disgraceful anomaly in the
English law, which left the practice of that art entirely
without legal or any other kind of regulation. The College
of Physicians scorned the idea of having anything to do
with it. The College of Surgeons did not actually preclude
their members from practising the branch, but they did not
patronize it by examination of candidates and granting
licences to practise it. The Society of Apothecaries, whose
members were the medical men most employed on these
occasions, were never examined when admitted as apothecaries how far they were acquainted with the branch of the
profession they would be frequently called upon to practise.
Worst of all, any broken-down washerwoman might call
herself a midwife and act as such, and no one had a right
to interfere with her calling, however ignorant she might
be of the art she professed to know. There was no provision whatever by any administrative arrangement for the
ignorant women's instruction or education.

Such was the anomalous state of midwifery in England
when I returned from Paris, where I had left schools and
public laws wholly and exclusively devoted to the promotion
of obstetrical knowledge, and especially to the qualifying of
well-educated females to act as midwives among the middle
classes of society, whether in the capital or in the provinces.
Although my endeavours to rectify what was wrong in
London was not successful to the extent of introducing the
superior system of the Paris school, I completely succeeded

in obtaining legalization, acknowledgment, and countenance for the obstetrical profession from the three medical corporate bodies in London, through the interference of ministers and the authority of parliament. I felt convinced that all my brethren in the profession had not witnessed without grief the evil consequences arising from the great oversight on the part of the legislature in this matter, and that they would gladly contribute in endeavouring to remove such a stigma on the profession.

I had in the autumn of 1825 promoted an obstetrical society which should take upon itself authoritatively, and through government, to obtain a proper remedy for an admitted defect in medical legislation. I was commissioned by the council of that society, which embraced the best obstetricians in London, to carry on through Mr. Peel, the Home Secretary, a correspondence with the College of Physicians, by which we ultimately succeeded in obtaining proper legislative regulation, both as regarded the College of Physicians itself and the College of Surgeons. The Apothecaries Company had already, of their own accord, adopted suitable regulations as regarded their own members. All these results were not obtained without a manifestation of ill-will on the part of the president of the College of Physicians, Sir Henry Halford, who had ventured to insert in one of his early replies to us, addressed to Mr. Peel, that "the art of midwifery was unworthy of the notice of gentlemen of academical education," a phrase which I took care should not go unnoticed in my official reply. . The reform, however, is not complete so long as a large number of ignorant, uninstructed women are suffered to attend the lower classes of married women, without any preliminary examination as to their fitness for the office, as is the ordinary practice in any other Christian country. This is a great blot in the policy of England.

The next official interference on my part, by which I attempted to bring about some important change and amelioration in an old public establishment in London, occurred not long after. In my capacity of secretary to the Board of Visitors of the Royal Institution of Great Britain, I had had occasion to remark and make some observations both to the board and to the general meeting of the members, on the clumsy and complicated manner of keeping the accounts, which were by rule submitted to the revision of the visitors before they could be adopted. The visitors had to examine the vouchers and see how they sustained the charges in the accounts. It was a source of dispute yearly among some of the members at their annual meetings, the finding out what the accounts really represented, there being not fewer than four columns of entries both on the credit and debit side ; so much so was this the case, that one little keen and persevering gentleman I remember, the late Mr. Sellow, used to be on his legs for an hour or two to ask for explanations and elucidation from the president or secretary, showing at the same time the absurdity of the system with such cogent arguments as to gain for himself the sobriquet of Mr. Sergeant Sellow. But Othello's occupation was clean gone when my pertinacious system of reforming absurdities removed every ground for the display of any Joseph Hume rhetoric. It was no difficult task for me to persuade the members of the board of the propriety of introducing some improvement in the manner of keeping the accounts, but as they were the accounts of the managers, and not our own, we could only suggest, not adopt, a difference in keeping them. Accordingly, at one of the first meetings which the visitors usually held to prepare for the anniversary meeting of the members, and before the Board of Managers had drawn up their accounts preparatory to their being submitted to us for revision, I presented to the manager, with the visitors' sanction, a new model for the presentation of their accounts, which model was by them approved, and liberty given to the visitors, through their secretary, to shape the accounts of the current year accordingly.

The following is extracted from the minutes :—" At a meeting of the Visitors of the Royal Institution of Great Britain, the Honourable Sir George Reece in the chair, 8th April, 1839, it was unanimously resolved that the thanks of the committee of visitors be returned to Dr. Granville for the very excellent report drawn up by him agreeably to the request of the visitors at their meeting of the 1st of April, which so ably described the present prosperous condition of the Royal Institution." The good result of this simplification substituted for the former mystification was not long in becoming manifest, for the principal secretary of the Board of Managers was thereby enabled to detect a petty system of fraud in preparing the managers' accounts, which ended in the discovery of a defalcation of £800 on the part of the assistant-secretary. The reverend secretary of the institution had the credit of the discovery, but my proposed mode of representing the state of the accounts put him in the way of accomplishing his detection of Fisher's defalcation.

During my period of office, which lasted nearly twenty years, and elicited the grateful thanks of the managers, I introduced another improvement in the manner of conducting the business of the anniversary meeting, by representing a fuller or more compendious report to the assembled members of the general proceedings in every branch of the institution, in lieu of the curt couple of paragraph reports of my predecessors. The improvement pleased the managers and satisfied the members, and I am very happy to behold the example followed with energy by my successor, so that at present we find that the Royal Institution of Great

Britain, which at the time of my accepting office was deeply
in debt, had in its account-sheet a mass of arrears of subscriptions which ended almost always in being cancelled, in
its annual report a long list of lamentations with as little
reference as possible to the scientific or literary sayings
and doings of the institution—now comes forward at the
annual meeting with a full report of its prosperous condition,
and the progress achieved in the past year by the zeal and
activity of its managers, the vigilant supervision of its
visitors, and above all by the talent and high reputation of
its permanent as well as occasional professors and lecturers.
The extinction of debt, and in its stead an investment of
several thousand pounds in state funds, an increase in the
number of books in the library, and of suitable appliances
in the laboratory, the extension of the time during which
the library has been made accessible to the members,
coupled with the facility of obtaining the desired volumes
through the courteous readiness of the librarian, and lastly,
the *tout ensemble* of the establishment, so well kept, and so
worthy of the popular favour it enjoys among the educated
classes of the western metropolis, justly constitute the Royal
Institution of Great Britain the leading scientific society
next to that which owns a royal Charles for its founder.

While on this topic I may be permitted to add, that I
consider this as one of the many happy periods of my life
during which I watched over the mutual interests of an
institution endeared to me by so many gratifying recollections of friendship, contracted with some of the most distinguished professors and prominent members before whom I
had the honour of venturing on two occasions, and
when I look back to that period and contrast the state I
found the finances of the society in, with the heavy arrear
of subscriptions from members in 1832, with that presented
in my last official report twenty years later, I feel a degree

of pride in having been permitted to co-operate with successive boards of active managers and vigilant visitors in effecting those salutary changes, not the less valuable because accomplished without strife and contention, by which an institution dear not to English only, but to all European and American men of science, from its connection with the imperishable discoveries of Davy and Faraday, changes I say which raised the Royal Institution of Great Britain to a higher state of efficiency than it could boast of at any former period of its existence.*

The next reform was a much more thorough and sweeping one, and refers to a somewhat later period of my life. The active part I have taken in the affairs of the Royal Society, as will have appeared already in the course of my narrative, induces me to gather up carefully all incidents in my life that have any reference to that subject, in order that that period of the history of the Royal Society which extends from the date of the loss it sustained by the death of its venerable president, Sir Joseph Banks, to the present phase may be complete. The vacancy in 1820 did not cause the disturbance among the fellows which subsequent vacancies in the presidential chair have given rise to. The electoral problem, on the contrary, seemed to have involved the society in a species of suspended animation, which lasted several years ; some of the fellows by their personal character and station in society, others from their exclusive reputation in particular branches of science, presented themselves to the notice of the voters at each subsequent anniversary meeting without commanding a lasting confidence. Many scientific

---

* On the day in which the new mode of keeping the accounts proposed by myself was adopted, the Royal Institution was in debt £1847 16s. 4d., with an excess of arrears of subscriptions from members of several years' standing. On the day on which I resigned, there were no arrears of subscriptions, and the institution had £5210 of funded property, besides £16,488 from other sources, making a total credit of £21,698.

names were passed over as lacking some of the desirable qualifications which members of high-bred communities look for in the gentleman who is to be over them.

Those fellows who remember the condition the Royal Society was in about the year 1830, when, after a severe struggle of parties, in an association which at the time acknowledged no special control, the presidential chair was awarded to a royal duke, cannot have forgotten the state of confusion and disorganization the Duke of Sussex was called upon to redress, and which he found fully and methodically set forth in an anonymous publication by myself entitled "Science Without a Head." That pamphlet served to secure the election of the royal duke, and thereby the society found a head at last. But what was the composition of the scientific body on which a head was at length imposed? At that particular time the Royal Society "for the diffusion of natural knowledge" consisted of 651 fellows, exhibiting a most incongruous mass of *savants*, who in the course of thirty years, since the commencement of the present century, had produced 464 memoirs. But not more than one in five of the number of so vast a total had any claim to the title of a *savant*, for the said 464 scientific memoirs, forming the volumes of the "Philosophical Transactions," were the actual production of only 103 fellows, the remaining 548 fellows consequently were *savants en crédit*, and nothing more. By separating the latter number of fellows into classes according to their station in life, I showed of what integral atoms that curious amalgam consisted, who might aptly be called the *fainéants* of the Royal Society. Of these, nine were bishops, sixty-three noblemen of every rank, twenty-five naval and thirty-five army officers, fifty-five physicians, eleven surgeons, and two hundred and eight whom we may call miscellaneous. On the other hand, among the real contributors towards the promotion of science, out of the total number of eighty-five fellows, there were one bishop, who produced nine memoirs; five navy and four army officers, who contributed thirty-three memoirs; six clergymen, who wrote nine papers; six lawyers, who supplied twenty papers; twenty-one physicians, who contributed sixty-five memoirs; nine surgeons, who afforded thirty-seven papers; and one of this class of fellows alone contributed one hundred and nine to the general collection.

This analytical view of the Royal Society served to show how easy it must have been to be made a fellow in those days; indeed, the process could not have been simpler or more expeditious. It consisted in sending round the ballot-box, or boxes, for frequently two such at one time were used, with the name of the candidate stuck on the outside, at any and generally at every ordinary weekly meeting of the society where a quorum of twenty-one fellows could be got together, sometimes it happening that fellows would have to be fetched out of the meeting of the adjoining Society of Antiquaries to complete the quorum. This process went on through the room all the while one of the secretaries was engaged at the president's table in reading the written scientific communications that had been presented to the society, occasioning a succession of interruptions neither acceptable to the author of the paper nor its reader, nor agreeable nor profitable to the listener.

The author of the " History of the Royal Society in the Nineteenth Century " * inveighed long and severely against such an absurd and unsatisfactory practice, as tending to level the first scientific society in England to the position of an ordinary club. He maintained that the election of fellows should take place once a year only, and should be limited

* " The Royal Society in the Nineteenth Century ; being a statistical summary of its labours during the last thirty-five years, with table, &c." By A. B. Granville, M.D., F.R.S. 1836.

to a select number of candidates proposed in the course of that or the preceding years ; that the certificate for ballot should distinctly set forth the grounds on which the candidate was recommended, his works and scientific pursuits, all which should be specified, the candidate in fact being favourably reported beforehand to the council for selection by one or more members of that scientific section of the council which was identical with that of the proposed candidate. The author of that work brought forward in support of his own view the example of the Institute of France, and suggested that the councillors should be divided into sections in accordance with the branch of science they were well known to excel in, a suggestion which was adopted and made part of the present new statutes. This classification of the councillors would serve other very essential and equally important purposes, namely, the securing of the effectual and impartial working of the society, and consequently its future reputation, and the reference of all the several papers read before the society to the judgment of that section of the council to which the subject of the paper referred, who would be bound to make a written or a verbal report to the meetings on the nature and merits of the paper, and on the propriety or otherwise of its publication in the "Transactions." Who can deny that since the adoption of this plan, or something very like it, urged by the author of the work before mentioned, the value of that renowned collection of scientific memoirs has risen a hundred-fold in the estimation of all the continental *savants* and academics (as I can testify from having very recently visited the greatest number of them), as well as in that of the English lovers of science ?. Compare the volumes as at present published—their well-finished engraved illustrations, and above all the regularity with which they have been issued during the last few years—with any equal number of the volumes of "Transactions" during the several years before the reform suggested, and who can fail to declare how infinitely superior the one series is to the other?

Not less important were the two next suggestions for the improvement of the Royal Society, advocated with as much energy as I was master of, and in which I was supported by a large number of working fellows. The first being the introduction of academical discussions at all the ordinary meetings, whether on the paper read, or any other scientific subject, as well as on all such matters as concerned the affairs and proceedings of the society in general; and the second, referring to the finance of the society. I contended in my work, that in lieu of the short verbal announcement made by the treasurer at the general meeting, without the production of a single voucher or other document in support or elucidation, which had been the case up to 1830, there should be a distinct balance-sheet printed, properly audited, and sent round to all the fellows some days previous to the election of officers, in order that they might be prepared when necessary to discuss it.

It will scarcely be believed that down to 1830 no such financial control was possessed by the fellows at their anniversary meetings, and yet, judging by the total sum expended in the course of five years (1830-35) subsequent to the adoption of the control I advocated, viz., £22,140, it is manifest that the measure was adopted very judiciously by the council, and indeed that it ought always to have existed.

Such were the principal points requiring reform which I strenuously indicated in my first publication already named, and more forcibly insisted upon a few years later in the subsequent and more important volume just analyzed. That lapse of five years proved a period of great contention within the society, which had enlisted the acrid pen of a

late eccentric astronomer, and the more sober and logical
one of a well-known mathematician, who I trust is still
amongst us—a period moreover which brought contributions to the *Times* on analogous subjects. Among others
which appeared in that paper was one signed "Socius," to
which a full and categorical reply was inserted on the following day, signed "Socius Alter," which was justly attributed to the author of the " Royal Society in the Nineteenth
Century." That author has happily survived all the hatred
and malice excited by his reforming volumes, as he has also
survived the shame he shared with all the fellows at the
discreditable proceedings permitted to take place at an
ordinary meeting of the society, when the chairman of the
evening suffered a flagrant violation of the then existing
statute to take place—the carrying of an irregular and
ridiculous motion proposed by a new-fledged fellow of about
one or two years' standing of the class lawyer (*fainéants*),
namely, to recall a vote of thanks accorded at a previous
meeting to the author of the work mentioned above. That
motion was carried by a small number, who thus inflicted a
disgrace on our society in which I participate like every
other fellow, none of our subsequent councils having had
the manliness to expunge the irregular minute of the whole
transaction from their registers, or to return to the un-
thanked author that which they had refused to thank him
for. But he has lived to seé all his suggestions adopted
one by one, as a late president, the amiable Marquis of
Northampton, who headed the reforming party in council,
used to tell me at his *soirées* while those reforms were in
progress : " You see, my dear doctor, that we are profiting
little by little by your suggestions; all the rest will come
by-and-by." And come they did at last ; for unquestionably the constitution, the mode of working, and the position
of the Royal Society in 1870 differ vastly from the Royal

Society of 1830, which now offers to the world the model of what such an association should be.

I am aware that by this personal statement I expose myself to the charge of selfishness, but when I reflect on the manner in which the council treated the works which had pointed out their defects and shortcomings, as well as the manner in which those imperfections could be remedied, I shall, I trust, be pardoned for proclaiming personally my own case, which by a violation of the rules and the statutes even then in force in the society, I was prevented from properly developing at an extraordinary general meeting convened on the requisition of the required number of fellows—twenty-one—whose names I might well be proud to repeat, to show how I was prepared to sustain my protest against all the irregular proceedings on the part of the authorities on the occasion in question. Those heartburnings, however, are now extinguished, and it is with no other than feelings of good-fellowship that I look back on all the fellows who resented my mode of endeavouring to do good to the society by reforming its shortcomings.

As I must be naturally desirous to eschew every occasion for again reverting to this disagreeable, and certainly not a creditable period in the history of the Royal Society, I shall close my own historical account of it by a reference to what my readers will doubtless consider as a redeeming feature in the sombre reminiscences of past days. The relation of the naked facts will explain my meaning. While the English *savants* were at loggerheads among themselves as to a fresh selection of a president in 1838, the society being still unreformed and under objectionable as well as ill-adapted statutes, a notion was started by some well-intentioned fellows of placing at their head one of the, perhaps I might say, most conspicuous public men in the State of the day. Popular, eloquent, and sagacious, of

whom England indeed felt proud, and who had at that very
period relieved himself by the resignation of a great public
trust.   While the generality of the fellows rejoiced at such
a prospect, I, on the contrary, trembled for the eminent
individual, for his fame and peace of mind, were he to be
plunged suddenly into such a vortex of difficulties as the
Royal Society, constituted as it then was, presented to the
world.   I therefore took the liberty of addressing to that
eminent person the following private letter :—

" To the Right Hon. Sir Robert Peel, M.P.

" 16, Grafton Street, Berkeley Square.   25th Oct. 1838.

" Sir,—Public rumours and newspaper reports have
lately assigned to you the possible occupation of the chair
of the Royal Society.   Much as I may desire, in common
with many of the old fellows, that a person in every way so
eminently qualified to fill that post should consent to honour
it with his superintendence and patronage, I cannot conceal
from myself that far more important duties to his country
await that person incompatible with the discharge of those
of president of a great national assembly of men of science
which, reduced to its present state, will need every effort
that a new head can make to uphold it.   Still, assuming it
as possible that on being proposed for election you may feel
disposed to accede to the wishes of many of the most respectable fellows, I have deemed it a duty, as I considered
it an honour, to request your acceptance of a copy of a work
I published on the history, proceedings, resources, and progress of the Royal Society since the commencement of the
present century, and I respectfully solicit your attention to
the facts and statistical averments it contains, that you may
be directly acquainted with the real condition of an institution over which you may be called to rule.   The picture
is not a cheering one, nevertheless true, for not one of the

allegations therein recorded has ever been gainsaid in the course of the three years which have elapsed since their publication to the world. To save you some trouble, I have taken the liberty of marking in red ink particular passages, and of making also certain particular references. In the present step I have no other object in view than that of preventing the possibility of any eminent person from being by circumstances led to take a charge the many and complicated difficulties of which may perchance have escaped his attention. And on the other hand I hope to convey to that eminent person, and the public generally, my vindication of British science from the attack of those who, with singular obstinacy, keep proclaiming in their diatribes its pretended state of degradation.

"I have the honour to be, &c.,

"A. B. GRANVILLE."

A reply to my letter was not long in coming :—

"Drayton Manor. Oct. 31st, 1838.

"SIR,—I have the honour to acknowledge the receipt of your letter, and I thank you for the volume to which it refers. It has not accompanied your letter from London, but I procured and read your treatise at the time of its publication, and have it here. The presidency of the Royal Society would be 'incompatible with the parliamentary duties I have to perform, and which are particularly onerous at that period of the year when the services of the president are most useful to the society. But I have another, and a stronger, objection to the acceptance of the office in the very improbable event that it should be proffered to me. I am decidedly of opinion that in the interests of the Royal Society, and for the character of men of science in this country, the chair should be filled by some distinguished man who has devoted his time and faculties to some branch or other of science. I, for one, shall not acquiesce in the selection of a mere honorary president.

    "I have the honour to be, Sir,

      "Your most obedient servant,

        "ROBERT PEEL.

"To Dr. Granville, M.D., F.R.S."

I consider it a fortunate circumstance that my letter, intended to put Sir Robert Peel on his guard on the question of the presidency of the Royal Society, should have elicited from so competent an authority another weighty opinion to be added to the many that had been already made public respecting the most fit person for the superintendence of the first scientific body in Great Britain.

CHAPTER XV.

Count Woronzow—Serious illness of Dr. Hutchinson—He is succeeded by Dr. Lee—Elected a member of the Athenæum Club—Parliamentary committees—The Gardner Peerage—Statistics for friendly societies—Death of my father—Accept a proposal to go to Russia—Incidents of the journey—Capo d' Istria—Effects of flowery pekoe—Return to England.

WHILE occupied with extra professional pursuits, the report of my successful visit to Wilton House kept creeping up to the metropolis with exaggerated appreciation, adding still further to my obstetrical engagements, several of which, however, I was compelled to forego, or rather to decline, not wishing to fetter myself in my movements by any compulsory fixture in the capital. I was nevertheless glad to receive the congratulations from the select few who expressed the great interest they naturally took in the prosperity of the house of Herbert, to which they were related, among whom I welcomed most gratefully those of Count Michael Woronzow, whose devotion to his rescued sister was unbounded. Sudden emergencies compelled the count and countess to repair to Russia, and they made application to me for a physician to reside with them at Odessa, to take care of the two children, as well as of the father and mother, for three or four years. At the end of that time they proposed to revisit England, agreeably to an understanding with the emperor, who had conceded that after an interval of four years the count should be at liberty to absent himself from his post, as general commanding in Bessarabia and governor of Odessa, to come and visit his

aged father.   In the choice of a medical gentleman for this
family I was fortunate enough in recommending Doctor
William Hutchinson, who had ably conducted the "London
Medical and Physical Journal."   How he was appreciated
by the family, an extract from a letter from the count, dated
the 1st of September, 1824, and some concluding phrases
in a letter from the doctor himself to me, dated the 13th
of September, 1824, will fully show.   Unfortunately, both
letters, but that from the doctor especially, are descriptive
of such an impaired state of health in the latter person, that
an immediate substitute for him had become a peremptory
necessity.   However, I prefer to let them speak for themselves, especially as the concluding part of Dr. Hutchinson's
communication to me expressed his feelings of great thankfulness for the manner in which he had been treated, and
I am glad of the opportunity of quoting an indisputable
authority for the statement I have published elsewhere in
allusion to certain misrepresentations of the general character of the Russian nobility to be read of in some recent
book of travels in their country :—

                    " Bialatzertikoff.   Sept. 13th, 1824.

   "MY DEAR SIR,—I believe I mentioned to you in my
last letter that I had suffered severe hæmoptysis at Odessa.
Since that time I have always had more or less cough,
difficulty of breathing, and vague pains in the chest,
although I confined myself wholly to the house during the
winter and spring.   During this summer I have several
times had more or less hæmorrhage from the lungs, and a
few weeks ago this occurred to the extent of about one
hundred ounces within thirty hours.   With such a state of
my lungs my life must be of but short duration in so dry
and sharp an atmosphere as that of this climate, with its
hot summers and severe winters and bitter north winds.
This I have just mentioned to Count Woronzow, and I have

advised him to seek another physician without delay. He calculates again on your kindness and active and important exertions, and I believe intends to write immediately to Lady Pembroke as well as to yourself about it. It will not be possible for any one to arrive here soon enough to enable me to quit before the winter will be established, and hence I must pass that season here. But I hope my departure will not be delayed longer than the first spring weather. It is for other reasons desirable that whoever replaces me should arrive as soon as possible, as the duration of my life is extremely uncertain, and there is not a physician in this part of Russia in whom the count could have sufficient confidence to place him at ease in regard to the welfare of his family. Every circumstance with regard to my connection with the count's family concurs to render my leaving it a cause of deep regret to me. My sense of duty would have incited me to have made any sacrifice as concerned myself, but in persisting to remain now I should expose the count to the imminent hazard of being suddenly left without any source of adequate medical aid. The count has just mentioned to me that it is a matter of necessity, that whoever replaces me should be acquainted with the practice of midwifery. I ought to mention to you that I have obtained considerable sums of money by practice extraneous to the family of the count, who has also made me considerable presents at different times, so that the regular appointments of the count have not been above half what I have actually acquired. You may make use of this information in your negotiations for my successor.

"Believe me, &c.

"WILLIAM HUTCHINSON.

"Dr. Granville."

The case appeared serious, and to admit of no delay. Doctor Robert Lee of Savile Row, a graduate of Edinburgh,

who had learned obstetrics from Dr. Hamilton, had for
some time attended with me the practice of midwifery at
the Westminster General Dispensary, working assiduously,
and visiting many patients in my stead. I asked him
whether he would like to pay a visit to Russia, and he
accepted. I immediately communicated with Lady Pembroke, and on my statement of his qualifications she
accepted him, referring him to Lord Pembroke for a proper
arrangement as regarded the conditions of the appointment, his *honorarium*, travelling expenses, and the nature
of his duties as a physician to the family of Count Woronzow.
I described to the Countess of Pembroke the doctor's
character and abilities, as they had fallen under my notice
on many occasions, and mentioned to her how he had
increased his experience in the obstetrical art and cognate
practice by attending for a year or two at my dispensary.
On this recommendation Dr. Lee was appointed to succeed
Dr. Hutchinson, and I had the satisfaction of seeing him take
his departure in a couple of days for Odessa, *via* Germany
and Poland, in which chief city and port of Bessarabia he
arrived on the 8th of January, 1825, to relieve his suffering
brother practitioner from a climate that was threatening his
existence. Thus was I fortunate in being the means of
saving one friend's life, of promoting the worldly interest of
another medical friend, and in so doing conferring a valuable
obligation on more than one other friend whom I highly
respected and wished to oblige. Doctor Robert Lee has
himself published an interesting narrative of his journey to
Odessa, and though he has entirely omitted to state the
circumstances under which he came to be engaged in that
transaction, he is happily alive and well, and still in practice
in London, to vouch for the accuracy of my own statement.
His first introduction to my acquaintance was a mere
accident, to which some allusion was made when I spoke of

my professional visit to Lady Melbourne at Whitehall. I now further remember (having recently conversed with the doctor) that on the occasion referred to in the first account, when Lady Bessborough had brought down the reluctant Dr. Warren from his bedroom in Brook Street to Whitehall, Dr. Lee got out at Melbourne House and was invited to be present at the consultation between Dr. Warren and myself, and he verbally informed me (this 23rd of June, 1871) that the doctor was the reverse of courteous towards me both in language and manner, but that I stoutly, though respectfully, maintained my opinion, viz., that other means of treatment would have been adopted had the nature of the complaint been properly investigated and defined.

One little event happened in the early part of 1824 which was calculated to show how truly Lady Ellenborough described the feeling of gratitude expressed in her letter after we parted, for on the first opportunity that occurred to her on which she could again evince that feeling, she did so in the most delicate and, as it turned out for me, flattering manner :—

"MY DEAR DOCTOR GRANVILLE,—As I observed this morning that the hesitation you felt in becoming a member of the new literary club proceeded from prudential motives, allow me the pleasure in the present instance of obviating that difficulty. A lively recollection of your goodness to us while we were fellow-travellers induces me to hope you will believe me :—

"Yours very sincerely obliged,
"A. ELLENBOROUGH.

"February, 1824."

This flattering incident in my life was occasioned by a proposition having been made that I should become one of the original members of the Athenæum Club, as will appear from the following letter :—

"Dear Sir,—It will afford me much satisfaction to nominate you a member of our new club, which has very recently been projected, and already attained much popularity. The persons eligible are authors known by their scientific or literary works, artists of eminence, and noblemen and gentlemen distinguished as patrons of science, literature, or the fine arts. A committee was formed on Monday last to choose members, and we shall assemble again next week. Be pleased to communicate this letter to Mr. Faraday, No. 21, Albemarle Street, who has undertaken to act as our temporary secretary, and will insert your name and give you a list of the original members already nominated.

"Believe me, dear Sir, very truly yours,

"Joseph Jeykell.

· "Spring Gardens. Feb. 19, 1824.
"Dr. Granville."

The admission was communicated to me by a second letter :—

"Dear Sir,—There was a mistake, too long to detail, as to the form of your nomination at our projected club, but it is rectified, and at a committee held at my house this day you were admitted a member.

"Yours, dear Sir, very truly,

"Joseph Jeykell.

"Spring Gardens. Monday evening,
"March 8th, 1824."

There is an interesting circumstance in connection with the first letter which could not fail to strike me. In Mr. Jeykell's residence in Spring Gardens, where I beheld assembled some of the most enlightened and clever people, all well and not a few nobly born, when on the point of constituting themselves into a friendly and literary club, there was one who had considered it a distinction to accept from this highly-talented assemblage the spontaneous offer of the post of honorary secretary for the occasion, who ten years before, when the personal attendant on Sir Humphry Davy, had performed for me a homely office, which I had accepted as a pure courtesy on his part, though it had been presented to him as a duty.

My practice now had reached its culminating point, and Sir Walter Farquhar's prediction was gradually becoming a reality. We may pretty safely conclude that a medical man's character and reputation in London are advancing in the estimation of the public when Parliament considers it of importance to obtain his opinion, and invites the assistance of his knowledge and experience in the investigation of some great question submitted to the consideration and judgment of either of the two Houses. I have already had occasion to refer to the evidence I had been called upon to give in reference to the quarantine laws as a supposed impediment to the free action of foreign trade with England. I am now about to quote another example of such references by Parliament to the knowledge and experience of a private medical man, with the view and hope of obtaining from him the means of coming to a correct and, as far as it is possible, satisfactory inference on which to found highly important principles and conclusions. This was precisely the case in the treatment by the House of Peers of what has been commonly called the Gardner Peerage, involving one of the most interesting questions that can be submitted to the consideration of men in authority on whose judgment is to depend, not only the possession or otherwise of wealth and honours, but what is of yet greater consequence, the honesty and character of the parties concerned. The House of Lords, to whom a petition was referred from a person named Alan Legge Gardner, who claimed the barony of Gardner, contrived through the persevering astuteness of men "learned in the law" to so complicate the question, that its solution was left as legally doubtful as it was before all the parliamentary parade. That parade commenced in May, 1825, and was protracted for many months without producing any satisfactory results.

Lord St. Helens, thinking the question one which might interest me, very considerately sent me a note requesting my acceptance of a printed minute of evidence in the Gardner claim. Its perusal did not satisfy me of the justice of the Lords' conclusions. They were illogical, and subsequent experience proved them to have been erroneous. The physiological question was one too far above the intelligence of attorney or solicitor general, but it was simultaneously brought by myself before a more competent tribunal at the time, viz., the Westminster Medical Society, where it formed the subject of a keen and well-conducted discussion by the members, who at the end of a long debate came to a conclusion the reverse of the one arrived at by the peers of England. The several nights' debate at the Westminster Medical Society was regularly and *in extenso* given both in the "Lancet" and the "Medical Gazette," if I remember rightly ; and I am not ashamed to avow that among the speakers who impugned the decision of the peers on the debated question, I was foremost in protesting against them, backed by a host of modern as well as more remote examples and authorities. I certainly had no expectation while supporting a plain physiological proposition, that I had been defending the individual respectability and interest of parties, then entirely strangers to me, implicated in the question, but into whose intimate society worldly circumstances threw me four or five years later.

Not long after this episode of my life, it came to pass that a select committee of the House of Commons, presided

over by Thos. P. Courtenay, was sitting on the laws respecting friendly societies, to which I was summoned, and before which I produced a number of registers kept by myself, and corresponding reports from certain public institutions with which I had been professionally connected, which reports served to illustrate important points of certain public questions then under parliamentary inquisition. The documents in question were considered of such value as to induce the committee to desire Mr. Finlaison, Actuary of the National Debt Office, to examine and report his conclusions therefrom at one of their subsequent meetings. On that occasion Mr. Finlaison was asked whether he had examined the books produced by Dr. Granville, to which he replied that he had, and he exhibited the result as calculated therefrom, adding the following observation :—
" From Doctor Granville's registers, with time and due care, I confidently hope to lay down more accurately the mortality among infants of the lower orders in London ; and when this is done there will be no difficulty in answering the question the committee have in view." Such is the brief account I, can give of the part I have had in contributing, by means of carefully-collected facts through a series of years and by personal experience, to the accomplishment of some very important questions of state policy connected with subjects in close alliance with natural science.

Although selfishly engaged in everything connected with myself and the onerous duties of my profession, I had nevertheless omitted no opportunity of directing my inquiries homeward to Milan, whence I had not received any direct tidings for some time. Impatiently desirous to know how my aged father bore his heavy years and the official labours to which I knew he still clung, I wrote to my eldest sister, who resided in Paris with her husband, and who I was aware kept up a continuous correspondence with our family in Milan. Her reply to my last inquiries, after giving me an indifferent account of our father's health, added a piece of information which she thought would make up by its gratifying nature for the other unsatisfactory news, whereas it only accounted for the existence of that bad health, and threatened us with that something worse which was soon to follow. I give an extract from my sister's letter, which, however, was written in French:—" Paris. I forgot to tell you in my last letter that while I was in Milan papa received the *médaille d'honneur* for his services, which is equivalent to a decoration. It is a gold medal attached to a gold chain, is worth a thousand florins, and carries with it an annual pension of that amount. It is much esteemed amongst the chief officials, and the gift has caused many to be jealous of our good father, who was most excited about it. Never did I see a man, so cool and sedate as he is, trouble himself so much because of the delay there has been in investing him as a chevalier. The ceremony cannot yet take place owing to the absence of the Viceroy Eugène, who will have to be present. This delay causes him such anxiety that he may die before it takes place, that he has lost his appetite and cannot sleep. Our dear brother John, with all his reason, is unable to calm him. It is very flattering for papa, because in the city of Milan there are only three thus honoured." This was written on the 11th of October, 1825: six months later my sister had the painful task to perform of forwarding to me another and most distressing enclosure, containing the account of our beloved parent's death. She writes from her home in Paris:—" The fears I expressed as to the illness of our dear father are only too soon realized. Confined to my bed for more than a month with an inflammatory nervous fever, which brought me almost to death's door, I could not in any way inform you of the sad loss we

have lately suffered. Now that I am a little better I discharge the duty of announcing to you his death, which took
place on the 11th of April of this year. Although the news
I received respecting him was not very satisfactory, I depended upon his constitution, which when I left him in
September appeared tolerably strong ; but dropsy made
such progress that in spite of the skill of Dr. Defilipi he
at last succumbed. So, my dear Augustus, we have lost
both our dear parents by the same malady" (in allusion to
my good mother's death, already mentioned in my account
of my arrival at Madrid).

A time was approaching when it would be my turn to try
the climate so unfavourably spoken of by Dr. Hutchinson in
his letter of the 13th of September, 1824. As I anticipated,
the Count and Countess Woronzow came back to England to
spend some time with their father and sister, who was now
completely restored and blessed with the comfort of beholding her "dear little Sidney," so fervently recommended
to my care when her own life was in peril five years before,
now grown into a tall young man, whose studies and application to political science gave early promises of his after
attainments. "Why not under the circumstances come
with us yourself?" said the count to me one day at Pembroke House, when they were discussing their proposed
return to Russia. "Your patients of importance will soon
be going into the country. Come, continue your treatment
of my dear wife, who feels already better, and would much
regret to be placed in other hands. You have been, we
may say, a little about the world, but not in Russia. Here
is an entirely different country, which well merits your
attention. Much has been written in your country, I
mean England, about Russia and the Russians. I wish you
would come and see if it is true or not what has been
asserted in the works of Mr. Liall and Dr. Clarke. Above

all, I should like you to make acquaintance with our system of medicine, that you might suggest a better course than that we have adopted in the instruction of our young students for the army and navy, since you have been a sailor yourself in your adventurous career." Such, or as near as possible, were the words Count Woronzow addressed to me in the presence of his venerable father, with whom I had been in the habit of daily communication for some time. The old count, who was then visiting his daughter in Privy Gardens, joined his son in pressing me to accede to his request (for I considered it as such, though worded in the form of a question). "And who will take care of your excellency?" I inquired. "At your age you cannot dismiss, but on the contrary must call for the aid of the doctor who has taken care of you for so long." "Oh, as for that," replied the old gentleman, "you can go without fear; you will find me on your return where you have left me, living and doing well. One does not die rapidly at my age. I am only eighty-five; between that and a hundred there is plenty of time." In short, the affair was settled there and then; that is, I said, "Yes, for three months, but not longer, dating from the month of August."

The count seemed indisposed to make an offer of remuneration, but I suggested the following plan: " A mutual friend from among our acquaintances shall be named, to whom I will submit my fee-book of the current year, and on the amount of fees therein represented he will suggest the *honorarium* to be paid to me for my three months' attendance. Travelling expenses each way, with a travelling carriage and a servant, and to reside as a member of the family during the whole of my sojourn in St. Petersburg." The adjudication arrived at was one thousand pounds.

On the 20th of September, 1827, the party, consisting of

the count and countess and myself, a lady's-maid and a valet, together with an official feldjäger attached to General Count Woronzow, set out on the journey to St. Petersburg. My readers must rest satisfied with this mere indication of a long narrative concerning a part of my life which I have fully detailed in two thick volumes, the contents of which require not to be repeated here. The younger readers, when they reach this part of the record of my life may, if they care for it, fill up the hiatus by referring to the former work.* My older readers, who remember the former work, either in itself or through its innumerable reviews, will consider that narrative as continuous with the account of the journey to St. Petersburg now undertaken through Flanders, the Rhenish provinces, Russia, and Poland, and on my return through Siberia, the federated states of Germany, and France, as forming part of the present work, which thus far may be deemed to be accomplished, although some people may be inclined to believe rather that I must rejoice at any plausible excuse of saving myself a great deal of trouble and labour on the present occasion, not having to repeat what has been so fully told before. However, as I shall have to tell a great deal more on the subject of the Russian capital, and some particulars of its government and ministers affecting my own interest, when I shall have to give an account of a second visit to St. Petersburg, in consequence of a professional summons thither to a distinguished patient in 1849, I shall reserve till then the remarks I may have to make subsequent to the first visit.

The journey I found myself engaged in little resembled any of the various journeys and excursions I had hitherto performed, either alone or in the company of friends. There were no difficulties as to horses to encounter, or contentions

---

* "St. Petersburg: A Journal of Travels to and from that Capital, &c." 8vo. 1828-9.

with postmasters or postillions. The trouble of paying for passports and *visas* never occurred, or had to be bribed for. At each hostelry of consequence the travelling party was instantly accepted and waited upon. Nor at any station in which Count Woronzow determined to rest a day or two do I remember to have missed remarking the *empressement* with which his arrival was welcomed by some great local authority or his delegate, through the foreign country we passed, and of course more conspicuously so once we crossed the frontiers at Polangen. What was mere politeness and compliment before became a matter of discipline or etiquette, for in no nation in Europe are military officers of a superior rank treated with more consideration and respect than in Russia. But my present was distinguished from any of my former peregrinations by a feature I need not hesitate to confess pleased me more than any of the advantages just enumerated. Like an expert and provident commander who has to undertake a long and not an easy journey, Count Woronzow had attached to his suite a culinary *fourgon*, with attendant cooks and marmitons, to supply us twice every day with such ample repasts that we might be envied by those who live at home at ease and amid plenty. Nor did this species of selfish enjoyment involve, as might be expected, any detriment to the houses of entertainment at which our party halted, for the feldjäger was instructed to leave in each case a certain sum as an equivalent for the trouble given.

One remarkable person I may allude to as having joined our party. This was Capo d' Istria, whom I first met during my visit to Corfu, of which he was a native. His talents as a diplomatist need not be alluded to here, but a physical feature peculiar to him was ethnologically so curious and unprecedented, that I cannot forbear recording it. I allude to the enormous size of his ears, which measured in length nearly five inches, with a corresponding breadth and thickness. One might consider such a fact as a mere monstrosity or accidental hypertrophy of the parts in all their integrity. But that was not the case, for the count assured me that the same peculiarity had existed proportionately since his birth, therefore it must be looked upon as an exceptionally peculiar ethnological case.

Much as was done to render the journey as little irksome and tedious as possible, the seventeen hundred and sixty-five miles of which it consisted did not occupy less than one month and five days, and for myself I confess, notwithstanding all the convenience I had secured for reading in my solitary little britzska, I was very glad when I found myself in the snug and well-appointed suite of rooms which had been made ready for us in the palatial residence of Count Woronzow, situate in one of the widest and most showy quarters of the capital, called the Malamorskoy. It was the 27th of October, and winter had set in at St. Petersburg since the middle of September ; my surprise therefore was equal to my delight when I found myself in a genially warmed atmosphere directly I left my carriage under the *porte cochère* and ascended to my rooms, accompanied by a valet who spoke French, and who had been chosen for my own service. He conducted me to a bedroom, which I found equally and as genially warm as the apartments, although I perceived neither fire nor the semblance of a chimney.

The special object that brought me to St. Petersburg was the state of health of the countess, and to the prompt recovery of the same was my professional attention directed from the first day of our arrival with gratifying and not very remote results. She was not long in recovering her strength the moment she had shaken off that species of nervous fever under which she had suffered for some months immediately after her late confinement. As soon as the invalid began to

find herself better, the count and countess opened their vast
and splendid *salons* to receive their numerous relations as
well as a select circle of friends and acquaintances. Being
special favourites of the reigning imperial family, sometimes
one, sometimes another of the grand duchesses visited the
countess, who not unfrequently, when I happened to be
in the room, did me the honour to present me to them as
her *médecin intime de Londres.*   This sort of introduction
gradually extended to other branches of the aristocracy in
St. Petersburg, to which circumstance I may attribute the
several consultations I was called to professionally. Nevertheless I abstained from any serious engagement which
might possibly interfere with my own special patient, and
it was my wish to avoid exciting the ill feeling of the
principal physicians in the place, with some of whom I
became intimately acquainted, especially after my admission as a member of the Medico-Chirurgical Academy, as
well as of the Imperial Academy of Sciences, before which
latter scientific body I delivered a lecture on my Egyptian
mummy, the preparation of which, arranged in mahogany
cases, I had taken with me from England in order to exhibit
them to the *savants* of foreign countries.

I have so fully described in my former work the active
life I led during the time I remained stationary in St.
Petersburg, collecting materials in every quarter for the
compilation of that extensive work, which it was my intention to publish on my return to London, that I need not
touch upon any of these topics again. One part which is
there omitted may properly be here introduced, being important in a medical point of view. I allude to the state
of my own health, induced by my mode of life in St.
Petersburg, or perhaps caused by the nature of its climate.
It may readily be surmised that, living in a princely
mansion, with everything down to the minutest want

satisfied, and pampered—for such is the correct word—
with the best of a French *cuisine*, not improved by
an occasional mixture of some stchi or batvinia (Russian
dishes), many of my very old dyspeptic annoyances returned, among which were a great tightness in the head
and nervousness, with a deficiency of peristaltic action
to a most inconvenient degree. Bodily exercise, that
is, walking out, was out of the question. Driving out in
a sledge or drosky served me but little as a substitute
for muscular movements, while the confined air of the
apartments, in which the thermometer was constantly
ranging between 65° and 75° of Fahrenheit, was not refreshing. I brought to mind my Parisian rule, that cheerfulness and constant occupation keep off nervous dyspepsia;
but in my present case I felt that something more than
simple dyspepsia was brewing, which required vigilance on
my part. I altered my daily diet, returning to simpler
nourishment, and promoted by suitable remedies a healthier
action of the liver; further, in spite of the intensity of the
prevailing cold, I insisted on walking to all the markets and
places of popular interest, accompanied by a good-tempered
and kind companion, one of the count's aides-de-camp, a
Caucasian prince, who had volunteered to be my cicerone,
and to whom I am indebted for obtaining the many
valuable and interesting statistics which I have recorded in
the second volume of " St. Petersburg." Still, one symptom, or train of symptoms, puzzled me, while I suffered
from an incessant tremulousness, with great depression of
spirits. To no assignable cause could I refer this strange
sensation, except that it occurred every morning soon after
breakfast, at which I partook of nothing beyond a couple
of eggs and some toasted bread, accompanied with two
cups of tea. I came to the conclusion that my nervousness depended on the direct influence the Russian tea had

on my nerves. However diluted, I invariably found that the tea I drank had a strong and perfumed taste. The countess insisted that it was mere fancy on my part, for the tea was part of what came regularly to St. Petersburg from Pekin through the Russian frontiers at Kiakhta, "from which," she added, "we were distant about eight thousand miles. Pekin is seven hundred and fifty miles further, so this tea we have on our table has had to travel eight thousand seven hundred and fifty miles, to do which it would occupy many months. Surely during that long period of time whatever objectionable matter might be found in the young or newly-gathered tea-leaf must have vanished. Try again." I did so, drinking it much more diluted with milk, but to no purpose. But the count and the countess were obliged at last to admit that I seemed to get more nervous and incapable of application every morning. It was at length determined that I should leave off tea and take chocolate, which, as a matter of course, gave me a headache from indigestion, until at last I was reduced to a plain *bouillon* and toasted bread, which formed my breakfast for the remainder of the time I continued in St. Petersburg.

It was natural that I should endeavour to investigate this physiological phenomenon, and try to ascertain whether in reality genuine tea obtained from the warehouse whither the Kiakhta Telegas conveyed their Pekin produce would give rise to the strange effect I experienced. To the warehouse in question, therefore, I was driven, and here a new case being opened, the secret was at once divulged in the appearance of innumerable little blooms, remarkable for their whiteness and from their being largely mixed with the dark tea-leaves, emitting a most nauseous effluvium, and characterizing the sort of tea I had been made to drink as belonging to the class of pekoe, a simple infusion of which would act on my nerves as poison. Of this fact experiments made by myself on the effect of concentrated extract of what is commonly called green tea on young dogs and domestic cats had sufficiently satisfied me before in England.

After seven weeks' stay, my patient being quite restored to health, the moment had arrived for me to return to my post in London. Even at this distance of time, now forty-five years since, I cannot revert without a shudder to the two or three first awful nights I passed in posting back from Russia in my own carriage—a travelling britzska placed and properly secured on a double-bodied sledge, which compelled us to take six instead of four horses, and all these cattle kept together by thin ropes, gathered within the left hand of a single driver, who drove the horses as much with his long whip as with his shrill and perpetual whoops. My Fahrenheit thermometer, at zero when we left the capital, very soon sank two or three degrees. The constant rolling and pitching of a vessel in a storm can alone convey the idea of the sort of inconvenience we were going through, with the additional chance in the present case of being overturned into compact snow. At each post station (and there were only four) before we should reach the place we had decided to stop at, the mere time expended in changing horses was sufficient to freeze our double-bodied sledge to the snow so fast that one-third of the population of the village was called forth to release us by means of long poles thrust under the back portion, and so raise us in the midst of the most deafening clamour. In this guise we passed Opolie, Yewe, Dorpat, and Volmar, to enter Riga on the 15th of December, the fifth day after leaving St. Petersburg.

But I must not dwell upon the disagreeableness of the present journey homewards, leaving my readers to suppose there were not some compensations for them. The first and most important of these was the fact that a gentleman, a young merchant settled in Russia, had offered to accompany me on my return journey to England—an offer gladly accepted, as it procured me the advantage of a pleasant companion, well acquainted with the northern languages, though not much with the countries we were to pass through. Another advantage, which was common to us both, was, that the carriage we were travelling in was one I had purchased from an English resident in St. Petersburg accustomed to make frequent journeys to Paris and back, who had had it built in that city by the first carriage-builder of the day. It possessed all the conveniences which a traveller could desire who does not wish to make many stoppages, and who wished to travel at night. In the middle of the carriage a bearskin lined the lower part, and an ingenious contrivance was made for spreading a bed on either side. A solid apron, with a movable part made of stout leather, met the German glass-blind from the top, which would have closed the traveller in almost hermetically had he wished it. Suspended inside I had a double-scale thermometer and a mariner's compass. Note-books and pencils fitted one of the many pockets, while in others were folded maps, post directions, and my passport, besides the official Russian paper authorizing me to post with so many horses. In a select pouch all the apparatus was placed for smoking, either with Latakia tobacco in a long pipe, or with cigars, and in this pouch travelled my pocket edition of Horace. In other recesses immediately fronting us, and quite handy, were two thick crystal goblets and a few bottles of sherry, and one of brandy, in case of emergency. As I had determined to travel by night as well as by day, I ordered a large lamp to be fitted to the back of the carriage, to enable me to read, and which served at the same time to keep the hands warm of the poor half-frozen courier placed in the dickey behind. He had received instructions to fill the several ample leather pouches that hung suspended and locked outside the carriage with every kind of portable provisions, including tea and soup.   To him I had given a large sheepskin great-coat, providing myself at the same time with a complete wrapper of the warmest sables, a courteous gift from one of my few Russian patients.   There was only one slight drawback to all these wise provisions.   My said courier was one of the greatest ninnies I had ever met in the whole course of my life, though a Pole !

The most remarkable feature in my homeward journey was a visit to the capital of Poland, well worth seeing, and, in my estimation, like an oasis in the deserts of north-east Europe, for Warsaw is truly suggestive of the superior comforts a polished society procures for a population surrounded by many discouraging circumstances.   The courteous reception by the Grand Duke Constantine possibly served to put us in good humour with everything we beheld around us ; but all the impressions we received while in Warsaw, with the advantage of having been well recommended, and consequently able to form accurate judgments, warrant me in proclaiming my admiration of the city and the people.   But our journey offered to us many other objects of attraction and enjoyment.   The crossing of the wild Dwina, now frozen over, which only a few weeks back we had seen covered with sailing merchant vessels, with a bright sun lighting up the wide expanse of ice and snow everywhere, was a sight truly magnificent. The greatest care is taken by municipal regulations, rigorously enforced, to prevent accidents during the incessant traffic on the river.   The police take special care of all travellers, as it is not considered safe to run across the ice with loaded carriages or with too many horses. We were too glad to be out of the way of any risk, so we gave up to the police the task of drawing our sledge and carriage from one side to the other, and they provided us with a smaller and slighter sledge for our own personal use.

Our progress was more satisfactory after we had dropped the cumbersome equipage of a double-bodied sledge, and returned to the more natural and comfortable rolling on four wheels, even though we had to drag through heavy sand for many a long track before quitting Poland. Entering Silesia at last, and then Saxony, till we reached Dresden, my attention was much engaged and interested in beholding a variety of scenes, people, and manners that were entirely new to me, especially in the last-named city, justly considered the Florence of Germany. Here, of course, my undivided attention was given to a minute examination of the magnificent collection of pictures, housed in a curiously yet judiciously arranged edifice since rebuilt to great advantage.

All these sources of enjoyment I confess were embittered by the perpetually recurrent reflection, that having exceeded, unavoidably on my part, by a few days only, the leave of absence granted to me by the Lord High Admiral when I left England, some of the *kind* professional friends I had left behind me might not be sorry to have the plausible excuse to damage my interest as a half-pay officer, as it unfortunately happened. But how to hurry on faster when I found that at Kalisz, on the Polish frontier leading into Prussia, I was yet many miles from London, and my travelling qualities did not improve, my reader may determine. Much as this matter weighed on my mind, I did not allow it to interfere with my determination of having an interview with Professor Meckel, the great anatomist at Halle, with whom I had some important business to transact; of being introduced to Goethe at Weimar, and having a very interesting interview with him; and, lastly, of executing a scientific commission with Professor Soemmering, at Frankfort. At Paris it was natural that I should pay visits to my old friends and professors, nor could I be insensible to the honour proposed to me by Lord Granville, of a presentation to Charles the Tenth, the last of the Bourbon kings.

My first care on reaching London was to report to the Admiralty my return, and to show I was once more within their jurisdiction—a step required to ensure the regular quarterly payment of my half-pay. In my official communications I explained the causes of a trifling excess of a few days that had occurred beyond the leave of absence granted to me by the Lord High Admiral. Almost the very next care was an interview with Mr. Henry Colburn, the well-known publisher, with whom before my departure for Russia I had entered into a sort of engagement to supply him with materials for a new work on a subject which at that time seemed to attract universal attention in this country. That engagement at the present interview was more explicitly drawn up in a regular form, to be carried out with as little delay as possible. I insisted on the introduction of a certain number of illustrations, the originals of which I could supply, with maps and plans of cities, and a certain number of statistical tables; and I left to Mr. Colburn's own taste and judgment the style of bringing out, with all the most attractive appliances of typographic art, a work which was estimated to form two thick volumes.

The public in general, and all the leading reviewers to head them, did full justice to the liberality and taste of the publisher. For my part I am bound to declare, that not on the present occasion only, but on more than one subsequent occasion, I have been indebted to my publisher for similar conscientious and profitable exertion. The late Mr. Henry Colburn was the publisher of three of my principal works, and in each case I owe him thanks for the style in which those volumes were introduced to the public. He was a particular man, I admit, the said Mr. Colburn, but honourable in his dealings, thoroughly master of his *métier*, a good authority to rely upon as to the public taste and judgment, and although shrewd, always straightforward.

CHAPTER XVI.

1826—33.

The Admiralty and the medical officers—How to trick them out of their half-pay—I am selected as a victim, and defrauded of my subscriptions to the widow and orphan fund—The insult of a junior secretary contradicted by his superior—Outbreak of cholera in England—Publish the "Catechism of Health"—Viscount Palmerston seized with cholera—Novel mode of treatment—No rest for a foreign secretary—Another minister attacked.

THOSE who have read "St. Petersburg" know that it is far removed from the category of such as are called medical or professional works. Perhaps in the thirteen hundred and sixty-one pages of which the two volumes consist, it would be difficult to find materials for a strictly medical pamphlet; yet in the course of the half-dozen years that followed the publication of those two volumes, I can with sincerity and justice declare. that I owe to them a larger accession of new patients to my list than I could anticipate even from any positive and special publication devoted solely to the consideration of human health. Of course there is a solution to this puzzle, and my readers will have no difficulty in finding it out. The prompt manner in which the publication was effected, set me quite free to devote my attention strictly to my professional engagements; and at the commencement of the London season of 1829, I found myself as regularly restored into my ordinary groove as if I had not been absent a single day from my post. It was when in the enjoyment of the serene and placid course of my domestic affairs that an act of most glaring injustice on the part of superior officials against me was perpetrated

with the utmost *sang froid* possible, which ended by de-
priving me of my half-pay, and removing me from the list
of medical officers in the navy—a measure which involved
immediate loss to my wife and children of certain pecuniary
allowance as widow or orphans, on account of which I had
been made to contribute from the very first day of my
entering the service, in order to keep up and increase the
funds from which those pensions were derived. A simple
narrative of circumstances will suffice to show the gross
injustice of these combined acts, when I mention that in a
pecuniary point of view they have occasioned me to this
day an absolute loss of 3,865*l.* sterling.

In 1826, the Board of Admiralty found themselves
burdened with a list of medical officers of all ranks, the
half-pay of whom formed a heavy charge in the navy
estimates. It was their ambition to have a larger fleet of
men-of-war afloat than any other maritime nation. They
would insist on building a great number of useless ten-gun
brigs, called "sea-coffins," giving them abundant patronage of
naming commanders, lieutenants, and medical officers, much
beyond the need of the time ; and now after the peace,
when Nelson and his brother naval chiefs had swept off the
surface of every sea even the shadow of a hostile sail, there
remained a list of eight hundred medical officers on half-
pay, for whom there was no work or any public service to
appoint them to, but who, nevertheless, had an indisputable
right to their half-pay for life. In such an emergency what
was to be done? How can this heavy list of doctors be
lightened by three or four hundred of them at the least
cost? To the economist this was a puzzle, but a mode to
overcome all difficulties was nevertheless devised, the merit
of which rumour in my time ascribed to the keen and
shrewd secretary, Mr. John Wilson Croker. If from
ignorance I deprive any other gentleman of the credit of

the invented dodge about to be put in practice, I can only say that I regret it. "Suum cuique." I for one believed the fact as I have given it, and it was worked in this guise. An *ex officio* circular, dated the 14th January, 1826, was sent from the Victualling Board to every medical officer on the Navy List, informing them that the Right Honourable Lords Commissioners of the Admiralty had determined that a certain number of surgeons should be sent out to each of the foreign stations, with the view of their being placed in such vacancies as might occur in the respective ships on the station, and that " those surgeons of the Royal Navy who had served shortest periods since their promotion should be first selected for that service, and so on in succession." From this measure it was expected that a considerable number of the younger medical officers, from considerations of finance and domestic interest, would refuse to serve, and so make themselves amenable to dismissal from the service, thereby lightening the half-pay list. The contrary, however, took place, and so many were the junior medical officers who accepted the offer of full pay as supernumerary surgeons, that besides the difficulty of finding ships on foreign stations in which to appoint them temporarily, it was found that, while the half-pay list became less, the full-pay list became larger; the result of which was the recall of their circular of the 14th January, 1826, and the substitution, January, 1832, of a general measure by which every medical officer on half-pay would never be called upon to serve who should signify his acquiescence to receive a commuted allowance less than the half-pay to which he was annually entitled, and thus the great scheme ended.

But in the interval the working of the circular of the 14th of January, 1826, was brought to bear on my own case in a manner that elicited expressions of surprise and undisguised condemnation from more than one servant of the crown, who had an opportunity of perusing my case as drawn up by counsel and presented to succeeding Boards of the Admiralty, including Lord Minto and Sir James Graham, whose strange deliberation on the subject I possess in the form of a short epistle from Sir James. Mine was an appeal to Sir James, then at the head of the Admiralty, against the wrong decision of his predecessors in office, to which protest Sir James replied in a private letter to me of the 16th of January, 1834, that he and his colleagues could not alter the decision adopted by their predecessors, because they thought they had decided according to the facts and merits of the case. Now, the appeal showed that the said facts were precisely the other way, and the merits of the case had been consequently misjudged. As an answer to the allegation of injured eye-sight in my case, Sir James brings forward an observation, no doubt suggested by the Junior Secretary, that I had but a short time before undertaken, and did perform successfully, an operation of a most delicate nature on a female in the presence of several eminent surgeons. Precisely so; but he omits to notice the fact that a certificate of surgeon Earle was among the documents which accompanied my appeal for restoration to the service, which stated that he, Mr. Earle, was obliged to assist me in tying up some of the minutest bleeding arteries, which I could not see. And again, Sir James tries to meet my allegation of injured health, and consequent debility, by this illogical refutation: that my state of health enabled me to bear the fatigue of an extensive practice in London. Truly so, or I should not get bread for myself and family to live upon. But the fatigue of a London practice is undergone with means of conveyance, which saves bodily fatigue, with a well-appointed diet, with the attentive solicitude of relatives and domestics, with a temperature under control, and, finally, with an occasional rest in a well-ordered home for a day or two. How are all these counteracting circumstances against fatigue from work to be found in active life on board a man-of-war? A little better logic would have spared Sir James the pain of using a wrong argument in support of an act of injustice.

By the legal statement just alluded to, accompanied by its corresponding documents from public offices, it resulted, 1st. That I was selected for immediate appointment considerably before my turn, in violation of the provision contained in the circular of the 14th of January, 1826, there being no fewer than ten or twelve well-known medical men in London settled in practice who had not been applied to, although junior to myself. For example, Mr. James Clark, who was my junior, and yet had not been appointed supernumerary surgeon to any ship, but left to the enjoyment of his well-sustained practice in London. 2nd. That my allegation of ill-health, supported by great numbers of certificates from physicians and surgeons of the first eminence in London, certificates which have been invariably taken into consideration in all cases of appointment to active service, were disregarded, quite overlooked, and my allegation set entirely aside, instead of being submitted to a proper impartial medical board for inquiry, as it is customary in the royal navy. 3rd. That to appoint me to any vessel in the West Indies was a wilful and direct violation of a resolution from an authorized board of medical officers who had invalided me home from that station as totally unfit for service in such a climate; the official documents of which medical survey were actually in the hands of the Commissioners of the Victualling and Transport Boards when they signed the warrant (three days after my return from leave of absence), namely, on the 9th of January, 1828, appointing me to a vessel stationary in the West Indies, and on the most unhealthy island, in which I had suffered from an attack of yellow fever, besides other ills due to the climate, as stated in the medical survey.

But it was decided that no remonstrance on my part should prevail, and accordingly, on the 23rd of January, 1828 (sharp work, indeed, no time wasted), a finale was put to this transaction between the authorities of the royal navy and a humble member of it, who had ruined his health in the service, the merits and justice of which finale I leave to my readers to determine :—

" Victualling Office.   23rd January, 1828.

" SIR,—Having laid before the Commissioners for Victualling His Majesty's Navy your letter of the 21st inst., I am to acquaint you that with reference to your letter of the 18th inst., the Board has caused your name to be removed from the list of medical officers of the royal navy.'

" I am, Sir,

" Your most humble servant,

" M. WALLER CLIFTON.

" To Dr. Granville."

Knowing as I did the engines that had been at work in bringing about the issue I have just recorded, perhaps it was a folly to prolong the contest, especially with the Admiralty, where one of the two hostile gentlemen I alluded to at the commencement of this narrative was an active subaltern ; still it was natural that I should protest before a superior tribunal against an official resolution which I considered as too important, and to myself fatal, to come from what I looked upon as a subordinate board, and I therefore did remonstrate, a step which brought an official negative reply with the gratuitous interpolation of an impertinence which, after all, instead of wounding my feelings, as no doubt it was intended to do, led to my being able to produce a document from the superior government officer in whose department was the naval medical branch, which my children will be proud to possess, and which forms an appropriate conclusion to my story of the loss of my rank and pay in the English navy :—

Mr. John Barrow to Dr. Granville.

"31st January, 1834. Admiralty.

"Sir,—Sir James Graham having communicated to my Lords Commissioners of the Admiralty your letter of the 30th inst., I have received their lordships' commands to acquaint you, that the subordinate Board you mention acted entirely under the direction of the Board of Admiralty, and your case and *conduct* being truly represented by the Victualling Board, with the whole correspondence, which is on record at this office, my lords required no further statement from you to decide on the prayer of your late memorial."

Dr. Granville to John Barrow, Esq., Admiralty.

"16 Grafton Street. February 3rd, 1834.

"Sir,—I have to acknowledge the receipt of your letter, dated the 31st ultimo, which you addressed to me by the command of the Lords of the Admiralty, in reply to my letter to Sir James Graham, marked 'private.' From the term and spirit of your letter I plainly perceive, that so long as the personal misrepresentation which first led to the glaring act of injustice against which I complain continues to prevail, my chances of redress must be very insignificant, and far better it will be for me at present to yield as the weaker party to the stronger. It is now more manifest than ever that my last memorial was not properly investigated by the Admiralty, neither have the open charges of partiality and violation of rules brought by me against the late Victualling Board, one influential member of which is still regulating (though in another capacity) the fate of the medical officers in the navy, been duly inquired into. This

conviction of my mind would have been sufficient to dis-
courage me from noticing any further your present communication, were it not for one expression in it relative to my
'conduct.' Respecting that expression, perfectly uncalled
for by the occasion, I might very properly have called upon
you for an explanation, but that the enclosed printed copy
of a certificate which I happen fortunately to possess,
written by the late medical commissioners of the Victualling
Board, and given to me before personal feelings of hostility
were suffered to sway the public acts of that Board, sufficiently indemnify me for any mortification which you might
have meant to produce by the uncalled-for insertion of the
word I have noticed."

" *Certificate from the Medical Commissioners of the
Victualling Board of His Majesty's Navy.*

"These are to certify that Dr. A. B. Granville has held
the rank of full surgeon in His Majesty's navy from the
year 1808 ; has served in a great variety of climates and
stations, and has distinguished himself as a medical officer
of superior merit. I further certify, from my personal
knowledge, that he went through a regular course of
elementary instruction and examination previously to his
entering His Majesty's navy, and that he is eminently well
versed in the different branches of medical science ; and
that during the whole period of his service afloat he discharged his duty as an officer and a gentleman in a manner
creditable to himself and satisfactory to his superior officers,
as well as to the Board under whose immediate orders he
has been employed.

"Given under my hand at Somerset Place, this 3rd
day of February, 1822. (Signed) J. Weir,
Medical Commissioner, R.N."

We are apt in this country to stare and turn our eyes up,

uttering at the same time objurgations at the turpitude of certain public functionaries in foreign lands, wondering how certain violations of right and justice can be perpetrated with impunity as we are told ; what will foreigners say of us when they learn that an important department of the government of this country engage experienced and ex- pensively-educated professional men to give their services during their lifetime for the preservation of the health of their sailors, in return for which service a pecuniary remuneration pledged to be, paid to them in full while on active service, and in part only in future when not on service, and that such engagements are thrown to the winds when- ever it suits the said authorities to repudiate their engage- ment, and so filch the deluded medical men of what they were bound to pay them?

Nor were these the only considerations that made me feel keenly the harsh return I received for my past services. The mortification was much greater at seeing myself thus ab- ruptly excluded through hostile feelings in high places from a service with which many high associations were connected, of friendship contracted with officers who have earned for themselves an imperishable name, such as Sir Edward Parry and Captain Liddon of Arctic fame, with both of whom I had been intimate in His Majesty's frigate *Maidstone* in 1811.

But soon more serious and important matters were to attract and engage general attention, respecting which the medical profession was called upon to take an immediate lead. Cholera from our north-eastern counties was making a stealthy yet manifest progress towards the capital, and had excited great alarm, exaggerated by some injudicious and absurd descriptions and prognostications. After ascending the Volga to Moscow, and thence to St. Petersburg, to reach the shores of the Baltic, visiting Riga and Stetting, the cholera came suddenly on Hamburg in the autumn of 1831. While the latter city was suffering severely under this epidemic, it broke out in Sunderland, whence it travelled to London, settling first among the shipping in the Thames, and by the end of 1832 it had possession of the metropolis. A great outcry was raised, and the sanitary movement was initiated. The College of Physicians issued rules for preservation from cholera, and other medical writers propagated their own views on the subject in medical journals. So soon as the dreaded malady had made its appearance in the metropolis, a certain number of medical men formed themselves into a committee at the west end of the town, intending to visit and treat gratuitously all patients of the industrial classes afflicted by the disease, and administer to them suitable remedies in each case. I selected for my district Lower Chelsea and Fulham, as most within reach of my own residence. The committee used to meet every evening and report progress, making comparisons between different reports, and many were the interesting facts and conclusions which our reports enabled us to draw from them. On my part, thinking that what the humbler and more exposed classes required was information as to the proper mode of living and as to the nature of the new disease, I undertook the pleasing task of publishing a popular work in simple language and of a portable size, entitled "The Catechism of Health;" or simple rules for the preservation of health, to which were added clear notions on the character and treatment of cholera. This work, which was published in the September of 1831, soon after the appearance of cholera in London, treating of every topic connected with health and sickness, with medicine, diet, air, exercise, must have proved welcome to that portion of the public for whom it was intended, inasmuch as four editions were published in that month by Bentley.

We had occasion to remark that the disease, which seemed

to have crept in with no stint into the humble abodes of the working classes in our district, had scarcely made any impression upon the higher classes, either aristocratic or public characters. This apparent immunity on their part, however, did not last long, and not a few members of the aristocracy and of the government were added to those whom the epidemic had not spared. Among these I had soon to reckon one of my ordinary patients, whom I had on several occasions attended—I mean Lord Palmerston; and after him, at a distance of only a few weeks, another distinguished member of the government—Viscount Goderich, of whose family I had had the honour of being the medical attendant for some time.

On the 4th of April, 1833, Lord Palmerston was brought to his house in Great Stanhope Street in a hackney coach, having been taken suddenly ill as he was leaving his office in Downing Street. The state in which I found his lordship when I entered his bedroom, scarcely half an hour after the summons to Grafton Street had been despatched, showed me at once with what sort of ailment I had to deal. The daily witnessing of patients attacked by cholera by the members of the Cholera Committee had made our eyes expert in recognizing the disorder. His lordship had been partially undressed and laid on his bed, where he was lying on his back; his head raised high on the pillows. His face was deadly pale and shrunk—the eyelids closed; both knees were drawn up almost to an acute angle with the surface of the abdomen, which I uncovered and felt all over, occasioning indications of pain when pressed, however gently, on my part. I nevertheless obtained the conviction that the pain as well as the attitude of the limbs were not occasioned by an attack of inflammation, but by spasmodic contraction of the muscles of the abdomen, to which part now and then the patient would direct both his hands, giving signs by his countenance and a shrill cry that the part was in pain. The whole surface of the body was icy, as was the tongue in a remarkable degree; respiration faint, and at long intervals; the pulse extremely small, and beating with long intermissions; very rigid. But for the contraction of the legs and thighs Lord Palmerston's state would have reminded me of that in which I had observed persons who had just been drawn out of the water and saved from drowning. One of the other symptoms we had to contend with was sickness, which rendered almost useless every sort of stimulant, for it was almost immediately rejected, except the stimulating alkaline drops recommended by me in the "Catechism of Health" under similar circumstances, and the nature of which was a combination of camphor, pure liquid ammonia, and essence of rosemary. This stimulant alone succeeded in diminishing notably the spasmodic action of the stomach. In my anxious moments of this treatment I had, fortunately, the advantage of a most excellent nurse in the old faithful housekeeper of his lordship, devoted to her master and grateful to him, who had invariably sent me to attend her during occasional illnesses. Her grief and tears did not prevent her from affording me every assistance.

Under such alarming and discouraging features of the case, I shall not scruple to enter into the detailed history of the treatment adopted where ordinary and common measures inspired no confidence. It was the inspiration of the moment, and may serve as a guide and encouragement to those who come after me under the like circumstances, not to despair however desperate the attack of the disease may appear. The patient was entirely stripped and placed in a prone position. A long band of thick flannel, four inches wide, was spread over and all along the spine from the joint in the back of the neck down to the upper portion of the sacrum, the band being held firm by the housekeeper at the upper, and by the valet at the lower end. Over this band I passed lightly up and down a heated flat-iron, such as is used in laundries. The first indication of any effect from this addition of heat to the spinal marrow was the relaxation of the contracted lower extremities, so that the pronation of the whole body became complete. His lordship had not spoken a word since he had been brought home, and had only uttered a more or less subdued cry now and then. We could only judge by other symptoms than his expressions whether the measure we were adopting was producing any salutary effect or not. On this point we were not long kept in suspense. It was remarked that he breathed more freely and at more regular intervals; in the mean while the pulse in both wrists became more sensible, and with scarcely any intermission. Presently a deep sigh was heaved—a deep inspiration, I mean—and the whole skin visible to us assumed a rosy tint, and felt warm to the touch. I now directed that he should be turned on his back, leaving the warm flannel on the skin when raised up to his pillows. Some of the stimulatory alkaline drops were now given, which were retained. An immense eructation of gas escaped from his mouth, another very deep inspiration followed, and my lord was heard to say "I am better." An ample cataplasm of linseed meal, with a small quantity of mustard powder sprinkled upon it, was applied to the whole surface of the abdomen, from which all vestige of spasmodic contraction or indication of pain on pressure had wholly disappeared. My lord was safe! Instant and positive silence was imposed, and every person except the housekeeper and the valet was required to leave the chamber, and his lordship to the chance of sleep. "We must have no unnecessary expenditure of power," I whispered into his ear when I left him.

Before I left the house that day Lord Palmerston seemed to me to have got over the danger of a sudden extinction, and I flattered myself he would recover. Directions were given to the servants to reply to all inquiries, that Lord Palmerston had been taken suddenly ill with a severe attack of the prevailing influenza, notice of which was forwarded in my name to the Foreign Office, with a note from myself to Sir George Shee, the under-secretary, requesting him at the same time to communicate the information to both his lordship's brothers-in-law, Lawrence Sulivan, Secretary at War, and Admiral Bowles. The name of cholera was not to be mentioned, an injunction I solemnly gave to the porter as I entered my carriage on leaving Stanhope Street. It was considered prudent to adopt such a course instead of alarming the public with the real name of the disease, at that moment an object of horror to Londoners. Accordingly, the public journals, the "Times" and the "Morning Post," of the 8th of April, 1833, announced the illness of the foreign minister, the "Morning Post" stating that "Lord Palmerston has been indisposed during the last few days," &c. The "Times" repeated day by day the same account as the "Morning Post;" and on the 17th of April, Wednesday, it states that "Viscount Palmerston continues confined to his residence in Stanhope Street."

All official or any other communications with the patient were strictly to be avoided, and no person however connected with his lordship was to be admitted to his chamber in my absence. I visited the patient frequently in the course of the day, and remained till late at night in attendance, although my own residence was in almost an adjoining street.

I have mentioned the principal reason for having entered into the particulars of my treatment as an encouragement to my co-professional brethren, but there is what must be considered of much more importance under any circumstance in which this formidable illness may appear. A sound reason for detailing the treatment is the introduction of a remedial agent which my brethren will admit to be new, and to the physiological influence of which they will join me in ascribing the prompt restoration of animal heat to the whole system, through the agency of an artificially excited action of the spinal nerves and vessels.

The complaint went its usual course, and Lord Palmerston was able to return to active life after a short period, though not very strong, yet as eager for work as if he had never suffered more than a few hours' illness. Indeed, it became evident to me that I should have to interfere more absolutely in the proceedings which I perceived going on in the establishment in reference to my patient. Lord Palmerston was not yet in a state to leave his bed from sheer debility, but there were parts of the day in which I allowed him to attend to some of the lighter occupations of his ministerial duties. He was permitted to receive a few of the official despatch boxes, to open them, and to peruse some of the contents in the presence of Sir George Shee, to whom he was to dictate a brief *précis* of the reply the despatch might require. But my lord, quite impatient under this slow process of doing business, so contrary to his usual habits, had insisted on a more active mode of proceeding, and I found him one morning in his dressing-gown sitting up in bed, the surface of which was positively strewed all over with many of the said despatch boxes, one of which had already received his attention, and was closed with the slip of paper hanging outside at the end of the box, having inscribed on it the name of the individual or office for which the contents were intended, or a brief indication of the nature of the despatch or official papers inserted, with a slight indication of the sort of reply they might require in Lord Palmerston's judgment.

But even this serious infringement of the rules I had laid down for his speedier convalescence were soon exceeded, and all attempts at preventing excitement and fatigue of the brain baffled, for in lieu of simply indicating his personal views and opinions of the nature of certain despatches he had perused, I found him actually now writing down in pencil the entire document, intended as an official reply to those he had received. Against these proceedings I seriously as well as firmly protested, urging as an argument that I was individually responsible for his safety in the eye of the public, not less than of his family, and that in a constitution so weakened by the serious attack he had just escaped from succumbing to, the exertion of the brain to which he exposed himself for some hours could only lead to but one result—a fatal one. "What is the use of your under secretaries?" I asked. "To give me double work," was his reply: "when I commit to them my ideas, I leave them to embody them in suitable phrases. They are both clever, sharp enough, and with much command of their pen; but what they tell and write, however instructed, is not what I should have said or written. I dare say you saw in passing through the drawing-room just now, Pozzo di Borgo. He has been here eagerly, and I may say kindly, to inquire after me every day, I am told, since my attack. The fact is, he is looking to a reply to a proposition he has made in the name of his government, which I am not in a hurry to submit to my colleagues for consideration. The reasons may be enumerated, but not distinctly told; and that was the official document I was writing just as you came in and as usual began to grumble at me. However, be easy, I will in future attend more strictly to your rules, and let me have more of that delicious drink that you have so cleverly invented."

The attack of another of the most prominent ministers of the day, to which I have made a simple allusion, was of much less importance, although at its outset sufficiently so to alarm his lordship's family. Lord Goderich, who was spending the summer at a villa near Highgate, with a view of being near his official department in London, was attacked with symptoms of illness, that led the local medical man to declare it to be cholera. It was on a Sunday that the attack took place, and I was hastily called out of St. George's Church to visit his lordship, whose carriage was in waiting at the church door. My professional acquaintance with Lord Goderich was of some years' standing, and I was perfectly aware of the state of his constitution. It was found on meeting the local medical attendant, that my lord was labouring under what was afterwards denominated cholerine, a mild form of cholera, resembling, if not identical with, what Dr. Sydenham called " cholera morbus," or English cholera. The complaint proved troublesome and exhausting, but gave way to the ordinary treatment under the assiduous co-operation of his local attendant, aided by the vigilance of his devoted countess, who had had unfortunately some regretful experience in illness with her young family. Lord Goderich was in fact restored to his daily occupations in the course of two or three weeks. As Earl of Ripon, I shall have to say more of my patient in the following pages under much more agreeable circumstances.

CHAPTER XVII.

Complexity of incidents—Statistics and contributions to scientific knowledge—Insanity—Martin's plan to improve the Thames—His scheme adopted in part by the Metropolitan Board without acknowledgment.

As I near the time of winding up my long account, and I look to the still thick volume of manuscript notes remaining by my side, which must be referred to in order to complete my narrative, I seem to get so bewildered that I can hardly perceive the chronological order I have hitherto followed, so much has one event been the effect of another. Labour of the mind also did not fail to intervene amidst adventures and ordinary domestic occurrences, and these have engrossed attention so as greatly to interfere with my professional or other obligatory duties. However, by taking comprehensive views of the period of my life now to refer to, I think I can best exhibit the nature of the multifarious work I was called upon to share in.

Some time in the spring of 1826 I received a summons to attend a Committee in the House of Commons on Friendly Societies, by order of the chairman, Mr. Courteney. I have already had occasion to refer to this committee, before which I was examined, when my evidence enabled the actuary of the National Debt Office, Mr. Finlaison, to draw certain inferences deemed important for some practical operations concerning friendly societies in general. On the present occasion my evidence was again sought on the recommendation of Mr. James Mitchell, an able mathematician, an actuary, I believe, and a lecturer on benefit societies. Mr. Mitchell addressed to me a letter on the 17th of March, 1826, asking for information as to "the probable number of children a woman will be likely to have according to the age at which she married, beginning at the earliest age and going on to fifty." A memoir on this subject afterwards appeared in one of the very useful and creditable volumes of the Obstetrical Society of London. In that memoir will be found an extensive *résumé* of my experience and opportunities of observation as regards Mr. Mitchell's principal points of inquiry. Setting aside the more practical points of midwifery, and looking only to the physio-statistical portions of the tables which accompany the memoir, there will be found even more curious facts and inferences than Mr. Mitchell contemplated when he referred with much friendliness of feeling to some former production of my pen. I may say that I am proud of those tables, the like of which I may assume the profession has not met with elsewhere.

From the period just referred to until the end of the year of the cholera, which had sufficiently occupied my time, I applied myself for a couple of hours in each day to the publication of an illustrated work on an analogous subject to that referred to in the preceding observations. This task I believe I accomplished with the approbation of the scientific world. In the first place I published an initiatory work,* and in the second place I laid before the public the result of several years' study, dissections, and designs from nature connected with the problem in hand,† and laconic and Latin descriptions accompanied the illustrations, which were lithographed and coloured by a skilful artist under my

* "Prolegomena of the Development and Metamorphoses of the Human Ovum." London, 1833.

† "Graphic Illustrations of Abortion, &c." A large quarto with fourteen coloured plates and forty-five figures. London, 1833.

immediate supervision, and with the natural preparations invariably present. This work cost me 400 guineas, and I was not likely to find readily a speculative publisher who would take on himself its publication. On the other hand, a sufficient number of eminent medical men in all branches of the profession pressed me to publish it by subscription. Headed with their names, a list of nearly 400 members was presently filled, who not only readily added their names, but did so in language or by letters, all of which I preserve with no little satisfaction, conveying a degree of approbation which the reviewers uniformly re-echoed. I was made to understand that by this new work I had placed within reach of the less instructed obstetricians, and supplied to a future generation of young medical practitioners, a source of information which they could only hope to gain after many years' personal experience. The "Lancet" called it "a splendid work. Every point in the text which could be advantageously illustrated by original drawings is made the subject of a beautiful reference to nature." The Magnus Apollo of the "Medico-Chirurgical Review," Dr. James Johnson, not always the mildest of reviewers, after discussing the mechanism of the work and its illustrations, concludes by saying that "twelve plates, containing forty-five anatomical figures, have been produced, lithographed, and coloured by Mr. Perry, rivalling the most successful efforts of French, German, or Italian artists." The "Medical Gazette," the third member of the dreaded aristarch medical triumvirate, had its own saying, thus: "It is a splendid volume, which in an especial manner deserves the patronage of the public. As we have been under the necessity of sometimes differing from Dr. Granville, it affords us pleasure on this occasion to speak in terms of unmingled commendation." (Valeat quantum, &c.) It was flattering also at the time to find the officers directing the libraries of the two medical colleges in London, and of other public scientific bodies, applying for the work. As one condition of the subscription was that after 400 copies the stones should be (as in fact they were) defaced in my presence and that of three of the subscribers, all chance of procuring a single copy in the trade was done away with.*

I must not omit to mention the various steps I had taken with the view to enlist the attention of the Lord Chancellor to a plan I laid before him on the treatment of insane people, which plan had been favourably viewed by some of the promoters of the Bill introduced by Lord Granville Somerset on that subject. But my brethren in the profession did not deem all these acts on my part sufficient. They looked for further exertions in the cause, and that I ought not to relax my efforts in any way. Thus, having heard me deliver the "First Oration" on medical reform before the British Medical Association; having sent me before parliamentary committees to give practical evidence on that subject; commissioned me to attend deputations to ministers and to draw up memorials for their instruction, even in the case of the united corps of medical officers for the poor, it was considered that my vigilance in caring for the interests of the medical profession had been sufficiently tested, which (it was at one time suspected) I appeared inclined to overlook or to put on one side. I mention all this to show that I was not unmindful of my own calling in the midst of other occupations. One of these was my attendance on the sick at the Royal Naval School at Camberwell, which I should have scorned to neglect or discontinue to attend gratuitously because of the scurvy treatment I had

---

* On one or two occasions I have noticed the work mentioned as forming a prize gift offered to a successful candidate in midwifery by a professor of that art, who must have given his own copy, or provided himself with some extra copies while the subscription was proceeding.

received from the Admiralty. For this service the unanimous thanks of a general meeting of the friends and supporters of that college, moved by Admiral White, and carried (Sir George Cockburn being in the chair), were a sufficient reward. The following is another letter imposing on me fresh duties, which I welcomed with equal satisfaction, making up my mind to fulfil them to the best of my abilities:—

" 32, Sackville Street. Oct. 10th, 1829.

"SIR,—I have the pleasure to inform you that at the first meeting of the Westminster Medical Society, held on Saturday last, you were elected to be one of the presidents thereof, and to request you will meet the rest of the Committee next Saturday evening, at half-past seven o'clock precisely.

"I am, Sir, your obedient servant,

"F. F. BAKER.

" Dr. Granville."

Immediately after my election I submitted to the Society a proposition of a character interesting to a body of enlightened members of a medical assembly, among whom were some of the most experienced as well as learned practitioners. This acquired a greater degree of interest from the fact that it had come to be noticed and discussed in a most earnest manner in the Upper House of Parliament. Nor was I mistaken in my estimate of the ability of my co-members to treat such a question with eagerness and talent. According to the printed Report published in the " Medical Gazette " of the 12th of December, 1829, which proceedings extend to an adjourned or second meeting, the question propounded by myself met with an exhaustive examination, and terminated by affirming the opinion fully developed in a long discourse by the proposer. The case which gave rise to the consideration of the question will be long remembered under the name of the "Gardner Peerage Question." Were it likely that the legal profession would accept the recommendation from a humble practitioner of medicine, whose impressions from study and observations lead him to prefer Nature's laws to the dicta of Chancellors and Q.C.s, I would respectfully advise them—" Ere you again interfere with a complicated problem like the one you discussed in perfect darkness on that memorable occasion, cast your eyes on and read through the discussion referred to in the 'Medical Gazette.'"

In 1837, by way of bringing forth and exercising the faculties and talents of my social electors, I propounded for their consideration a very important question, the discussion and consideration of which turned out as much for the good of the public in general as it reflected credit on the members of the society in particular. I allude to the detection, by means of a series of chemical experiments, of the presence of a considerable quantity of arsenic employed in the manufacture of stearine candles, with the object of rendering them hard and giving them the polish of first-class sperm candles, a process fraught with double mischief, first from the injurious effects produced by the inhalation of the arsenical vapour during the combustion of the candles, and secondly from the facility it afforded to the evil-minded of extracting, by the simple process of melting the candle, a sufficient quantity of arsenic to poison a person without the fear of detection from discovering the source whence the poison had been obtained. These experiments and their conclusions I had published by direction of the Westminster Medical Society, and having been distributed to each foreign minister at our Court, elicited from their respective governments the most earnest expression of gratitude.

Another very important society, the British Medical

Association, of which I was the vice-president, was making strenuous efforts to improve the medical status in England. Its president had insisted on considering me his right-hand man in this question. I accepted the task, though it involved me in more work than I had time for, but I had not the courage to refuse work to a man who was so indefatigable himself in the same undertaking. Here is a specimen :—

"Dulwich. 28th May, 1838.

"MY DEAR SIR,—Lord John Russell has appointed Saturday to receive the deputation of the Council of our Association, of which you were named a member, and I sincerely hope you will be able to accompany us to White-hall. Doctors Grant, Farr, Marshall Hall, Davidson, and some others compose the deputation. I send you a copy of my letter to Lord John, that you may be acquainted with our intention, and consider what further information we may be able to extract from his lordship.

"Believe me, &c.;

"G. WEBSTER, Pres."

As the letter to Lord John Russell exposed in a simple yet admirable manner the views and intentions of the Association, I shall not consider a small space misapplied by inserting a copy in this place :—

"Dulwich. 24th May, 1838.

"MY LORD,—At a meeting of the Council of the British Medical Association, held in their chambers in Exeter Hall on the 22nd inst., a deputation was appointed to wait on your lordship with the hope of ascertaining, 1st. Whether it be the intention of Her Majesty's government to recommend that the remaining portion of the valuable mass of evidence should be printed which was taken before the Select Committee of the House of Commons appointed in the year

1834—' to inquire into and consider the laws, regulations, and usages regarding the education and practice of the various branches of the medical profession.' The Council consider that the publication (unfortunately so long delayed) of the important facts and opinions collected at so great expense to the country, is indispensable towards forming a just and correct judgment as to the details of any legislative enactments for accomplishing a reform of the existing laws and practice of the medical colleges and corporations. 2nd. Whether it is probable that any measure of medical reform will be introduced during the next session of parliament under the sanction of Government; and if not, whether, should such a measure be brought forward by any member unconnected with Her Majesty's government, they would sanction, or be likely to sanction its principle without pledging themselves to its details. I take the liberty of adding for your lordship's information, that the British Medical Association consists of a large number of legally qualified physicians and surgeons residing in London and in different parts of the kingdom, who have associated themselves to uphold by every means in their power the respectability and best interests of their profession, to promote necessary and salutary reforms of its laws and regulations, and for various friendly and benevolent purposes. In therefore soliciting for the deputation the favour of a short interview, I trust your lordship will not consider the time unprofitably employed in affording them such information as it may be your lordship's pleasure or in your lordship's power to communicate on matters so generally and deeply interesting to the medical profession.

" I have, &c.,

" G. WEBSTER, M.D., Pres."

These various exertions on our part bore their good fruit,

although not immediately. It is now on record how and when our legislature undertook and accomplished the reformation of all the abuses as well as the reparation of the various defects existing in medical legislation. Our medical annals after that date tell sufficiently how successful the various steps taken, and measures adopted, proved in accomplishing the desired objects of the profession. It is to them that the present condition of the medical faculties in the three kingdoms bears a superior character to what they could boast of during the first quarter of the present century. But there was yet the great blot in a humanitarian point of view in the practice of medicine in England, which many agreed with me in desiring to see removed for the credit of the profession, and yet more for the sake of humanity. I need hardly name the treatment of the insane in public not less than in private asylums; in the latter indeed more especially. This had always been a subject to which I had devoted attention, and which I had studied while resident in Paris in 1817 under Hebreard, Esquirol, and Pinel: studied it, I mean, more ethically than professionally.

The physical or medical treatment of the disease insanity may be fairly open to a collision of methods; but only one plain method of ethical treatment of the patient is admissible—the *suaviter in modo*. In this respect I grieve to record that no country had more to learn than England at the time I speak of. It struck me that the machinery of the British Medical Association might be made subservient to the obtaining a declaratory Act which should secure a fair and humane treatment of the afflicted creatures confined in lunatic asylums. I have entered largely into this important subject in my publication of an account of the Lincoln Lunatic Asylum, in the second volume of a work of mine, "The Spas of England." I there quote the opinion of the then Bishop of London, who had noticed and recommended with much eloquence the innovation, happy and great, in the treatment of the insane, which he found exemplified in the asylum of Lincoln, under the superintendence of Mr. Hill, who had long preceded the late physician of Hanwell Asylum, Dr. Conolly, in adopting the humane treatment of the insane in order to insure a prospect of an amelioration of or recovery from the malady. The experiment had been tried in my native country, as the late eminent surgeon and philanthropist, John Bell of Edinburgh, testified by publishing in one of the journals of the day a detailed account of the arrangements of some of the lunatic asylums in Italy, pointing out the advantages derived from the adoption of a humane system of treatment as contrasted with the results of a harsher method continued in England until within the last few years, when the Society of Friends proved in their Retreat at York that a treatment of mildness and gentleness was the one most eminently calculated to produce beneficial results.

But besides this great object, the members of the British Medical Association, with their president, vice-president, and council, aimed at ensuring a just and equitable legislation respecting the right of declaring any person to be *non compos* who was such, and consequently a fit subject for seclusion, and to protect people against any possible or probable exercise of a tyrannical application of the right of personal coercion under the power or authority of any parliamentary act on lunacy. About this time I addressed a memorial to the Lord Chancellor on the subject, in all its aspects and branches, which found its way into the "Times" newspaper,* and stirred up the public interest, so that a member of the lower House of Parliament considered it his

---

* "Times," Friday, April 8th, 1842: "The New County Lunatic Asylum Inspection Bill."

duty to introduce a bill for the better regulation of the practice and usages concerning lunatics and lunatic asylums. This was deemed a most timely opportunity for the members of the British Medical Association to aid in promoting an object they had so much at heart, but at the same time in freeing from one or two drawbacks affecting the interests of the lesser grades of medical practitioners which militated against the value of the measure. Accordingly our president decided that a petition should be addressed to Parliament with reference to what was known as Lord Granville Somerset's bill, and he wrote to me thus :—

" 15th April, 1842.

"My dear Sir,—Will you draw up the substance or heads of a petition as you would wish to be presented to Parliament on Lord Granville Somerset's bill, and bring it to the council meeting on Tuesday next? As far as I remember, neither in your speech at the Association, nor in your letter to the 'Times,' which is a very able and admirable one, do you notice another insult in the bill, viz. : that in future no general practitioner shall sign a certificate as to the state of a lunatic patient. Surely this should be noticed and reprobated.

"G. W.

" Since writing I find that Dr. Dyke of Corsham, and Mr. Crosse of Norwich had both written to his lordship on the subject of the clause, and that in reply they had received the following note from his lordship :—

" 'Clarges Street. April 7th, 1842.

" ' The bill I have introduced into Parliament contains no clause to alter the existing law as to certificates. I did not think upon the whole that I could make an alteration without producing greater evils than benefits.' "

This question, like that of the medical reform advocated

by the British Medical Association, came to a successful issue in the course of time, and after amelioration and additions terminated in a satisfactory legislation in force at this day, though in my opinion not sufficient.

On the 20th of April, 1836, the Earl of Euston, M.P., requested my attendance at his residence in Grosvenor Place, where after a few preliminary observations on the part I had taken in questions of interest to the public by my practical testimony before several Committees of the House of Commons, he proceeded to say that some influential persons, friends of his, and other respectable inhabitants in the City, had expressed a wish that a committee or society should be formed to inquire into the nature and merits of a plan proposed by Mr. John Martin, the eminent painter, for purifying the water of the Thames, the source whence nearly all the water companies derived their supply. He named the Duke of Rutland, Sir Frederick Trench, the Honourable Rice Trevor, Sir Edward Lytton-Bulwer, Mr. Alexander Mackinnon, Daniel O'Connell, Sir H. Morley, Bart., Sir Augustus Clifford, General Sir Patrick Ross, Isaac Lionel Goldsmith, and many of the most eminent merchants in the City as having agreed to meet for the purpose indicated, and that it had been suggested that I should be requested to attend, " an object," added his lordship, " which was left to me to see successfully accomplished." Lord Euston in conclusion asked me if the proposition was agreeable to me. My reply in the affirmative was immediate, and I added that I should consider it an honour to be of any service to the meeting. I had had in fact more than one conversation with Mr. Martin himself on his idea of improving the condition of the Thames water by discharging the town sewage through two parallel tunnels north and south, and creating two splendid embankments or quays over them, affording noble sites at the same time for palatial edifices. These conversations took place on Sunday evenings, when we and many eminent artists and men of science used to assemble at the hospitable *conversazione* of the industrious Pickersgill, the esteemed painter, in Soho Square.

Before I took leave of Lord Euston I undertook to summon some of the gentlemen he had mentioned, as well as some of my own friends, to a meeting to take place at his lordship's residence, at which meeting I arranged to read a detailed report on the meditated enterprise.

As it was proposed, so it was done. A meeting was held on the 23rd of April, 1836, at which I read a report I had drawn up at the request of a committee, wherein I developed briefly a scheme as the basis for a working company, to be denominated the "Thames Improvement Company," whose objects were to be: 1st. The total and simultaneous subtraction of all filth and every kind of ordure from the river, leaving the water in the purest state; 2nd. The establishment of an extended and magnificent public walk along both banks of the river, constituting quays unequalled in any capital in Europe; 3rd. The improvement of wharfage property; 4th. The saving of a vast quantity of the most fructifying manure, which, employed on cultivated soil, would nearly double its produce, and bear a high price in the agricultural market.*

In order to add the authority of science and experience to the assertions contained in my report concerning the fourth of the before-mentioned objects, I supplied information (for which I had prepared suitable materials during a long inquiry into the matter) in the appendix on the following subjects: 1st. A calculation of the amount of human

* " Report of a Committee of Gentlemen appointed to take into consideration Mr. Martin's plan for the Improvement of the River Thames." Presented at a General Meeting held at the Thatched House Tavern, April 23rd, 1836, by A. B. Granville, M.D., F.R.S.

impurities that enter the River Thames in the metropolitan district; and 2nd. Memoranda of the nature, value, and application of human impurities, deduced from facts and agricultural experiences.

The report, with all its substantiatory accompanying documents, was ordered to be printed, and found its way among the general public, creating no little stir and interest in the City. A copy was presented to each member as he entered the House of Commons on a call day; and 1 stood in the lobby to see that this was done. In the interior, in the mean time, a bill was read a first time, establishing the Thames Improvement Company.

With the view of being fully prepared to meet the investigation before the committee, which might be expected to come on in the course of six weeks or two months, the managers of the company were directed to collect not only in this country, but on the Continent, all such indisputable evidence as was likely to assist us in going through the committee satisfactorily and creditably. The commission was intrusted to myself to execute, as more conversant with foreign transactions referable to the desired end. I may as well terminate all I shall have to say on this matter by observing that I performed a journey of many hundred miles through the agricultural districts of central Europe, and returned with a vast mass of information on the points of inquiry, which I embodied in a report read before the subscribers, and with the contents of which Earl Everton was so well pleased that he insisted on defraying the cost of publication of an abstract.*

In the report I took care to state that Viscount Palmerston had materially assisted me in my inquiry, by supplying

* "Dr. Granville's Report to the Board of Directors of the Thames Improvement Company, dated January, 1837, containing all information respecting the value of human manure among foreign nations, &c." London: Printed by order of the Board.

me with letters addressed to several British ministers at
the court of the nations I should have to visit, instructing
them to put me at once in direct communication with the
proper authorities, with the view of facilitating my inquiries,
and of obtaining all authentic documents in support of any
information granted; and I owe it to his lordship's memory
to declare that I am almost entirely indebted to his sagacity
and foresight in offering me the letters of introduction
alluded to for the full success of my expedition.   In saying
" full success " I am in error, for the evidence I collected
never came before the committee of the House; nor did
the bill, which ever since has continued in single blessed-
ness in heaven knows what part of the House of Commons,
our directors not being prepared to meet the standing orders,
which required a previous deposit of a certain proportion of
the capital to be invested.   It was " no pay no success "
with the poor Thames Improvement Company, and the bill
was dropped.

But the vigilant eye of those who watch over the interests
of the millions was not likely to close in the face of such
unparalleled demonstration of an obtainable boon to the
multitude as our plan had supplied, and, presto ! the
Metropolitan Board (recently created), putting itself in the
room of the paralyzed Euston Company, seizing hold of the
idea of Martin as well as of the full development and
statistical information of Dr. Granville, undertook to realize,
(with the aid of four millions and a half of civic rates, and
after a long period of years), the Euston project, without in
a single instance having the honesty to acknowledge the
sources whence they' had derived their wisdom.   Rather
worse than that, indeed, for overlooking all considerations
of that sort, they had the courage to ask the ratepayers of
London to contribute a supplementary sum of £10,000, to
be presented to their acting engineer as the originator of

the plan they had adopted! Poor Martin was dead and gone, and could not protest, but the individual who had assisted him in developing and bringing before the public his grand original idea, since carried out by the civic authorities with the millions of pounds Parliament empowered them to abstract from metropolitan tills and sachels, was not yet dead, and he forthwith, on hearing of the proposed gift to the wrong person, published and sent to the Lord Mayor and other civic authorities, as well as to the Metropolitan Board, a protest against the proposed measure as unjust.* Of this work I published the historical part only, as my object was to show to whom the merit of the plan really belonged, and not to put those who had filched the plan and its adjuncts in possession also of the practical information we of the Euston scheme had collected at much trouble and expense, and knew how to put into profitable action should we be able to procure money, a consummation the authorities have not yet been able to accomplish. †

But now again, after a lapse of more than thirty years, during which little advance has been made either in the house of legislature or out of it to profit by the investigation promoted and carried on by Lord Euston and friends, a new and loud complaint is set up by Mr. John Lascelles, of Manchester, against the universal state of pollution of our rivers and water-courses. The injury and danger to the public health are set forth categorically, as we of the Martin plan had shown in 1836, but on the present occasion without any of the specific demonstrations such as we exhibited

* " The Great London Question of the day, or can Thames sewage be converted into Gold ? " 1855.

† Well did an able writer observe, treating of the use to be made of what pollutes our rivers : " It rests with ourselves whether the ordure that now pollutes our rivers shall henceforth fertilize our fields, and ceasing at length to breed disease and death, shall spring up strangely transmuted in rich crops of the life-sustaining grain."—"Times," 13th September 1849.

in our published report before alluded to. The remonstrances of Mr. Lascelles offer only generalities, unsupported by specific facts and the all-powerful statistics which distinguished the report in question. The mischief to be remedied, however, requires no fresh or stronger evidence than we possess of its existence. The remedy is the question. We have successfully applied such by adopting Martin's plan. What more generally applicable remedial measures can be suggested to submit to Parliament for adoption? No commission or associations of individuals has yet suggested any better plan for legislation on this most vital point of the sanitary question. It will be said that observations like these are beside my province, as having no reference to my personal existence. Most readers, however, will opine differently when they shall have reflected on the active part I have taken in the consideration of the general question.

I am sensible that I have entered too largely into professional matters, all the while intending only to prove that after having written many pages of general desultory political and superficial matter, I was not likely to overlook my own individual share in those transactions which referred to my profession. Zealous to preserve the character of a laborious medical man, I ventured to take a survey of a few of my professional exertions—the narrative of which may possibly in the opinion of some of my readers be deemed to have been better calculated for a chapter in some new history of medicine in the present century than suited to the many-hued pages of an autobiography. I can only reply with a humble " Peccavi," which confession comes accompanied with an assurance that such medical divagations shall not again occur through the few of my remaining chapters.

CHAPTER XVIII.

THEODORE HOOK is a name that requires no particular introduction to—I was going to say London, but it should be English readers, for who that reads English has not read some of his many smart conceits? His " Sayings and Doings," like the " Household Words " of a more modern *bel esprit*, has become a familiar phrase. As a relative to the Farquhar family by the marriage of his brother to a daughter of the medical baronet of that name, we frequently came in contact, although he professed not to be particularly fond of medicos. Still medicos may be, and are occasionally, useful in rendering services to people of more value even than the remedies which save life, if intended to maintain character. Theodore esteemed that an early act of mine on his behalf, soon after his return from the western hemisphere, had proved useful to him in the sense just referred to, and our intimacy continued from that day. Belonging to the same club, opportunities for meeting were frequent and easy, although I never joined his little snug corner table in the coffee-room of the Athenæum, where three or four choice spirits revelled in calembours and smoking-hot bishop! Theodore, one day in June, 1828, paid me a visit in Grafton Street, when I had just got rid of my morning consultations, and addressed me thus: " I have

been told that you have got into a *brouillerie* with a neighbour of yours at number four in this street; in fact, that
you are in open rupture with Henry Brougham on account
of some trick (so like him) to prevent you from obtaining
the professorship of obstetrical medicine in the university
in Gower Street, of which he is president or chairman;
and that he has purposely kept back from the consideration
of the council many, or I believe all, the testimonials in
support of your application, which would have rendered
the election of your competitor more than problematical,
but which, I am assured from a member present, was
carried *d'emblée*, as your letter of application for the chair
was completely destitute of any document in support. Are
these facts? Because if you affirm them as such, I tell
you at once that I shall consider it my duty to expose the
whole affair in ' John Bull.' "

I was still smarting so (I confess it) under the unexpected and unmerited disappointment thus alluded to, that
I experienced a degree of satisfaction at the chance thus
offered to me of publicly exposing what *primâ facie*
appeared (and as it proved ultimately) to be an intrigue
against me, purposely adopted for a particular end, that I
at once said, " I accept the offer of your assistance in this
matter, and will put you *au fait* of all the circumstances
of the case, including documents and correspondence,
leaving it to your judgment and sense of right to represent
the affair in whatever light your pen may please to ensure
the exposure of a knavish trick." The following day my
statement, with all the *pièces justificatives*, as he styled
them, were in the hands of my friend. Those who at that
time enjoyed the pleasure of perusing "John Bull," a
periodical sparkling with wit, may possibly recollect how
Theodore Hook treated the subject in question, and how he
handled the new-fledged chancellor and peer in that matter.

My own task is only to relate the whole story as it got into general circulation, being in fact part of my own story, and an illustration of one among the not few disappointments I have met in life.

The council of what was then called the University of London, in April, 1827, made known by advertisements that they were ready to receive applications from properly qualified candidates for the chairs of professors, which applications were to be accompanied with such testimonials as the candidates intended to rest their claims upon, and by which alone the council declared they would be guided in their selection, canvassing being strictly forbidden. My friend, Dr. A. T. Thomson, being well acquainted with Mr. Brougham, chairman of the council, induced me to become a candidate for the professorship of midwifery, as he was himself a candidate for the chair of materia medica, and offered to introduce me to Mr. Brougham. Accordingly shortly afterwards I had that honour at his residence in Grafton Street. I did not solicit his vote, but simply explained that among my testimonials there were some of foreign origin, would they be accepted with others of English origin, which I wished likewise to present? On receiving an affirmative answer, I remarked that in a day or two I should have the honour to transmit to him through Dr. Thomson, my formal application for the professorship of midwifery, supported by a certain number of testimonials, and our visit came to an end. To show that this was not a hole-and-corner manœuvre, I think it right to bring forward other documents, proving how openly I presented my claims to the chair I was desirous to occupy. They are letters from the Marquis of Lansdowne and Lord Auckland, both members of the council and of the committee of education. The former, under date of the 22nd of November, 1826, states that he thought it due to the interest of the proposed university (and he believed most of the gentlemen whose names are upon the council have pursued a similar course) not to promise his support to any candidate for a professorship until the period of election arrived, a determination he communicated to several applicants who had addressed him; but he begged to add that "he is fully aware of Dr. Granville's high reputation and great qualifications for such a situation as that which he seeks, and that it gives Lord Lansdowne great pleasure to find Dr. Granville would be willing to accept it." The Earl of Auckland's sentiments on the question were thus expressed :

"I beg to acknowledge your letter with one that I have received from Sir Gore Ouseley, and I have had great pleasure in recommending your application to the consideration of the committee to which this subject refers. At the same time you must be aware that we are only digging the foundations of our buildings, and probably no decision will be very immediately made ; but you may be assured that your application will not be lost sight of.

"Yours very faithfully,

"AUCKLAND."

A few days after, my official application to the council, addresssed to H. Brougham, Esq., M.P., as chairman of the council, was delivered to him in person, together with the requisite testimonials in two packets. Of the receipt of these I never had any official acknowledgment, although I made more than one inquiry at the University Chambers in Furnival's Inn. At length, wishing to be assured that the papers were in Mr. Brougham's possession, I wrote to the acting secretary, Mr. Coates, who on the 16th of May (eighteen days after my letter) replied as follows :—

"I have delayed answering yours of the 29th of April,

until I heard from Mr. Brougham that your testimonials
were in his hands, as well as the letter addressed to the
committee applying for the chair of obstetrical medicine and
surgery.   Mr. Brougham informs me that he holds it, and
will immediately present it with the other documents.

" Furnival's Inn. 10th May, 1827."

So it appeared that while the testimonials of the other
candidates and competitors had been lying daily before the
council, working their influential effect, my own were closely
enshrined in Mr. Brougham's pocket.   In the mean time,
week crept on after week, the election took place (that is,
the selection by the council was made), and Dr. Davis,
Mrs. Brougham's medical attendant, got the professorship.
Anxious to repossess myself of my valuable documents
after this decision, two days after the result of the election
had been made public, I applied in person at the University
Chambers to have them returned to me by the secretary.
I was requested to call again.   Two other visits proved
equally unsuccessful ; still the documents were not forthcoming, and each time some frivolous excuse was made to
account for their detention, until, becoming more and more
pressing on Mr. Secretary, his sense of honour and candour
prompted him to declare, that in order to clear himself from
every appearance of neglect, he was bound to state that he
had never seen the documents in question, and that consequently they were not and had never been in h's
possession.

Here was a *naïve* confession by the responsible official
of the council—who had been present at the election, when
it would have been his duty to read aloud to the members
at the board of electors my twelve testimonials, justifying,
while they supported emphatically, my application as a
candidate for the chair—telling me in plain words that he
had never seen the important documents alluded to ; and

yet when questioned by a friend (as we shall see presently) on the report spread, that at the meeting of the council my individual application had been passed over, as being unsupported by testimonials, Mr. Brougham replied, with the amenity and pleasing manners which are said to be peculiar to him, "I can assure you that in the selection from among the candidates the council took full notice of every testimonial in their favour." "Oh, vir bonus et simplicis veritatis amicus!" would Cicero have called the worthy M.P. ?

To Mr. Brougham alone then could I apply as a last resource if I desired to gain possession of my documents. In order to do this with due effect, I deemed it expedient to obtain from the secretary the purport of his verbal assertion to me. Accordingly I addressed to that gentleman the following letter :—

" " *To Mr. Coates, Acting Secretary of the University of London.*

"13th August, 1827.

" SIR,—Although you candidly admitted at our last interview that you had not seen, and consequently had not in your possession the several testimonials, English and French, which I forwarded to the council of the University of London through Mr. Brougham, in support of my application for the professorship of midwifery, I cannot refrain from again, and for the fifth time, appealing to you as the only official organ of the council I know of, for an explicit answer on the subject of the papers in question, which I officially claim on the present occasion, and which I trust you will be able to restore to your obedient servant,

" A. B. GRANVILLE.

" P.S.—My official application to the council was placed in the hands of Mr. Brougham on the twenty-fourth of

December, 1826, and annexed were the following certificates :—

From

"Sir Henry Halford, P.C.P.
"Dr. Maton.
"Sir Humphry Davy, P.R.S.
"Sir Gilbert Blane, Bart.
"Sir Everard Home, Bart.
"Professor Chaussier, Paris Maternité.

"Professor Serres, Paris Pitié Hospital.
"Capuron, Lectr. on Medi.
"Tadilot, Physician, Hosp. Sick Children.
"Baron Cuvier, Natural History."

To this letter the following reply was received after a fortnight's delay :—

"University of London.

"Sir,—I beg leave to repeat to you what I said when I had the pleasure of seeing you here, that I am unable, until Mr. Brougham returns to London, to restore your testimonials to you.

"Yours, &c.

"Thomas Coates.

"Furnival's Inn. 17th August, 1827."

Mr. Brougham at length returned to town, but the documents came not with him, and the acting secretary again declared that the papers in question were not and had not been in his custody, and that as I had caused them to be delivered into Mr. Brougham's own hands, the application for their restitution should be made to him.

My journey to Russia intervened to prevent me from applying on that subject to Mr. Brougham until the 28th of January, 1828, when I did so, citing the secretary's extraordinary declarations. A mere promise to look after the documents came in reply, which had not been fulfilled even after a third and a fourth letter from myself had been written. Four months and a half after this correspondence I wrote, on the 28th of June, that unless the papers were forthcoming, an *exposé* of the affair would be published, and legal proceedings instituted for their recovery ; as for any explanation of so extraordinary a transaction, I renounced it altogether. This last communication proved the most stimulatory of those that had passed with Mr. Brougham, inasmuch as it brought a common friend, General Sir Robert Wilson, with a proposition for an interview with Mr. Brougham at his own house.

The interview took place with no other result than another promise. I however elicited on this occasion the following facts : Firstly, that he did not contradict the assertions of the acting secretary ; secondly, that he would not say positively that he had executed his trust of delivering to the council my application and annexed documents, as he had undertaken to do; thirdly, that the only explanation of the irregular transaction he could give was that the testimonials must have been lost in his house ; and lastly, that when I presented to him copies of the said testimonials for his perusal, he declared that he did not recollect having read them, or having heard them read before. All these facts I supplied to Theodore Hook in a condensed letter, accompanied by copies of the testimonials alluded to, in order that he might judge whether, under an ordinary and equitably conducted mode of electing, or rather selecting, a professor for a practical branch of science among other candidates for the same chair (and I believe there was only one who competed—namely, Mrs. Brougham's own medical attendant), the candidate who could exhibit such testimonials as I tendered would not have had every reason to expect that success which a canny device so triumphantly marred.

I must add as a corollary to this story, which forms a

fitting end to it, soon after Henry Brougham had been raised to the high dignity of Chancellor of England, I received through his private secretary one of the packets containing some of the foreign certificates, with many apologies and an avowal that they were found in the new chancellor's private box. Two years later a second packet was sent me in the same way (and with the same apologies) containing the English testimonials, but two of the most important of the latter were missing, which I had added to the rest for the purpose of identifying my person (as a stranger by birth), namely, the diploma of my alma mater, and the licence of the Royal College of Physicians in London, dated November, 1817, which constitutes me a member of fifty-four years' standing of that royal college; in fact, senior member.

In reply to a letter from myself concerning this inexplicable imbroglio, my friend Professor Thomson, who had been elected to a chair in the new university, informed me that my memorial to the council, after a delay of fifteen months, like its attendant testimonials which I had committed into the hands of Mr. Brougham, never went further than Grafton Street, his residence.

What other inference could Theodore Hook and his thousands of readers draw from this pretty story, than that I had been cleverly (query honourably) tricked out of the professorship I solicited, and which I should have considered as a great professional distinction? It may be readily imagined that, being satisfied of the truth of the story, the editor of " John Bull " made a pretty free use of the name of the president of the Gower Street university Sunday after Sunday. In such a course, however, he was not inspired by me. I left him to act on his own judgment, for however much my *amour propre* might feel mortified, I harboured no vindictive feelings against the offender; nay, the very reverse course I soon had an opportunity of adopting proved the nature of my feelings on the occasion, for in learning some time later from my friend Dr. Birkbeck, that he and Lord Brougham had founded a Society for the Diffusion of Useful Knowledge, I dedicated personally to him my popular "Catechism of Health," just written, as an apt publication for the industrial classes, for which he returned me his thanks in a holograph note from Grafton Street. Howbeit I had to bear at the same time a slap on the face from the facetious editor of the "John Bull," who laughed at my ultra-Christian forbearance.

Nor was this the only infliction I had to bear from the fact of my dedication, since it brought upon me also the ponderous crushing weight of a hostile review in the "Quarterly Review," by no means inclined to favour either Stinkomalee, as they used to call the institution in Gower Street, or Theodore of the "Bull." I recognized the hand of the medical reviewer at once. I had before castigated him in reference to plagiarism from my own writing, and he now took his revenge. To make it still more bitter to me, he induced the good and honest proprietor of the review to present me, several days before the publication of the number, with an early copy containing the damning article, which I need not add excelled in misrepresentations and false quotations. The notice I took of this little impertinence was a short note of thanks to Mr. John Murray, thus worded :—

"DEAR SIR,—I am very sensible of your great and considerate kindness in presenting me thus early with a copy of the new number of your quarterly, containing a truly ridiculous article on a work of mine, 'The Catechism of Health.' I give you and the writer joy of having so delightful a bantling among the many that grace the nur-

sery of that wonderful trimestrial propagating machine.   I
shall not reply to so witty a production, but advertise it and
the learned periodical in which it appears as far as money
and influence can circulate the fact of its birth in the news-
papers.

"I remain always truly yours,

"A. B. GRANVILLE

(fearful of adding M.D., in terror of Dr. Macmichael).

"John Murray, Esqre."

It was an unfortunate coincidence in my present position
as a physician looking for advancement in public estimation,
and considered as an authority worthy to be consulted by
ministerial committees, that I should have unwittingly come
into collision with a second lord chancellor, having previously wrangled with a former one, Lord Lyndhurst, at
the bar of the House of Lords, on a question (as I stated
before) where common law was pitted against the law of
Nature.   I was thus squeezed in as it were between two
formidable powers of the State, though my insignificance
and the care I took to keep clear of their fangs, and the
lapse of time also, so diverted their attention from those
fortuitous incidents, that no evil accrued to me; rather, I
should say, the reverse, as a curious, and for myself an interesting, *rencontre* will show, and which I may as well
recount in this place, at the risk of being charged with
anachronism.

I was called to Sloane Street to treat a lady suffering
from the effect of a sudden transition from the mild climate
of Spain to that of London—from light malaga to heavy
port.   At that time Lord Brougham, who occupied the
woolsack, was residing in the same house in Sloane Street,
where he carried on his ordinary official business, and where
every morning and evening the judicial as well as the
cabinet messengers waited upon him with despatches.

My patient was all right in the course of eight or ten days, but in the interval she informed me that Lord Brougham had told her he knew her doctor quite well, and he would be glad of an opportunity of meeting me again. Upon this she had remarked to him, " In that case I will contrive to have a little dinner party for you to meet at." " Capital," observed Lord Brougham ; " the earlier the day the better ; and if you, dear good lady, will permit me to add a third guest, I think I can promise you the presence of the famous Lord Chancellor Lyndhurst. At least I flatter myself that if I propose in your name that he should be one of the charming party you intend to give, his lordship will be most happy to join it."

I copy from my diary of August, 1831, my account of this choice dinner party, which, together with my reflections, I committed to paper at once : " I dined this day at the table of Madame d'Acuña, a very handsome Andalusian lady, sometime settled in London, and who has been for some days under my professional care. Lord Brougham, an intimate acquaintance of the lady, had requested her to arrange a *petite partie quarrée* at dinner, that he might meet me, as he told her he knew her doctor well. My Lord Lyndhurst, the ex-chancellor, was of the party. I sat at the bottom of the table at the lady's request, Lord Brougham took the chair. There was also present a young gentleman, a Mr. Alfred Montgomery, sickly-looking rather, and thin, having a slight hesitation or impediment in his speech, but otherwise a *fashionable;* excellent company for either a table or a drawing-room. Lord Brougham, who was all *empressement*, studiously affable, to the guests, was during the dinner *très-vif*, clever, ever on the *qui vive*, full of anecdotes and observations, or quiet as suited the subject, referring to it or quitting it in three different languages. His demeanour was that of a man who had never done

anything else but live in fashionable society, loved its fri-
volities though he accepted its more serious obligations,
and was not loth to gather the applause of his auditors by
appearing perfectly *au fait* with every art, thing, or conversation that could add distinction to a man of the world.
My Lord Lyndhurst, on the other hand, with some degree
of polite and softened, not austere, reserve (as I should have
anticipated from a knowledge of his public and judicial
character), appeared sufficiently gay, inclined to enjoy himself, as well as make the company with him quite pleased
and contented. He entered into the mirth of the others,
shared with the rest of the guests the prevailing satisfaction
of the moment without appearing to be carried away entirely by the occasional wit and the repartees, or the mer-
curial and endless agitation of his noble colleague. His own
remarks and his replies, not less than some of his critiques
of a few of the sentiments uttered by Brougham, partook
more of a sedate reflection, yet they were sufficiently prompt
and spontaneous as not to assume the garb of sententious
pedantry. Both eminently enjoyed the treat of being in
company with the handsomest woman possible, who on her
part conducted herself in a manner to surprise me, and to
secure for herself the most strict consideration. Both lords
were exceedingly polite and considerate towards myself,
commencing by allusions to the 'Spas of Germany' and
'St. Petersburg,' the talent shown for writing, and for
accurate descriptions. I could not help profiting by this apt
opportunity of throwing out a little sarcastic allusion to
Lord Lyndhurst for his venture in cross-examining Nature,
and endeavouring to bewilder her in my poor person when
under his lordship's examination at the bar of the House of
Lords, in the Gardner Peerage case. 'Ah, dear doctor,'
said he, 'physicians and lawyers have different logics.' The
doctor on the present occasion could not afford more time

to listen to either logic, so I took my leave before the party broke up.

"The manner of the two great orators towards one another was *on ne peut plus* cordial, and wore the semblance of sincerity. On the part of Lord Lyndhurst, much of his conversation and bearing towards Brougham implied evident admiration of his talents. One instance of which particularly, in reference to himself, Lord Lyndhurst seemed delighted to bring forward. Brougham not only accepted the incense with pleasure, but took up the subject, and hesitated not in going on with it all in commendation of himself. I do not think that either is sincere towards the other, and I believe that each has an object or a by-play to enact in their present respective position when *vis-à-vis* with one another. Still, in appearance that would not be suspected.

"Lord Brougham, among many curious facts connected with his former and present habits of living, mentioned to me that for a few years, when in chambers, he never went to sleep without having his pipe in his mouth after he had got into his bed. He is temperate, drinks sparingly, eats little, and has seldom required a doctor; although he takes pills of his own accord, and occasionally a dose of rhubarb or magnesia. I reminded him of the occasion on which I had ministered a slight correction to his knowledge of chemistry (acquired at Edinburgh University), when we were both before the Privy Council in 1827, on the subject of granting a prolonged patent for the manufacture of artificial mineral waters at the Brighton Spa. His lordship contended in opposition to the patent that he had all his life drunk artificial mineral waters, inasmuch as he never went to bed without drinking a glass of soda water. 'In that case I must inform the Privy Council that Mr. Brougham never drunk artificial mineral water, for what he drank was water and carbonic acid.' He was pleased to remember the

fact, and deemed the correction a proper one at the time.
At our dinner in Sloane Street, however, with the brilliant
black eyes of the hostess shot here and there over the
company, my lords neither spared the champagne, the
paxarete, or the maraschino."

Such of my readers as can remember the excitement
produced by the trial and consequent incarceration of a
noted empiric with an aristocratic name, who had on a
sudden inspiration exchanged a painter's palette and indifferent brushes for the more profitable handling of pots
of ointment and rubbing, are aware that the medical profession had their attention on that occasion directed to
the study of counter-irritation. That physiological principle,
brought conspicuously into notice by that famed trial and
its preliminary investigation before a coroner's jury, at
which I was present (*tempore* Wakley), had been adopted
by the incriminated Doctor St. John as a means of defence.
Hence the large number of communications which appeared
in the medical journals, as well as in separate memoirs on
the subject, need not excite surprise. Among the members
of the medical profession who took a chief part in the
investigation, I may reckon myself as not among the least
interested. Some chance coincidents contributed to give
me a part to perform : the knowledge of the defendant's
antecedents on the one hand, and a long practical acquaintance with what are called counter-stimulating agents on the
other, a subject I happened to have been studying ever since
I attended Professor Rasori's lectures *Sul contrastimolo* in
Italy. My acquaintance with the defendant's antecedents
came about in this manner. Being in conversation one day
with Sir Gore Ouseley, not long after his return from his
embassy to Persia, he mentioned to me that among the
several applicants who came to him with the view of finding
the means of emigrating to that country in hopes of pro-

curing a living, a gentleman had presented himself as an artist, who thought he might readily find employment in that benighted country.

"And what, may I ask, is the branch of the arts you profess, sir?" "Portrait painting, full size," was the reply. "In that case I can tell you at once that Persia is no country to make your fortune in. Look round my room. Here are the full-length pictures of the last two shahs, and one of the two present first ministers. Here is the very last I brought from Teheran, full length, and strikingly like the original; in fact, I imagine you must have seen him in public in London not long ago. Can you paint like that, Mr. ——? I beg pardon, I did not catch properly your name when the footman announced it." "St. John Long is my name; I am connected with noble families." "Ah! but that will not help you in Persia. It is only your brushes and colours and skill in drawing that can be of use; and there I can tell you you have no chance of competing with such colourists as you see here suspended before you. If your pictures are inferior to these, they will be rejected; if superior, they will not be accepted, for there is in Persia as much detestation of superiority in any art or profession as there is in England of what you call professional jealousy, especially against a foreigner. Depend upon it, Mr. St. John, you would lose both time and money, and subject yourself moreover to much mortification. Are your means large enough to enable you to waste an indefinite number of years for the chance of making your way as a painter by dint of perseverance?" "Why no, Sir Gore, else I should hardly try to do better for myself by leaving my country." "Then permit me to offer you sound advice. Remain where you are, and strive on with your brushes and colours. Good morning." "In such a case," added Mr. St. John, "I know what remains for me to do. An ancestor of the

St. Johns has left behind a memorandum teaching us a precious secret for curing many formidable complaints by rubbing external remedies on the parts affected. I'll cast aside canvas and brushes, and take to physic." "You mean," added Sir Gore, smiling, "a little charlatanry, I suppose. There again you are at fault, Mr. St. John. The Persians are the greatest quacks in the universe in the way of illness. Of all the eastern nations, they are probably the most ignorant in such matters; but no man, however learned, can compete with the old Persian hags for curing, or pretending to cure, the most desperate diseases. So you have no chance there." "What a barbarous nation your pet Persians must be, Sir Gore, of whom you have written with the enthusiasm of a poet!" observed the visitor, and the interview concluded.

The coroner's inquest brought this old story back to Sir Gore's recollection, and he thought I might like to add it to my memoranda on professional matters. The nobly connected St. John Long was not long in discovering that although it is easy to assume the character of an M.D., its illegitimate exercise will lead to some ugly scrapes, and thence to the cells of Newgate. There Mr. St. John Long spent a certain time, receiving professional fees and giving consultations to titled patients, whose carriages might have been seen in files along the Old Bailey and down Newgate Street. A statuary group from the *ateliers* in the New Road stands now on a conspicuous spot in Kensal Green Cemetery, recording (opposite the memorial to Ducrot), in a long inscription, how genius and talent were cruelly oppressed and extinguished by envy and malice.

It was in the midst of the general commotion occasioned by the St. John trial that I took the opportunity of publishing my volume on counter-irritation,* with the view of

* "Counter Irritation : its Principles and Practice, illustrated by one

explaining on simple and physiological principles a system
or doctrine which was as old as the medical *ars longa* of
Hippocrates, and had nothing particularly striking or new
in it, except when misemployed, as it had been by our
aristocratic empiric with the intention of gulling the ignorant. The medical profession received with undisguised
approval this addition to our practical knowledge of thera-
peutics, and people can now understand what is meant by
counter-irritation. I took care in that work to give a
lucid and plain account of the effects produced on the
human frame while labouring under particular or special
complaints by certain liquid preparations of ammonia of a
definite strength, and mixed with one or two other aro-
matic stimulating ingredients. The operation or action of
the said ingredients on the human skin is similar to that
produced by an ordinary blister, but it possesses the great
superiority over the last-named application, of being able
to produce the required effect in as short a time as three or
four minutes, instead of as many, or perhaps double, that
number of hours. The rapidity of action is one of the
elements of its virtue as a remedy, and in this aspect I
claim the merit of having brought more ostensibly forward
agents much more active as well as more manageable
than those already adopted for the desired effect.

It was (to use a common phrase) a ticklish matter, while
publishing a new work on such a subject, how to avoid
trenching on empirical grounds. On the one hand there
was the apprehension that to divulge at once the nature of
the agents recommended might do harm, by placing in the
hands of the ignorant an agent of great power which might
do hurt instead of doing good. On the other hand, my
professional brethren might accuse me of wishing to keep

hundred cases of the most painful and important diseases effectually cured by
external applications." London, 1838.

secret my new remedial agents. I therefore adopted a neutral course, and I am glad I did so. The profession has received the preparations as well as the views of the writer, which establish their value and importance, and the "London Pharmacopœia," in its last edition immediately previous to the change in its title into that of "British Pharmacopœia," introduced under an officinal denomination the compound I originally recommended.

One illustration of the truth of the doctrine of counter-irritation, and of its successful application, was exhibited in a case so striking that I cannot hesitate to record it. The case commenced in a noted trial in one of the courts of law in Paris in which an English nobleman was defendant. His lady, subject since her last confinement to periodical attacks of spasm, accompanied with very acute pain in the loins, had been under the care of a notorious homœopathic and almost magnetic attendant of the Jewish persuasion in Paris. The attendance was of several months', I may say some years' duration, incessant and inexplicable. The demand for fees amounted to a preposterous sum, which was resisted, and hence the law-suit. A suitable professional remuneration in full discharge being tendered, it was declined, and the original demand insisted upon. The mystery in which Mordecai had involved his whole treatment, and the explanations he now and then vouch-safed, suggested to the defendant's lawyers the propriety of an arrangement which should entirely preclude the possibility of those disgraceful investigations, which in French courts not unfrequently furnish rich and mysterious materials for such novelists as Sandeau, Féval, and Sand. A compromise, I believe, terminated the litigation. It signified not an air-bubble to the quarrelsome Esculapius that his patient was just as much suffering from the original complaint now as she was when first the attendance commenced. The noble defendant had to pay the heavy bill, and bring his suffering lady to London. Here she was immediately placed in the charge of Sir Charles Mansfield Clarke, Mr. Copland, the well-known surgeon, and her own physician, Dr. Hugh Ley. Some other eminent practitioners were also occasionally consulted. There was connected with the case a sort of mystery, which arose from the fact that the attack accompanied the most agonizing pain, invariably came on at one and the same hour—eight o'clock in the evening, and that notwithstanding the stale trick under such circumstances, of altering the hands on the dial-plate, had been had recourse to, in order to test the genuineness of the periodicity of the spasm, the attack still persisted in coming on at the same time.

The case had proved one of the most important examples of what are commonly called nervous diseases, and it was suggested to the mother of the lady that I should be consulted, to know whether the patient was likely to be benefited by my ammoniated applications. I felt it due to the credit of the profession, as well as to the public, to procure the best information I could obtain respecting the origin and progress of the case. The public press in Paris during the trial for the recovery of the exorbitant fees for attendance—so exorbitant as to throw into the shade the notorious demand of a Piccadilly medical firm at the commencement of the present century against the executors of a certain antique duke of virgin-milk celebrity—had dilated to such length on the mystical character of the disease under treatment, and upon the many pretended metamorphoses it was said to have undergone hourly, that we on our side of the water were left without a guide to determine which way we should view the case, and how to treat such an undefined malady. I had a preliminary private conversation with the lady's mother, and then with the patient herself, who fortunately from the first had kept a record of her own feelings and notions as to the disturbances going on in her own constitution.

I found her considerably reduced in flesh, unable to walk upright, and altogether in a state of health far from satisfactory. Her written statement of the origin and progress of the complaint, including some particulars of the Israelitic doctor in Paris that astounded me not a little, was placed in my hands by the lady, and I promised to be in attendance any day fixed, at the hour of the expected attack, feeling confident that the acute sufferings of the moment, such as she had described from former attacks, would be greatly mitigated, if not altogether subdued and dispersed, by the use of my application.

The case is so curious in itself that; as an illustration of my doctrine and prejudice in such cases, I think it right to republish it in the present history of my life. For what does the case represent? A gentlewoman, mother of two children, the cynosure of her own circle, is suddenly stricken by illness consisting of acute spasms of the lower part of the spine (attended with the most agonizing pain), a part corresponding with the internal uterine region, and the attacks are renewed daily at the same hour of the day. Being abroad, she consults and is attended by a foreign medical man of notorious fame; but after months of unrelieved sufferings and waste of money, she comes back to her native air and medical advice and attendance with all the comforts and appliances that wealth can command and secure. Still the destroying, the painful spasm recurs, and nothing seems to make the slightest favourable impression on it. I am present at one of the attacks, to which I had been called, for one was expected. I heard my patient screaming as I was ascending the stairs to her bed-chamber, and the house-clock had just done striking the hour of eight. The lady's mother was present in the room, an attached friend, and two other lady-friends were likewise present assisting in the management and control of the suffering patient, who on my asking her as to the seat of the pain, replied that it pervaded at first both arms, then the neck, whence it ran down to the lower extremities, with at times cramp in the calf of the legs and shootings almost incessant in the hollow of the backbone (sacrum). With all these sensations there supervened a sense of constriction at her throat, as if she was about to be suffocated. She was lying on her face ; and her spine bone could not be kept still nor straight. It bent violently forward during the spasm, so as almost to double the spine and throw off the pressure of both my hands and those of one of the ladies applied to keep the spine straight. The scene was truly heart-rending, and not to be described in words. We all stood aghast at what was to come next. All the antecedents of the case were against hope ; the present occurrences were not more encouraging ; what does the future predict ? That is what we are about to see almost immediately.

If I have formed a right conjecture of the nature and character of the case, if I have not placed an exaggerated confidence in the anti-spasmodic counter-irritating virtue of the ammoniated lotion, in twenty minutes our suffering patient will suffer no longer. The bottles of the ammoniated lotion were forthwith brought up out of my carriage, and a suitable sized compress of linen several times doubled was applied first to the principal seat of the pain in the loins ; another such compress was applied a little higher up, and lastly one more was imposed in the nape of the neck. The lady complained of a new pain, like scalding fire, yet one which she rather liked ; presently she could breathe quite freely ; she liked the new pain outside, for she now

no longer felt the inward agony. Soon after, the contracted arms and legs became supple; she spoke more
cheerfully, said she thought she was already cured, and
remained at length quiet and silent. There was no blistering of the parts, but these were intensely red and intensely
hot. She was turned gently on her back and left to herself, after which time she fell asleep, and no further attack
of spasmodic pain at 8 P.M. came on again for eight days,
when a single application of the lotion sufficed to prevent
its endurance beyond a few minutes.

Dr. Hugh Ley, who attended on the following day after
my successful visit, could hardly believe the story told him
as here described. He thought it almost fabulous, but he
happened to be present when the fresh attack after the first
eight days came on, and witnessed the application of the
lotion to the part, as well as the instantaneous dispersion of
the spasm ; and so he was convinced.

The strongest, as it is also the most flattering, testimony
a physician can receive of his having accomplished his duty
successfully, is the one which conscientious and grateful
patients or their friends will address to him as a spontaneous expression of feelings of thankfulness for the
benefits received ; such a testimony it was my good fortune
to receive from the lady's husband three weeks after I had
taken leave of her. I have preserved the letter, not for
my own sake, or through vanity, but as a most impressive
admission in favour of the new system of medical treatment
I had been trying to bring into public notice, and for that
purpose alone have I resolved to insert it in this part of
my narrative:—

" June 22nd, 1835.

" MY DEAR SIR,—I cannot send the enclosed without at
the same time endeavouring to express the sentiment of

x 2

obligation which I feel to you, not only for your most valuable and valued services, but for the undeviating anxiety and attention which you have displayed during your attendance upon Lady ——'s difficult and trying case. To you she owes, as far as medical skill is concerned, her restoration to health; and I will only add that both she and I shall ever entertain the greatest gratitude for so inestimable a benefit.

"Believe me to be, my dear Sir, yours very truly,

"———"

CHAPTER XIX.

Joseph Bonaparte—My relationship to the Bonaparte family—Jerome Bonaparte—Prince Louis—The affair at Strasburg — Interview between uncle and nephew—Joseph seized with apoplexy—Prince Louis' *parole d'honneur*—The landing at Boulogne—Shock to Joseph—A chapter of secret history—Diplomatic spies.

I AM now nearing two of the most interesting epochs which served to give a colour to my noonday life it had not before, yet made no material or sensible change in my destiny. I went through each, taking my part in it without suffering the even tenor of my medical career and profession to be in the smallest degree changed or interfered with. I allude to my connection with the Bonaparte family, and to the stupendous change that marked the commencement of the revolutionary movement in my native country in 1848, and to which I boldly lay claim to having contributed by many years' writing and no trifling interference by personal influence and exertion. As regards the first, recent and curious revelations from the highest quarters within the last fifteen years have shed a broad light on the female lineage of my race.

In October, 1853, Joseph Napoleon published an historical fragment of his life in one volume, which forms the first of a series of ten volumes entitled "Mémoires et Correspondance Politique et Militaire du Roi Joseph." The work was edited by one of his aides-de-camp, Colonel du Casse, with the assistance and under the supervision of Monsieur Mailliard, who for a quarter of a century had been

Joseph's private secretary, and during his reign in Spain had filled the post of his home minister, with the rank of a grandee. In the first of those ten volumes, at page 42, we read as follows: "La maison que l'on montre à Ajaccio, dans laquelle Napoléon est né, appartenait originairement à la famille Bozzi, qui l'apporta en dot dans la nôtre."[*] So unexpected a piece of intelligence, though not likely to surprise me, since I was perfectly aware of the fact of members of our family being settled both in Corsica and Genoa, was nevertheless calculated to make me pay more attention to that branch of our genealogy, and accordingly I addressed proper inquiries to Monsieur Mailliard, with whom I had been in habits of intimacy for many years during his residence in London. His reply was not long in coming :—

"Monsieur de Pietra Santa, to whom I addressed myself, has been to me to tell me that the Madlle. Bozzi spoken of by King Joseph, was the grandmother of Charles Bonaparte, father of Napoleon the First. She was born in Corsica, but of a family coming from Italy, and that there are several families of the name of Bozzi in Corsica."[†]

In a work entitled "Memorie Storiche dell' Abbate Gerini," which was brought to my notice by Sir Anthony Panizzi in 1853, there is a copy of the memorial or petition which Joseph, then plain Giuseppe, Buonaparte, at the age of twenty years, presented to the Grand Duke of Tuscany in 1789, claiming to be admitted into the religious and equestrian order of San Stefano, as a member of a noble family descended from ancestors whom the Republic of Genoa,

---

[*] "The house shown in Ajaccio in which Napoleon was born originally belonged to the Bozzi family, from whom, as a marriage portion, it came into ours."

[†] We gather from a " Storia o Ragguaglio delle nobili Famiglie di Corsica," that the branch of the Bozzi therein named were from Genoa, consequently descended in a direct line from the Lombard stock, the only one in Italy.

then in possession of Corsica, considered as noble, and further alleging that "i Buonaparte di Corsica si trovano alleati in detta citta d'Ajaccio colle famiglie nobili Colonna, Bozzi, d'Ornano, Durazzo, Lomellini di Genoa, e si trovano godere dei diritti signoriali del Feudo Bozzi,"—that is, the property brought as her dower into the Bonaparte family when the great-grandfather of Napoleon I. married a Bozzi. Whether these statements can be construed or not into any claim of connection with the highly fortunate and exalted family therein referred to, especially as there does not exist another distinct family of the name of Bozzi in Lombardy, it is nevertheless a curious coincidence that chance, and many important circumstances, should have combined within the last forty years to bring me in contact (intimately in two or three instances) with more than one member of the French imperial dynasty. But the reference I shall afterwards bring forward to that family subsequent to their elevation to the imperial dignity in France does not allude or take cognizance of the fact I have related, inasmuch as I was not aware, nor was anybody aware of it until some time after my personal acquaintance with the several members of it had commenced. Had I been known to them by the name of my father's instead of that adopted from my deceased mother's family, under which my professional standing and reputation were attained, the result to myself might have been far otherwise.

Joseph Bonaparte, ex-King of Spain, arrived in England at the end of 1832. On reaching London he secured a handsome house in Park Crescent. He had only been a few weeks settled in London when his ex-Queen, Julie, sent him their second daughter, Princess Carlotta, widow of an elder brother of Louis Napoleon. The princess was the bearer of a letter from her own physician at Florence, addressed to myself, claiming my professional services on account of her health, which was stated in the letter to be in an indifferent condition and to require attendance, which was of course immediately bestowed upon it with the utmost care and attention. It chanced that in the course of this attendance, her father, known in this country as the Comte de Survilliers, falling ill himself also, his daughter recommended me for his physician.[*] That office I continued to fill from that time until the count left England finally for Italy, about the middle of 1840, where he died at Florence, aged about seventy-seven, keeping up an active correspondence with his London physician.

A continuous intimacy of seven years could not fail to procure me the acquaintance of móst of the surviving heads of this extraordinary family, including the one who until the great onslaught at Sedan sat enthroned in France from the second day of December, 1852, after having exhibited no great reluctance in the short course of his early years to engage his personal faith and adhesion to a fourth form of government, to all the previous forms of which he had equally pledged himself in turn—republicanism, ten years' presidency, imperial régime with personal government, and then Cesarism with responsible ministers and an independent Chamber of Deputies, when any such shall be possible in France!

---

* It was after his recovery from this illness that I received the first autograph letter, which I give in its original language as interesting perhaps to some of my readers :—

"Londres. Le 14 Janvier, 1834.

"Monsieur,—Je suis passé chez vous pour avoir le plaisir de vous voir et vous renouveller ma reconnaissance pour le vif intérêt que vous avez bien voulu me témoigner. Ma fille m'a chargé aussi de vous rappeler tous les soins que vous lui avez donnés. J'ai consulté le docteur Stokoe, ne connaissant pas les usages de ce pays, et j'espère que vous voudrez bien agréer le mandat ci-joint, et surtout ne pas oublier que je m'estimerais heureux toutes les fois que vous m'offrirez l'occasion de vous témoigner les sentiments d'affection que vous m'avez inspirés, avec lesquels je suis bien véritablement, monsieur, votre affectueux,

"Joseph, Cte. de Survilliers."

It is necessary to the verification of what I may have to state further in this matter, that I should introduce here as a member of Count Survilliers' family, with whom I have held a constant intimate intercourse, his private secretary, M. Mailliard. This honest, upright, and most trusty man, worthy of such a royal master, adhered to him with an unwearied zeal and loyalty in adverse not less than in prosperous fortunes, until death removed the eldest brother of the great Napoleon in 1845. There were other followers who had remained faithful to the exiled king, and who formed a select circle around him, with domestic attendants, some of whom were English. His establishment, in fact, was like that of a wealthy English nobleman; certainly not inferior in hospitality, inasmuch as agreeable guests at his daily table were never wanting, including some well-known military officers both English and French, with occasionally an American, and two or three London civilians specially acceptable to our host on account of their eminence in law or general literature, but chiefly for their *bel esprit* and fluency in the French language.

I remember meeting often Lucien Bonaparte, and occasionally his eldest son, Prince Musignano, who, as a son-in-law and the progenitor of nearly a dozen grandchildren, had the right we might say to be part of the family circle. King Jerome, ex-King of Westphalia, paid also one or two visits, coming purposely from across the Channel, not always on a disinterested errand as I understood. With respect to another of the count's brothers, Louis, King of Holland, whose state of health had always been too indifferent to enable him to move about like the rest of the family, the intercourse between the two brothers was confined to epistolary correspondence.

One day, early in the winter of 1835, I found my illustrious patient much depressed at the receipt of a letter from his brother, King Louis, written the previous Christmas, at the tenor and spirit of which he expressed himself much pained. The star of Louis had never shone propitiously. His unlucky family circle was broken up when he reconducted his Queen Hortense to Paris from the baths of Arrens in the Pyrenees, and he never after the 10th of September, 1807, consorted again with that remarkable princess and most excellent mother. A widower in October, 1837, and having declined a second matrimonial alliance, he wrote in better spirits to Joseph, who replied to him on the 23rd of June, 1838 : " Mon cher frère,—J'ai reçu ta lettre, par laquelle tu m'annonces que tu as conservé ta liberté. Je t'en fais mon compliment. A notre âge c'est ce qu'on a de mieux à faire lorsqu'on a cessé d'être marié." *

During the early part of King Joseph's settlement in London, Prince Louis, his nephew, was absent in Switzerland or elsewhere. His presence in London had not attracted much attention. It was only after his exploit at Strasburg in 1836, and his return from exile in America which had followed that adventure, that the prince took up his abode once more in London in a sumptuous palace in Carlton Gardens.

Having made up his mind to settle altogether in Europe, and if possible in Italy, Comte de Survilliers paid a short and last visit to the United States for the purpose of disposing of his large and magnificent palace at Point Breeze, his vast territorial possessions on the Delaware, and of better securing his large investments. In this determination of proceeding once more across the Atlantic, where he successfully accomplished his object, Comte de Survilliers avowed

---

* " MY DEAR BROTHER,—I received your letter in which you tell me you have preserved your liberty. I congratulate you. At our age it is the best thing one can do when once one is free."

to me that he had not been a little influenced by Prince Louis' ill-judged attempt in Alsace. In his " Quelques Mots sur le Roi Joseph," Louis Napoleon has declared that " cette affaire eut lieu sans l'autorisation et sans la participation de Joseph."[*]   He should have gone further in his avowal, and confessed that the news of its occurrence threw the uncle into a state of great irritation, and that he was often heard to exclaim, " Well, then, all chance is now lost of our family being readmitted into France as French citizens, which is what we have demanded of the king and the Chamber.   Ce vaurien à tout gâté."

Louis Napoleon has admitted that when Joseph heard of the affair he was " extremely displeased ; " but he goes on to say, " in 1837 he returned to America.   When he came back again he found his nephew in England, and restored him all his affection."   The last passage forms a part of a biography of Joseph, written after his death by Louis when emperor, which, to say the least, is inaccurate.   King Joseph was not in America in 1837.   I can answer by a reference to my own journals, *de die in diem*, that from January, 1837, to the end of July, 1838, I hardly missed a day without seeing him professionally or *en ami;* and as regards any " affection " exhibited by the offended uncle towards the guilty nephew, if by that term be meant the reconciliation, which certainly did occur (though at a much later period than the nephew would make us believe), that event took place under such solemn circumstances as rendered a subsequent breach of its conditions by the nephew the more to be deplored.

After an absence of a few months, the Comte de Survilliers returned to London to Thomson's Hotel, Cavendish Square, on the 2nd of December, 1839, where he desired

---

[*] " That affair took place without either the authorization or participation of Joseph."

my attendance. The object of the summons was soon explained by the count, who declared that it was not in consequence of ill-health he had required to see me, but from a wish he felt to have me present at the first interview he was about to have with Prince Louis on the subject of his conduct at Strasburg, " which " (Joseph added) " I can never forget nor forgive. After the many protestations he had made never again to compromise our name, I hesitate to receive any explanation or promise he may be disposed to offer without a witness more impartial from his position than any member of my suite, to whose testimony I may refer in case of need."

Flattering though the proposition was, it was also slightly embarrassing; but I should not have known how to extricate myself without seeming lukewarm in the interest of a person who had won for himself the good-will and general esteem of all who knew him by his highly honourable demeanour while in this country, his candid and trustworthy character, and kind, genial, and straight-forward mode of intercourse. The sudden announcement of Prince Louis put an end to all such reflections. The count at once introduced me as his *médecin* and *bon ami* (his doctor and good friend), whose presence need not prevent any communication the prince might have to make. Although I wrote down in my diary (to which I am now referring) directly I drove home the greater part of the conversation which ensued, it would be superfluous to repeat the whole of it in this part of my narrative.

The prince commenced by protesting that his uncle had been strangely deceived by false reports and hostile journals as to the motive and intention of the Strasburg affair. " Votre neveu s'est exposé pour votre cause. Personne ne comprendra que votre neveu et ceux qui avec lui ont exposé leur vie et leur bien pour remettre l'aigle sur nos

drapeaux soient traités par vous en ennemis. Je vous
avais déjà écrit cela dans une lettre quelque peu de temps
après l'insurrection de Strasbourg, à laquelle vous m'aviez
répondu, et dont je fus vivement peiné. J'espère que vous
reviendrez à des sentiments plus justes à mon égard."

The count in reply insisted on the absurdity of the
attempt in the first place, and next on the presumption on
the prince's part in putting himself forward immediately
after the death of the Duc de Reichstadt, as the representative of the Napoleon dynasty, in defiance of the proclaimed
law of succession of the 27th of November, 1804. But the
count more emphatically dwelt on the irreparable damage
inflicted on all their own kindred, whereby all chances of
being relieved from the law of perpetual banishment from
France had been demolished.

"Crois-tu" (the Count went on to say), "crois-tu que si
le peuple français aurait voulu de nous, pendant les trois
jours de Juillet il serait aller chercher le cadet des Bourbons
qu'il déteste ? Tu es fait pour tout gâter! Nous sommes
d'accord sur les questions fondamentales, mais nous différons
sur l'exécution. Je dis qu'il ne faut rien précipiter ; qu'il
faut se résigner et attendre tous du temps. Tu, au contraire
impatient, veux accélérer les événements. Eh bien, tu as
vu à quoi cela t'a mené et nous tous avec."

"J'avais sollicité" (insisted the prince) "de nouveau du
Roi Louis-Philippe la faveur de rentrer en France, non pas
comme prince, mais comme simple citoyen. Pour réponse
on renouvela la loi de bannissement contre notre famille !
La mort du Duc de Reichstadt ranima en moi les sentiments de mes droits, et j'ai vu le moment d'agir arrivé.
La trahison seule a empêché mon succès."

"Pour moi, au contraire" (reiterated the count), "cette
mort m'inspira un autre devoir, celui de rester plus que
jamais fidèle à la déclaration du peuple français de l'an

douze de la République, jusqu'à ce qu'il plaira à la nation d'en décider autrement."

The interview was likely to last much longer, with faint prospect of its ending in pacification. Neither party was warm, but both positive, though uniformly courteous towards one another. It seemed to me that the hour of reconciliation between uncle and nephew was far distant. Louis Napoleon has undertaken the task of supplying us with a kind of biography of his uncle, in which he shows himself an inaccurate as well as an imperfect narrator. The details of that period of his uncle's life which are interwoven with those of his own the biographer passes over in entire silence, while the concluding part is purely imaginary. The bitterness of heart the count experienced at that act of foolhardiness of his nephew, which had marred for ever the hope of his uncle re-entering his beloved France, was a feeling which Joseph had often been heard to declare "était plus fort que lui." Nor was it likely to be softened down by the information which used to reach the count of a fresh plot being concocted in Carlton Gardens, where a number of strange persons of many nations and characters were known to congregate daily, amongst whom Comte de Survilliers pointed out to me one who had published a defence of the revolt at Strasburg, and who was destined, from a *maréchal de logis* in the 4th regiment of hussars, to become duke, minister of the interior, and finally ambassador of France to the court of St. James's.* That person Comte de Survilliers considered to be a spy of the Paris police, employed by Louis-Philippe to betray Prince Louis, an opinion shared by many people in London, but without foundation; still a writer, who in defending his patron's violation of French territory at Strasburg, declared that

* Persigny.

among a great many officers in garrison of all grades, those who spoke of "leur fidélité à leurs serments étaient le petit nombre," and who further on utters the following opinion : " Depuis quarante ans le serment donné aux gouvernements qui se succèdent l'un à l'autre n'est devenu qu'une formule, et n'a put rester un engagement d'honneur." Such a writer, I say, duke as he is, could be but a bad counsellor for the nephew of Joseph Bonaparte.

We must not therefore attach much importance to the " Quelques Mots sur le Roi Joseph," already alluded to, which the ex-Emperor Napoleon III. has inserted in the second volume of what he has called " His works."

However, the lucky arrival in London of Jerome, the ex-King of Westphalia, on a visit, with the presence also for a few days of another relative, Arrighi, Duke of Padua, served to mollify the good-hearted uncle at last. A further interview with the nephew took place at Hanover Lodge in their presence, when a fresh engagement to abstain from all sorts of political " entreprises téméraires " (échauffourées) was entered into by Prince Louis.

" Je crains ton entourage, Louis," said the count. " Defais-toi de tous ces mauvais conseillers qui te volent et te trompent. Garde ton argent pour des temps meilleures ; ne le gâche pas en subventions au ' National ' et au ' Journal du Commerce,' et attend tout du temps."

" *Je vous le promet, mon oncle.* Tout ce que l'on dit est de l'exagération. Quant à moi, je suis bien décidé de ne plus jamais m'immiscer dans des complots politiques." And the uncle and the nephew embraced each other.

In retracing in his memory this remarkable scene, the *ci-devant* emperor will remember all this conversation, and many more assuring words he pronounced than I have recited, for they were followed by that very reconciliation to obtain which he had solicited the intercession of more

than one individual having a degree of influence with his
offended relative, and I may name among them his advocate,
Crémieux, and myself, his physician.[*]

In an account of the rejoicing that took place at Hanover Lodge not many days after the auspicious event, this
portion of the unpublished page of his own biography
will be brought to the emperor's recollection. Comte de
Survilliers, finding himself surrounded by so many members
of the Bonaparte family, was desirous that they should partake with him in his joy. A full-dress banquet was therefore ordered for the 16th of February (we were in the year
1840), at which were present Joseph, ex-King of Naples
and Spain ; Jerome, ex-King of Westphalia ; Prince Louis,
eldest surviving son of Louis, ex-King of Holland ; Prince
Lucien Murat, second son of the dethroned King of Naples ;
Count Mandelsloh, Minister of the King of Würtemberg,
in attendance on Jerome, brother-in-law of his sovereign ;
Colonel Vaudry, the leader of the revolt at Strasburg ;
Prince Bacciochi, nephew of the prince of that name who had
married a sister of the Emperor Napoleon I. ; Baron von Stal-
then, chamberlain of the King of Würtemberg, in attendance
on King Jerome ; Monsieur de Leonsthern, a great traveller
recently arrived from Mexico and China ; Dr. Stokoe, who
had been physician to Napoleon at St. Helena ; Monsieur
Mailliard, *ci-devant* Grandee of Spain, and the count's private
secretary ; Monsieur Thibaut, the faithful treasurer of King
Joseph ; his daughter ; and lastly myself.

There was only one toast, and no speeches ; but many
" touchez-là " between ex-royals, princes, grandees, and
commoners, all seemingly truly rejoicing at the hearty
reconciliation (so interesting to the Bonaparte family) between the direct and the presumptive successor to the

* This was written a few months before the lamented death of the imperial
exile.—ED.

imperial crown of France, should that dynasty ever again be recalled by the French people.[*]

All went off merrily as a marriage bell, and I, the least of those who shared in the general joy, felt it perhaps more sincerely from the conviction I had long entertained that the shaking health of my illustrious patient could not long withstand the pressure of these perpetually recurring shocks to his nervous system. Henceforward everything went on evenly and agreeably at Hanover Lodge. The intercourse between Carlton Gardens and that villa became frequent, and on many occasions I noticed early meetings of the prince's friends closeted with himself in the lower apartments before the count had left his own rooms upstairs, and of course unknown to him. These meetings appeared to me to be always seriously engaged in animated conversations or discussions as I passed through the apartment. Among the persons present I recognized General Montholon and Colonel Vaudry, and the editor of the "National," but on not a single occasion did I observe M. de Persigny, although at Carlton Gardens he was everything, yet in bad odour with the count.

What the object of those deliberations was, at which there were convened now and then persons recently arrived from Paris, and returning thither in a day or two, I never learned, nor was it my business to investigate. Prince Louis had by this time become popular, and gave frequent dinners at Carlton Gardens. His dark green *coupé*, in imitation of that of the Great Napoleon, with the imperial arms, was to be seen at the door of many of the principal mansions in London during the day, while at night some of

---

[*] " Le peuple veut l'hérédité de la dignité impériale dans la descendance directe, naturelle, légitime et adoptive de Napoléon Bonaparte, et dans la descendance directe, naturelle et légitime de Joseph Bonaparte et de Louis Bonaparte, ainsi qu'il est réglé par le Senatus Consultum, Loi du 28 floréal, ann. xii."

the brilliant *salons* were open to him; in one of these, that
of a baronet's wealthy daughter (now a peeress), whose
name is synonymous with charity and benevolence, I met
him.

I am tempted to copy from my diary the account I find
in it of this agreeable *rencontre*:—"2nd February, 1847.
Piccadilly.   I was much pleased at the reception at Miss
Coutts's last night, and spent a very pleasant evening.
The lady herself was most amiable.   Prince Louis, who
was standing by her side, near the fireplace, was very cordial; also Lord Brougham came across the room as soon
as he saw me, and shook hands heartily; and a host of
other people engaged my attention very soon.   The Duke
of Wellington came in shortly, when the prince was
introduced by the lady of the house.   I spoke several
times in the course of the evening to Miss Coutts.
She has a charming, pleasing manner, seemed particularly courteous to Prince Louis, whom she introduced to
everybody."

My own accidental meetings with the prince were necessarily frequent, and I reckon it among my gratifying reminiscences that of having been sufficiently often in the
prince's company to enable us both to become acquainted
with one another's character.   Prince Louis was aware that
his uncle extended his personal confidence in his physician
to the degree of frequently claiming his services in the
settlement of family affairs; as in the instance, for example,
of a daughter of Lucien and first cousin of Louis, married
to an English diplomatist, but separated just then from her
husband.   To her, at my intercession, the warm-hearted
uncle came forward in such a way as to save both mother
and children for a better fate, as the documents in my possession testify.

"Le Dr. Granville peut vous dire," she writes to her

brother, the Prince de Canino, "que mon oncle était disposé, lui avait même promis, de me donner les moyens d'aller en Italie et de payer toutes mes dettes." A son, not as " wise " as his father, I rescued by means supplied by the count, and through my professional and firm interference, from sickness and a plot to confine him in a private lunatic asylum.*

There was no reserve, therefore, between the Bonaparte family and the count's medical adviser, the advantage of which state of things was not long in making itself manifest.

On June the 15th a pressing message at daybreak summoned me to Hanover Lodge, where I found the count labouring under a sudden apoplectic seizure, which had made him speechless, drowsy, insensible, and paralyzed on the right side of the body. The danger was imminent, and so the appliances for relief were immediate. The count, a person by nature predisposed to fulness of blood in the head, had partly brought on the present seizure through intense head application, having sat up that same night until twelve o'clock with Monsieur Crémieux, the well-known eminent *avocat*, who had arrived a few days before from Paris with the count's will, which he had prepared by his direction. In my attendance on the count I had the benefit of the advice of Sir Henry Halford and Dr. Chamberlain, both of whom I called in consultation after the first

---

* " The will of Her Imperial Highness Princess Letizia Bonaparte, lately residing at Viterbo in Italy, daughter of the late Lucien Bonaparte, Prince of Canino, and relict of the Right Honourable Sir Thomas Wyse, K.C.B., formerly a Minister of the British Cabinet, M.P. for Tipperary and Waterford, and deputy-lieutenant of Queen's County, was proved in Her Majesty's Court of Probate, on May 19, by Signor Dominico Falcioni, the sole executor. The personal property in England was sworn under £4000. The will is translated from the Italian. Her Imperial Highness was a native of Milan, and was married in 1821 to Sir Thomas Wyse, by whom she leaves a family."—The Times.

day of the attack.   After a steady, though slow, recovery, in two or three weeks my patient was in a fit state to go and spend a short time of his convalescence at Newnham Paddox, the seat of the Earl of Denbigh, who considerately placed a great portion of his mansion at the service of the ex-king and his small retinue.   It was my intention as soon as the patient should have gained sufficient strength to travel, to send him to some of the thermal baths of Germany, with the view to assist in restoring the tone of the paralyzed limb, and improve his general health.

At Newnham Paddox I used to visit the count every other day by the Rugby express.   On our return from the country it was decided in consultation that the patient should repair to the baths of Wildbad, but as the count was anxious to determine at the same time whether he should return and settle in England, as he wished, or go to his wife and daughter in Florence, which the family would have preferred, another consultation of relations and medical advisers was held, at which, by request of Prince Louis, his own physician, Dr. Conneau, was admitted, to whom I explained *viva voce* my view of the case, and the good result I expected from the bath recommended.

While in consultation, the Duc de Padoue (Arrighi), a relative, entered the room, and placed in my hands a letter he had received from Baron Larrey, concerning the question about to be discussed, requesting me to read it to the meeting.   I have preserved the holograph, which I now produce :—

                                            " Paris, 1840
"Monsieur le Duc,—Comme j'avais un mémoire à lire à l'Institut le lendemain du jour où vous vous êtes donné la peine de venir me voir, je n'ai pas eu le temps de tracer la réponse à la lettre que vous m'avez fait l'honneur de

m'écrire pour me demander quelques conseils sur la nature
du climat des villes de Londres et de Florence, et laquelle
de ces deux villes pourrait le mieux convenir à la santé de
M. le Comte de Survilliers, ayant conçu le projet de fixer
définitivement sa résidence dans l'une ou l'autre de ces deux
villes. Certes à moins de motifs particuliers et très-impor-
tants qui forceraient le prince à se fixer à Londres, cette
ville m'a paru offrir des grands inconvénients pour la santé
des personnes sensibles et accoutumées aux climats chauds.
1° Cette ville est constamment enveloppée dans un brouillard
épais, humide, surchargé de gaz hydrogène et de la combustion du charbon de terre, le seul combustible qu'on emploie
dans ce pays. 2° L'hiver y est d'autant plus fâcheux que
l'humidité prédomine toujours. Les effets de ces influences
sont dans le premier cas de prédisposer les individus aux
congestions cérébrales, et dans le second aux affections
catarrhales plus ou moins intenses et à la diathèse scor-
butique. Le climat de Florence est très-bon ; l'air en est
pur est salubre, et les campagnes qui environnent cette
ville sont ravissantes et très-riches par les productions de
tout genre, et surtout par les fruits délicieux qu'on y trouve.
Les maisons, et surtout les palais, sont construit de matière
à pouvoir tempérer les chaleurs de l'été. L'atmosphère est
condensée dans les appartements de ces palais par une
disposition particulière des fenêtres, qui permit l'entrée des
vents du nord et nord-est et s'oppose à l'introduction dans
ces appartements des vents du cercle méridional. La régime alimentaire usité dans cette contrée est très-propre à
entretenir l'élasticité dans nos organes et la fluidité dans
les liquides qui les parcourent, ce qui conserve la santé et
prolonge la vie. Au Caire et en Syrie, dont les climats ont
beaucoup de rapport avec celui de Florence, nous avions un
grand nombre de centenaires ; nous en avons compté plus de
trente dans la capitale de l'Egypte, et nous avons eu un

Samaritain au camp devant St. Jean d'Acre lequel était
venu présenter au Général Bonaparte sa sixième généra-
tion.   Il avait cent vingt ans révolus (voyez mes com-
pagnons, &c.).

"Veuillez, je vous prie, faire agréer mes respectueux
hommages à sa majesté, et recevoir pour vous, Monsieur le
Duc, l'assurance, &c.

"Bon. LARREY, M.D."

The tenor of this letter decided the question as to the
count's ultimate and fixed residence.   By the middle of July
Comte de Survilliers was able to walk unsupported, take
an airing for an hour or two in an open carriage, until at
length, having recovered his faculties—his vision wholly,
and his hearing in part—he became able to settle his
worldly affairs with Monsieur Crémieux, and sign his will,
I witnessing his signature.   Prince Louis was assiduous
in his inquiries, but he was not, neither was any one,
admitted into the presence of thé sufferer until such
time as considerable progress had been made towards
recovery, and the count able to go from one apartment
to another.   My own peremptory recommendation that
the patient should proceed to the hot baths of Wildbad,
in the Black Forest, was now accepted, and my advice
was taken.

And now comes that episode in the life of the count
which is entwined with an unpublished page of the "Bio-
graphie de l'Empereur Napoléon III.," a page which
recalls a fact suppressed *by order*, as calculated to embarrass
the readers in the choice of a right appellative to be affixed
to the conduct about to be described.   The principal state
rooms and adjoining cabins were retained on board the
Batavier, a Dutch steamer, to convey the count and suite
to Rotterdam, and thence by a Rhine boat to Carlsruhe.

Passports had been procured from the Dutch, Baden, and Wurtemburg authorities, through whose states the party would have to pass or reside in. Sunday, July 26th, 1840, was the day on which we were to set off from the south side of the river, below London Bridge, and the whole party were conveyed to the vessel and embarked. On deck they were joined by Prince Louis, who had come to bid adieu to his uncle. A meeting had taken place the night before, during which the count had recalled to the prince's recollection the solemn promise he had given not to embark in any fresh plots which (he added) " comprommettaient l'honneur et le nom de la famille Bonaparte, et rendaient plus difficile la réhabilitation en France de telles de ces branches qui désireraient y rentrer."

On the present occasion we were standing on the quarter deck in front of the state room. The count, supported on one side by his secretary, whilst my hand was under his right arm on the other, stood facing Prince Louis, who seemed at the moment affected by the scene. Before him he beheld the eldest brother of the great founder of his dynasty, who had himself filled two kingly thrones, now a wreck in health and prospects, having no country of his own to live in, about to quit one strange land to proceed to another equally strange to him, with but a faint hope of returning quite recovered—perhaps not at all! The prince must really have felt the precarious situation of a most excellent relative, from whom he was about to part perhaps for ever. But the bell for visitors to leave the vessel sounded, and the nephew and uncle separated — Joseph still holding the hand of Louis, repeating these words : " Point de complots, entends-tu ? Garde ton argent pour des meilleurs occasions ! Quand la France voudra de nous, elle saura nous appeler."

" Soyez tranquille, mon oncle," was the reply ; " vous

pouvez compter sur moi," retreating one or two steps in the meanwhile.

"Vrai?" cried the uncle, with tears in his eyes.

"*Ma parole d'honneur*," exclaimed the prince, with one hand on his heart, and he was gone. I hear those words ringing in my ears even now as I am writing a circumstance which I recorded in my note-book in the state room of the steamer, whither we immediately withdrew, my patient perfectly exhausted, as he himself declared.

We reached Wildbad on the 2nd of August, and in the very first week I noticed a visible improvement in the power of using his right leg and arm, and of clutching another man's hand, trying to squeeze it, a simple test which served my purpose for estimating the rate of increase in muscular power. At twelve o'clock on the 10th of August, the King of Wurtemburg arrived at Wildbad, and desired my immediate attendance. On entering the room where the king was with a single aide-de-camp, he at once addressed me in French. "I have just received a despatch containing sad news, which may be fatal to your patient, King Joseph," and he went on to say that Prince Louis, with a party in arms, had landed at Boulogne last Thursday, the 6th, from a steamer coming from London. After a short conflict with the military and the authorities, during which it is reported that the officer who tried to arrest him was shot, the prince was captured and lodged in prison. "And now," observed the king, "how are we to break such miserable news to your patient, or how is it to be concealed from him?" In reply I declared that the sudden communication of such an event to the count might prove instantly fatal. I insisted upon the necessity of keeping from his knowledge for the present the untoward event, and "until I shall have prepared him to receive it with less chance of mischief." So orders were given that no " Galignani," nor any French newspaper, should be admitted into the count's apartments. But the unfortunate sufferer, while spared for a time from this painful news, was not equally fortunate with regard to other distressing family tidings, for King Jerome, who had come to see his brother, had brought him the intelligence of their brother Lucien's death, and by-and-by a letter was read to the count, stating that Jerome himself had made up his mind to make his submission to Louis-Philippe. Coup sur coup! The news of the death of Lucien, to whom he had been much attached, afflicted the count greatly, and now the defection of another brother seemed too much for his nerves. Fortunately the arrival of young Jerome Napoleon, Prince de Montfort, eldest son of the ex-King Jerome, a charming young man, afforded some pleasure to my afflicted patient; and when in a few days he left, his younger brother, Napoleon Joseph, now Prince Napoleon, a youth about eighteen years of age, full of spirits, came to enliven our circle on the 17th of August.

Both these young princes had received their education at the military college of Ludwigsburg, the elder of the two having been fellow-collegian with my son, whom I had the misfortune to lose at the age of one-and-twenty. I mention this fact merely because it served to place me at once on an agreeable footing with the young princes, especially with the eldest, who expressed his great sorrow upon learning the fatal accident which had deprived me of a most promising son. A stronger contrast I have never met with in the course of my long life between two brothers, as I beheld here before me. While Jerome Napoleon, Prince de Montfort, had the appearance, gait, manner, and notions of a true aristocrat of the 'Teutonic type, the younger brother, Prince Napoleon, professed the most opposite principles to those of his great ancestor and own brother, being in fact a determined republican, and violently opposed to Cæsarism. He used to say, and often repeat to good Mr. Mailliard, his uncle's secretary, "Fi! de toute cette canaille de Juillet! Il va pleuvoir bientôt des baïonnettes; vous allez voir: Et alors Vive la République!"

We were then a few years yet from 1848, and the bayonets did indeed and in truth rain not unlike thick hail at that epoch. But what did they serve for? To set up a republic one day to pull it down again the next, and thus elevate his cousin to the Cæsarism he detested.

At length it became impracticable to keep the news of the Boulogne affair from the knowledge of the count, and accordingly I undertook to communicate it to him one day during which he had appeared to be much better in every respect. The effect of such a communication soon made me regret having made it. For the first moment he stood aghast, then literally screamed out, "Impossible! Pas vrai! pas vrai! Oh pauvre nom de Bonaparte, que tu as baissé aux yeux de la France!" And his voice was becoming husky, his face red, his breathing difficult. I endeavoured to soothe and tranquillize him. I had him put to bed, placed ice water at the back of his head—for it is the cerebellum, and not the brain, which in such cases is in danger. He felt grateful for the application, which presently produced sleep. I had promised not to leave him, and I remained in the room some hours, when, after a long and agitated sleep, he awoke in the morning of the 6th of September, talking coherently but pronouncing his words with difficulty. There was not a moment to lose: we were approaching a fresh stroke of apoplexy. I directed him to be cupped forthwith. The rescue from the threatening symptoms was almost immediate. But I need not proceed any further with professional details, simply adding that four days after this dangerous paroxysm I was able to declare that my patient was in a fit state to undertake his return journey to England, which we reached after a whole week's travelling, and a most tempestuous passage of nearly forty hours crossing from Rotterdam to London, where the whole party arrived on the 17th of September, the count weak in body, but his mind normal, able to walk slowly, to grasp firmly with his right hand any hard object of a moderate size, and feeling more cheerful and happy, as he declared, at finding himself once more in this " happy land."

Here ends, I may say, an unpublished chapter in the life of two men more famous perhaps than many of the notabilities whom the political tornado that shook Europe during forty years brought up to the surface. It may be asked, were the facts here recorded worth collecting and being made public ? I answer, Yes, most emphatically. Are facts, irrefragable facts, demonstrative of the character of one, at all events, of the two sovereigns herein depicted, holding in his hands the fearful privilege and power of wielding six hundred thousand bayonets and thousands of cannon against the peace and well-being of millions of people, to be ignored when, on the contrary, the knowledge of those facts would serve to put those millions on their guard against fresh deceptions ?

Between Louis Napoleon and the writer of this episode in his life there cannot subsist any personal feeling. The last time we met, namely, when the prince was about to leave London for the second time on his return to take his seat in the Assembly in Paris on his second election for the Département de la Seine, we shook hands in Piccadilly as we had done on ordinary occasions. On his election as president I made it the subject of a congratulatory epistle. . Again a few congratulatory words were addressed to the president when he reached the throne. I had hoped that the declarations I had often heard expressed by the prince in the presence of his uncle, " that the monarchical form of government in England was the best, the safest, and the most endurable," would now be put to the test in France. Hating democracy as he most cordially does, the writer of these lines rejoiced to see a prince who had had such abundant opportunities of putting in practice the monarchical system he had so much eulogized, placed in a position to apply that system to his own country.

Now for a small account of a species of contraband diplomacy, which, although dating from 1835, comes apropos of the revolution of 1848, in which Prince Louis took a lead. A series of documents are in my possession, forming an instructive as well as interesting record of part of the secret history of Louis-Philippe's interesting reign. The collection, which might have found a most appropriate place in Louis Blanc's clever " Histoire de dix Ans," and which that astute historiographer would have doubtlessly so employed had it got into his possession, has no chance at present of seeing the light of day. The story itself of the papers, though brief and simple, is almost a romance. A middle-aged nobleman, Count Rh—in, every way qualified in person, rank, manners, and talents, was sent by Metternich secretly to Paris in 1835 *en voyageur*, to reside there as his emissary, to watch, study, and report on all questions of political interest likely to be of use to the crafty Cæsarian minister. He was to be introduced at court by the Austrian ambassador (kept in ignorance, of course, of the motive), and to put himself in communication with the king and Monsieur Thiers, but not with de Broglie, Minister for Foreign affairs, with whom Metternich did not sympathize. The duke was to be kept absolutely in the dark of the plot, which was confined to three persons only. The Austrian emissary was to be the medium through whom the secret correspondence was to be conducted, and it is amusing to notice by these letters how, while the plotters seemed to act harmoniously together for one and the same object, each secretly communicated on certain occasions his own individual opinion and judgment on his colleagues to the secret emissary. Thus we have the character of Monsieur Thiers openly dissected in an interview between the king and the emissary; while in one of the emissary's reports to Metternich of an interview with Thiers, he divulges the private opinion of the latter as to the character and abilities of his sovereign.

The plot appears to have been ingeniously contrived. In order to make matters quite safe, Herr Graf Rh—in conceived the brilliant idea of dispensing with a hired secretary, and employing as his amanuensis a lady he had known some time, to copy the several letters and despatches received and sent out. Madame ——, who not long after had occasion to consult me, was a highly educated, clever German lady, and lent herself most gracefully to this occupation. Noticing after a short time how important the successive papers she was busy in copying were becoming, she judged that she might as well employ part of her time in making an extra copy for her own private purposes, in case of a rainy day, as she had no great faith in the Graf's sunshine. Accordingly a second copy of all the papers was made, and when death parted the two friends, and Metternich got possession of all the documents and papers left by his clever emissary, Madame remained possessed of the fruit of her nimble and untired pen. Thus a whole *petite comédie* terminated as cleverly as it had been skilfully devised.

Why and how her papers came into my possession it is no part of my duty to divulge. As I before hinted, these documents would impart a surprising and interesting character to a new " Histoire de dix Ans," while they would better prepare us for the advent of that fresh republic in France which ended in and with Cæsarism. The following list of the papers forming the collection will not prove uninteresting, and will excite political as well as ethological reflections. One of the *pièces* in the appendix, called " Liste d'Agents Secrets " (all of whom we are to understand were paid by the respective courts to which they reported their espionage), shall never go out of my hands. If the name of these spies are correctly reported, one may feel humbled rather than hurt at having received and honoured by our confidence and friendship ·people deemed worthy of both. The first on the list (only so, I suppose, because in an alphabetical list his name required to be placed at the head of the letter A) was a count who, during the whole of the years of his exile from Naples (as I had been made to believe) frequented my family, and never missed one of the *soirées* I used to hold at my house, faithful, no doubt, to his work of "reporting progress.."

The authentic copies of letters in my possession are as follows :—

1re. Kœnigworth, 11 Sep., 1835.
Le Prince Metternich à son Agent Diplomatique à Paris.   *Pièce ostensible*, with a P.S. confidentiel.
2me. Du même au même, 2 Oct., 1835.   Pièce confidentielle.
3me. Du même au même, 30 Oct., 1835.   Pièce confidentielle.
4me. Du même au même, 30 Oct., 1835.   Pièce sensée confidentielle.
5me. Prince Metternich à son confidant, 9 Jan., 1836.

1re. Conversation de Louis-Philippe avec le confidant de Metternich.
2me. Conversation du confidant de Metternich avec Mons. Thiers.
3me. Conversation de Mons. Thiers avec le confidant de Metternich.
4me. Conversation du même avec le même.

Appendice.—Note du confidant au Pr. Metternich, 15 Juin, 1837.

Extrait d'une note préliminaire de l'acte d'association du Comité Révolutionnaire Français, avec celui de la Jeune Europe, fait à Ste. Pélagie le 10 Avril, 1835 ; communiqué au Pr. Metternich.

Liste d'Agents Secrets de plusieurs Cabinets en 1836, fourni par l'Emissaire particulier du Pr. Metternich. (They are sixty in number.)

N.B.—Tout le dossier de ces différents documents occupe quarante-huit pages d'une écriture fine (8vo, large).

CHAPTER XX.

1835—54.

Singular absence of information on a subject of importance—A tour among the springs of Germany—Presentiment of my son—His death—A visit to Buxton—The mineral springs of England—Bournemouth—Excuses for leaving England—Kissingen : efficacy of its waters—Gastein—German mode of treatment—Dr. Grimm.

THAT sprightly and spirited trifle from the pen of Sir Francis Head, which, under the title of " Bubbles from the Brünnen of Nassau," caused such a stir, and sent shoals of the upper ten thousand to Germany in the year 1835, suddenly inspired me with the idea of visiting during the summer months all the other Brünnen of that vast region of Europe, besides the very few paraded by the worthy baronet : Ems, Wiesbaden, and the " source of beauty," with the " fountain of snakes " adjoining. My own persuasion of the medical benefit to be derived from mineral waters, especially of some of the continental springs, was not a new conviction. I had had sufficient experience in the treatment of particular diseases by means of those medicinal auxiliaries to know, that were the attention of my professional brethren in England to be properly awakened, both they and the public in general would welcome the information, test its facts and their value, and finally accept the whole as a novel, scientific, and acceptable branch of medical treatment. I put to myself this question : Which are the works in the English language published of a sufficiently recent date and worth that can be referred to and made available for bringing about the result mentioned above ?

I looked round the great reading-room of the British Museum, that garden of literature, into which once entered you luxuriously sit before a well-appointed desk, ready to collect and treasure up into your memorandum book whatever knowledge you can gather from the thousands of volumes within your own reach, or from any other which you desire to have brought to you by prompt attendants from the many inner halls of that gigantic library. Here you can pick and choose, transcribe and collect, whatever can help you in the prosecution of any projected work you may happen to be engaged in, and sure it is that the process will be one of cramming rather than of depleting.

It turned out otherwise in my case, and I came away with the conviction that no standard printed work, elementary, practical, and descriptive, giving a continuous and special account of the various mineral springs throughout Germany, combining the *utile dulci*, was to be found at the epoch I refer to. A subsequent search in the libraries of the Colleges of Physicians and Surgeons in London proved equally fruitless. In fact, the reality being that English bibliography was deficient in modern scientific and practical works on mineral hydrology. Thus did I conclude after ample search in 1836, and hence the determination at once taken to carry into effect the plan of visiting, studying, and experimenting upon the sources of mineral waters in Germany, which produced for the public the work mentioned in the note.* Accordingly, accompanied by my two sons, Augustus and Walter, still *in statu pupillari*, I set out for Germany from Paris early in the summer of 1836, in the same carriage that had served to bring me home from Russia a few years before, fitted up with all the conveniences which posting days demanded, taking with me a plan previously studied and sketched out for a tour of about four

* "The Spas of Germany." 1837.

thousand miles, with the intention of visiting and describing more or less fully forty principal mineral springs in that country, besides others of minor importance. The public opinion of my professional brethren concerning the two volumes I afterwards produced is expressed in a few short sentences, which I hope an author may be permitted to repeat without being taxed with vanity: "They (the volumes) are a remarkable acquisition to the invalid and the traveller, not less than to his professional brethren in England. They contain a scientific analysis of the several spas of Germany, which they describe minutely; and they present to the reader an itinerary over a pleasant route in which the companionable qualities of the writer are no slight recommendation. Not that he sacrifices utility to amusement with the view of captivating his reader; far from it, for there is enough and to spare of the real solid, matter-of-fact business introduced everywhere to constitute a work having at the time of its appearance no competitor in English literature on the same subject treated in the like manner;" on a subject, too, as I stated in the preface of the first edition, perfectly new. Thirty chief or principal springs, divided into geographical groups, were visited and inquired into personally in the course of the entire tour, which lasted four months. The information collected in that period fills one thousand pages, in which are views of some of the most salient objects, as well as itinerary maps to guide the traveller. One feature especially I will venture to signalize as perfectly original in this work, namely, the introduction of what I have called a chemico-pneumatic thermometrical table, embracing at one view the analysis or composition of each mineral water as taken from the spring. How tedious and surfeiting would it not prove to readers to have had their attention arrested (on every occasion of the introduction of a new spring) by the names, nature, and quantity of its mineral ingredients in the middle of an interesting or instructive description! Some publications of a like nature to the "Spas of Germany" have appeared since in imitation of it, and this great defect is found in them, namely, a perpetually recurrent insertion of abstracts of chemical analysis, which render the perusal of the works almost repulsive. Now, by the use of a single general table devised as mine is, all such repetitions in the body of the work are obviated. The table enables us at a glance to judge of the nature of every spring, to see at once the most prevailing and characteristic ingredients in them, and lastly, to sum up the respective quantities of solid substances held in solution in a common measure of mineral water.

Another feature which distinguishes the present from the rest of the treatises on mineral waters is the essay which precedes the first volume, entitled " Popular Considerations on the Use and Powers of Mineral Waters." Being on the point of laying before the English reader a whole catalogue of foreign waters, which, judging from the complicated nature of the mineral ingredients they contain in solution may à priori be deemed to possess some action on the system of those who drink them, it became an almost absolute duty on my part to enlighten them how to use the waters as remedies, whether internally or as baths; what diet to follow during the treatment, with many other considerations I need not repeat again. Those considerations for the present stand unique in the history of hydrological works. I felt qualified to give the result of positive and direct experience, and not merely didactic recommendations. The date and appearance of the two volumes in question, and the favourable reception they met with from the press, are circumstances so near our own time that I needed to have

done no more than give their title and date in the chronological order of my other published works.

My own feelings would induce me to pass over in silence
the period during which I was going about the world gathering materials for a new work destined to be associated with
the most painful period of my life—the ever-recurrent me-
mento of an irreparable and fatal loss which has embittered
my days. On determining to set off to Germany, my eldest
surviving son, Charles, just recovered from a dangerous
fever, hoping that his leave of absence from his post of
lieutenant and adjutant of the 89th Foot, then stationed in
Ireland, which was about to expire, might on application
to Lord Hill be prolonged some weeks, entreated me to
take him along with his brothers, that he might revisit the
scenes of his collegiate life in the military school of Ludwigsburg, near Stuttgart.   But I had, in a private interview with
Lord Granville Somerset, learned that no further extension
would be granted beyond the present one, given on the
score of illness, as, he added, "the Medical Board reports
him at present improved."   The regiment was on the point
of sailing to a foreign station, and the two or three weeks
he had yet of his leave would not enable him to accomplish
what he so much desired without the risk of losing his rank,
and possibly subjecting himself to dismissal from the service.
Unwilling that he should face such a risk after his success
in the service and the flattering reports made to the Commander-in-Chief of his diligence and military knowledge, I
decided it could not be.   Still he pleaded long and earnestly,
repeating his own dire forebodings that if we parted we
should never meet again on earth.   It was a bitter moment,
a moment of suspense, which a sense of stern duty alone
put an end to.   No, it could not be ; and so we parted.
Many affectionate letters from him followed me, until, as I
was on my return home, a letter from my constant friend at

the Foreign Office, so often mentioned, reached me at
Berlin, detailing an accident by which my boy had perished
—drowned, in Dampton Bay, from a sudden seizure of the
heart while bathing on the recommendation of Sir James
Macgregor, who had attended him professionally after we
had parted. My wife was then in Paris, and no relative
was at hand to attend to the dead. Old friends kindly
assumed the pious part of the absent relatives, and so the
dear remains were temporarily received in the parochial
cemetery at Broadstairs, whence, on my return to London,
I had them removed to the catacombs in Kensal Green,
where, after twenty-five years, in a twin-niche, was deposited in 1861 the dear mother he had loved so well; a
third vacancy by the side of the last, yawning with its dark
maw waiting for its future occupant, who tarries behind to
console himself with the words of the prophet Isaiah : " The
righteous is taken away from the evil to come. He shall
enter into peace."

I have already in the " Spas of Germany " detailed this
painful episode in my life, and to the perusal of it in those
two volumes I might refer my present readers. But no ;
the heart is bleeding still, after thirty-five years, as if the
wound had been only fresh inflicted. Had I taken my
beloved and most worthy son along with me, he might now
be by my side, a superior officer, helping me to sketch
more accurately the varied scenes of my life, and cheer up
his now almost decrepit father. But it was not to be.

An intended visit to my medical friend Sir Charles
Scudamore, who was following at Buxton with his London
patients the example I had just set him in attending my
London patients at the Spa of Kissingen, in Bavaria, first
brought to my knowledge that my laborious task on the
" Spas of Germany " was considered at Buxton to be the
chief cause of its waning glory. Indeed, I had at times

experienced some qualms of conscience as to whether I did not owe it to my adopted country to try to make amends for whatever damage to English interest that work of mine might have produced, and so exert myself in remedying any such mischief, by doing for the mineral springs of England what I had done for those abroad. Had such an inspiration needed a stimulant to convert it into a reality, that agent was not long in presenting itself before me on my first appearance at the Grand Hotel in the aristocratic spa of Buxton. " You wish to see Sir Charles Scudamore, I am informed, sir ? A room, the last in the hotel at present vacant, has been kept for an expected friend of Sir Charles." And then accosting me nearer, with peculiar grace, the comely lady added, " May I venture to ask whether I have the honour of ·addressing the author of ' The Spas of Germany ? ' I bowed assent. " Then permit me to tell you that your book has done for us and other similar establishments in the country, what the report of a raging of small-pox or scarlet fever would have done if propagated in this place. All the lame and limping people, the nice elderly gouty gentlemen who have always so many wants we are glad to provide for, the many invalided officers of the late Peninsular war—dear good creatures, the nervous courtiers and their ladies—all, in fact, and everybody, now turn up their noses at the mention of Buxton. They must go to Wiesbaden or Baden, or I know not to what other *bad*-en place for their recovery ! As to this hotel, I assure you such changes have brought about our ruin. Our landlord is about to give up the place, and the one who has just retired, Mr. Shaw, declares that we may as well shut up at once and go digging."

" Then I think your landlord and his predecessor are both wrong and precipitate in their judgment. Let them wait a year or two after the publication of a fresh work by the same author who has done all the mischief, in which new work the nature and value of the watering and sea-bathing places in England will be set in contrast with those of Germany, and you will sing, dear madam, a different song when next we meet. Nor shall I have less reason to rejoice to find that I have effected many favourable changes in your mode of managing the baths and treating your guests the patients—changes which will render your establishments as attractive and popular as those over the sea. In truth, my present visit to Sir Charles has the double object of greeting him and of studying a little the nature of the bath he specially patronizes, as being one of those which, under the more general title of 'The Spas of England,' I meditate soon to write upon."

After the lapse of thirty years, remembering what I said to my handsome interlocutrix, the well-bred representative of the Duke of Devonshire's interest in the Grand Hotel at Buxton in 1840, I think I may venture to ask whether any prediction could have been more completely realized, not as regards Buxton only, but also Bath, Harrogate, Scarborough, and for not a few of the sea-bathing places, with the addition of some entirely new resorts for invalids, many of which were wholly unknown before the researches I undertook regarding medicated springs, climates, and sites to suit people of weak health, without the necessity of banishment from home. Who had ever before heard of our iodine spa in this country until I singled out Woodhall near Lincoln, where scrofulous patients can find the same medicated water as at Kreuznach in Rhenish Prussia? Who had ever dreamt of such a Nice-like haven as Bournemouth before I undertook to investigate the natural peculiarities of our south coasts, and pointed out to the owners of the land in the place just named (mere heaps of sand fetching five shillings an acre) the very *locale* for a sanatorium, where now building land fetches twice and thrice as many pounds per acre as it before fetched shillings?

"I have no hesitation in stating," I said, at the conclusion of a speech in answer to a toast drank at a banquet given in February, 1841, by the members of Poole, Christchurch, Dorchester, and some of the owners of the land, who were present at the hotel at Bournemouth to welcome my visit and hear my report of its capabilities,—"I have no hesitation in stating, as the conclusion of all my observations, notes, and experiments in every nook and corner of your district, that no situation I have had occasion to examine along the entire south coast possesses so many capabilities of being made the very best invalid's sea-watering place in England. For you, Mr. Chairman, for Mr. Drax (the member), Sir George Jervis of Christchurch, Messrs. Skittle, Sydenham, and others who have a personal interest in this question, my assertions will prove satisfactory, and the more acceptable because founded on truth. I see present my friend, the clever editor and proprietor also, I believe, at all events the clever writer of the 'Salisbury Herald,' Mr. Halpin. To him will belong the pleasing task of giving publicity to the professional judgment I have this evening expressed; the more satisfactory to him as he was the one to suggest to the owners of the property the measure you adopted for ascertaining the real worth of your property.

"I look upon Bournemouth and its yet unformed colony as a perfect discovery, not only as a sea-bathing place, but, what is of more importance, as a winter residence for the most delicate constitutions requiring a warm and sheltered locality at this season of the year. As such I hold it superior to Bonchurch, St. Lawrence, or Ventnor in the Isle of Wight. Although situated ten miles less to the south than the extreme coast line of that island, Bournemouth has

the superior advantage of being as many and more miles to
the westward, which make amends for the trifling difference
in regard to its southern position. But the Bourne has
other claims of superiority over Ventnor, being in the centre
of a beautiful curvilinear sweep of the coast (which should
be called Bourne Bay, and not Poole Bay), the two extreme
points or ends of which, equidistant from the Bourne, serve
to protect the latter place from the direct influence of the
two most objectionable winds that blow. But above all is
Bournemouth superior to the Isle of Wight from its entire
exposure to the south in a position protected from all easterly
winds.

"I hardly need touch upon its superiority as a bathing-
place, should you or your visitors be inclined to turn it
into one, as the sands and the form of the beach generally
are better than in the majority of sea-bathing places on the
neighbouring coasts. It is as an inland and sheltered haven
for the most delicate invalids that I would call your special
attention to the great capabilities of Bournemouth, for you
would look in vain elsewhere for that singular advantage
which is here presented to us, of two consolidated banks of
sandy cliffs clothed with the verdure (like those of the
Black Forest) of pine trees, planted here twenty-five years
ago by a provident landowner, running inland from the sea,
with a smiling vale between them watered by a rapid brook,
the Bourne—which divides them just enough to allow of
complete ventilation, with sufficient coolness during the
summer months, yet affording sheltered spots for the erection
of residences, not only for convalescents free from positive
disease, but for patients also in the most delicate state of
health with reference to chest complaints. For this special
class of invalids, the many glens which run across the
western cliff, and which I pointed out to one of your
architects, afford beautiful retreats, surrounded by balmy

and almost medicinal emanations from the fir plantations, which are found so beneficial in all cases.

"In fact, gentlemen," I went on to remark, "you have a spot here which you may convert into a perfect blessing for those among the wealthy who are sorely afflicted with disease, and who do not like to tear themselves from home to go in search of distant foreign salutary climates. I have pointed out to you in the course of our rambles all that is requisite to be done to make the place perfect, and it will be your own fault if Bournemouth does not soon become an object of attraction and admiration."

It was not likely that I should part with my attentive audience without giving them some wholesome advice as to the manner of disposing of their promising possession, and therefore I added in conclusion: "You must take care not to commit the blunders that have been committed in many other of our sea-bathing places. You must not let in strangers, speculators in bricks and mortar, or contractors, to erect long streets of inferior lodging-houses, with 'parades,' 'crescents,' and 'terraces' interminable, with all the dwellings facing the roaring sea, and confronting every severe gale that makes the window frames of a poor invalid's bedroom rattle by night as well as by day, and shakes his own frame in bed also. The laws of climate, of locality, of aspect for houses, of site, and for arrangement, have hitherto been overlooked, neglected, and misunderstood in this country. My own experience, abroad as well as at home, has enabled me to lay down certain principles on all those important points, which can only lead to success by producing satisfaction. Those points I have explained to you and to the gentlemen surveyors who were good enough to accompany me in my examination, to whom I showed how they may be made applicable to Bournemouth in order to be triumphantly accomplished."

This speech was concluded on a snowy winter night over thirty years ago. Some of my hearers are still living ; the provincial papers, which reported the proceedings in full, are in existence ; they, and better still, my present readers who may have visited, or heard of, or experienced the benefit of a residence at Bournemouth, and the thousands besides that year after year have crowded that winter asylum and contributed to make it famous (though they may never read my present statement) ;—all such witnesses will testify that in this one striking instance, at all events, the author's work* has proved a source of public benefit, and so put me all right again with the " Belle " of the Grand Hotel at Buxton.

There is one talent which the writer of a long and diversified narrative of worldly occurrences possesses in common with a scene-shifter during the performance of some grand dramatic representation—I mean the art of varying by unexpected shifts and transformations the scene of the drama from gloom to cheerfulness or the reverse ; from a picture of distress to one of merriment ; from a dismal dungeon to resplendent halls of enjoyment. Such is my bent and course at this moment. I have given glimpses of the spas of England sufficient to show what they are intended to represent, and what they are good for ; and we will now change the decoration and the scene by bringing the reader into the very centre of the spas of Germany, thus accomplishing to a moderate extent the duty of an autobiographer, of referring in turn to the several works he has published. I designedly say, referring, for to do more, or to enter into the nature and scope of such works would be on my part an absurd and gigantic pleonasm. A short preliminary deviation will be permitted, to put me straight with my readers. More

* "The Spas of England, and Principal Sea-bathing Places." London, 1839–40.

than once I have been charged with a capricious tendency
or a restless love of change, both of country and home.   I
hear people say : " He has no sooner succeeded " (beyond
his deserts, the ill-natured ones will add) " in settling himself—an alien—in this great metropolis as a respectable and
respected physician, forming most enviable professional
connections with some of the best families, than, disre-
garding all personal considerations, off he starts, first to
Italy, then to Russia, next to Germany, and we know not
how many times to France, besides running through the
whole length and breadth of England, leaving behind him,
to take care of themselves as best they may, the people who
relied on him in case of illness."

Thus plainly put, the proposition is against me, and in-
volves a merited condemnation, for which reason I deem it
a duty to notice it.   I am not so indifferent to public opinion
as not to feel how important it is to my character not to
allow such an impression as conveyed above to pass unnoticed, still less unexplained, and I consider the present a
suitable occasion for disposing of the charge by adequate
explanations.   For there are more narratives in store to
come forward of flights through England and to foreign
countries equally amenable to the aforesaid criticism, yet
equally explicable and pardonable on the same grounds.
And what are they?   In not a single instance but one of
all my wanderings, subsequent to my final settlement in the
capital in 1818 as a candidate for public patronage, have
I absented myself for any but objects strictly professional.
The exception was my visit to my own family in Milan,
whom I had not seen for a period of sixteen years.

By no other selfish purpose was the absence complained
of occasioned when not positively summoned to attend a
pressing case of illness in a distant foreign-country or in
any of the English counties far remote; my journeys

in every case being either for the purpose of affording immediate succour to some ailing person, or of acquiring a practical knowledge of the many means for improving the health of my patients, and finally to cure them, by methods or agents that could only be obtained away from London, or even away from England. To these results I had committed my reputation as a medical man when I recommended as a treatment in many important cases of disease, the use of foreign baths and the drinking of mineral waters, either abroad or in this country, and I proceeded to the one or to the other to witness the working of my own recommendation, to assist by my own supervision when possible or required, and by suggestions calculated to make the recommended treatment perfectly successful, and so hasten the desired consummation. When the straightforward account I am about to commit to the world of my ups and downs of life shall have been read, it will be admitted that the whole course of my professional career has been an uninterrupted study for the advantage of such persons as had trusted themselves to my care, even while I was absent. I have already mentioned what share I had in bringing into notice one of the mineral springs in Germany, which has since become one of the most frequented and famous, not on account of any of those attributes which have made and still sustain the popularity of Baden Baden and Homburg, for at Kissingen (the spring I refer to) there are no such temptations. The fame of Kissingen stands on the well-established fact, that the many maladies to which the weaker sex are liable find their relief and cure. I am not afraid of being suspected of puffing, but I am desirous, as one who has intimately studied the branch of the profession which relates especially to the female portion of the creation, to let it be known as my conviction before I quit this earthly scene, as I have already left the professional calling, that with the assistance of the internal use of the powerful Ragozi, judiciously administered with baths of Pandur (alone or mixed with a third spring called the Soolen), with the application in the form of a bath of carbonic acid, to be had in abundance, and lastly with the plunging for two or three minutes into the Wellenbad (one of the most powerful restoratives of nervous energy I am acquainted with) ; I say that with such aids, either partially or generally resorted to, there is no defect or failure or morbid condition in the female system, married or single, that has not given way or been put to rights to the full of my knowledge and experience.

It has been a frequent source of satisfaction in my old age to run down the long list of this class of patients I have had the happiness to restore to health. This assertion I am confident will meet many assenting nods of confirmation from my fair readers. In the very outset of my career as a medical hydrographer, I brought the Spa of Kissingen fully before the profession and the public. After watching the effects of the various springs to be found in this highly favoured place in a great variety of complaints for the space of six seasons in succession, upon a large number of cases recommended by myself and by such of my brother practitioners as had taken pains to make themselves acquainted with the subject, it was natural that I should not only publish in the little volume on Kissingen * the result of my observations, but continue to patronize and recommend the spa in all suitable cases. The bare inspection of my medical register would satisfy the most incredulous of the utility of mineral waters, and they would be surprised at the wonderful regularity with which happy results followed the proper employment of the various mineral resources of

* " Kissingen ; its Sources and Resources," London, 1846.

Kissingen. The lists of the complaints cured include many of that proteoform class which are commonly denominated nervous. It would be an easy task to quote letters from grateful patients testifying by personal experience the truth of what has been advanced, but I consider such a measure both superfluous and inexpedient.

When a watering-place known in 1836 to only a few natives of the country in which it lies, as was the case at my first visit to Kissingen, becomes in the course of a few years the rendezvous of sovereign princes and branches of royal families from different parts of Europe, and even from beyond seas; when we find gathering at this same place hundreds of the aristocracy of Russia, France, Germany, Italy, and England, and not a few of the notabilities in science, literature, and the arts, together with remarkable military and diplomatic characters, all of them equally anxious to adopt and strictly to follow the same plan of water treatment for the space of four or five weeks; we may justly conclude that the mineral springs of the place are *bonâ fide* remedies for diseases not otherwise curable, and are the motive which brings together such an assemblage of invalids at the new favourite Spa of Bavaria.

From the year 1840 I had been in the practice of attending at this spa for the space of about three of the summer months in every year, down to 1868, keeping a strict account of all the patients I attended, of their different ailments, progress, and the ultimate result. In the course of that time thirty-two thousand patients attended the spa from all parts of Europe and America, according to the official list (Kurliste) published daily. Of that number, about one-sixth part were English, that is, five thousand four hundred belonged to that nation, and were principally attended by myself. This number of patients, it may be supposed, afforded me ample opportunity to test the virtue of the several springs (there being four essentially different). The history of their cases being carefully recorded by daily observations, were after each season collated, and the names, as well as that of their complaints, indexed, so that to this day I can refer to any individual case I treated, and how many of them successfully, during the period here alluded to. Their histories fill twenty-three thick volumes of the same form of my volume descriptive of Kissingen, of about four hundred pages. My brethren will admit, I am certain, that with such data it was a plain professional duty on my part to communicate so much knowledge to the profession.

I should think it unnecessary to proceed in the same course of reflection with regard to Gastein, were it not that propriety prompts me to refer to the name of an individual eminent in his career, who has, in the most direct and distinct manner, benefited to the extent of obtaining a complete cure by the use of that bath. My readers will not have forgotten "My dear, dear Sidney" of Wilton House, on the memorable night of the 22nd of February, 1822. Dear little Sidney was in 1836 a big as well as a great man, and a minister to boot. In the midst of incessant application and work his health had given way, and I had had frequent visits from him in the morning (as we were living in the same street) on account of his health. What still remained after a recovery from a positive attack of illness was a total prostration of the nervous system, meaning by this term that débile condition of his physical nerves, as the late Dr. Baillie used to call them, in contradistinction to fancy nerves. And this state of Mr. Sidney Herbert, I promised him, his mother, and his sisters, would be completely and absolutely remedied by the cautious use of the bath of Gastein. Some, if not all, of those sisters are, I hope, still alive to attest the truth of what I assert, and the country at large fully knows, and must remember,

what excellent use my lamented friend made of his restored
health in the service of the people he loved so well. I
promised Lady Pembroke to time a second visit I intended to pay to Gastein with that of her son, so as to
enable me to superintend for the first days the application
of that powerful water, that he might avoid the danger of
any attack in the head, to which I had exposed myself
inconsiderately in the first personal experiment I had made
with the bath, the strength of which water is really for
midable. However, "Dear Sidney" was restored, with
the full use of his firm limbs, which enabled him to ramble
about those Alpine recesses and take a sketch of Gastein,
which I made use of with his permission as an illustration for my chapter on Gastein, my account of which I may
specially and confidently recommend to my professional
brethren.

These several illustrations of the worth of mineral waters
may fairly be referred to by the author of "The Spas of
Germany," as proofs of the desire he has ever experienced
when employing his pen of being useful to the myriads of
his fellow-creatures, by detailing the many and often singular
methods by which Providence brings about such a blessed
result. How right, then, it was that in thankfulness for so
many blessings every year being presented before me, I
should have appealed to those patients who enjoyed them,
to aid me in erecting a suitable house of prayer—a church,
in fact, for divine worship according to Anglican rites, which
I found celebrated in a stable loft when I first visited Kissingen in 1836 ! The appeal was not made in vain : a handsome
and commodious edifice has since risen, duly consecrated,
in which divine service has been since celebrated twice each
Sunday, from the commencement of June to the 15th of
September, supported by voluntary contributions and
donations. The entire cost of the building and appur-

tenances being paid and any debt extinguished previously
to my relinquishing Kissingen, the sacred trust was committed to the Colonial and Continental Church Society, whose
zeal and continued exertions in successfully promoting measures for religious worship among English communities in
foreign lands are well known. That I have humbly contributed to the spiritual as well as to the bodily benefit of my
patients who visit Kissingen, will ever form a pleasing
recollection, which will follow me to my grave.

To an indifferent spectator, not a sufferer himself from
any formidable disease, a day in Kissingen presents him
with a spectacle more impressive than the most showy
dramatic procession. I may commence by saying that it is
almost always fair weather in Kissingen during the months
of what is called the " Kur." The blessed sun is the great
helper in such matters, and no sooner have its rays tipped
with gold the verdant hills on either side of the valley,
through which flows the sluggish Saal, and in which the
springs are found, than an alarum from a band of
brazen instruments awakens both the sound and the un-
sound inhabitants to rise, and for the latter to repair at
once to the fountain of health. Two of these, the principal
springs, the Pandur and the Ragozi, are quaffed in goblets
holding each about four ounces of water, either at its
natural temperature of 45° Fahr., exceedingly pleasant to
the taste and refreshing from its effervescence, or warmed
slightly by dipping the glass for a couple of minutes into a
copper basin of water kept ever on the boil for that
purpose on the spot. But for any further description or
instruction I must refer my readers to the volume already
mentioned, as I do not feel disposed to go over the same
ground again.

It is a local fashion, or rather the habit of the German
physicians authorized to practise in the place, to plant

themselves under and against some particular tree close to the pavilion (due to the liberality of King Ludwig) under which the two principal springs are situated. This tree, henceforth sacred to the man who chose it, marks the spot where they listen to all such of their patients who choose to consult them on his or her malady. The applicants are speedily dismissed with their laconic instructions, and thus a long file of them are to be observed going up to the oracle, whisper a few words, answer two or three questions, and being dismissed for another and yet another waiting in their turn to go through a like ceremony. The farce is sufficiently ludicrous : that it can be of any use to either party except the doctor, may be readily conjectured from the fact that the pulse is never felt nor the state of the tongue ever inspected, for in truth what lady patient, though she be a German, would open wide her mouth *sub divo* and exhibit its interior?

I suppose that my brethren of the Alemannic race would refer me for an explanation of their mode of consultation to the primitive ages of gastrology, in the times of good Hippocrates and Galen, when patients placed themselves in front of their own dwellings and waited for the passing of the great healer, who inquired into and prescribed for the case. A much more selfish feeling guides the German. He has only to pay his medical counsellor once for all at the end of the treatment, and may in the mean time go up to the oracular tree to interrogate its deity as many times as he pleases, albeit he is often dismissed with only two words and very little comfort.

I adopted a very different practice. Each of my patients was visited every day at home. His symptoms and condition noted down in a little day-book left with the patient, in which the kind of water to be drunk, and the quantity, the baths to take, and their temperature, and many other

A A 2

particulars respecting the pulse, state of the tongue, &c.,
were registered, and this day-book I carried away home
when patient and physician parted company at the conclusion of the season.   As each book began with a brief
description of the case as it appeared at first sight, written
in Latin, I had little apprehension of doing harm to the
patients by enlightening them too much on the nature of
their ailments, whilst to myself a collection of such records
has proved of much interest and advantage in a professional
point of view.   But such a *ratio medendi* could only extend
to about twenty or five-and-twenty patients daily, and that
number I was able to visit each day by having my own
carriage, which I brought with me from England, when I
found the distances rendered it an absolute necessity.

It would be only repeating myself were I here to give
a description of the scene which presents itself to the eye
at six o'clock A.M., the first hour at which patients are
expected to attend. "Le spectacle," as a Frenchman would
say, " qui s'offre à un étranger," is one of the most interesting we can imagine.   The grand pavilion, the alleys, the
colonnade, parterre, which were an hour before in the still-
ness of the grave, now resound with the Babel-buzz of many
tongues, scarcely drowned by the harmonious resonance of
the orchestral instruments close at hand. It is a scene full of
interest, for here some hundred individuals, leaving behind
home comforts and probably home affections, seek relief
from bodily sufferings by going through the same process
they see hundreds of other fellow-sufferers do, with an
earnestness and precision that bespeak their faith in the
remedial efficacy of the measures they are adopting.   And
what encouragement, in truth, is it not to an invalid to
behold many who were as ailing as himself when they
arrived, and perhaps worse, getting now gradually and daily
better! and to others who associate or group together day

by day at the wells, to talk over their own case, to be able
to form comparisons between their own and other people's
cases, deriving comfort in consequence! Speaking professionally, I assert that this daily operation of the mind
among a congregated mass of well-educated persons labouring under chronic or recent functional ailments, is calculated
to, and does, produce wonderful sanative effects. Nor is
another of the peculiarities of this mode of treating maladies
less useful or encouraging in the way of obtaining successful
results ; I allude to the knowledge of the fact that many
among the nameless crowd are persons of high standing in
society by rank, learning, and talent; persons not likely to
be easily swayed by mere fanciful appreciation of fashionable doctrines or prejudices. Such a fact itself forms an
additional encouragement to faith in the virtues of the
mineral water treatment. Hence I hold the distribution
of a list of arrivals of new visitors, setting forth their
rank and profession, which takes place early every morning
at the springs and promenade, to be productive of a good
effect, besides supplying a fund of curious, amusing, and
often interesting information.

Doctor Grimm, an eminent physician connected with the
Berlin court, was present at Kissingen in 1854, when we
had occasion to converse on these metaphysical considerations connected with the treatment of disease by mineral
waters. We were sitting in a long line of patients resting
on chairs for a while (against their doctors' orders), and
noticing particularly the people as they went by. I had
the " Kurliste " of the day in my hand, Dr. Grimm, himself
a Prussian, had I might fancy his " Almanach de Gotha "
by heart. Thus informed, we watched and scanned the
most notable of the persons as they marshalled up and
down before us. They had each their particular history,
but I cared not to keep it in remembrance.

"But now look there," said Dr. Grimm. "Here comes one who, if I am not mistaken, will in a few years hence become a very influential character in Austrian political questions; whether for good or for evil depending on the mind and calibre of whoever it will be his destiny to encounter during his career of a state minister. We have his name here inserted," and Grimm read to me, "Seine Excellenz Herr Graf von Hohenthal, Königlicher Sächsischer Wirklicher geheimrath, ausserordentlicher Gesandter und bevollmächtigter Minister am Königlichen Preussischen Hofe."

"By-the-by," I said to Dr. Grimm, "this reminds me of a gentleman and his wife of the name of Beust from Dresden, whom I attended last year at the Hôtel Bellevue. Mr. or Baron Beust was said to be Minister of Public Works in Dresden, and to have an elder brother prime minister of Saxony."

"Quite correct," said Grimm. "We consider him in Germany a statesman equal to Metternich, and his Saxon countrymen look upon him as a man of first-rate genius entirely lost at the petty court of Saxony. For such a mind a vaster field is needed to expand and work out his destiny."

"I am inclined to believe you, for I remember what the sister-in-law, Baronne Beust, used to tell me. She herself appeared a most interesting person, as much endowed with intellectual accomplishments as she was gifted with natural charms, and she looked forward to a great destiny for her relative." Looking to the political affairs of the Austro-Hungarian empire within the last few years, the presentiment of the fair baroness has become a matter of history.

My friend Dr. Grimm was Leibarzt seiner Majestät des Königs von Preussen, General Stabsarzt der armee und geheimer ober Medicinalrath. He was a hale man of about forty years of age, and likely to live as many more. Yet I doubt whether he looked forward to paying another visit to Kissingen twelve years later, under circumstances very different from the peaceful scene we were now surveying together. We never dreamt of the great battle of 1866, when his valuable services would be put in requisition. The good doctor's acquaintance with the English language was such as to make our discourse a matter of difficulty, and he preferred the French language, "the common idiom," as he called it, "of travellers." We therefore had frequent recourse to it, as in the present instance when I quitted him, saying, "Ah, voilà la Princesse Esterhazy qui descend de sa barouche," and I proceeded to meet the princess, who went through the usual doses, walking the while, in which latter exercise I escorted her but a short time, her highness being presently surrounded by numerous friends, admirers, and relatives, for her arrival had been duly recorded in the "Kurliste" of the day— Prinzessin Esterhazy, *née* Louise Gräfin Almasy, ambassadrice," &c.

Our acquaintance had commenced in London under some ridiculous misunderstanding, arising from a supposed personal likeness in me to her husband, which some pretended was really striking (with the exception of a glass eye), a likeness, by-the-by, which had caused me some droll vexations in London. On subsequent occasions, however, my personal acquaintance with the prince became direct and official, he having had the commission of remitting to me in the name of his sovereign, Ferdinand, an enamelled clasp with a large letter F in brilliants on a blue ground, to be worn on the left breast. With the princess herself our summer acquaintance ended in a letter from her in reply to one or two from myself, occasioned by some *contretemps* that supervened in the transmission of some *petits souvenirs* sent by the ambassador's messenger, or by private hands, in both which instances we were equally disappointed. Here is her letter:—

"Vienne, ce 12 Août.

"Il me fut impossible, cher M. le docteur, de répondre plutôt à vos deux aimables lettres, et je laisse à votre amour propre la croyance que je fus bien contrariée par mon silence. Il se trouvait déjà au commencement de l'hiver une lettre pour vous en route, mais mon ambassadeur l'avait portée pas plus loin que Ratisbonne, tout au plus à Nuremberg, ce que les gazettes vous auront appris, car le Prince Esterhazy me rapporte la lettre à Vienne avec la malheureuse croix brisée en pièces. A mon retour à Vienne j'ai trouvé le petit paquet que vous avez eu la bonté de m'envoyer par la Chancellerie de l'Etat; mais il est décidé que je ne dois pas porter une croix Anglaise, car je l'ai trouvé brisée en huit pièces. Le cœur Anglais me resta seul et en entier. Je voulais donc vous envoyer une seconde fois la croix, mais il fallait qu'un ambassadeur devienne malade dans notre capitale pour entraver encore une fois mon intention. Malgré tous ces contretemps je vous remercie infiniment de votre complaisance, et j'espère que j'aurais l'occasion de vous remercier moi-même au courant de cet été à Kissingen, où je compte de me rendre au commencement du mois de Juillet. Venez-y et envoyer d'aimable Anglaises et Anglais. Adieu, dans l'espoir d'avoir le plaisir de vous revoir.

"LOUISE C^{TESSE.} ALMAZY."

Two periods in the year 1838 deserve to be noticed, as full of personal interest, not unmingled with much that refers to public advantage. The season for visiting the British Association for the Advancement of Science, of which I was a life member, and which was to meet in August in its migration at Newcastle, had arrived, and a most agreeable arrangement had been made of reaching that destination by a large steamer named the *Ocean*, which was lying conveniently at a wharf at Blackwall. We embarked and steamed off on Friday the 17th of August. It was perhaps the first argosy rich with an intellectual freight that ever left that almost unknown littoral, for therein were assembled the heads of the different sections of the Association, celebrated professors and members of every learned society in England, including not a few of the dons and square caps of Oxford and Cambridge. The principal saloon was crammed. I heard the name of Martineau mentioned ; and on the table lay her recent "Society in America." I directed my attention to a part of the saloon where a party were taking their breakfast, and amongst them I beheld the fair authoress herself much fêted, though the other works which were to cast a

greater *éclat* on her name in subsequent years had not yet
seen the day nor thrown a new light on political economy.

At a luncheon given by Mr. Greenhow, the geologist,
Miss Martineau being among the guests, I had the
advantage of being introduced to the gifted authoress,
an introduction that naturally led to interesting conversations on subjects which my own early travels suggested,
and which she mentioned it was her great desire and
intention to perform at no distant period. It is surprising
(some say not) how quickly and sympathetically this communion between a man made wise by age and experience
and this highly-gifted maid of Norwich was brought about.
I esteem this fortuitous meeting with Miss Martineau as a
good fortune. It certainly made the passage from London
to Newcastle very pleasant, and placed us on a footing as
if we had been acquainted for years. We have never met
since! I do not think I can accuse myself of having
adopted laudatory language in speaking favourably of
this clever Englishwoman, because she had herself commenced our acquaintance by a very flattering opinion she
expressed to me and others on a work I had very
recently published respecting Germany, a country Miss
Martineau said she was " very anxious to visit, as Madame
de Staël had done," whose memory Miss Martineau seemed
to me to revere to an almost superstitious degree.

During the different meetings of particular sections of the
Association, I took a slight part in their transactions and
diverse academical labours and investigations whenever
they offered any temptation, either on account of the subject
matter treated, or in view of listening to some eminent
reader or speaker. My business was with the medical
section, and in it I took my part most earnestly, and I fear
in some degree perhaps in a manner chargeable with a
fractious and touchy disposition in my address, having

thereby contributed, no doubt with many more testy speakers, Scots and Northumbrians, especially in having brought about that state of oratorical bewilderment both in the section itself and (by adjournment) at the general meeting also, which led to the entire suppression of the medical section from the original scheme of the British Association. But how could a physician (for example) of age and experience be expected to listen unmoved to medical rhapsodies uttered in public with unabashed temerity, and not refute them? Such was the case in one instance as regards my encounter with a *savant* and M.P., which, while it lasted, was a fierce one, albeit it never interrupted the respect and esteem the two litigants entertained for one another. Sir John Bowring had just returned from the Levant, and a certain return called for by Parliament had just informed the world that he had received a consideration from one of the principal branches of the government, to the amount of some thousand pounds, for visiting Syria, Turkey, and other parts, as well as for looking into the public accounts of France and Belgium. What must have been my astonishment to hear Sir John (thus qualified) at one of our meetings, 24th of August, 1838, in the medical section, utter such expressions as these: " that the doctrine of contagion in plague was an illusion to be laughed at," while the existing European records of recent date had almost overwhelmed us with contrary evidence?

Sir John had brought me a letter of introduction from my good friend Angeloni, the Italian *litterate* and staunch advocate of Italian independence, then residing in Paris. It were useless to reiterate all the arguments, or to recall the many examples of destructive plague introduced into several districts of Europe, owing to the relaxation or absence of quarantine laws. The latest melancholy reports laid before

government respecting Noia, Malta, Cephalonia, and of some
of the lazarettes of the Mediterranean ports were quoted in
vain. Neither did all the official documents corroborating
my assertions appear to be of any avail. "Had not Sir
John" (asked his supporters) "travelled in Turkey and
Syria, &c., by order of Lord Palmerston, to collect evidence
and all requisite information, for which the public had paid
suitable compensation on the recommendation of the Right
Hon. the Secretary of State for Foreign Affairs?"

In the face of all these observations directed at me, what
other line of debate could I have adopted but to urge my
opponent to make use of more substantial arguments, and to
oppose facts to facts, such as I had alleged, in the room of
mere idle declamation or of other matters foreign to our
discourse. Our warmly-contested discussion did not conclude with the adoption of any positive resolution by the
section, but served to revive at the distance of a few years
later the identical question in the House of Commons,
much in the same way or spirit it had been conducted at
Newcastle, although it terminated more consistently with
truth and for the interest of that very national trade which
injudicious people were nearly destroying utterly by consigning England to the list of infected nations.

The attendance at Newcastle was not "all work and no
play," neither was it the converse, as some captious auto-
crat from Printing-House Square took pains to make its
readers believe in the spirited columns of the leading
journal. The nobility and gentry of the neighbouring counties and the neighbourhood of Newcastle itself dealt out
their unstinted and gracious hospitality to the strange
visitors, making them welcome within their own cheerful
and well-appointed mansions. His Grace of Northumberland, at his princely castle of Alnwick, led the way. The
Earl and Countess Tankerville were not backward in

affording to the southern *savants* curious in natural history an opportunity of observing, as closely as it was safe to do so, and from under a most hospitable roof, the still surviving wild bulls which have added celebrity to Chillingham ; while Lord Ravensworth, a nearer neighbour, received his guests all day and entertained them with a *féte champêtre* in his enchanting grounds at Ravensworth Castle.

To the gentry no member of the Association had greater reason to be grateful for acts of politeness and good offices than myself, who was received by the charming family of the Brandlings at Low Gosforth, close to Newcastle, yet away from its smoke and noise. More than one member of that agreeable family may survive to peruse this acknowledgment of their kindness and attention to the writer, who at their table had the good fortune to dine by the side of the great Scotch Teniers, David Wilkie, who, with Sir Thomas Brisbane, Edheim Bey, Andrew Combe, and other notabilities, often adorned the cheerful and animated circle round the Brandling table.

An invitation to dine at Alnwick Castle was turned into a *séjour* of three days at the suggestion of the duchess, joined to the very tempting offer of Lord Prudhoe, who had just returned from Egypt, to exhibit before me a fine collection of interesting antiquities, including specimens of mummies, which he had displayed in a series of rooms on the ground-floor of a colonnade on one side of the *Cour des Princes*, or principal court of the castle, where one beheld two feudal pieces of ordnance standing one on each side of the entrance into the vestibule and great staircase.

Both at the meetings of the Association and at his own table the duke had conversed seriously with me concerning agricultural science, His Grace being a model farmer, whilst I, since the scheme of the Martin's Thames Improvement Company, had paid much and varied attention to the composition of manures, as described in some of my writings. On this account the duke submitted that I was bound to remain at Alnwick a short time longer, that he might drive me round to his farms, and show me how he had engaged his attention on agricultural matters. This was accordingly done on the 22nd of August, 1838. An open phacton, with a pair of smart horses driven by the duke himself, attended by his "Master of the Horse" and two grooms, took us round twelve miles of a walled *enceinte* inclosing several farms and a vast domain in the highest state of cultivation.

In the act of explaining to me some of the particulars of one or two of his model farms, I had occasion to allude to a "Petition" I had very recently circulated for subscribers' names, addressed to the general committee of the Association for establishing an agricultural section in the society. The idea struck His Grace as a very appropriate and necessary measure, and his name was therewith added to the petition, which I generally carried about in my pocket. His name was followed by one hundred other names, and the petition for the creation of a new section for agricultural science was deposited by me with one of the local secretaries the day after.

It was rather a curious coincidence that Her Grace the Duchess, whose guest I thus found myself to be, had been among the first distinguished patients I was called upon to visit with the celebrated physician and anatomist, Doctor Matthew Baillie.

It was about the middle of the year 1838 that my intercourse with Lord Palmerston recommenced, during a strange eruptive epidemic rife among the better classes of society in London. There had been some cases among well-known and distinguished persons that had proved fatal, so that people began rather to quake when any of their friends became attacked. Lord Palmerston, who had enjoyed the best of health since the cholera up to the 17th of June, 1838, requested my attendance at the Foreign Office on that morning, and received me in his *sanctum sanctorum* —I mean his own innermost bureau in that retired part of his office which looked over the park, and in which he used to shut himself up in front of a tall standing desk daily to read more attentively the despatches or official papers he had received and opened in his own spacious receiving-room. Here, in this contracted and innermost *sanctum*, he wrote all his replies and notes, never sitting down to do it ; and upon this high four-legged desk I had to indite my brief prescriptions or directions. There was a little settee in one corner, and a single chair by its side, so that two people might rest if required, but I would defy any third person to find room in this *vrai cabinet*.

" You do not enjoy a very large proportion of pure air, my lord, in this snug box," I said.

" No ; I get that in the morning early, when I take a ride round the park, enough to last me for the day. I cannot write in a large room, it prevents me reflecting, and as I never require an amanuensis, but send all my *brouillons* to the under-secretaries to get them copied by clerks, my little snuggery here I find quite sufficient. No foreign minister or other applicant of any sort is admitted within these four walls. Possibly you will have to see me again more than once. Mine, indeed, is more of a surgical than a medical case, for which reason I rejoice that you combine so well the character of both branches of the profession. I do not care for the public knowing I am undergoing medical treatment, and therefore I have asked you to come to me here."

My attendance continued daily from June to September, and had become at last tedious and disagreeable to both patient and doctor. I had pretty well exhausted all my

chatty and desultory subjects, including those connected
with science, physiology, and chemistry, of which Lord
Palmerston, an old *élève* of the High School of Edinburgh,
had imbibed much knowledge. I had no other subject left
for a pleasing conversation with my patient, until at last
his lordship entered into the consideration of some political
questions, at which I had reason to rejoice, since it offered
me most propitiously a chance of divulging my views of the
Italo-Austrian question, which was just commencing to
engage the attention of English statesmen and legislators
with more or less judgment, yet with a scant amount of
historical or statistical knowledge of Italian affairs, respecting which we were destined to read not long after so many
extraordinary speeches from Brougham, Smythe, Disraeli,
and sometimes even from Lord Palmerston himself.

At length I was able to take my leave, as I considered
him for the time quite cured, but with the promise that in
the course of a week or two I would renew my visit to
give him some general directions for the preservation of his
health, and (I might have added, though I did not just
then) " for giving satisfaction to your clerks in Downing-
street, who grumble sadly that your lordship keeps them
for hours from their dinner two or three days in the
week."

With all the bantering way Lord Palmerston had, and
his apparent readiness to enter into any humorous attempt
to make light of what in reality was serious, his lordship
had a remarkable and distinctive feature in his ostensible
character, which at once served him to maintain that sort
of insular and unapproachable position which precluded all
possibility of establishing familiarity, or even mere domesti-
city. He thus kept himself aloof from all entanglement
and compromise when the accredited diplomatic angler
approached the official estuary of this Foreign Minister of

State, to cast his hook into a pretended clear stream, his lordship suffered him to fondle with his line under water. Full play was allowed before the last jerk was given to the hook, which invariably returned to the mortified angler without either the bait (all swallowed) or the prize, leaving behind only aslight quiver on the water, as if it were merely a smile. The fact is, that in all that Viscount Palmerston undertook to handle and carry to a conclusion satisfactory to himself, he considered his own judgment preferable to that of the best man, nor would anything make him deviate from it, though his resistance was so managed as never to be mistaken for mere obstinacy.

To this peculiarity of character may be attributed more than one great failure in his lordship's foreign policy. Carried into private life the same characteristic feature has produced disastrous results. One glorious opportunity of immortalizing his name Lord Palmerston had had thrown in his way, by sharing in the bold and original device of an Italian state minister whom Sir Robert Peel, in addressing the House of Commons in June, 1861, considered to have been the most conspicuous statesman that ever directed the destiny of any nation on the Continent in the path of constitutional liberty. Lord Palmerston, ignoring, or affecting to ignore, the difficulties and dangers which encircled the course of the great Italian minister, Cavour, questioned his policy, and censured his conduct. The magnificent scheme of the regeneration of twenty-five millions of long-enslaved Italians was too grand in my lord's conception, that it should be permitted to emanate from any other than his own brain. Hence all his friends in the House, whether liberal or indifferent, taking the hint from their leader, who had bestowed the damaging praise of a faint approbation on Sir Robert Peel's proposed commendation of

Cavour's genius and sagacity, proceeded to abuse the Italian cause as it was proceeding steadily under the councils of that long-headed statesman and the troops of Charles Albert, the constitutional sovereign of the north of Italy.

He was "a treacherous and midnight assassin;" "the Piedmontese robber;" "the violator of Austrian rights made sacred by old and solemn treaties;" at the same time the Italians were declared to be incapable of enjoying political liberty! Brougham, Smythe, e tutti quanti, joined in sneering at the great work going on, perfectly ignorant of Italian history, or perverting its pages for a purpose, as I demonstrated in my second letter addressed through the press to Viscount Palmerston.*

However, the question was beyond the cavils of parliament, hesitating ministers, or blundering politicians. A provincial government in my own native city had already broken the Austrian yoke, declared allegiance to Charles Albert as he was passing downwards into Italy and stopped at Pavia to receive a royal address. His Majesty declared that he was determined to conduct the military operations with the utmost activity until Italy was completely freed from the foreign yoke. And so Italy is. What a marvellous result! what other analogous example in ancient or modern times can history offer to our admiration, and how deeply and for all time to come will those born in my fatherland declare themselves indebted to that Savoyard prince, who risked his whole to rescue us Italians from a long-enduring and shameful thraldom that had rendered

* "The Italian Question : a Second Letter to Lord Palmerston, G.C.B., M.P., &c., with a refutation of certain misrepresentations by Lord Brougham, Mr. Disraeli, and 'The Quarterly Review' respecting the rights of Austria and the Lombardo Venetians," 1848. A former letter, addressed equally to Lord Palmerston, was intitled "On the Formation and Constitution of a Kingdom of Upper Italy." 1848.

our name a political cypher, our country a geographical expression, a mere accident, our own nationality a mere by-
word for scholars, artists, and antiquaries, unacknowledged
as of any weight whatever in the political balance of Europe!
But now there is a kingdom of Italy! What green cloth
shall again invite the heads of European puissances around
it, to determine on the fate of any one other member of the
European congress and throw aside or affect to take no
account of the majesty of Italy? Into how many combinations or alliances shall not my native land be asked or
invited to enter henceforth with the influence, the weight,
and the prestige of a first-rate ruling power? She, poor,
dear, beloved country, whose name we, her unfortunate
helots, were almost ashamed to pronounce! Oh, the
glorious change! Thanks to the Divine Disposer of worldly
events, and next, to those staunch, inflexible, sharp-witted
patriots who knew how to bring about those events which
had been so often dreamt of but never attempted in serious
earnestness.

To Vincenzo Gioberti, a professor of the Turinese University, and afterwards President of Council and Minister for
Foreign Affairs, appertains the glory of having first struck
the right spark that was to fire the pent-up combustible.
It is remarkable how quickly a group of earnest patriots
who had determined to begin were able to bring about important results. History will tell more in detail all the
transactions through which the actual roots of the Italian
kingdom were planted.

In a mere record of my own doings in this world I need
only refer briefly to those political transactions herein alluded
to which were in connection with the glorious cause I took
a part in, and in which I can justly exult. The very
moment I learned that "La Società per la Confederazione
Italiana" had been established, and that the opening of its

first congress would take place on the 10th of October, I addressed a letter of adhesion to the president of the society. My letter, after other matters, called the attention of the assembly to certain publications in England which have reference to Italy, especially in a publication by Mr. Whiteside, barrister, entitled " Italy in the Nineteenth Century," and also in the " Quarterly Review," which attaches much importance to the work.

Matters went on after the meeting of this assembly in a steady manner, until an actual constitution was set up and a house of deputies elected, who accepted an hereditary monarchy with responsible ministry in the royal family of Savoy, as I had all along advocated and maintained in every one of my public writings.

That once accomplished, it became me as a new subject of Charles Albert, from choice and free will, though not by born allegiance, to submit to the sovereign the expression of my adhesion, as I had done in the case of the spontaneous popular assembly which had proclaimed the independence of my native country. I therefore addressed a first letter to his Majesty, placing myself entirely at his disposal, and when circumstances had called me again, a month later, to defend with my pen the rights of Italy to independence, not less than the just claim she had to choose her own sovereign, I did not hesitate to repel the pretended arguments of certain false and ill-informed politicians in England, by addressing to the English Minister for Foreign Affairs my second letter, a copy of which the Italian minister in London, Count de Revel, forwarded to Charles Albert, from whom, as well as from the president of the Parliament, I received appropriate acknowledgments and thanks.

I owe it to myself in an affair of such weight and from which such important consequences have resulted, to leave

a record of the language I considered it my duty to hold
with the august personage whose political rights I was
endeavouring to uphold as far as a private individual
subject could with his pen.   My following address to
Charles Albert on this occasion, the original of which will
be found in the Appendix, was more explicit :—

   " SIRE,—By the courtesy of your majesty's minister,
the Count de Revel, I had the honour of placing under
your majesty's eyes about four weeks since the copy
of a publication I had addressed to the Minister for
Foreign Affairs in this country, Lord Palmerston, written
in English, entitled, On the Formation of a Kingdom
in Italy in the north, under a constitutional monarch
selected from your royal house.   It is an old favourite
project from my youth, which I have always had at
heart and cherished, and on account of which I suffered
not a little both under the French and Austrian system.
The pamphlet in question had scarcely appeared, when
most of the high-placed public men of England set up in
arms against its principles and recommendations, some
laughing at the idea of 'Italian Independence,' others
scouting the notion of the Italians being capable of enjoying
political liberty; most politicians contending that the rights
of Austria to the territory they occupied in the peninsula
was their own by hereditary and indefeasible law, not fit
for mediation as proposed between the courts of Turin and
Vienna.   The complete ignorance that prevails in this
country respecting the true nature and character of the
Italians on the one hand, and the unceasing machinations of
Prince Metternich to prop up the Austrian interest on the
other hand, have tended to keep the English community in
perfect ignorance as regards the Italian question.   With a
view to mar this species of plot against our rising fortune,
and expose the errors disseminated by tricky orators and

paid writers, and on the same occasion to demonstrate the right we possessed to a national independence, well merited indeed after the noble and arduous efforts due to your majesty, I addressed a second epistle to the same lord, a copy of which in its original language (which we are aware is well known to your majesty) has been forwarded to Minister Gioberti, who will probably agree with me that, translated into Italian, the said pamphlet might offer some advantage to the country.

"May God lead your majesty on to a fortunate issue in the noble cause of Italy so worthily commenced, checked only for a moment, and now again smiling with promises of success.   Once Lombardy delivered from the stranger, and the throne of your majesty, as the sovereign of a united kingdom planted in my native city of Milan as the capital, I shall hasten from the banks of the Thames to salute the national banner, to revisit my paternal Lares, and beg your majesty to accept me among the number of your subjects who consider themselves happy to serve so good a king in such a great public cause.

(Signed)   " The Chevalier Auguste Bozzi-Granville." *

* I had before this been made Knight of St. Maurice, as well as of the Crown of Wurtemberg and of St. Michael of Bavaria, which latter entitles me and my descendants to the prefix of " von " or " de " before our name, which, however, I have never taken.

CHAPTER XXII.

A journey to Russia—Icebound—Reception by Prince Tczernicheff—Society in St. Petersburg—A Russian christening—The Waterloo medal—Its acceptance by the Emperor, and singular disappearance.

In the midst of the movement and bustle which the intrusion of the Italian news and commotion had occasioned in my tranquil *ménage*, I had a hint given me that it was possible my presence on the Continent might soon be required on professional business, and that if I took a decidedly partisan side in political questions of such high interest I might be made to suffer personally, considering how unscrupulous and revengeful the foreign police were acting under superior orders. The hint was not thrown away, for it so happened that just about that time (we were then in the spring of the year 1849) I had received from the Princess Tczernicheff, the wife of the Russian Minister of War at St. Petersburg, a proposition for me to proceed to the Russian capital in order to attend her in the summer. To such an arrangement I could not have any possible objection. With the Russian people my intercourse had always been of the most friendly kind, and my work on St. Petersburg had secured me their good-will. I had therefore only to look askance at the chancellerie of Prince Metternich and his myrmidons, and keep clear of his clutches. This, in the event of my deciding to accept any such engagement, was of no difficult accomplishment. I had only to choose the sea instead of a land line of communication with Russia. When, therefore, a downright proposition came from the princess, who was very pressing in her request, not concealing her apprehension of danger at her own situation, and when the prince himself, as well as their friends in England, joined in the solicitation, I yielded, and undertook to be in St. Petersburg at the appointed time, weather and wind permitting. The middle of June was the expected period, and for the occasion I had the good fortune of securing the services of one of my best nurses, who has remained in the family ever since.

The arrangement over the water I may say was of the easiest; not so the one on this side, although I was happy in finding able substitutes in my profession to undertake the charge of ordinary patients, no engagement of the same sort existing on my list, I having for some time relinquished the active practice of that branch of my profession. A series of homely letters will best describe my voyage, which proved not uninteresting. They were addressed to my wife and youngest daughter Paulina, the only one of our children left to us, the others being grown up and scattered about the world. I sailed from Hull on Sunday, the 6th of May.

"At sea. Tuesday, 8th May, 1849.—My dearest Mary and Lina,—Not knowing whether we shall be admitted for a long stay at Copenhagen or not (as there appears to be some ill-feeling towards the English on the part of Denmark), and as they may subject us to the recently established quarantine in their ports on account of the cholera, I commence my letter while on our slow, slow way to that capital through a rough sea, and with the wind, which has been incessant, directly in our teeth; so that instead of ten or twelve miles an hour, the utmost of our progress through the water is five and a half miles. At this rate we shall not get to Copenhagen in a hurry. The weather is extremely fine overhead, the sun shining brightly. You may judge by my handwriting whether I am tossed up and down and from one side to the other while I am inditing this letter, it being a matter of difficulty to write steadily or at all. All the passengers more or less, except three or four of us, have been ill all along, but especially on the first day, Sunday. The *City of Aberdeen* is a splendid ship for size and its accommodation, but she is a horrible sea boat, rolling and pitching ten million times more than our old *Batavier*. The effect on myself on Sunday was to make me heavy in the head, muzzy, and very sleepy. I did nothing but sleep on a sofa, and it was all I could do to keep up and awake during prayers, which were read, and after them a sermon, very impressively by Captain Knocker, who is a lieutenant in the navy on half-pay. He and I were in the same English fleet at the capture of the Russian fleet at Lisbon at the end of 1807, and went together at that time from the Tagus to Spithead, when I was promoted to a full surgeon and soon after fell in love with a certain young lady who shall be nameless, with whom I have been well acquainted and happy ever since. Can you, Mary, remember the circumstance? The only passenger of any note on board is the gentleman whom you saw in the same carriage with me in the train, a most gentlemanly man, acquainted of course with all my acquaintances and many of my patients, being a brother of Mr. Cox of Hillingdon. We had a long chat together. What an appalling death that of Horace Twiss! While you and I were standing on the platform together that morning, I held in my hands the dismal article in the journal which gave an account of that sudden disappearance of our friend. Such is life! And how true it is that we ought always to be prepared to quit it!

" 10th May: in the Kattegat. You Londoners can hardly form an idea of the serenity, beauty, and softness of the air we are enjoying at this moment, with a sea calm and blue as a sapphire, the sun warm and brilliant, though the wind is cold still. I feel invigorated already. . . . 6 P.M. We have just arrived safe, with splendid weather and in the best health, at Copenhagen, anchored opposite the Marine Promenade, which is full of beaux and belles staring at us. We remain the night, and probably to-morrow."

From the same to the same.

"Off Copenhagen. 11th May, 1849.—I broke off my letter suddenly last evening on our arrival before the capital, that I might avail myself of the opportunity of a Danish passenger going on shore immediately to post it, with the chance of its going off the same evening, so that it will reach you about the 15th—the very day we expect to reach St. Petersburg, that is, two days later than we calculated on reaching that place had not the wind been all along dead against us; for although a steamer makes its way despite of wind and sea and, I may now add from experience, icebergs, its onward progress is much retarded when all those impeding elements are to be overcome. Copenhagen makes no show on the sea-side, especially at that part by which we approached it from the north. There are so many advanced batteries and fortified isles and wet docks which mark the city, that you might fancy yourself before any indifferent military maritime town. The expanded and extended view which most important cities of sea-board display along the shore, Copenhagen offers only (and that in a moderate degree) when you have passed it a little way further south as you proceed into the Baltic, as I had occasion to verify this afternoon, when we left our anchorage at 3 o'clock under the most charming sky, with a fresh breeze and a warm sun, and started upon the second half of our adventurous voyage. Copenhagen is unquestionably seated in a most unfavourable aspect, presenting its whole face to the broad, blighting east and the chilly north, the sun in its meridian scarcely warming the interior of its streets and squares, and in the western descent lighting up its suburbs and fortifications only on the land side. It stands, moreover, on an island, and these circumstances combined give it a doubtful character for health. I felt the chilling and depressing effects of this combination of unlucky physical features soon after our arrival ; for having remained on the paddle-box for an hour or so, to watch the approach to the town, and on our coming to an anchor under the gaze of thousands of eyes surveying us from the ' Lange Linie,' a species of marine promenade, I was not long in experiencing the untoward effects of the chilling atmosphere, which made me beat a retreat below in the saloon, where I endeavoured to restore again the natural heat I had lost by donning my wraps and getting near the fire till tea-time, though I did not escape the almost inevitable and usual result of such an exposure, viz., a severe cold in the head within the twenty-four hours, which has plagued me the whole evening after and to this moment of writing. A great treat, which indeed I had forgotten to expect on visiting Copenhagen, and which I enjoyed most intensely, was the inspection of what is called the Thorwaldsen Museum. You recollect we saw at Munich, in churches, in the king's palace, and at the Glyptothek, some of this sculptor's magnificent productions. These are all here reproduced, whether in their original marble or in plaster, besides some hundred originals by the same indefatigable sculptor, who was a Dane by birth, and died in this city at the age of seventy-four, after having resided in Rome the best part of his life, where he acquired an immense fortune and an imperishable name. When it became known that he had settled to return to his native place, his countrymen determined to give him a triumphant national reception.

As Thorwaldsen approached Copenhagen (this occurred ten or fifteen years since, I believe), hundreds of boats in procession went out to meet him, headed by the principal people of every rank and station and profession. Nothing could equal, they say, to this day the splendour of such a reception, which moved the good old man to tears. On the outside wall of this Thorwaldsen Museum, which has been erected by subscription since his death, in shape, size, and architecture resembling a great Egyptian temple, the representation of the marine procession in all its stages, the landing of Thorwaldsen, and his reception by the king, has been painted in fresco with figures of the size of life. Altogether I may say that this visit to the receptacle of the works of one of the greatest sculptors of modern days is worthy the laborious voyage to the revered cradle of the artist. As I spent most of my time in the museum (and it was too short), you may imagine that we had little spare time left to go anywhere else. Our time was limited to four hours, but with the aid of one of the heavy one-horse flys—somewhat like those at Brussels—we, Mr. Cox and I, under the escort of a *valet de place*, while the vessel was taking in seventy tons of coal, contrived to see the interior of the principal royal palaces, stables, and the Frei Kerche, or principal Lutheran church, to the top of which we ascended to survey the city and take in a panoramic view of its streets, squares, principal edifices, and the surrounding country. The general view is not more striking or impressive than was the survey of its interior. The country is not pretty, nor is the aspect of the inhabitants, male or female, very prepossessing. I saw no indication of wealth, still less of luxury. The ladies appeared to wear dresses of the fashion prevailing among us ten or fifteen years ago. The appearance of the men, even the *bourgeoisie* and better classes, with clothes of coarse materials, ill-made, and the

absence of all clean linen about the face was very unfavourable. The men are bulky, with round, thick waists, almost all
alike, short-necked, bull-headed, red-faced, light hair, with
peculiarly blue eyes—a very distinct race, decidedly, from
other European people. The ladies not particularly attractive. The general aspect of the capital is by no means ugly.
It is remarkable for large wide streets flanked by extremely
lofty houses several stories high. The shops are placed on
what would be the first floor, opening on the streets, with
many steps to get to them. Under these are lesser shops,
level with the street—'the Oster Gade,' for example (a
sort of Regent Street)—which are tolerably splendid.
But passengers on the pavement have no chance of peering
into their interiors, and can only judge of their wares by
what is displayed behind the large panes of glass forming
the square, flat, ordinary windows of the lower floor of each
house. In many parts one could fancy himself in some
large provincial town in France or Belgium; but in other
places the streets and squares have a physiognomy entirely
their own. They consist of rough-hewn stones without pave-
ments; and along each side of the street deep gutters or
open sewers convey the entire drainage from the houses. Over
a few of these drains a wooden covering is laid, movable at
pleasure, for the convenience of carts or foot passengers.
In many parts they are left uncovered, and then besides the
stench which is generally prevalent in consequence, there is
the disgusting sight of all that falls out of sinks and wash-
tubs to proceed in streams down to the port, with the water
of which it mingles to scent the landing-place, not very
sweetly even for such deadened olfactory nerves as the
chlorine gas has left me.

"May 12th, 1 o'clock, P.M.—We are running fast, steaming northward to reach the Gulf of Finland. Various
reports reached the captain as regards the state of the ice,

the upshot of which is that we shall not find the sea free from ice at Cronstadt before the 15th or 16th.

" May 13th, Sunday.—We are yet 350 miles from Cronstadt, entirely owing to the contrary winds and the slow steaming power of the vessel. It is not likely that we shall reach our destination before Tuesday afternoon. On awakening this morning at my usual hour of six o'clock, I found it was snowing very hard, and the wind blowing fresh, the prospect all around us very dismal. But soon after breakfast the sun again came forth to cheer us, and by the time we had congregated together in the saloon, the first as well as the second class passengers with the crew, for divine service, the weather became moderate and serene. We had an excellent sermon from a young chaplain who is proceeding to St. Petersburg to relieve the Rev. Edward Law, brother of my friend and patient, William Law. Soon after the sea began once more to swell, the sky to be cloudy and threatening, and we were again tossed about finely, when in your imagination I dare say you concluded I had reached my destination. I have never suffered so much from cold as I do now, and am not prepared with any clothing to face the quarter deck. Still I go up to it for the sake of a walk, but I invariably come down with a fresh cold in my head, and sneezing and coughing. I have often longed for my Greek capote.

" 14th, Monday.—The weather became less boisterous in the night, and it is now twelve by the sun (not 10.30 with you). We are going to our luncheon, and you, I suppose, have not long finished breakfast. The cheerful sun and a moderate breeze have raised our spirits, my own especially, for I cannot divest myself of the anxiety I experience at every apparent delay at the heavy responsibility I incur. We observed in the distance two large vessels coming down the Gulf of Finland, full sail, looking as if they had just left Cronstadt, and we augur from it that as we approach that port to-morrow morning we shall find an open sea; if so, we hope to be at anchor by two'o'clock, and unless detained by official forms we may be at the Palais Tczernicheff by dinner time to-morrow, the 15th.

"11 o'clock at night.—It is truly remarked that the tide of human life never runs smooth, and the same may be said of the sea. We were rejoicing at the prospect of going through clear water, having at sunset made the port of Revel, not more than 150 miles from Cronstadt. The sunset was most brilliant, when, whilst writing, a terrific thump on the side of the vessel, which stopped the engines, made us all rush upon deck one after another. I cried out, 'A touch, a touch,' thinking only that we might possibly have got on one of the numerous shoals or sandbanks with which the gulf is strewed on either shore. But on reaching the deck we discovered that the great thump had been occasioned by a huge iceberg running against the side of the vessel, fortunately not at right angles. The spectacle before us at this moment was grand in the extreme. The twilight, which at this time of year never ceases in these latitudes, threw a warm and picturesque light on the scene, and showed us as far as the eye could extend a field of frozen water of dazzling white and blue tints, broken up into huge masses, each of the size of our two drawing-rooms put together, floating sometimes together, at other times apart, through which our brave *City of Aberdeen* made her way, breaking, cracking, pushing, and dispersing the various pieces of ice, which, as they rattled passing along the side of the ship, produced a solemn, rumbling noise, like that of subterranean thunder. But we soon became accustomed to both sound and sight, except the one we should have wished to prolong, that of some groups of two or three seals or of some single indi-

vidual, all in every stage of age and development, presenting themselves in a variety of graceful attitudes on some
iceberg here and there, viewing us pass unmoved, or
tumbling headlong into the pool of water by their side with
something like a baby cry. Nothing was more charming
than this impromptu comedy, or more impressive than the
notion it suggested that these interesting creatures, with
their smooth, well-chiselled forms and intellectual eyes,
were at that moment working within their well-rounded
cranium a problem as to what this *catalysis* in their kingdom could mean or portend. I had determined to remain
up all night and continue on deck to enjoy this grand new
and striking scene, but at three o'clock I got very cold,
and went to lie down, dressed, on one of the sofas in the
saloon. At four o'clock Mr. Cox came down to tell me we
had broken both paddle-wheels. We were standing motionless: not a vestige of blue water was to be seen; the sun
was up, huge icebergs or ice fields indeed encompassed us,
and the vessel lay immovable, giving us not inaptly though
but a faint specimen of that much more awful scene in which
poor Sir John Franklin has possibly found a grave at the
North Pole.

"15th May. — On examination it was found that the
iron circle of one of the wheels was torn asunder. Whilst
proper artificers were set to mend it, the captain took
counsel with us principal passengers as to the best and
most prudent course to adopt as soon as the damage should
be repaired; whether to endeavour to continue onwards, or
to retrace our way through the free channels we had come,
and take shelter in the port of Revel. You may easily
imagine, dearest Mary, that this state of hesitation to me,
who am the only passenger tied to time, was a consideration
of great anxiety. On the supposition that the captain
would really go back to Revel, I made up my mind to land

and set off post to St. Petersburg in a gentleman's carriage then on board, which would have been intrusted to me. The distance is two hundred miles, and I could post it in twenty-five hours. But even our way back to Revel was not free from danger of the ice we passed since eleven o'clock last night, so the point was finally determined in favour of going on to Cronstadt. Fortunately, the wind becoming somewhat favourable, we were able to set some of the sails, and with them (putting out the fires, the paddles consequently fixed) we broke at a slow, solemn pace the surrounding fields of ice, noticing at the same time that most of it, from its dirty surface and the marks of footsteps, must have been detached from land, and consequently showing that further up towards the land we were bound to, the mass of ice must have moved and given way to come down into a wider sea. Be that as God may please, we are again, and have been for some hours, in the direct track. Some ice is seen on our left far off, but we avoid its course, and trust in Providence not to be further impeded, still less to be made fast or jammed in the midst of icebergs. Of course all chances of reaching Cronstadt this evening are done away with, too fortunate and happy if we do so to-morrow.

"16th May, 12 P.M.—Another twenty-four hours are gone, and not only are we not at Cronstadt, but at breakfast time this morning so fast beset and bound all round by thick ice, that we trembled for the safety of the ship. In attempting to push through, as we beheld clear water a long way ahead of us, the flimsy wooden floats of the paddles kept snapping off one after another like glass. Near us we knew lay a shallow shoal, on to which we feared being drifted irresistibly by the ice. A little beyond on our right were three small desert isles, and between them and us a seal disporting himself in the sun on the hard ice, his natural region, in mockery as it were of our

distress and presumption in intruding upon his domain. At
breakfast all was dejection. The captain said nothing, but
looked unutterable things. My fellow passengers gazed at
each other. I felt for the disappointment of my waiting
patient. But the fear for life soon silenced that sensation.
Thank God! the repaired paddles backed us out of the
midst of the ice, and we were once more in clear water;
and after making two more attempts to see if we could discover a fresh opening in the ice to carry us into the living
water we beheld before us, we gave up for the present all
further attempts, and are now lying-to afloat, waiting the
chance of a change. You can easily imagine, dear ones,
whether at this moment I feel at all happy or at my ease
as I think of the anxiety of the princess and her family.
The luncheon bell has just sounded. I leave off writing,
but shall not partake of the repast.

"Four o'clock, P.M.—At last the attempt has proved
successful, thanks to the great heat of the sun, which fortunately shone forth in all its splendour, and the wind also,
which became stronger and favourable. We chose the
weakest point we could discover in the ice, broke through
cautiously where it was stronger, and aimed at reaching a
very distant spot on the horizon, which through our spy-
glasses looked like blue or living water. After meandering
for three hours through this maze or labyrinth of icebergs,
we did at length emerge into the clear waves, all the sea
open before us, the lighthouse of Cronstadt in sight at this
moment, seven o'clock, P.M. At nine we shall be at anchor,
but we shall not move off up the Neva till to-morrow,
making exactly two weeks since we left London.

"Cronstadt, Friday, 18th May.—Embarked in a small
steamer for St. Petersburg, and at the landing-place opposite the English commercial hall was an officer of the État
Major waiting to inquire if I was on board the steamer.

Upon showing myself he instantly galloped off to announce my arrival, and presently young Prince Leo, with his military tutor, appeared on the mole. I stepped on shore, and was soon driven to the prince's palace with the young prince, where I was most warmly and cordially received by the princess, her daughter, and Prince Tczernicheff himself. I was soon installed in a most sumptuous apartment in connection with the princess's extensive rooms, where I dressed and dined. Got into a most comfortable bed, slept over all my voyaging troubles, and here I am quite well, 19th May, after breakfast, concluding my long epistle, which must be in the post-office *viâ* France within an hour. God bless you both, and return me as good news as I send you.—A. B. G."

On reading over these epistolary records of my life in the Russian capital, revisited for an occasion that required particular and precise attention, I find the reality of "things as they were" so perfect that if I am to say what I did during the summer months of 1849 in that city, I cannot adopt a clearer or more straightforward line of narrative than the preceding letters represent. I shall therefore continue to hold the same course awhile longer, until I have accomplished the important object for which I had been called a second time to the banks of the Neva.

"This day last week I posted my first letter, a journal, in fact, of my proceedings from the day we left Copenhagen to the moment of my arrival and installation in this magnificent palace. I shall follow the same plan in this and any subsequent letters until I start for Kissingen or home. As I told you, every preparation to lodge me in the most luxurious manner possible had been made. Bed-room and dressing-room, and an adjoining *salle* in which my writing-table is placed, provided with every species of stationery, a profusion of secretaires

and drawers, and a large breakfast table, couches and set-
tees, a splendid French clock on the chimney-piece, and
flowing drapery at the windows to exclude at bed-time the
wandering horizontal sunshine. Here I receive my visits,
several of which, from medical men high in the army, I
have already had. The aspect of my rooms is excellent,
and as we have no night, or darkness at all events, from the
first to the last of the twenty-four hours, my rooms look
perpetually gay, whether I am going to bed or getting up.
For although I feel quite ready and do go to bed between
eleven and twelve o'clock, the day is already begun, and I
can read plainly without my excellent carcel-lamp, which
is lighted as a matter of course in the evening, and left
burning, though I am never in my rooms till bed-time.
This being the Hôtel du Ministre de la Guerre (the post
my princely host occupies), is furnished, warmed, lighted,
and served throughout the year at the expense of the
government, and consequently everything is done with profusion and well. On the day of my arrival we dined at
home. In the evening the Grand Duchess Constantine
came with her husband, and remained to play cards till
twelve. The princess told me privately that Her Imperial
Highness intended consulting me about her own health
before I left for England.

"Upon having my first serious conversation with my
patient last Saturday, the princess told me she proposed
that the expected event which had summoned me from
England should take place at a country house about one
hour distant from town, on one of the islands in the Neva,
lent to her by the emperor for the occasion. This information rather disappointed me, but as I am to visit the said
country house in company with the prince, to see if I
approve of it first, the question remains suspended for the
present. There was a grand dinner here to-day, which

took place in the state apartments on the first floor; a splendid suite of rooms like those, Mary, you and I remember in the Tuileries. There were present, Countess Nesselrode, Prince and Princess Bariatinsky, General Boutourline and his lady, Princess Sherbatoff, General Baron Wrewsky, aide-de-camp to the emperor, Baron de Loevenstein, my old friend Doctor Ardnt with his bride (Miss Chillingworth), who has exchanged her situation as governess in Madame Boutourline's family for that of the wife of the first civil physician in the capital, full of wealth and honours, master of a magnificent hôtel of his own in one of the most fashionable streets near the court. He is an excellent man, with a European reputation, and lived most happily with his first wife, whom I knew well. The present wife may be about twenty-six years of age, whilst he admits to be sixty-three, though in appearance he might really pass for forty. He is now undergoing the routine of fifteen dinners, which it is the fashion to give to a recently-wedded pair for the first half of the honeymoon by the families most intimate with the husband, and as the doctor is known to almost all the higher families, at the houses of many of whom I have since dined myself, I have necessarily met the lady as often, and discoursed with her in her native tongue. She speaks excellent French, but not one word of Russ. The prince introduced me to the English *chargé d'affaires* and to all his principal guests, who dispersed in about half an hour after dinner was over, such being the practice here as well as in France and Germany.

" Sunday, 20th May.—The prince sent me his carriage to go to church and fetch me from it, for which I was very thankful, as the English church is some distance, and the sun intolerably hot. After service I had a short conversation on the state of the English colony in the capital, and on certain rumours concerning the emperor, who is still absent in Hungary. In the afternoon a carriage fetched me to see Princess Bariatinsky's baby. . . . .

"The family went to the Russian play, which I declined, being Sunday, and I spent the evening pleasantly with the princess and a few relations.

"Monday 21st.—After my daily visit to the princess, I walked out with young Prince Leo, who comes regularly every morning after breakfast to ask me to walk with him for half an hour or so. He took me to see some of the new public buildings erected since my last visit. St. Petersburg has doubled in extent and fine edifices during the last twenty-one years. The prince had put his carriage and four at my disposal for the entire morning, that I might go and pay my visits of *etiquette*, especially to the leading doctors, and also to one or two English families.

"On Tuesday we dined at Madame Boutourline's. After dinner Dr. Pellican, the chief physician of the army, and Dr. Ardnt, both in attendance on the youngest child of the handsome mistress of the house, requested me to visit her with them in consultation, which took place at once in presence of the father and mother and the English nurse. The emperor had unfortunately left for the army two days before my arrival, and the empress had gone into the country the same day I arrived, and all the grand duchesses are out of town likewise. In the evening I escorted some of the ladies to the French play in one of the *théâtres de la cour*, and to-day we have been to visit the country house offered for the use of the princess, and report upon it. The prince had the admiralty state barge ordered, steered by nine pairs of oars and escorted by a colonel of marines, flags at the fore and abaft, &c., in which style we rowed up the Neva and down by a smaller branch for a short distance, a succession of most splendid views of St. Petersburg before my eyes, such as I had never imagined to find there, and I wonder how the Russians can be at all astonished at our river and its banks,* or at the sight of Venice or even Constantinople. I know nothing equal to the panoramas I witnessed this day. I can well understand the thrill of pleasure with which the fair partners of the worn-out ministerial or government *employés* hear their husbands propose a summer '*aux Isles!*' The house I went to see is not in a fit state to receive the princess, and I am not at all disposed to approve of it. It is far from ready, and appears damp. On our return in the afternoon we dined with Princess Bariatinsky, a most gorgeous banquet, served in princely style. Here I made several more acquaintances, and sat by the charming mother of the little sick girl I had prescribed for, who was very grateful, and in whose carriage I went after dinner to see the child, who was now doing well. I gave full instructions to the English nurse, who whispered to me, ' You have saved the child, sir.'

"May 24th.—The physician-in-chief of the army came in his carriage to fetch me to visit a new general military hospital erected since my first visit to St. Petersburg, and which had been suggested by Prince Tczernicheff himself, who has superintended the whole construction. We were received by about twenty medical officers, all in their uniform, as was my guide, and by the colonel-governor of the hospital. It is an immense and handsome building, capable of containing 1400 patients. I examined several patients, and tasted the food prepared for them. Everything was excellent. The establishment is quite perfect of its class, and my commendation of it gave the prince great pleasure, as he assured me. We dined quietly at home after our fatiguing morning.

* This was written, be it remembered, before our embankments were made.

"The principal occupation this day (Friday) has been a minute and extended visit to what is called here the 'État Major,' an immense establishment connected with the administration of the army, something like what we call the Horse Guards, but how gigantic! like every public establishment in this wonderful country. I went through every branch of the gigantic official development under the prince's own guidance. Eight hundred *employés* of all classes live and work together and are fed in the building, besides four hundred officers who attend daily at certain fixed hours. The sections in which military maps are constructed, fortification drawings effected, designs of military encampments devised, besides the department of the portable field press, are parts of this great department of the administration of their army of which the Russians are not a little proud."

"St. Petersburg, May 30, 1849.—Since last Saturday, when I posted my second letter to you, nothing particular has occurred beyond the ordinary events of a life passed in comparative idleness. We are still here, and do not leave for the country house before Saturday. I objected to the princess's apartment being on the ground floor and exposed to the north, and I am therefore to revisit the house and make fresh arrangements before the family leave town. Last Sunday I dined with my old friend the Countess Laval, where of course I met a prince and sundry counts, one of the latter son-in-law of the old countess, who has just reached the age of eighty-eight years, yet still as brisk and intellectual as when I first knew her years ago. We had a splendid dinner, and she made me promise to pay her frequent visits when I shall be in attendance on Madame Tczernicheff, as the house we were about to inhabit was at a short distance from her own in the country. I remained some time after dinner, and returned home at half-past nine and went to my room, as all the family, including the princess, had gone to the Russian play. Being Sunday, I was glad to spend the rest of the evening by myself.

" On Monday, the 28th, I went to the Alien Office to procure my *billet de séjour*, a permission granted on showing your passport and a certificate of the English consul of your identity. I got clear in less than half an hour, but it is impossible to have the faintest conception of all the difficulties, ceremonies, processes, examinations, papers, which a stranger has to undergo before he can obtain permission to remain, even after his admission into the territory at the frontiers or at Cronstadt. It is now even more strict than ever, owing to the general disturbances on the Continent. The principal officer asked me whether I had been in Russia before. On my answering in the affirmative, he inquired at what time, and I said about twenty-one years ago, in 1828. 'No,' says he, exhibiting a file of papers he had brought from an inner room. 'Do you know this signature?' pointing to the corner of a large blue printed paper. 'Yes, it is mine.' 'Well, look at the date; it is 19th November, 1827; namely, twenty-one and *a half* years ago, and not twenty-one only since you were here, and this is your *billet de séjour.*' I replied—'True, you are more exact than the police of the ancient République de Venise;' and I took my leave, paying for my new *billet de séjour* a tax of eighteen shillings. I shall have many more such ceremonies to go through to get away. What a country!

" During my absence General Boutourline called for the second or third time at my rooms to ask me to attend his niece, which I find also the princess is anxious I should consent to, it being considered from past experience to be likely to be a difficult case. I am myself not at all willing to attend any case before that of the princess, far less this one, as should anything adverse happen, it might have a bad effect upon her. I trust therefore they will not press it. I dare not go out in the daytime except to post my letters to you, the heat and sunshine are so great. I thought this evening I would saunter out along the principal streets and the quays of the beautiful canals. This I did from ten till twelve, the light of day being scarcely dimmed. The sight of all these gigantic buildings, swelled even to larger proportions by the additional light of the moon, is really magnificent. I walked for two hours in ecstasy: neither was I a solitary being in the streets, for thousands of droskies and people were on foot. Shops lighted up, billiard tables, clubs, palaces in a blaze of light, all showed the active life that was going on near and around me. There was a little fresh air, but on the whole the night was as hot as the following day. Vegetation bursting around, and the trees, bleak and leafless a few days ago, are now out in the luxuriousness of the middle of summer. To-day I dined with the Princess Meschersky. The lady had arranged the dinner with the view of procuring me the pleasure of meeting the principal physician-in-ordinary to the empress, who came from Tzarsco-çelo, where her majesty resides. I was much pleased with the man, and found him clever, shrewd, and intelligent, full of information, well acquainted with modern literature—including the English. I showed him one of my works, the famous coloured plates on the female constitution, which he admired greatly, and regretted the libraries had not a copy of it. The work made a great impression on him, as novel and original. He had never heard it mentioned among my other works, for the plain reason that it was never sold. As you, Mary, know, it was published for a limited number of subscribers. I imagine this very clever physician of the empress, who is covered with stars and resides in the imperial palace when in the country, has imperial equipages and servants, receives about twelve thousand roubles a year, or four hundred and eighty pounds, something like the sum I make in three months, with all my liberty and independence. There are two English physicians settled here : not one of them is known even by name in the circles I frequent. They only practise among the English. In former times none but English were employed, and preferred ; now the contrary is the case. The Emperor Nicholas has been striving to make the higher classes really Russians, and nothing but Russians or Russian Germans hold the sway. This extends even to the nurses. They say the English are too extravagant, and that they can procure as good nurses from Germany for half the money.

"It is the dinner hour, and I must dress, but I leave this letter open for anything that may occur before Saturday.

"Thursday, May 31st.—I read last night of the atrocious attempt made against our queen. Here also there has been detected a sort of conspiracy, and about forty young officers and civilians have been arrested and are now in the citadel to be tried. But not a word of the affair has been allowed to transpire in any of the papers. It was a mad scheme quite. From what I hear and read (for we have all the papers in the house), it would seem that my prediction, which you will recollect I told you of last month, is about to be fulfilled. I said that by the end of May the whole of Europe would be in arms. Is it not so ? Italy has now after all a better chance than ever. The emperor is still at Warsaw. The guards keep going off from here to different parts of the empire. The religious and military ceremonies of state in the Imperial Military Medical Academy, of which I am a member, by-the-by, I am to attend in my uniform next Tuesday.

"Friday, 1st June.—A regular engagement to attend the

countess in question was entered into yesterday, and I saw
the patient both yesterday and to-day. I am packing up
for the country house, exactly thirty-five minutes distant
from town.

"Saturday, 2nd.—We are in the very hurry of packing.
I take but few things, as I shall come to town daily. We
dine *en ville, en gala;* in the evening to the French play,
and at ten or eleven (all daylight) set off for the villa."

"Sunday, 3rd June.—After closing and posting my letter
yesterday, I went into the great cathedral of St. Isaac with
M. de Montferrand, who has been twenty-five years engaged
in this gigantic work, has realized a large fortune, and is a
grand seigneur. One of the most striking features on
entering the interior of the church (to which no one is
admitted except on strict business) is the exceedingly beautiful, strong, yet simple scaffolding by which you may ascend
to every height of the works, from the pavement to the
highest cupola, nearly two hundred feet from the ground. To
all these various parts I ascended with Montferrand without
being giddy in any place, except perhaps when I looked down
through the crevices of the boards on which I stood to see
some of the eminent painters paint their historical figures of
saints on the ceiling of a chapel one hundred and fifty feet
above the ground. There was not the smallest vestige of
danger in any part. It is impossible to describe all I have
seen of splendour in marble and precious stones and gold
employed in the decoration of this magnificent temple.
Montferrand gave me a copy of his great publication of the
various parts of this immense edifice, which will exhibit
better than I can do all its marvellous beauty when we
meet. I went to the grand dinner, and then to the French
play. The princess's *calèche* took me afterwards to the
country house, whither the whole family had preceded me
a few hours before. It was a most lovely night (day rather,

sans soleil), and I enjoyed the sight of the river and islands, on which are scattered all the principal villas of the seigneurs of St. Petersburg.

"Monday, 4th June.—I visited Madame O., whom I have agreed to attend, and whom I found had the good sense to promise to obey me, and to desist from eating and drinking everything to an enormous extent. After, I visited the President of the Imperial Academy of Sciences, Count Ouvaroff, who since my last visit to this city has been appointed Minister of Public Instruction, and lives in the house of the *Ministère*, which, like that of our prince, is of the most gigantic size, and splendidly furnished. Lucky these ministers are besides ; having coals, lights, and many servants, all paid for by the crown. He received me most cordially as an old friend, and proposed various projects of visits, &c., which I declined for the present, until the princess is doing well after the event is over.

"To-day, being Whit Monday, everybody is out, all the churches full, all the streets crowded, and not a few drunkards about. The truly Russian or Muscovite dress displayed on the occasion gives animation and interest to the scene, but oh ! how ugly both males and females are ! the latter more especially. With the exception of the high-born ladies I meet at the dinners (and these are not a few), I have not seen a good-looking woman on any day or in any class of the population. We had a grand dinner at home to-day ; people crowd out to see us, and keep their equipages waiting, either in the road before the house or (in the case of relations) in the great coach-yard behind the gardens. They play at whist *de préférence*, for money invariably, and set off at eleven or twelve o'clock to return home.

"Tuesday, 5th June.—I rose early, to go at ten o'clock, by the wish of the prince, who is the head of the establish-

ment, to see the Medico-Chirurgical College, at which all the
medical officers for the army are educated from first to last
for nothing.   Dr. Kruber, the secretary to the general who
commands the Institute, came to fetch me, and I started at
that early hour in uniform and orders, taking with me the
great diploma given me twenty-one years ago by order
of Nicholas, which constitutes me an honorary member of
the academy.   On presenting myself to the President in the
public theatre, where all the people were assembled at a
public examination in Latin, I claimed the honour of taking
my seat among the members as one of them, and not as a
stranger.   They rose and made me take a seat next to the
President, on his left.   After the examination, which was
conducted in a most creditable manner, I was accompanied
all over the various parts of the establishment by the
respective heads of each, and when concluded I found my
visit had lasted three and a half hours, so that I was
perfectly exhausted, but at the same time pleased at the
immense improvement and great changes that had taken
place since my last visit.

" 6th June.—One of my two anxieties is over.   Countess
O. is safe, and both she and the baby are doing well.
Another great dinner to-day, Prince Tczernicheff, Prince
Dolgoroucky, Prince Gagarine, Prince Meschersky, and
Prince Bariatinsky, princesses less by two, with the rest of
the party made up of counts, barons, &c.   I left soon to
run up to my patient at St. Petersburg.

" Thursday, 7th June.—A curious ceremony, at which I
was present, takes place in all Russian families when a wet
nurse is to be employed.   Madame O. would not nurse her
baby herself, and I had to choose a substitute from three
young women brought from the country.   The baby,
properly dressed, is brought by the head nurse into the
room and given to the mother ; then the wet nurse is

introduced, and asked by her if she is willing to take charge of her baby.   On the nurse answering in the affirmative, she makes the sign of the cross over her face, and stoops to kiss the hand of the mamma, who places a silver coin in the hand of the nurse, saying aloud, ' I consign this baby to your care ; be you as a mother to him,' and the woman sits down and proceeds to the duties of her office.

" Here nothing is heard of but war and rumours of war. All the regiments of guards, foot and horse, are *en marche* for the frontiers.   Every day one or two regiments leave, and all the young men of family, who are of course in the army, are eager to follow.   The husband of the lady I am now attending, who is one of the aides-de-camp of the Minister of War, hearing that a school-fellow of his, Count Strogonoff, one of the emperor's aides-de-camp, has just been killed in a battle with the Hungarians, has petitioned the prince to appoint and send him to the field of battle in his stead ; and yet he is very fond of his wife and children! Upwards of forty-four thousand men of the guards have left town, yet there remain still as many more behind, all lodged in most splendid barracks.

" June 17th, Sunday.—I am very anxious about the princess.   God grant this day may end prosperously for her !   3 o'clock.—The event is over, and a pretty little girl is added to the prince's family.   Some curious superstitious ceremonies were gone through by the Russian attendants (unknown to the patient), proving to me how *arriérés* this people are.   At dinner to-day, all the members of the family being assembled, I was thanked, and my health drunk by the prince.

"20th June.—I went yesterday to the christening of Madame O.'s baby.   The prince, after the ceremony and *déjeuner*, took me home, and again told me, as he has done before, with many others, that they wished I would establish myself in St. Petersburg, that I should have an immense practice. I shall ask the princess immediately to get my name announced in the Gazette, as it requires ten days before I can go, and I shall drive to the English consul and get my English passport made out for Germany. I would not exchange my English home for all the wealth I could be offered here !

"The ceremony of private christening I had never seen before. It is imposing, and conducted with the greatest decorum. Some of the nearest relatives are invited, besides the godfathers and godmothers, who by the ceremony become relatives as it were, the title being held in great regard in Russia and the Church, which forbids marriages between them. The priest, who brings a clerk, a man in plain clothes, is in his ordinary dress, beard and hair dishevelled, and hanging down, having a stole of red silk ; and subsequently, when most of the prayers are read and the real ceremonial part begins, he puts on the more pontifical over-tunic of gold brocade. The room is prepared for the ceremony : on a table between two windows a little altar is dressed, having two chased images and two candles, a bottle of oil with a camel-hair brush, a pair of scissors in a little red case, and a new shirt and cap. In the centre of the room is a portable font, large and deep enough to receive the baby with ease. It has the form of a gigantic egg-cup, of gold ; on its edge three lighted tapers, in the shape of a triangle, are fixed. Before the font the godfathers and godmothers stand during the entire ceremony, and in front of them the priest nearly the whole time. The father and mother, who had previously received their guests in an adjoining room, are quitted by the latter and shut into the room, as they must never be present at the ceremony. Being ranged on one side of the room, the priest reads several prayers out of the missal he holds in his hands before the altar. Then he reads a prayer in front of the godfathers and godmothers. At one period the latter turn their backs to him, and then in front again. All this time the infant lies in the nurse's arms on a cushion richly covered with lace and coverlets. It is already stripped. During these prayers the safety of the emperor and every individual grand duke and grand duchess, old and young, is prayed for in a very long litany, which is the practice at all religious ceremonies and in all churches. The child is then transferred on its cushion, and covered, to the godfather. The prince who stood as such behaved remarkably graciously and well throughout the ceremony, preserving a devout appearance, and holding a lighted taper, as did the godmother, which the priest had previously handed to them.

"The priest, after reading some other invocations over the water (which in this instance I insisted upon should be warm, though it was against the rules), crosses it with his hand over the surface three times, breathing at the same moment the sign of a cross with his mouth over the surface. This being done he takes the baby with one hand, while with the other he closes the eyes, ears, and mouth, and as rapidly as possible plunges the infant in and out of the water three times. After the last time, being wiped and restored to his cushion on the hands of the godfather, he puts on the new shirt and cap, and proceeds to anoint his forehead, eyes, ears, &c., with a brush dipped in the sacred oil. This is performed on two occasions, more prayers are read, and the ceremony is concluded, after which the company adjourn to the room where the parents have been locked up, the godfather and godmother leading the way, and restoring the baby in the most formal manner to the parents, with many felicitations. In the mean time the nurse, dressed smartly, and followed by a footman who has a large silver waiter on which is a napkin and several

champagne glasses laid down at full length, makes the round
of the company, beginning with the godfather and godmother,
offering them a glass of champagne, which she pours from
a bottle in her hand. The glass of champagne drunk,
with a toast to the new Christian's 'health and long life,'
the empty glass is returned to the tray, each guest deposit-
ing at the same time a note of one, two, three, or more
roubles as a present to the said nurse. A *déjeuner* follows
the ceremony, which in this case lasted one hour and a half.

"I visited Princess Mechersky in the evening, and afterwards received a message from the Grand Duke Héritier."

Before relating what took place at my interview with the
Cesarewitch, I must state that a unique copy of the Waterloo
medal by Pistrucci, struck in soft metal, and richly electro-
typed in gold by that celebrated artist, had been presented
to me in lieu of honorarium for many years' attendance on
him and his family. When I left England I took this
medal with me, with the intention of offering it to the
Emperor of Russia, whose brother, the Emperor Alexander,
was one of the four powerful allied sovereigns depicted upon
it, and to whose united arms the glorious conclusion of a
war of forty years was due. At that time neither Her
Majesty Queen Victoria nor any one else was in possession
of a perfect copy. I had requested to be allowed to present
it to his imperial highness, the emperor being absent with
the army in Hungary. The morning of the 21st of June,
1849, at 12 o'clock, was the time appointed to receive me,
and it was arranged by Prince Tczernicheff that his carriage
and four should convey me and Prince Waldimir Bariatinsky, his son-in-law, who was to accompany me to the
Palais d'Hiver. I took with me the Waterloo medal to
present to the emperor through his Imperial Highness the
Cesarewitch, an intention I had already communicated to
the whole of the Tczernicheff family, who had ample time to

admire the medal. On my arrival, the aide-de-camp de service, who had been informed by Bariatinsky of my coming, and who stood by the door of the inner room, requested me to wait. In less than three minutes the door of the inner room opened, two general officers with red cordons came out, and I was desired to enter. The reception I experienced was most cordial. His imperial highness took me by the hand in the most frank manner, saying, " I am delighted to see you at St. Petersburg, cher Monsieur Granville;" and he at once inquired after the health of Princess Tczernicheff, and " la petite nouvellement née," both of whom he informed me I had "treated admirably." Having satisfied him on these points, I took the liberty of asking after the Grand Duchess Alexandrina, a sweet child I had admired at Kissingen.

" Ah, mon Dieu! Vous avez donc du savoir comme elle a été malade? Depuis voilà à peu près six semaines elle a eu la fièvre, et aucun remède ne paraît lui faire du bien. Vous ne la reconnaitriez presque plus si vous la vissiez à présent."

I expressed my deep regret. A few more observations next followed concerning the many improvements I had observed in the capital since my first visit in 1827-8, and then I said, " Je tiens en mes mains un objet rare et d'une haute valeur comme objet d'art et de politique en même temps, lequel je désirerais présenter à sa majesté l'empereur qui se trouve dans ce moment absent de St. Pétersbourg, et je ne sais de quelle manière le lui faire parvenir. J'espérais cependant que son altesse impériale, une fois qu'elle aurait su et approuvé cet objet, voudrait bien se charger de la mettre en mon nom aux pieds de son auguste père."

I then opened the box and explained to his imperial highness that it was the first complete copy of the famous Waterloo medal, which the English government had caused to be executed by the celebrated Pistrucci of Rome, whose name was doubtless familiar to his imperial highness.

I first showed the grand duke the obverse side of the medal (which was handsomely framed in choice wood, and under glass, having a pivot in order to facilitate the examination of both sides without touching the gilt surface), explaining to his imperial highness the various symbols and allegorical figures; and afterwards the side on which the heads of the four allied sovereigns are sculptured in relief, whom the grand duke at once recognized and named. While looking at the obverse of the medal, his imperial highness admired the splendid display of art in the equestrian figures of Wellington and Blücher. But more particularly was he struck by those groups of Titans precipitated from heaven by the thunder of Jupiter Tonans, which represents the universal defeat of all the bad genii of revolution, demagogie, and anarchy.

" Oui, oui! " exclaimed the grand duke suddenly, " c'est très-beau ; et ce qui est plus, c'est très-vrai! Malheureusement c'est tout à recommencer! Ainsi, Monsieur Granville, vous voudriez offrir cela à l'empereur ? "

" Voilà précisément quel serait mon désir."

"Eh bien, je m'en charge. C'est vraiment très-beau, et l'empereur l'approuvera beaucoup ; et vous en aurez des nouvelles."*

From that hour to this in which I am writing these words, I have never had one word of official acknowledgment that the medal had ever been received; though, through Prince Tczernicheff, I learned before I left Russia that the Emperor Nicholas on his return had expressed great admi-

---

* "Yes, yes! it is very fine ; and what is more, very true. Unfortunately it has all to be done again.   And so, Mr. Granville, you wish to present this to the emperor?"   "That is exactly my wish."   "Well then, I will undertake it.   It really is very fine ; the emperor will highly approve of it, and you will hear about it."

ration of the medal, which he accepted as a present, and had given directions to the Ministre des Apanages dirigeant le Cabinet de sa Majesté Impériale, who was Prince Pierre Volkonsky, to acknowledge its acceptance, that is to say, with a token of the emperor's munificence, as is customary at the court of Russia. Be that as it may, nothing ever reached me; and this is not all, for on making inquiries several years afterwards as to the fate of the medal, I learnt that it is not to be found, either in the late Emperor Nicholas's collection, in that of the reigning emperor, or in that of the Imperial museum of the Hermitage!

I leave my readers to draw their own conclusions from these facts, by which it would appear that the emperor and his successor have been deprived of a magnificent object of art, estimated by the best authorities to be worth some hundreds of pounds, as a copy issued from the eminent artist's own hands, struck in metal, and I have lost the honour of an acknowledgment from the emperor by this example of ministerial morality in Russia, A.D. 1849.

CHAPTER XXIII.

THE CLOSE OF A MEDICAL LIFE!

It has fallen to my lot to close the autobiography of my father. I wish the task could have been undertaken by abler hands; but it being considered that as the only one of his surviving children who remained with him to the last moment of his life, I should be the one best suited to such a duty, I have undertaken it with mixed feelings of satisfaction and diffidence, well aware of my inability to do full justice either to the manuscript left in my hands, or to the notes and journals from which these concluding pages are partly taken.

After the interview with the Cesarewitch, just described, my father was called in consultation on the case of the Grand Duke Michael, brother of the Emperor Nicholas, who had desired to see him. The grand duke had just passed in review a train of artillery, which was leaving the capital for Hungary, at which review my father was near him and witnessed scenes of violence of temper towards generals and aides-de-camp hardly equalled in a lunatic asylum. It was in this state of mind he found him, and advised cupping, a regulated diet, avoidance of exposure to the sun or fatigue, the administration of certain medicines, and abstention from mineral waters containing steel, of which he had, since a visit to Kissingen, partaken of rather freely. His physician, the younger Sir James Wylie (who has since died suddenly) assented reluctantly, but did not carry out the advice. The grand duke, unrelieved by any remedial measure, joined the army, rode out in the sun,

and fell from his horse in an apoplectic fit, from which
he died scarcely two months after the consultation, aged
forty-eight.

During the time he remained in Russia, my father was
consulted by many families of distinction, and many propositions were made to induce him to settle in St. Petersburg ;
but he was too thoroughly an Englishman at heart to entertain for one moment the thought of relinquishing his home
in his adopted country, and declined all such offers, as he
had done on his first visit twenty-one years before, though
he fully appreciated, as he had done then; the kindness,
hospitality, and consideration with which he was welcomed
everywhere.

When the princess was in a fair way towards recovery,
my father accepted an invitation from General Boutourline
to accompany him to Moscow before his final departure from
Russia. Before, however, leaving St. Petersburg, I find he
gave a public lecture in French at the Medico-Chirurgical
College, and soon after started with the general for a flying visit to the ancient capital of the empire. But what
to many would have proved too short a time for observation
was sufficient for my father to fill several volumes of notes.
When travelling, it was his habit to be always pencil in
hand, noting down everything he saw or heard, to be
stored away for future siftings. Thus he gathered during
a stay of a few days only, sufficient information for a contemplated second work on Russia, to be entitled " The Two
Russian Capitals, or Sketches of the Present State of St.
Petersburg and Moscow." This proposed work, however,
which, from the headings of the chapters now before me,
was likely to have proved of great interest, never went
beyond a rough sketch, in consequence of Mr. Henry
Colburn, who by a clause in the agreement for " St.
Petersburg " had bound my father not to write a second

work upon Russia, refusing his permission except on inadmissible terms, although the former work was then out of print. For this reason the book was never written.

It was during this visit to Moscow that his attention was drawn to a new stimulant, used with much success as a vigorous excitant, which he afterwards introduced into England, writing a small volume upon the subject, which was published in 1858, under the title of "The Sumbul, a New Asiatic Remedy."

Upon his return to St. Petersburg he remained but a few days to take leave of his numerous friends and give his parting instructions for the benefit of his patient. He always retained feelings of the greatest esteem for the family with whom he had resided, and kept up an uninterrupted friendship with them to the end of his life, which closed twenty-one years later, only one month before the princess died at Rome, a widow, in the arms of the daughter at whose birth he had been present.

I cannot dismiss this subject without recording what I find my father has written as a tribute to the memory of Prince Tczernicheff : " He enjoyed the most universal popularity that a man in his station has ever enjoyed. Everyone esteemed and loved him, and gave him a most exalted character for uprightness, excellency of heart, goodness and kindness to all his dependents and officers, always glad to do good and render service."

On the 14th of July, 1849, my father took his final leave of St. Petersburg, reaching Cronstadt by steamer, then on to Stettin and Berlin, and so to Kissingen, where he arrived on the 21st, to find many of his English patients awaiting him. After remaining here a few weeks he set out for London, which he reached on the 1st of September, when my mother and I met him, and drove him to his house in the country where we resided in the summer.

The next ten years of his life were not unmarked by many trials and many sorrows, all of which he bore with that true spirit of Christian fortitude and resignation which was ever conspicuous in his character. His industry and perseverance in all he undertook were indefatigable, and I have never known him to be for one moment without mental occupation of some sort, even when not engaged in his profession. Taking always a keen interest in political events, it will be easily imagined that the state of Europe in 1853 greatly occupied his attention. The policy of English ministers, as regarded the Eastern question, then beginning to agitate Europe, he considered to be founded upon wrong premises, knowing as he did the state of the emperor's health, which had been no secret while my father was in Russia. The discussions carried on with Nicholas were shaped on the usual metaphysical grounds : my father considered that ministers should have been guided instead by a knowledge of the physical condition of the disputant, and it was in the hope that the prognosis of an experienced physician might put them on their guard, by revealing the undoubted state of the case, that he addressed the following confidential letter to Lord Palmerston from Kissingen, whither he had gone at the end of June, as was his yearly custom :—

"Kissingen, Bavaria. July 6th, 1853.

"My Lord,—Failing in my endeavours to meet with your lordship at the appointed interview at the House of Commons on the 22nd ult., at which I proposed to make a *vivâ voce* communication of some importance to the government, as I thought, concerning the present political discussions with Russia, I stated in a second note, written at the moment of my departure from England for this place, that I regretted the disappointment, inasmuch as the subject of the intended communication, from its delicate nature, did not admit of being committed to paper. I think so still. But, on the other hand, the necessity of the government being put in possession of the communication appears to me to become every day so much more urgent, that if it is to be of any use it must be made at once, or it will fail to direct ministers in time, as I think the communication is capable of doing, in their negotiations with Russia, and in their estimation of the one particular element which, I apprehend, has first provoked, and is since pushing on, the emperor in his present reckless course. Mine is not a political, but a professional communication, therefore strictly confidential. It is not conjectural, but positive, largely based on personal knowledge, and partly on imparted information accidentally obtained. It is not essential I should say from whom, for I take the whole responsibility upon myself, inasmuch as the whole but confirms what I have myself observed, studied, or heard on the spot. The western cabinets find the conduct of the Emperor Nicholas strange, preposterous, inconsistent, unexpected. They wonder at his demands ; they are startled at his state papers ; they cannot comprehend their context ; they recognize not in them the clear and close reasoning of the Nestor of Russian diplomacy, but rather the dictates of an iron will to which he has been made to affix his name ; they view the emperor's new international principles as extravagant ; they doubt if he be under the guidance of wise counsels. Yet they proceed to treat, negotiate, and speak as if none of these perplexing novelties in diplomacy existed on the part of a power, hitherto considered as the model of political loyalty. The western cabinets are in error. The health of the czar is shaken. It has become so gradually for the last five years. He has been irritable, passionate, fanciful, more than usually superstitious, capricious, hasty, precipitate, and withal obstinate—all from ill health, un-

skilfully treated ; and of late deteriorating into a degree of
cerebral excitement, which, while it takes from him the
power of steady reasoning, impels him to every extrava-
gance, in the same manner as with his father in 1800 ; as
with Alexander, in Poland, in 1820 ; as with Constantine,
at Warsaw, in 1830 ; as with Michael, at St. Petersburg, in
1848-9.   Like them, his nature feels the fatal transmission
of hereditary insanity, the natural consequence of unnoticed and progressive congestion of the brain.   Like them,
he is hurrying to his fate—sudden death from congestive
disease.   The same period of life, between forty-five and
sixty years of age, sees the career of this fated family cut
short.   Paul, at first violent and fanatical, a perfect lunatic
at forty-five years of age, is despatched at forty-seven in
1801.   Alexander dies at Taganrog in December, 1825,
aged forty-eight.   For five years previously his temper
and his mind had at times exhibited the parental malady
by his capricious and wayward manner of treating the
Polish provinces.   He died of congestive fever of the brain,
during which he knocked down his favourite physician, Sir
James Wylie, who assured me of the fact at St. Petersburg
in 1828, because he wished to apply leeches to his temples.
Constantine, eccentric always, tyrannical, cruel, dies at
Warsaw suddenly in July, 1831, aged fifty-two years, after
having caused rebellion in the country by his harsh treatment of the cadet officers.   I saw and conversed with him
on the parade and in his palace at Warsaw in December,
1828.   His looks and demeanour sufficiently denoted to a
medical man what he was, and what his fate would be.   It
has been said that he died of cholera ; again, that he had
been despatched like his father.   The physician-in-chief of
the Polish military hospitals assured me some years after
that he had died apoplectic, and in a rage.   Michael, after
many years of suffering from the same complaints which

afflict his only surviving brother, became, in 1848-9, intolerably irritable, violent, and tyrannical to his own officers of the artillery and engineers, services of which he was supreme chief. In July, 1849, he consulted me at St. Petersburg. . . . To complete this disastrous picture of the grandchildren of Catherine, their mother, Maria of Wurtemberg, a most exemplary princess, died apoplectic in November, 1829, scarcely more than sixty-five years of age. The attack, mistaken for weakness, was treated with stimulants and bark by her physician, Buhl, and bleeding was only had recourse to when the mistake was discovered—but too late to save. . . . During my second sojourn in St. Petersburg, in 1849, for a period of ten weeks, what the opinion was of the emperor's health, what acts of his came to my knowledge which bespoke eccentricity, what were the sentiments of his physician, Dr. Mandt, who, homœopathist as he is, and exercising a most peremptory influence over his master, leaves him, nevertheless, unrelieved, except by mystical drops and globules—what transpired of political doctrines and opinions, or, in fine, what I gathered afterwards at Moscow on all co-equal points, must be left to your lordship's conjecture—not difficult after all I have divulged. To go further would be like a breach of trust, and of that I shall never be guilty. In all I have related there is nothing that has been committed to me as a privileged communication; while the imperative requirements of the moment calling for its immediate divulgement, I hesitate not to make it under the firmest conviction that my fears and anticipations will be surely realized. If so, then the method of dealing with an all-powerful sovereign so visited must differ from the more regular mode of transacting business between government and government. For this purpose it is, namely, to put Her Majesty's ministers on their guard accordingly, that I have determined to place in your lordship's hands the present professional information, which must be considered as so strictly confidential that I shall not sign it with my name. That I have selected your lordship as the channel of my communication, rather than the Minister of Foreign Affairs, to whom more properly it should have been addressed, will at once appear natural to your lordship. In my capacity of once and for some years your lordship's physician, . . . your lordship has known me personally, and is convinced that what my pen commits to paper may be taken as coming from an honourable man and your obedient servant."

By return of post an acknowledgment was received in Lord Palmerston's handwriting :—

"11th July, 1853.

"MY DEAR SIR,—Your letter of the 6th has been duly received.

"Yours, ..."

But this timely professional warning was unheeded, as events but too truly showed. Who knows how many thousand lives and millions of money might have been saved if, on receipt of the above warning, instead of continuing for months together all sorts of unprofitable arguments, peremptory language and peremptory action had been employed, leaving no time to the imperial and real " sick man " for the infliction on his own people, and those of the three nations allied against him, of that irreparable mischief which by the Crimean war he was suffered to perpetrate ? It was thus that Pitt dealt with Paul. But— there was no Pitt then. · This I find was so firmly my father's conviction, that at an interview with Lord Palmerston subsequently, on the 23rd of February, 1854, on matters of a private nature, in answer to his lordship's question before they separated, as to whether he still adhered to his opinion and prediction about the Emperor of Russia, he replied, that before July, 1855, when the emperor would be fifty-nine years old, what he anticipated would have happened. "Let but a few reverses overtake the emperor," he added, "and his death will be like his brother's—sudden." And so it proved : Alma, Inkermann, Balaklava, shook the mighty brain. Eupatoria completed the stroke, which anticipated my father's prognosis by only a few weeks. The prediction of the pathologist was accomplished. On the 2nd of March, 1855, the Emperor Nicholas expired, and my father's letter to Lord Palmerston, dated Kissingen, July 6th, 1853, had become an historical document.

Having previously acquainted his lordship on the 3rd of March of its intended publication, the letter appeared in the "Times" of March the 5th, and was copied by a large number of daily and weekly journals. As it may be supposed, this letter was a nine days' wonder. Everyone was full of it, and on referring to my father's journal I find he was for a time beset by people stopping him in the street and addressing him at the club, whilst many frightened patients came to tell him their parents had died apoplectic at the fated age, and they wished to consult him as to their own chance of life !

This *prediction*, as it was, or *foresight*, as it should have been called, was merely the result of careful study of a subject which had long occupied him, and which resulted in the book he published in 1854, entitled " On Sudden Death." This important statistical work cost him many weary months of incessant labour, turning over the " Black Book " in the Registrar General's Office in Somerset House. It was a subject of deep interest to him, involving as it did so much of the study of life, so much of the result of disease. The work, which was very generally and favourably reviewed, he had intended should be followed by a second volume to be entitled " On Longevity," some of the unpublished manuscript of which is in my possession.

In 1859 my father's last work on mineral waters appeared, " The Mineral Springs of Vichy," the result of a rapid excursion from Kissingen in the summer of 1858. Nothing had then been written in England upon those waters, and he thought an account of them might not prove unacceptable in a country where patients were beginning to seek relief at those springs. The book was written in his usual easy and popular style, fitted for the perusal of all, contained much matter of general interest, from actual personal investigation of one who had for years made his indefatigable study those " stupendous gifts of Providence for the relief of human bodily suffering," which he was wont to consider all mineral waters to be.

It was whilst at Kissingen, in July, 1859, that my father received the news of Mr. Hamilton's death, the early friend who through so many years had ever proved his staunchest supporter, one to whom he had been indebted for many acts of sincere friendship, and for whom he long and deeply mourned. Sorrows were now indeed coming on apace. My mother's health, which had been failing for some time, began utterly to give way, and after two years of great sufferings this devoted wife and most exemplary mother to our inexpressible grief died almost suddenly, on the 1st of November, 1861. My father never seemed quite himself after this blow. The world began from that moment gradually to lose its interest for him. At times he rallied, but it was always to return to the same idea, as to the probable time of his own death, and re-union with those " not lost, but gone before." He went about his usual occupations, attending to his old patients, some of more than forty years' standing, but he relinquished by degrees his profession in London, continuing only at last his practice at Kissingen, to which Spa I invariably accompanied him. It was soon after the death of my mother that he again had great pecuniary losses from the failure of a firm in which he had embarked large sums of money for the establishment of one of his sons. One great satisfaction, which he has himself alluded to, was yet in store for him, this was the opening and consecration, in August, 1862, of the English Church of All Saints in Kissingen, the first Anglican Church in Roman Catholic Bavaria, which owes its existence entirely to my father's unremitting zeal for a number of years in overcoming all difficulties with the Bavarian government, and in securing by his untiring exertions the subscriptions of those through whose munificence the church was built, and finally, after failing in the offer made to the Society for the Propagation of the Gospel, delivering it over in 1868, free of debt, into the hands of the Colonial and Continental Church Society, who since his death have erected a brass tablet to his memory in the sacred edifice as the founder of the church.

Of the last few years of my father's life but little now remains for me to say. His last published work appeared in 1865, at the most critical period of the great London sanitary question of the day—of water, sewage, and manure, and has already been mentioned in these pages. It was written with the desire to do justice to a departed man of genius, whose plan for effectually freeing the Thames from pollution and of applying the polluting matter as a source of profit to the land, the Metropolitan Board of Works have adopted without the smallest reference or allusion to him, or to those patriotic individuals who early came forward with their money and influence to support and, if possible, bring to a happy issue so original and national a scheme, undertaken by them in the form of an intended joint-stock company, of which my father was one of two managing directors, and was the loser of a considerable sum of money, that company undertaking more than thirty-five years ago to carry out every one of the measures which the Metropolitan Board of Works have now all but accomplished "piece meal," as their own architect has declared before Lord Robert Montagu's committee.

In 1863 my father completed his eightieth year, and until then, as he has often assured me, he had never felt an old man. From that date age seemed to creep upon him fast. His bright clear intellect was undimmed, but his bodily health became enfeebled, though he was able to continue his summer visits to Kissingen as late as the year 1868, when he had a most brilliant season, surrounded by numbers of his old patients, amongst whom were the Russian family he had gone to St. Petersburg to attend in 1849. All seemed to have come to Kissingen to consult him for the last time.

On our return to England he determined never to leave it again, and having finally relinquished practice he commenced writing his autobiography. Amongst his immense bulk of diaries and correspondence he soon became so absorbed in memories of the past as to lose almost all interest in passing events, except only as they might affect his friends or his children. And so the time passed quietly in London, but the end was drawing near. His mind, always imbued with a deep sense of religion, began to dwell much on that other world to which he was fast hastening. Simple and childlike was his faith. He would never allow that the deepest scientific researches ever conduced to scepticism : he saw the hand of God in everything, and as rapidly increasing infirmities came upon him he seemed only the more patient, waiting for the time when he should be summoned to his rest.

In 1871 we left London to spend the winter at Dover, hoping that the sea air might give him strength, which at first it did; but he was not able to write for so long together as formerly, or to read aloud to me as was his custom, and it is to this circumstance I owe being in any way in a position to finish the work he had begun, for in anticipation of never completing it himself, he would relate to me as we two sat alone in those long winter evenings how he would wish me to proceed with the book when he was gone.

Soon after the New Year of 1872, the first symptoms of his last illness showed themselves; * palpitations of the heart, and great difficulty in breathing, quickly followed by a bronchial attack, the progress of which he himself watched as he would have done one of his own patients in conjunction with that able Dover practitioner, Dr. Sutton, whose kindness and attention were unfailing to the last. But my father, with all his experience and scientific knowledge, knew the end had come, and it was with difficulty he could be induced even to take nourishment. " The end has come," he would repeat; and so it was. After five weeks' intense suffering, with a heart prepared for the great change, he passed away on Sunday, March 3rd, without a sigh, conscious to the last, and whispering in my ear, " Light, all light," as he most truly fell asleep in Jesus. . . .

My task is done! To dilate upon my father's character, which to the most refined and polished manners

---

* Whilst going through that portion of my father's manuscript which gives an account of his state of health when as a young man he was leaving England to study in the Paris hospitals in the year 1816, I cannot but be struck with the extraordinary resemblance of the symptoms, identical in every respect with those of his last illness. It would almost seem that his youth, his wonderful determination and energy had power to overcome and keep in abeyance throughout his long life a malady which once more asserted itself when age had come—the mainspring of life, the desire to live was gone, and the fiat had gone forth that it was his " Time to die."

united a nature all nobleness and kindness, incapable of retaining a resentment, would be a labour of love, but it would be but a daughter's tribute to a loved and revered parent's memory. I prefer quoting in conclusion portions of a letter from Sir Charles Douglas, one of his oldest patients and friends, the words of which may, I think, yet find an echo with many who are still living :—"I have known your father above forty-eight years ; during the last forty-two, very well. I had the highest admiration for his talents and learning, and in my experience (long and varied) of the most renowned medical men, I never knew one of whose powers, resources, skill, attention, and care in illness, chronic or acute, I could compare with his. To his long experience in the most varied practice he added to the last all the vigour of youth, combined with the safety resulting from the most profound knowledge of his profession. It has for many years been a saying of mine, ' If Dr. Granville cannot cure, no human aid can avail,' and I have always entertained a grateful sense of the value of his medical advice to and care of me and mine. . . . Within a week I said to my medical attendant, who was urging me to leave town, ' I will go down to Dover and see *the* doctor ; he alone can do me good.' I hope his book will be published. You have the consolation that he lived to a good old age, and was, as a medical man, a blessing to thousands. I know he employed much time in still higher thoughts, and that must now afford you greater consolation than all. I will only add my own poor prayer,

" REQUIESCAT IN PACE."

APPENDIX.

SIRE,—Per gentilezza di questo signor Ministro Conti di Revel, presi la libertà già da quattro settimane di porre sotto gli occhj di V. M. un esemplare d' una prima lettera scritta in inglese e indirizzata a Mylord Palmerston, Ministro degli Affari Esteri, "Sulla Formazione d'un Regno dell' Alta Italia" governato da un Rè constituzionale della Real Famiglia di vostra Maestà.

E desso un antichissimo mio projetto ch' io ebbi mai sempre a cuore e in favor del quale scrissi molto e molto sofrii, sì dai Francesi che dai Tedeschi; onde poi preferii l' Esiglio in questo paese al vivere sotto il dominio dell' Austria. Appena comparve il detto opuscolo che fuori si scatenarono nei giornali gli fautori dell' Austria deridendo il progetto nostro; negando i diritti dei Lombardi all' indipendenza; chiamando imbecilli gl' Italiani come non atti alla libertà; biasimando altamente tutto ciò che a favor di essa avea V. M. eseguilo; e finalmente dichiarando che l' Austria possedea il territorio dell' alta Italia per diritti indisputabili, sia pervetusta eredità, che per virtù dei trattati del 1815 sinegava al tempo stesso che vi fosse luogo a una qualsisia mediazone fra vostra Maestà e la corte di Vienna.

Da un lato l' ignoranza totale che quì regna circa l' indole ed il vero carattere degli affari dell' Italia; e dall' altro lato il gran desiderio di sostenere il partito Austriaco che varie persone altamente poste e frequenti commensuli del. Principe di Metternich, esprimono in discorsi in scritti e colle stampe, tendono a mantenere il popolo Inglese in generale, nell' inganno sù di ogni cosa riguardante la questione· Italiana.

Onde sventare una così iniqua trama contro la causa nostra; far cessar gli errori confondere i dolosi scrittori ed Oratori ignari; dimostrar la validità dei nostri diritti alla nazionalità ed a un tempo stesso la leal condotta di vostra Maestà nella presente nobile ma ardua intrapresa; lo mi misi a scrivere una seconda lettera al detto ministro degli affari esteri Mylord Palmerston nella quale assumendo, per così dire ·la carica di negoziatore a nome dell' Italia mi son fatto un dovere di trattare l' intiera questione di maniera a non lasciar più addito alle soperchierie di quei molti che ci son nimici in Inghilterra.

Forse questo secondo sforzo che parimenti depongo davanti V. M. meriterà quell' accoglienza che lo spirito almeno, se non l' esecuzione dell' opera sembrerebbe richiamare da V. M. Oserei credere che voltato senza indugio nell' Italiana favella, potrebbe questa seconda Epistola esser di qualche vantaggio al nostro paese.

Faccia Iddio che V. M. possa condurre a felice esito la nobil causa degli Italiani così degnamente incomminciata per un sol instante infelice, ma ben tosto renduta ad un più fortunato avvenire Purgata la Lombardia dai Forestieri e piantato il Trono di V. M. come sovrano del Regno Unito nella mia natia città di Milano, io correrei di buona voglia a salutar il Vessillo, a rivedere i miei patrii Lari ed intercedere da vostra Maestà il privilegio di esser posto nel numero di quelli che ci stimano felici di servir un tal Principe nelle cose pubbliche.

LIST OF THE SEVERAL WORKS AND PAPERS WRITTEN BY DR. GRANVILLE,

ACCORDING TO THEIR RESPECTIVE DATES OF PUBLICATION.

1812. CRITICAL OBSERVATIONS ON SIX OF THE PRINCIPAL CHARACTERS REPRESENTED BY JOHN KEMBLE AT THE THEATRE ROYAL, MANCHESTER.

1813. L' ITALICO : a Literary, Scientific, and Political bi-monthly publication. Supported by the English Government.

1814. IL PATRIOTA ITALIANO.

1814. AN APPEAL TO THE EMPEROR OF RUSSIA ON ITALY. Written in three languages.

1817. AN ACCOUNT OF THE LIFE AND WRITINGS OF BARON GUYTON DE MORVEAU, the Reformer of Chemical Nomenclature.

1818. REPORT ON THE PRACTICE OF MIDWIFERY AT THE WESTMINSTER GENERAL DISPENSARY.

1819. FURTHER OBSERVATIONS ON THE INTERNAL USE OF THE HYDROCYANIC (PRUSSIC) ACID IN PULMONARY COMPLAINTS, &c.

1819. ON THE PLAGUE AND CONTAGION, WITH REFERENCE TO THE QUARANTINE LAWS : in a Letter to the Right Hon. F. Robinson, M.P.

1819. ON A NEW COMPOUND GAS FROM DROPSY. Read at the Royal Society.

1820. AN HISTORICAL AND PRACTICAL TREATISE ON THE INTERNAL USE OF HYDROCYANIC ACID IN DISEASES OF THE CHEST. Second Edition. Much enlarged.

1820. A CASE OF PROTRACTED HEADACHE CURED BY CARBONATE OF IRON.

1820. REPLY TO PROFESSOR BRAND'S CRITIQUE ON PRUSSIC ACID.

1823. PROGRESS OF MEDICAL SCIENCE IN THE YEAR 1822, ENGLISH AND FOREIGN.

1825. AN ESSAY ON EGYPTIAN MUMMIES, WITH OBSERVATIONS ON THE ART OF EMBALMING AMONG THE EGYPTIANS, &c.

1825. LETTER TO THE RIGHT HON. MR. HUSKISSON, M.P., President of the Board of Trade, on the QUARANTINE LAWS.

1825. EVIDENCE BEFORE PARLIAMENT ON THE THAMES IMPROVEMENT.

1828. ST. PETERSBURGH : a Journal of Travels to and from that Capital through Flanders, Prussia, Poland, Silesia, Saxony, &c. 2 vols.

1830. REFORM IN SCIENCE, OR SCIENCE WITHOUT A HEAD, AND THE ROYAL SOCIETY DISSECTED.

1831. The Catechism of Health, or Simple Rules for the Preserva-
      tion of Health and the Attainment of Long Life.

1833. Graphic Illustrations of Abortion, with Prolegomena of the
      Development of the Human Ovum.

1835. Report on the Thames Improvement Company, with many original
      Memoirs.

1836. The Royal Society in the 19th century, being a Statistical
      Summary of its Labours during the last 35 years.

1836. Report on Martin's Plan for Improving the Thames, &c.

1836. Report of a Journey through Central Europe for Agricultural
      Inquiries.

1837. The Spas of Germany. 2 vols.

1837. Report on Arsenicated Candles.

1837. Medical Reform : being the First Oration read before the British
      Medical Association.

1838. Counter-irritation, its Principles and Practice : illustrated with
      One Hundred Cases cured by External Applications.

1841. The Spas of England and Sea-bathing places. 3 vols.

1843. The German Spas revisited.

1846. Kissingen, its Sources and Resources.

1848. On the Formation of a Kingdom in Italy. First Letter to Lord
      Palmerston.

1849. The Italian Question. Second Letter to Viscount Palmerston.

1849. Letter to the Duke of Wellington on the Nelson Column.

1849. Description of a Rostral Column to Lord Nelson, with a Design.

1854. Sudden Death !

1858. The Sumbul, a new Asiatic Remedy.

1859. The Mineral Springs of Vichy : a Sketch of their Chemical and
      Physical Characters, and of their Efficacy in the Treatment of Disease.

1860. Dr. Todd and the late Member for Ashton.

1861. Obstetrical Statistics of the Industrial Classes of London.

1865. The Great London Question of the Day : Sewage v. Gold.

INDEX.

INDEX. 435

THE END.

BRADBURY, AGNEW, & CO., PRINTERS, WHITEFRIARS.

A CLASSIFIED CATALOGUE OF

HENRY S. KING & CO.'S PUBLICATIONS.

CONTENTS.

HISTORY AND BIOGRAPHY.

AN AUTOBIOGRAPHY AND OTHER MEMORIALS OF MRS. GILBERT, FORMERLY ANN TAYLOR. By Josiah Gilbert. In 2 vols. Post 8vo. With Steel Portraits and several Wood Engravings. [*Preparing.*

PERSIA; ANCIENT AND MODERN. By John Piggot, F.S.A. Post 8vo.

SARA COLERIDGE, MEMOIR AND LETTERS OF. Edited by her Daughters. 2 vols. Crown 8vo. With 2 Portraits. Price 24s. Third Edition, Revised and Corrected. With Index.

"We have read these two volumes with genuine gratification."—*Hour.*
"We could have wished to give specimens of her very just, subtle, and concise criticisms on authors of every sort and time —poets, moralists, historians, and philosophers. Sara Coleridge, as she is revealed, or rather reveals herself, in the correspondence, makes a brilliant addition to a brilliant family reputation."—*Saturday Review.*

"These charming volumes are attractive in two ways: first, as a memorial of a most amiable woman of high intellectual mark; and secondly, as rekindling recollections, and adding a little to our information regarding the life of Sara Coleridge's father, the poet and philosopher."—*Athenæum.*
"An acceptable record, and presents an adequate image of a mind of singular beauty and no inconsiderable power."—*Examiner.*

SAMUEL LOVER, THE LIFE AND UNPUBLISHED WORKS OF. By Bayle Bernard. In 2 vols. Post 8vo. With a Steel Portrait. [*Preparing.*

65, Cornhill; & 12, Paternoster Row, London.

A MEMOIR OF THE REV. DR. ROWLAND WILLIAMS, With selections from his Note-books and Correspondence. Edited by **Mrs. Rowland Williams.** With a Photographic Portrait. In 2 vols. Large post 8vo.   [*In the Press.*

POLITICAL WOMEN. By **Sutherland Menzies.** 2 vols. Post 8vo. Price 24*s.*

"Has all the information of history, with all the interest that attaches to biography."—*Scotsman.*
"A graceful contribution to the lighter record of history."—*English Churchman.*

"No author could have stated the case more temperately than he has done, and few could have placed before the reader so graphically the story which had to be told."—*Leeds Mercury.*

THE LATE REV. F. W. ROBERTSON, M.A., LIFE AND LETTERS OF. Edited by **Stopford Brooke, M.A.,** Chaplain in Ordinary to the Queen.

I. In 2 vols., uniform with the Sermons. Price 7*s.* 6*d.*

II. Library Edition, in demy 8vo, with Two Steel Portraits. 12*s.*

III. A Popular Edition, in 1 vol. Price 6*s.*

NATHANIEL HAWTHORNE, A MEMOIR OF, with Stories now first published in this country. By **H. A. Page.** Large post 8vo. 7*s.* 6*d.*

"The Memoir is followed by a criticism of Hawthorne as a writer; and the criticism is, on the whole, very well written, and exhibits a discriminating enthusiasm for one of the most fascinating of novelists."—*Saturday Review.*
"Seldom has it been our lot to meet with a more appreciative delineation of character

than this Memoir of Hawthorne."—*Morning Post.*
"He has done full justice to the fine character of the author of 'The Scarlet Letter.'"—*Standard.*
"A model of literary work of art."—*Edinburgh Courant.*

LEONORA CHRISTINA, MEMOIRS OF, Daughter of Christian IV. of Denmark : Written during her Imprisonment in the Blue Tower of the Royal Palace at Copenhagen, 1663—1685. Translated by **F. E. Bunnett,** Translator of Grimm's "Life of Michael Angelo," &c. With an Autotype Portrait of the Princess. Medium 8vo. 12*s.* 6*d.*

"A valuable addition to history."—*Daily News.*
"This remarkable autobiography, in

which we gratefully recognize a valuable addition to the tragic romance of history."—*Spectator.*

LIVES OF ENGLISH POPULAR LEADERS. No. 1.—STEPHEN LANGTON. By **C. Edmund Maurice.** Crown 8vo. 7*s.* 6*d.*

"Mr. Maurice has written a very interesting book, which may be read with equal pleasure and profit."—*Morning Post.*
"The volume contains many interesting

details, including some important documents. It will amply repay those who read it, whether as a chapter of the constitutional history of England or as the life of a great Englishman."—*Spectator.*

HISTORY AND BIOGRAPHY—*continued.*

CABINET PORTRAITS. BIOGRAPHICAL SKETCHES OF STATESMEN OF THE DAY. By **T. Wemyss Reid.** 1 vol. crown 8vo.   7s. 6d.

"We have never met with a work which we can more unreservedly praise. The sketches are absolutely impartial."—*Athenæum.*

"We can heartily commend his work. —*Standard.* "The 'Sketches of Statesmen' are drawn with a master hand."—*Yorkshire Post.*

HISTORY OF THE REVOLUTION OF 1688. By **C. D. Yonge,** Regius Professor, Queen's Coll., Belfast.   1 vol. Crown 8vo.   Price 6s.

ALEXIS DE TOCQUEVILLE. Correspondence and Conversations with NASSAU W. SENIOR from 1833 to 1859. Edited by **Mrs. M. C. M. Simpson.** In 2 vols., large post 8vo.   21s.

"Another of those interesting journals in which Mr. Senior has, as it were, crystallized the sayings of some of those many remarkable men with whom he came in contact."—*Morning Post.*

"A book replete with knowledge and thought."—*Quarterly Review.* "An extremely interesting book."—*Saturday Review.*

JOURNALS KEPT IN FRANCE AND ITALY. From 1848 to 1852. With a Sketch of the Revolution of 1848. By the late **Nassau William Senior.** Edited by his Daughter, **M. C. M. Simpson.** In 2 vols., post 8vo.   24s.

"The book has a genuine historical value."—*Saturday Review.* "The present volume gives us conversations with some of the most prominent men in the political history of France and Italy. . . Mr. Senior has the art of inspiring all men with frankness, and of persuading

them to put themselves unreservedly in his hands without fear of private circulation."—*Athenæum.* "No better, more honest, and more readable view of the state of political society during the existence of the second Republic could well be looked for."—*Examiner.*

THE HISTORY OF JAPAN. From the earliest period to the present time.   Volume I., bringing the history down to the year 1864.   By **Francis Ottiwell Adams,** H.B.M.'s Secretary of Embassy at Berlin. Formerly H.B.M.'s Chargé d'Affaires, and Secretary of Legation at Yedo. Demy 8vo.   With Map and Plans, price 21s.

THE NORMAN PEOPLE, AND THEIR EXISTING DESCENDANTS IN THE BRITISH DOMINIONS AND THE UNITED STATES OF AMERICA.   One handsome vol.   8vo.   Price 21s.

THE RUSSIANS IN CENTRAL ASIA. A Critical Examination, down to the present time, of the Geography and History of Central Asia. By **Baron F. Von Hellwald,** Member of the Geographical Societies of Paris, Geneva, Vienna, &c., &c.   Translated by **Lieut.-Col. Theodore Wirgman, LL.B.,** late 6th Inniskilling Dragoons; formerly of the Austrian Service; Translator into English verse of Schiller's "Wallenstein's Camp." In 1 vol., large post 8vo, with Map. [*Nearly ready.*

HISTORY AND BIOGRAPHY—*continued.*

BOKHARA : ITS HISTORY AND CONQUEST. By **Professor Arminius Vàmbèry,** of the University of Pesth, Author of "Travels in Central Asia," &c. Demy 8vo. Price 18*s.*

"We conclude with a cordial recommendation of this valuable book. In the present work his moderation, scholarship, insight, and occasionally very impressive style, have raised him to the dignity of an historian."—*Saturday Review.*	"Almost every page abounds with composition of peculiar merit, as well as with an account of some thrilling event more exciting than any to be found in an ordinary work of fiction."—*Morning Post.*

THE RELIGIOUS HISTORY OF IRELAND: PRIMITIVE, PAPAL, AND PROTESTANT; including the Evangelical Missions, Catholic Agitations, and Church Progress of the last half century. By **James Godkin,** Author of "Ireland, her Churches," &c. 1 vol. 8vo. Price 12*s.*

"For those who shun blue books, and yet desire some of the information they contain, these latter chapters on the statistics of the various religious denominations will be welcomed."—*Evening Standard.*	"Mr. Godkin writes with evident honesty, and the topic on which he writes is one about which an honest book is greatly wanted."—*Examiner.*

THE GOVERNMENT OF THE NATIONAL DEFENCE. From the 30th June to the 31st October, 1870. The Plain Statement of a Member. By **Mons. Jules Favre.** 1 vol. Demy 8vo. 10*s.* 6*d.*

"A very eloquent book."—*Examiner.* "Of all the contributions to the history of the late war—we have found none more fascinating and, perhaps, none more valuable than the "apology," by M.	Jules Favre, for the unsuccessful Government of the National Defence."—*Times.* "A work of the highest interest placed in an attractive form before English readers. The book is most valuable."—*Athenæum.*

'ILÂM ÈN NAS. Historical Tales and Anecdotes of the Times of the Early Khalifahs. Translated from the Arabic Originals. By **Mrs. Godfrey Clerk,** Author of "The Antipodes and Round the World." Crown 8vo. Price 7*s.*

"But there is a high tone about them, a love of justice, of truth and integrity, a sense of honour and manliness, and a simple devotion to religious duty, which however mistaken according to our lights, is deserving of every respect. The translation is the work of a lady, and a very excellent and scholar-like translation it is, clearly and pleasantly written, and	illustrated and explained by copious notes, indicating considerable learning and research."—*Saturday Review.* "Those who like stories full of the genuine colour and fragrance of the East, should by all means read Mrs. Godfrey Clerk's volume."—*Spectator.* "As full of valuable information as it is of amusing incident."—*Evening Standard.*

ECHOES OF A FAMOUS YEAR. By **Harriet Parr,** Author of "The Life of Jeanne d'Arc," "In the Silver Age," &c. Crown 8vo. 8*s.* 6*d.*

"A graceful and touching, as well as truthful account of the Franco-Prussian War. Those who are in the habit of reading books to children will find this at once instructive and delightful."—*Public Opinion.*	"Miss Parr has the great gift of charming simplicity of style ; and if children are not interested in her book, many of their seniors will be."—*British Quarterly Review.*

VOYAGES AND TRAVEL.

— • —

SCANDINAVIAN SKETCHES, Being Notes of Travel in the North of Europe. By **Mark Antony Lower**. 1 vol., crown 8vo. [*Preparing.*

ON THE ROAD TO KHIVA. By **David Ker**, late Khivan Correspondent of the *Daily Telegraph*. Illustrated with characteristic Photographs of the Country and its Inhabitants, and a copy of the Official Map in use during the Campaign, from the Survey of CAPTAIN LEUSILIN. 1 vol. Post 8vo., 10s. 6d.

ROUGH NOTES OF A VISIT TO BELGIUM, SEDAN, AND PARIS, In September, 1870—71. By **John Ashton**. Crown 8vo, bevelled boards. Price 3s. 6d.

"The author does not attempt to deal with military subjects, but writes sensibly of what he saw in 1870—71."—*John Bull.*
"The work of a thoughtful and observant man. . . . Well worth reading."—*Scotsman.*

"Possesses a certain freshness from the straightforward simplicity with which it is written."—*Graphic.*
"An interesting work by a highly intelligent observer.—*Standard.*

THE ALPS OF ARABIA; or, Travels through Egypt, Sinai, Arabia, and the Holy Land. By **William Charles Maughan**. 1 vol. Demy 8vo, with Map. Price 12s.

"Deeply interesting and valuable."—*Edinburgh Review.*
"A pleasant and agreeable book which will be read with much pleasure and profit."—*Civil Service Gazette.*
"Very readable and instructive. . . . A work far above the average of such publications."—*John Bull.*
"He writes freshly and with competent knowledge."—*Standard.*

"We can safely recommend 'The Alps of Arabia' to our readers. It is easily and pleasantly written, and conveys a good deal of valuable information on various subjects connected with the localities passed through. . . Much sensible advice is given to intending travellers, who would find its perusal a beneficial preliminary to a tour in the East."—*Glasgow News.*

THE MISHMEE HILLS: an Account of a Journey made in an Attempt to Penetrate Tibet from Assam, to open New Routes for Commerce. By **T. T. Cooper**, author of "The Travels of a Pioneer of Commerce." Demy 8vo. With Four Illustrations and Map. Price 10s. 6d.

"The volume, which will be of great use in India and among Indian merchants here, contains a good deal of matter that

will interest ordinary readers. It is especially rich in sporting incidents."—*Standard.*

GOODMAN'S CUBA, THE PEARL OF THE ANTILLES. By **Walter Goodman**. Crown 8vo. 7s. 6d.

"A good-sized volume, delightfully vivid and picturesque. . . . Several chapters devoted to the characteristics of the people are exceedingly interesting and remarkable. . . . The whole book deserves the heartiest commendation . . . sparkling and amusing from beginning to end. Reading it is like rambling about with a companion who is content to loiter, observing everything, commenting upon everything, turning

everything into a picture, with a cheerful flow of spirits, full of fun, but far above frivolity."—*Spectator.*
"He writes very lightly and pleasantly and brightens his pages with a good deal of humour. His experiences were varied enough, and his book contains a series of vivid and miscellaneous sketches. We can recommend his whole volume as very amusing reading."—*Pall Mall Gazette.*

VOYAGES AND TRAVEL—*continued.*

FIELD AND FOREST RAMBLES OF A NATURALIST IN NEW BRUNSWICK. With Notes and Observations on the Natural History of Eastern Canada. By **A. Leith Adams, M.A.**, &c., Author of "Wanderings of a Naturalist in India," &c., &c. In 8vo, cloth. Illustrated. 14s.

"Will be found interesting by those who take a pleasure either in sport or natural history."—*Athenæum.*

"To the naturalist the book will be most valuable. . . . To the general reader the book will prove most interesting, for the style is pleasant and chatty, and the information given is so graphic and full, that

those who care nothing for natural history as a pursuit will yet read these descriptions with great interest."—*Evening Standard.*

"Both sportsmen and naturalists will find this work replete with anecdote and carefully-recorded observation, which will entertain them."—*Nature.*

TENT LIFE WITH ENGLISH GIPSIES IN NORWAY. By **Hubert Smith.** In 8vo, cloth. Five full-page Engravings, and 31 smaller Illustrations, with Map of the Country showing Routes. Second Edition. Revised and Corrected. Price 21s.

"If any of our readers think of scraping an acquaintance with Norway, let them read this book. The gypsies, always an interesting study, become doubly interesting, when we are, as in these pages, introduced to them in their daily walk and conversation."—*Examiner.*

"Written in a very lively style, and has throughout a smack of dry humour and satiric reflection which shows the writer to be a keen observer of men and things. We hope that many will read it and find in it the same amusement as ourselves."—*Times.*

FAYOUM; OR, ARTISTS IN EGYPT. A Tour with M. Gérôme and others. By **J. Lenoir.** Crown 8vo, cloth. Illustrated. 7s. 6d.

"A pleasantly written and very readable book."—*Examiner.*

"The book is very amusing. . . . Who-

ever may take it up will find he has with him a bright and pleasant companion."—*Spectator.*

SPITZBERGEN THE GATEWAY TO THE POLYNIA; OR, A VOYAGE TO SPITZBERGEN. By **Captain John C. Wells, R.N.** In 8vo, cloth. Profusely Illustrated. Price 21s.

"Straightforward and clear in style, securing our confidence by its unaffected simplicity and good sense."—*Saturday Review.*

"A charming book, remarkably well written and well illustrated."—*Standard.*

"Blends pleasantly science with adventure, picturesque sketches of a summer cruise among the wild sports and fantastic scenery of Spitzbergen, with earnest advocacy of Arctic Exploration."—*Graphic.*

AN AUTUMN TOUR IN THE UNITED STATES AND CANADA. By **Lieut.-Colonel Julius George Medley.** Crown 8vo. Price 5s.

"Colonel Medley's little volume is a pleasantly written account of a two-months' visit to America."—*Hour.*

"May be recommended as manly, sensible, and pleasantly written."—*Globe.*

THE NILE WITHOUT A DRAGOMAN. By **Frederic Eden.** Second Edition. In one vol. Crown 8vo, cloth. 7s. 6d.

"Should any of our readers care to imitate Mr. Eden's example, and wish to see things with their own eyes, and shift for themselves, next winter in Upper Egypt, they will find this book a very agreeable guide."—*Times.*

"It is a book to read during an autumn holiday."—*Spectator.*

"Gives, within moderate compass, a suggestive description of the charms, curiosities, dangers, and discomforts of the Nile voyage."—*Saturday Review.*

VOYAGES AND TRAVEL—*continued.*

ROUND THE WORLD IN 1870. A Volume of Travels, with Maps. By **A. D. Carlisle, B.A.,** Trin. Coll., Camb. Demy 8vo. 16s.

"Makes one understand how going round the world is to be done in the quickest and pleasantest manner."—*Spectator.*

"We can only commend, which we do very heartily, an eminently sensible and readable book."—*British Quarterly Review.*

IRELAND IN 1872. A Tour of Observation, with Remarks on Irish Public Questions. By **Dr. James Macaulay.** Crown 8vo. 7s. 6d.

"A careful and instructive book. Full of facts, full of information, and full of interest."—*Literary Churchman.*
"We have rarely met a book on Ireland which for impartiality of criticism and general accuracy of information could be

so well recommended to the fair-minded Irish reader."—*Evening Standard.*
"A deeply interesting account of what is called a tour of observation, and some noteworthy remarks on Irish public questions."—*Illustrated London News.*

OVER THE DOVREFJELDS. By **J. S. Shepard,** Author of "A Ramble through Norway," &c. Crown 8vo. Illustrated. Price 4s. 6d.

"We have read many books of Norwegian travel, but . . . we have seen none so pleasantly narrative in its style, and so varied in its subject."—*Spectator.*
"Is a well-timed book."—*Echo.*

"As interesting a little volume as could be written on the subject. So interesting and shortly written that it will commend itself to all intending tourists."—*Examiner.*

A WINTER IN MOROCCO. By **Amelia Perrier.** Large crown 8vo. Illustrated. Price 10s. 6d.

"Well worth reading, and contains several excellent illustrations."—*Hour.*
"Miss Perrier is a very amusing writer. She has a good deal of humour, sees the

oddity and quaintness of Oriental life with a quick observant eye, and evidently turned her opportunities of sarcastic examination to account."—*Daily News.*

SCIENCE.

THE QUESTIONS OF AURAL SURGERY. By **James Hinton,** Aural Surgeon to Guy's Hospital. Post 8vo. [*Preparing.*

AN ATLAS OF DISEASES OF THE MEMBRANA TYMPANI. With Descriptive Text. By **James Hinton,** Aural Surgeon to Guy's Hospital. Post 8vo. [*Preparing.*

PHYSIOLOGY FOR PRACTICAL USE. By various Writers. Edited by **James Hinton.** 2 vols. Crown 8vo. With 50 illustrations.

These Papers have been prepared at great pains, and their endeavour is to familiarize the popular mind with those physio-

logical truths which are needful to all who desire to keep the body in a state of health.
[*In the Press.*

8

THE PLACE OF THE PHYSICIAN. Being the Introductory Lecture at Guy's Hospital, 1873-4; to which is added

ESSAYS ON THE LAW OF HUMAN LIFE AND ON THE RELATION BETWEEN ORGANIC AND INORGANIC WORLDS.

By **James Hinton,** Author of "Man and His Dwelling-Place." Crown 8vo, cloth. Price 3s. 6d.

MODERN PARISH CHURCHES; THEIR PLAN, DESIGN, AND FURNITURE. By **J. T. Micklethwaite.** Crown 8vo. Price 7s. 6d.

LONGEVITY; THE MEANS OF PROLONGING LIFE AFTER MIDDLE AGE. By **Dr. John Gardner,** Author of "A Handbook of Domestic Medicine," &c. Small Crown 8vo.

LITTLE DINNERS; HOW TO SERVE THEM WITH ELEGANCE AND ECONOMY. By **Mary Hooper,** Author of "The Handbook of the Breakfast Table." 1 vol., crown 8vo. Price 5s. [*In Press.*

THE PRINCIPLES OF MENTAL PHYSIOLOGY. With their Applications to the Training and Discipline of the Mind, and the Study of its Morbid Conditions. By **W. B. Carpenter, LL.D., M.D., F.R.S., &c.** 8vo. Illustrated. Price 12s.

THE EXPANSE OF HEAVEN. A Series of Essays on the Wonders of the Firmament. By **R. A. Proctor, B.A.,** author of "Other Worlds," &c. Small Crown 8vo. Price 6s.

"Perfectly adapted to their purpose—namely, to awaken a love for science, and, at the same time, to convey in a pleasant manner the knowledge of some elementary facts."—*Church Herald.*

"A very charming work; cannot fail to lift the reader's mind up 'through nature's work to nature's God.'"—*Standard.*
"Full of thought, readable, and popular."—*Brighton Gazette.*

STUDIES OF BLAST FURNACE PHENOMENA. By **M. L. Gruner,** President of the General Council of Mines of France. Translated by **L. D. B. Gordon, F.R.S.E., F.G.S., &c.** Demy 8vo. Price 7s. 6d.

"For practical men the volume supplies a long-felt want."—*Birmingham Daily Gazette.*
"The whole subject is dealt with very"

copiously and clearly in all its parts, and can scarcely fail of appreciation at the hands of practical men, for whose use it is designed."—*Post.*

A LEGAL HANDBOOK FOR ARCHITECTS. By **Edward Jenkins** and **John Raymond, Esqrs.,** Barristers-at-Law. In 1 vol. Price 6s.

"This handbook has been prepared with great care. The text is remarkably clear and concise. Architects, builders, and especially the building public will find the volume very useful."—*Freeman.*

"An exceedingly valuable treatise for the use of persons concerned in building. We can confidently recommend this book to all engaged in the building trades."—*Edinburgh Daily Review.*

SCIENCE—*continued*.

CONTEMPORARY ENGLISH PSYCHOLOGY. From the French of **Professor Th. Ribot.** An Analysis of the Views and Opinions of the following Metaphysicians, as expressed in their writings :—

JAMES MILL, A. BAIN, JOHN STUART MILL, GEORGE H. LEWES, HERBERT SPENCER, SAMUEL BAILEY.

Large post 8vo.   Price 9s.

THE HISTORY OF CREATION, a Popular Account of the Development of the Earth and its Inhabitants, according to the theories of Kant, Laplace, Lamarck, and Darwin. By **Professor Ernst Hæckel**, of the University of Jena. 8vo. With Coloured Plates and Genealogical Trees of the various groups of both plants and animals. 	*[In the Press.*

Second Edition.

CHANGE OF AIR AND SCENE. A Physician's Hints about Doctors, Patients, Hygiène, and Society ; with Notes of Excursions for health in the Pyrenees, and amongst the Watering-places of France (Inland and Seaward), Switzerland, Corsica, and the Mediterranean. By **Dr. Alphonse Donné.** Large post 8vo. Price 9s.

"A very readable and serviceable book. . . . The real value of it is to be found in the accurate and minute information given with regard to a large number of places which have gained a reputation on the continent for their mineral waters."—*Pall Mall Gazette.*

"A singularly pleasant and chatty as well as instructive book about health."— *Guardian.*

MISS YOUMANS' FIRST BOOK OF BOTANY. Designed to cultivate the observing powers of Children. From the Author's latest Stereotyped Edition. New and Enlarged Edition, with 300 Engravings. Crown 8vo. 5s.

"It is but rarely that a school-book appears which is at once so novel in plan, so successful in execution, and so suited to the general want, as to command universal and unqualified approbation, but such has been the case with Miss Youmans' First Book of Botany. . . . It has been everywhere welcomed as a timely and invaluable contribution to the improvement of primary education."—*Pall Mall Gazette.*

AN ARABIC AND ENGLISH DICTIONARY OF THE KORAN. By **Major J. Penrice, B.A.** 4to. Price 21s.

MODERN GOTHIC ARCHITECTURE. By **T. G. Jackson.** Crown 8vo. Price 5s.

"The reader will find some of the most important doctrines of eminent art teachers practically applied in this little book, which is well written and popular in style."—*Manchester Examiner.*

"Much clearness, force, wealth of illustration, and in style of composition, which tends to commend his views."—*Edinburgh Daily Review.*

"This thoughtful little book is worthy of the perusal of all interested in art or architecture."—*Standard.*

SCIENCE—*continued*.

A TREATISE ON RELAPSING FEVER. By **R. T. Lyons**, Assistant-Surgeon, Bengal Army. Small post 8vo. *7s. 6d.*

"A practical work, thoroughly supported in its views by a series of remarkable cases."—*Standard*.

FOUR WORKS BY DR. EDWARD SMITH.

I. **HEALTH AND DISEASE**, as influenced by the Daily, Seasonal, and other Cyclical Changes in the Human System. A New Edition. *7s. 6d.*

II. **FOODS.** Second Edition. Profusely Illustrated. Price *5s.*

III. **PRACTICAL DIETARY FOR FAMILIES, SCHOOLS, AND THE LABOURING CLASSES.** A New Edition. Price *3s. 6d.*

IV. **CONSUMPTION IN ITS EARLY AND REMEDIABLE STAGES.** A New Edition. *7s. 6d.*

THE PORT OF REFUGE; OR, COUNSEL AND AID TO SHIPMASTERS IN DIFFICULTY, DOUBT, OR DISTRESS. By **Manley Hopkins**, Author of "A Handbook of Average," "A Manual of Insurance," &c. Cr. 8vo. Price 6s.

SUBJECTS :—The Shipmaster's Position and Duties.—Agents and Agency.—Average.—Bottomry, and other Means of Raising Money.—The Charter-Party, and Bill-of-Lading. Stoppage in Transitu; and the Shipowner's Lien.—Collision.

"Combines in quite a marvellous manner a fullness of information which will make it perfectly indispensable in the captain's bookcase, and equally suitable to the gentleman's library. This synopsis of the law of shipping in all its multifarious ramifications and the hints he gives on a variety of topics must be invaluable to the master mariner whenever he is in doubt, difficulty, and danger."—*Mercantile Marine Magazine*.

"A truly excellent contribution to the literature of our marine commerce."—*Echo*.

"Those immediately concerned will find it well worth while to avail themselves of its teachings."—*Colburn's U.S. Magazine*.

LOMBARD STREET. A Description of the Money Market. By **Walter Bagehot.** Large crown 8vo. Fourth Edition. *7s. 6d.*

"An acceptable addition to the literature of finance."—*Stock Exchange Review*.

"Mr. Bagehot touches incidentally a hundred points connected with his subject, and pours serene white light upon them all."—*Spectator*.

"Anybody who wishes to have a clear idea of the workings of what is called the Money Market should procure a little volume which Mr. Bagehot has just published, and he will there find the whole thing in a nut-shell. . . . The subject is one, it is almost needless to say, on which Mr. Bagehot writes with the authority of a man who combines practical experience with scientific study."—*Saturday Review*.

"Besides its main topic, the management of the reserve of the Bank of England, it is full of the most interesting economic history."—*Athenæum*.

CHOLERA: HOW TO AVOID AND TREAT IT. Popular and Practical Notes by **Henry Blanc, M.D.** Crown 8vo. *4s. 6d.*

"A very practical manual, based on experience and careful observation, full of excellent hints on a most dangerous disease."—*Standard*.

THE INTERNATIONAL SCIENTIFIC SERIES.

Fourth Edition.

I. THE FORMS OF WATER IN RAIN AND RIVERS, ICE AND GLACIERS. By **J. Tyndall, LL.D., F.R.S.** With 26 Illustrations. Crown 8vo. 5s.

"One of Professor Tyndall's best scientific treatises."—*Standard.*
"Before starting for Switzerland next summer every one should study 'The forms of water.'"—*Globe.*
"Eloquent and instructive in an eminent degree."—*British Quarterly.*

Second Edition.

II. PHYSICS AND POLITICS ; OR, THOUGHTS ON THE APPLICATION OF THE PRINCIPLES OF "NATURAL SELECTION" AND "INHERITANCE" TO POLITICAL SOCIETY. By **Walter Bagehot.** Crown 8vo. 4s.

"On the whole we can recommend the book as well deserving to be read by thoughtful students of politics."—*Saturday Review.*
"Able and ingenious."—*Spectator.*
"A work of really original and interesting speculation."—*Guardian.*

Second Edition.

III. FOODS. By **Dr. Edward Smith.** Profusely Illustrated. Price 5s.

"A comprehensive résumé of our present chemical and physiological knowledge of the various foods, solid and liquid, which go so far to ameliorate the troubles and vexations of this anxious and wearying existence."—*Chemist and Druggist.*
"Heads of households will find it considerably to their advantage to study its contents."—*Court Express.*
"A very comprehensive book. Every page teems with information. Readable throughout."—*Church Herald.*

Second Edition.

IV. MIND AND BODY: THE THEORIES OF THEIR RELATIONS. By **Alexander Bain, LL.D.,** Professor of Logic at the University of Aberdeen. Four Illustrations. 4s.

"A brief and popular statement of the leading positions of psychology."—*Examiner.*
"Well worth study."—*Graphic.*
"The importance of this work cannot be overstated."—*Public Opinion.*

Second Edition.

V. THE STUDY OF SOCIOLOGY. By **Herbert Spencer.** Crown 8vo. Price 5s.

"Bound by no ties to any party, he attacks the cherished opinions of all with perfect impartiality. We lay down the volume with many temptations to desultory comment still unsatisfied ; it contains a great amount of interesting and suggestive matter, and our only fear is that it may have stolen too much of his time and thought from the working out of his principal task."—*Saturday Review.*

VI. ON THE CONSERVATION OF ENERGY. By **Professor Balfour Stewart.** Fourteen Engravings. Price 5s.

"One of the most popularly instructive of the series."—*Examiner.*
"A most valuable manual... The author has in a singularly lucid manner contrived to popularise some of the most intricate problems in the philosophy of the physical sciences."—*Iron.*

THE INTERNATIONAL SCIENTIFIC SERIES—*continued.*

VII. ANIMAL LOCOMOTION; or, Walking, Swimming, and Flying. By **Dr. J. B. Pettigrew, M.D., F.R.S.** 119 Illustrations. Price 5s.

> "A clear and comprehensive résumé of the present advanced state of our knowledge of animal locomotion, as shown by the most recent successful experiments and discoveries."—*Standard.*

VIII. RESPONSIBILITY IN MENTAL DISEASE. By **Dr. Henry Maudsley.** Price 5s.

IX. THE NEW CHEMISTRY. By **Professor Josiah P. Cooke,** of the Harvard University. Illustrated. Price 5s.

X. THE SCIENCE OF LAW. By **Professor Sheldon Amos.**

FORTHCOMING VOLUMES.

Prof. E. J. MAREY.
The Animal Frame.

{ **Rev. M. J. BERKELEY, M.A., F.L.S.,** and **M. COOKE, M.A., LL.D.**
Fungi ; their Nature, Influences, and Uses.

Prof. OSCAR SCHMIDT (Strasburg Univ.).
The Theory of Descent and Darwinism.

Prof. VOGEL (Polytechnic Acad. of Berlin).
The Chemical Effects of Light.

Prof. W. KINGDOM CLIFFORD, M.A.
The First Principles of the Exact Sciences explained to the non-mathematical.

Prof. T. H. HUXLEY, LL.D., F.R.S.
Bodily Motion and Consciousness.

Dr. W. B. CARPENTER, LL.D., F.R.S.
The Physical Geography of the Sea.

Prof. WILLIAM ODLING, F.R.S.
The New Chemistry.

W. LAUDER LINDSAY, M.D., F.R.S.E.
Mind in the Lower Animals.

Sir JOHN LUBBOCK, Bart., F.R.S.
The Antiquity of Man.

Prof. W. T. THISELTON DYER, B.A. B.SC.
Form and Habit in Flowering Plants.

Mr. J. N. LOCKYER, F.R.S.
Spectrum Analysis.

Prof. MICHAEL FOSTER, M.D.
Protoplasm and the Cell Theory.

Prof. W. STANLEY JEVONS.
The Logic of Statistics.

Dr. H. CHARLTON BASTIAN, M.D., F.R.S.
The Brain as an Organ of Mind.

Prof. A. C. RAMSAY, LL.D., F.R.S.
Earth Sculpture: Hills, Valleys, Mountains, Plains, Rivers, Lakes ; how they were Produced, and how they have been Destroyed.

Prof. RUDOLPH VIRCHOW (Berlin Univ.)
Morbid Physiological Action.

Prof. CLAUDE BERNARD.
Physical and Metaphysical Phenomena of Life.

Prof. A. QUETELET.
Social Physics.

Prof. H. SAINTE-CLAIRE DEVILLE.
An Introduction to General Chemistry.

Prof. WURTZ.
Atoms and the Atomic Theory.

Prof. DE QUATREFAGES.
The Negro Races.

Prof. LACAZE-DUTHIERS.
Zoology since Cuvier.

Prof. BERTHELOT.
Chemical Synthesis.

Prof. J. ROSENTHAL.
General Physiology of Muscles and Nerves.

Prof. JAMES D. DANA, M.A., LL.D.
On Cephalization ; or, Head-Characters in the Gradation and Progress of Life.

Prof. S. W. JOHNSON, M.A.
On the Nutrition of Plants.

Prof. AUSTIN FLINT, Jr. M.D.
The Nervous System and its Relation to the Bodily Functions.

Prof. W. D. WHITNEY.
Modern Linguistic Science.

Prof. BERNSTEIN (University of Halle).
Physiology of the Senses.

Prof. FERDINAND COHN (Breslau Univ.).
Thallophytes (Algæ, Lichens, Fungi).

Prof. HERMANN (University of Zurich).
Respiration.

Prof. LEUCKART (University of Leipsic).
Outlines of Animal Organization.

Prof. LIEBREICH (University of Berlin).
Outlines of Toxicology.

Prof. KUNDT (University of Strasburg).
On Sound.

Prof. LONMEL (University of Erlangen).
Optics.

Prof. REES (University of Erlangen).
On Parasitic Plants.

Prof. STEINTHAL (University of Berlin).
Outlines of the Science of Language.

ESSAYS, LECTURES, AND COLLECTED PAPERS.

NEWMARKET AND ARABIA; AN EXAMINATION OF THE DESCENT OF RACERS AND COURSERS. By **Roger D. Upton**, Captain late 9th Royal Lancers. Post 8vo. With Pedigrees and Coloured Frontispiece. Price 9s.

" It contains a good deal of truth, and it abounds with valuable suggestions."— *Saturday Review.*

"A remarkable volume. The breeder can well ponder over its pages. With all the skill which he used in unravelling the mysteries of the Stud Book, our author enters into the subject of defining first the probable origin of the Arab, and, still more interesting, the different tribes to which the best castes belong."—*Bell's Life.*

" Of the highest importance to breeders of race horses, and indeed to all who take an interest in horseflesh."—*Standard.*

"A thoughtful and intelligent book. . . . The author does not confine himself to mere statements of opinion, but quotes the undisputed logic of the 'Stud Book' to prove his case. . . . The worth of its statements is not to be denied. . . . A contribution to the history of the horse of remarkable interest and importance."— *Baily's Magazine.*

IN STRANGE COMPANY; or, The Note Book of a Roving Correspondent. By **James Greenwood**, "The Amateur Casual." Second Edition. Crown 8vo. 6s.

"A bright, lively book."—*Standard.*

"He writes in a free and easy style ; he appreciates the ludicrous, and weaves a yarn which grave and gay will laugh at or weep over by turns. . . . It has all the interest of romance."—*Queen.*

"Certainly presents striking pictures of too large a class of our London society— masses of hapless humanity, seething in this vast 'smoking cauldron.'"—*Telegraph.*

" Mr. Greenwood's book is to be welcomed as giving us the eye to eye experience of a keen observer. . . . He reveals to us things we had never dreamt of as existing within the bounds of the four seas that encompass our island." — *Glasgow News.*

"Some of the papers remind us of Charles Lamb on beggars and chimney sweeps. Our author's experiences are, however, much more varied."—*Echo.*

MASTER-SPIRITS. By **Robert Buchanan**. Post 8vo. 10s. 6d.

" Good Books are the precious life-blood of Master-Spirits."—*Milton.*

"The essay upon Dickens is in every way charming. . . . The essay upon Victor Hugo strikes us as the best in the volume, though there is also much that is very interesting in the chapters upon Danish literature, and upon the 'poets in obscurity.' Mr. Buchanan's volume is full of fresh and vigorous writing, such as can only be produced by a man of keen and independent intellect." — *Saturday Review.*

"A very pleasant and readable book."— *Examiner.*

"A series of light and bright papers, written with a beauty of language and a spirit of vigorous enthusiasm rare even in our best living word-painters."—*Standard.*

" Mr. Buchanan is a writer whose books the critics may always open with satisfaction, assured that whether poetry or prose be the vehicle of thought, the work will be both manly and artistic."—*Hour.*

THEOLOGY IN THE ENGLISH POETS. Being Lectures delivered by the **Rev. Stopford A. Brooke,** Chaplain in Ordinary to Her Majesty the Queen. [*Preparing.*

ESSAYS, LECTURES, ETC.—*continued.*

MOUNTAIN, MEADOW, AND MERE; a Series of Outdoor Sketches of Sport, Scenery, Adventures, and Natural History. By **G. Christopher Davies.** With 16 Illustrations by W. HARCOURT. Crown 8vo, price 6s.

"If the book has none of the dramatic grandeur of the epic, where the hunter's life is staked on the steadiness of his nerves, on the other hand it is pervaded throughout by the graceful melody of a natural idyl, and the details of sport are subordinated to a dominating sense of the beautiful and picturesque. The great charm of a book of this kind lies in its reviving so many of the brighter associations of one's early existence."—*Saturday Review.*

"Mr. Davies writes pleasantly, graphically, and with the pen of a lover of nature, a naturalist, and a sportsman."—*Field.*

"Will be read both for its charming little passages descriptive of English scenery, and as the production of an enthusiastic worshipper of home sport."—*Examiner.*

"The narrative portions are simply and graphically told, and the descriptions of scenery are so faithfully and vividly painted that they give the reader actual glimpses of many charming bits of landscape, and prove that the author has a keen eye for the picturesque, as well as some poetic taste."—*Sporting Gazette.*

HOW TO AMUSE AND EMPLOY OUR INVALIDS. By **Harriet Power.** Fcap. 8vo. Price 2s. 6d.

"Worthy of the attention of all interested in the comfort of invalids."—*Edinburgh Courant.*

"A very useful little brochure ... Will become a universal favourite with the class for whom it is intended, while it will afford many a useful hint to those who live with them."—*John Bull.*

STUDIES AND ROMANCES. By **H. Schutz Wilson.** 1 vol. Crown 8vo. Price 7s. 6d.

"Vivacious and interesting."—*Scotsman.*

"Open the book, however, at what page the reader may, he will find something to amuse and instruct, and he must be very hard to please if he finds nothing to suit him, either grave or gay, stirring or romantic, in the capital stories collected in this well-got-up volume."—*John Bull.*

SHORT LECTURES ON THE LAND LAWS. Delivered before the Working Men's College. By **T. Lean Wilkinson.** Crown 8vo, limp cloth. 2s.

"A very handy and intelligible epitome of the general principles of existing land laws."—*Standard.*

"A very clear and lucid statement as to the condition of the present land laws which govern our country. These Lectures possess the advantage of not being loaded with superfluous matter."—*Civil Service Gazette.*

AN ESSAY ON THE CULTURE OF THE OBSERVING POWERS OF CHILDREN, especially in connection with the Study of Botany. By **Eliza A. Youmans.** Edited, with Notes and a Supplement, by **Joseph Payne, F.C.P.,** Author of "Lectures on the Science and Art of Education," &c. Crown 8vo. 2s. 6d.

"This study, according to her just notions on the subject, is to be fundamentally based on the exercise of the pupil's own powers of observation. He is to see and examine the properties of plants and flowers at first hand, not merely to be informed of what others have seen and examined."—*Pall Mall Gazette.*

THE GENIUS OF CHRISTIANITY UNVEILED. Being Essays by **William Godwin,** Author of "Political Justice," &c. Never before published. 1 vol., crown 8vo. 7s. 6d.

"Few have thought more clearly and directly than William Godwin, or expressed their reflections with more simplicity and unreserve."—*Examiner.*

"The deliberate thoughts of Godwin deserve to be put before the world for reading and consideration."—*Athenæum.*

ESSAYS, LECTURES, ETC.—*continued.*

THE PELICAN PAPERS. Reminiscences and Remains of a Dweller in the Wilderness. By **James Ashcroft Noble.** Crown 8vo. 6s.

"Written somewhat after the fashion of Mr. Helps's 'Friends in Council.'"—*Examiner.*
"Will well repay perusal by all thought-

ful and intelligent readers."—*Liverpool Leader.*
"The 'Pelican Papers' make a very readable volume."—*Civilian.*

BRIEFS AND PAPERS. Being Sketches of the Bar and the Press. By **Two Idle Apprentices.** Crown 8vo. 7s. 6d.

"Written with spirit and knowledge, and give some curious glimpses into what the majority will regard as strange and unknown territories."—*Daily News.*

"This is one of the best books to while away an hour and cause a generous laugh that we have come across for a long time."—*John Bull.*

THE SECRET OF LONG LIFE. Dedicated by Special Permission to Lord St. Leonards. Third Edition. Large crown 8vo. 5s.

"A charming little volume."—*Times.*
"A very pleasant little book, cheerful, genial, scholarly."—*Spectator.*
"We should recommend our readers

to get this book."—*British Quarterly Review.*
"Entitled to the warmest admiration."—*Pall Mall Gazette.*

SOLDIERING AND SCRIBBLING. By **Archibald Forbes,** of the *Daily News,* Author of "My Experience of the War between France and Germany." Crown 8vo. 7s. 6d.

"All who open it will be inclined to read through for the varied entertainment which it affords."—*Daily News.*
"There is a good deal of instruction to

outsiders touching military life, in this volume."—*Evening Standard.*
"Thoroughly readable and worth reading."—*Scotsman.*

THE ENGLISH CONSTITUTION. By **Walter Bagehot.** A New Edition, revised and corrected, with an Introductory Dissertation on recent changes and events.' Crown 8vo. 7s. 6d.

"A pleasing and clever study on the department of higher politics."—*Guardian.*
"No writer before him had set out so

clearly what the efficient part of the English Constitution really is."—*Pall Mall Gazette.*
"Clear and practical."—*Globe.*

REPUBLICAN SUPERSTITIONS. Illustrated by the Political History of the United States. Including a Correspondence with M. Louis Blanc. By **Moncure D. Conway.** Crown 8vo. 5s.

"A very able exposure of the most plausible fallacies of Republicanism, by a writer of remarkable vigour and purity of style."—*Standard.*

"Mr. Conway writes with ardent sincerity. He gives us some good anecdotes, and he is occasionally almost eloquent."—*Guardian,* July 2, 1873.

STREAMS FROM HIDDEN SOURCES. By **B. Montgomerie Ranking.** Crown 8vo. 6s.

"In point of style it is well executed, and the prefatory notices are very good."—*Spectator.*
"The effect of reading the seven tales he presents to us is to make us wish for some seven more of the same kind."—*Pall Mall Gazette.*

"We doubt not that Mr. Ranking's enthusiasm will communicate itself to many of his readers, and induce them in like manner to follow back these streamlets to their parent river."—*Graphic.*

MILITARY WORKS.

THE OPERATIONS OF THE FIRST ARMY, UNDER STEIN-METZ. By **Von Schell.** Translated by **Captain E. O. Hollist.** Demy 8vo. Uniform with the other volumes in the Series. Price 10s. 6d.

THE OPERATIONS OF THE FIRST ARMY UNDER GEN. VON GOEBEN. By **Major Von Schell.** Translated by **Col. C. H. Von Wright.** Four Maps. Demy 8vo. 9s.

THE OPERATIONS OF THE FIRST ARMY IN NORTHERN FRANCE AGAINST FAIDHERBE. By **Colonel Count Hermann Von Wartensleben,** Chief of the Staff of the First Army. Translated by **Colonel C. H. Von Wright.** In demy 8vo. Uniform with the above. Price 9s.

"Very clear, simple, yet eminently instructive, is this history. It is not over-laden with useless details, is written in good taste, and possesses the inestimable value of being in great measure the record of operations actually witnessed by the author, supplemented by official documents."—*Athenæum.*

"The work is based on the official war documents—it is especially valuable—the narrative is remarkably vivid and interesting. Two well-executed maps enable the reader to trace out the scenes of General Manteuffel's operations."—*Naval and Military Gazette.*

THE GERMAN ARTILLERY IN THE BATTLES NEAR METZ. Based on the official reports of the German Artillery. By **Captain Hoffbauer,** Instructor in the German Artillery and Engineer School. Translated by **Capt. E. O. Hollist.** [*Preparing.*

This history gives a detailed account of the movements of the German artillery in the three days' fighting to the east and west of Metz, which resulted in paralyzing the army under Marshal Bazaine, and its subsequent surrender. The action of the batteries with reference to the other arms is clearly explained, and the valuable maps show the positions taken up by the individual batteries at each stage of the contests. Tables are also supplied in the

Appendix, furnishing full details as to the number of killed and wounded, expenditure of ammunition, &c. The campaign of 1870—71 having demonstrated the importance of artillery to an extent which has not previously been conceded to it, this work forms a valuable part of the literature of the campaign, and will be read with interest not only by members of the regular but also by those of the auxiliary forces.

THE OPERATIONS OF THE BAVARIAN ARMY CORPS. By **Captain Hugo Helvig.** Translated by **Captain G. S. Schwabe.** With 5 large Maps. Demy 8vo. In 2 vols. Price 24s. Uniform with the other Books in the Series.

AUSTRIAN CAVALRY EXERCISE. From an Abridged Edition compiled by CAPTAIN ILLIA WOINOVITS, of the General Staff, on the Tactical Regulations of the Austrian Army, and prefaced by a General Sketch of the Organisation, &c., of the Country. Translated by **Captain W. S. Cooke.** Crown 8vo, cloth. Price 7s.

History of the Organisation, Equipment, and War Services of

THE REGIMENT OF BENGAL ARTILLERY. Compiled from Published Official and other Records, and various private sources, by **Major Francis W. Stubbs,** Royal (late Bengal) Artillery. Vol. I. will contain WAR SERVICES. The Second Volume will be published separately, and will contain the HISTORY OF THE ORGANISATION AND EQUIPMENT OF THE REGIMENT. In 2 vols. 8vo. With Maps and Plans. *[Preparing.*

VICTORIES AND DEFEATS. An Attempt to explain the Causes which have led to them. An Officer's Manual. By **Col. R. P. Anderson.** Demy 8vo. 14*s.*

"The present book proves that he is a diligent student of military history, his illustrations ranging over a wide field, and including ancient and modern Indian and European warfare."—*Standard.*

"A delightful military classic, and what is more, a most useful one. The young officer should have it always at hand to open anywhere and read a bit, and we warrant him that let that bit be ever so small it will give him material for an hour's thinking."—*United Service Gazette.*

THE FRONTAL ATTACK OF INFANTRY. By **Capt. Laymann,** Instructor of Tactics at the Military College, Neisse. Translated by **Colonel Edward Newdigate.** Crown 8vo, limp cloth. Price 2*s.* 6*d.*

"An exceedingly useful kind of book. The design is not merely good, but well worked out in a style which makes the work a valuable acquisition to the military student's library. It recounts, in the first place, the opinions and tactical formations which regulated the German army during the early battles of the late war; explains how these were modified in the course of the campaign by the terrible and unanticipated effect of the fire; and how, accordingly, troops should be trained to attack in future wars." — *Naval and Military Gazette.*

"This work has met with special attention in our army."—*Militarin Wochenblatt.*

ELEMENTARY MILITARY GEOGRAPHY, RECONNOITRING, AND SKETCHING. Compiled for Non-Commissioned Officers and Soldiers of all Arms. By **Lieut. C. E. H. Vincent,** Royal Welsh Fusileers. Small crown 8vo. 2*s.* 6*d.*

"An admirable little manual, full of facts and teachings."—*United Service Gazette.*

"This manual takes into view the necessity of every soldier knowing how to read a military map, in order to know to what points in an enemy's country to direct his attention; and provides for this necessity by giving, in terse and sensible language, definitions of varieties of ground and the advantages they present in warfare, together with a number of useful hints in military sketching."—*Naval and Military Gazette.*

THREE WORKS BY LIEUT.-COL. THE HON. A. ANSON, V.C., M.P.

THE ABOLITION OF PURCHASE AND THE ARMY REGULATION BILL OF 1871. Crown 8vo. Price One Shilling.

ARMY RESERVES AND MILITIA REFORMS. Crown 8vo. Sewed. Price One Shilling.

THE STORY OF THE SUPERSESSIONS. Crown 8vo. Price Sixpence

MILITARY WORKS—*continued.*

STUDIES IN THE NEW INFANTRY TACTICS. Parts I. & II.
By **Major W. Von Schereff.** Translated from the German by **Col. Lumley Graham.** Price 7*s.* 6*d.*

"Major Von Schereff's 'Studies in Tactics' is worthy of the perusal—indeed, of the thoughtful study—of every military man. The subject of the respective advantages of attack and defence, and of the methods in which each form of battle should be carried out under the fire of

modern arms, is exhaustively and admirably treated ; indeed, we cannot but consider it to be decidedly superior to any work which has hitherto appeared in English upon this all-important subject."— *Standard.*

TACTICAL DEDUCTIONS FROM THE WAR OF 1870—1. By **Captain A. Von Boguslawski.** Translated by **Colonel Lumley Graham,** late 18th (Royal Irish) Regiment. Demy 8vo. Uniform with the above. Price 7*s.*

"Major Boguslawski's tactical deductions from the war are, that infantry still preserve their superiority over cavalry, that open order must henceforth be the main principles of all drill, and that the chassepot is the best of all small arms for precision. . . . We must, without delay, impress brain and forethought into the

British Service ; and we cannot commence the good work too soon, or better, than by placing the two books ('The Operations of the German Armies' and 'Tactical Deductions') we have here criticised, in every military library, and introducing them as class-books in every tactical school."— *United Service Gazette.*

THE ARMY OF THE NORTH-GERMAN CONFEDERATION.
A Brief Description of its Organisation, of the different Branches of the Service and their 'Rôle' in War, of its Mode of Fighting, &c. By a **Prussian General.** Translated from the German by **Col. Edward Newdigate.** Demy 8vo. 5*s.*

"A good translation of an instructive and suggestive book."—*Athenæum.*
"The work is quite essential to the full use of the other volumes of the 'German Military Series,' which Messrs. King are now producing in handsome uniform style. It has also the great recommendation of being of very moderate length, and, whilst stating everything with professional exactness, is singularly free from technicalities that might embarrass the general reader." —*United Service Magazine.*
"Every page of the book deserves attentive study . . . . The information given

on mobilisation, garrison troops, keeping up establishment during war, and on the employment of the different branches of the service, is of great value."—*Standard.*
"The essay is well filled with information, easy to read, but requiring study for its digestion. It is also a book which must be useful to the younger officers, and still more so to the older officers, who really have in their hands the management of the British army, and so large a part in moulding the institutions upon which it rests."— *Spectator.*

THE OPERATIONS OF THE GERMAN ARMIES IN FRANCE, FROM SEDAN TO THE END OF THE WAR OF 1870—1.
With Large Official Map. From the Journals of the Head-quarters Staff, by **Major Wm. Blume.** Translated by **E. M. Jones,** Major 20th Foot, late Professor of Military History, Sandhurst. Demy 8vo. Price 9*s.*

"The book is of absolute necessity to the military student. . . . The work is one of high merit."—*United Service Gazette.*
"The work of translation has been well done. In notes, prefaces, and introductions, much additional information has been given."—*Athenæum.*
"The work of Major von Blume in its English dress forms the most valuable

addition to our stock of works upon the war that our press has put forth. Major Blume writes with a clear conciseness much wanting in many of his country's historians. Our space forbids our doing more than commending it earnestly as the most authentic and instructive narrative of the second section of the war that has yet appeared."—*Saturday Review.*

THE OPERATIONS OF THE SOUTH ARMY IN JANUARY AND FEBRUARY, 1871.

Compiled from the Official War Documents of the Head-quarters of the Southern Army. By **Count Hermann Von Wartensleben,** Colonel in the Prussian General Staff. Translated by **Colonel C. H. Von Wright.** Demy 8vo, with Maps. Uniform with the above. Price 6*s.*

HASTY INTRENCHMENTS. By **Colonel A. Brialmont.**

Translated by **Lieutenant Charles A. Empson, R.A.** Demy 8vo. Nine Plates. Price 6*s.*

"A valuable contribution to military literature."—*Athenæum.*

"In seven short chapters it gives plain directions for forming shelter-trenches, with the best method of carrying the necessary tools, and it offers practical illustrations of the use of hasty intrenchments on the field of battle."—*United Service Magazine.*

"It supplies that which our own text-books give but imperfectly, viz., hints as to how a position can best be strengthened by means . . . of such extemporised intrenchments and batteries as can be thrown up by infantry in the space of four or five hours . . . deserves to become a standard military work."—*Standard.*

"Clearly and critically written."—*Wellington Gazette.*

STUDIES IN LEADING TROOPS. By **Colonel Von Verdy Du Vernois.**

An authorised and accurate Translation by **Lieutenant H. J. T. Hildyard,** 71st Foot. Parts I. and II. Demy 8vo. Price 7*s.*

*** General BEAUCHAMP WALKER says of this work :—"I recommend the first two numbers of Colonel von Verdy's 'Studies' to the attentive perusal of my brother officers. They supply a want which I have often felt during my service in this country, namely, a minuter tactical detail of the minor operations of the war than any but the most observant and for-

tunately-placed staff-officer is in a position to give. I have read and re-read them very carefully, I hope with profit, certainly with great interest, and believe that practice, in the sense of these 'Studies,' would be a valuable preparation for manœuvres on a more extended scale."—Berlin, June, 1872.

CAVALRY FIELD DUTY. By **Major-General Von Mirus.**

Translated by **Captain Frank S. Russell,** 14th (King's) Hussars. Crown 8vo, limp cloth. 7*s.* 6*d.*

DISCIPLINE AND DRILL.

Four Lectures delivered to the London Scottish Rifle Volunteers. By **Captain S. Flood Page.** A New and Cheaper Edition. Price 1*s.*

"One of the best-known and coolest-headed of the metropolitan regiments, whose adjutant moreover has lately published an admirable collection of lectures

addressed by him to the men of his corps."—*Times.*

"The very useful and interesting work."—*Volunteer Service Gazette.*

INDIA AND THE EAST.

THE THREATENED FAMINE IN BENGAL; How it may be Met, and the Recurrence of Famines in India Prevented. Being No. 1 of "Occasional Notes on Indian Affairs." By **Sir H. Bartle E. Frere, G.C.B., G.C.S.I., &c., &c.** Crown 8vo. With 3 Maps. *[Preparing.*

THE ORIENTAL SPORTING MAGAZINE. A Reprint of the first 5 Volumes, in 2 Volumes, demy 8vo, price 28s.

"Lovers of sport will find ample amusement in the varied contents of these two volumes."—*Allen's Indian Mail.*
"Full of interest for the sportsman and naturalist. Full of thrilling adventures of sportsmen who have attacked the fiercest and most gigantic specimens of the animal world in their native jungle. It is seldom we get so many exciting incidents in a similar amount of space ... Well suited to the libraries of country gentlemen and all those who are interested in sporting matters."—*Civil Service Gazette.*
"These volumes contain a good deal o amusing matter.—*Sporting Gazette.*

THE EUROPEAN IN INDIA. A Hand-book of Practical Information for those proceeding to, or residing in, the East Indies, relating to Outfits, Routes, Time for Departure, Indian Climate, &c. By **Edmund C. P. Hull.** With a MEDICAL GUIDE FOR ANGLO-INDIANS. Being a Compendium of Advice to Europeans in India, relating to the Preservation and Regulation of Health. By **R. S. Mair, M.D., F.R.C.S.E.,** late Deputy Coroner of Madras. In 1 vol. Post 8vo. 6s.

"Full of all sorts of useful information to the English settler or traveller in India."—*Standard.*
"One of the most valuable books ever published in India—valuable for its sound information, its careful array of pertinent facts, and its sterling common sense. It is a publisher's as well as an author's ' hit,' for it supplies a want which few persons may have discovered, but which everybody will at once recognise when once the contents of the book have been mastered. The medical part of the work is invaluable."—*Calcutta Guardian.*

THE MEDICAL GUIDE FOR ANGLO-INDIANS. Being a Compendium of advice to Europeans in India, relating to the Preservation and Regulation of Health. By **R. S. Mair, F.R.C.S.E.,** late Deputy Coroner of Madras. Reprinted, with numerous additions and corrections, from "The European in India."

EASTERN EXPERIENCES. By **L. Bowring, C.S.I.,** Lord Canning's Private Secretary, and for many years the Chief Commissioner of Mysore and Coorg. In 1 vol. Demy 8vo. 16s. Illustrated with Maps and Diagrams.

"An admirable and exhaustive geographical, political, and industrial survey."—*Athenæum.*
"The usefulness of this compact and methodical summary of the most authentic information relating to countries whose welfare is intimately connected with our own, should obtain for Mr. Lewin Bowring's work a good place among treatises of its kind."—*Daily News.*
"Interesting even to the general reader, but more especially so to those who may have a special concern in that portion of our Indian Empire."—*Post.*

TAS-HĪL UL KALĀM; OR, HINDUSTANI MADE EASY. By Captain W. R. M. Holroyd, Bengal Staff Corps, Director of Public Instruction, Punjab. Crown 8vo. Price 5s.

"As clear and as instructive as possible."
—*Standard.*
"Contains a great deal of most necessary

information, that is not to be found in any other work on the subject that has crossed our path."—*Homeward Mail.*

WESTERN INDIA BEFORE AND DURING THE MUTINIES. Pictures drawn from Life. By **Major-Gen. Sir George Le Grand Jacob, K.C.S.I., C.B.** In 1 vol. Crown 8vo. 7s. 6d.

"The most important contribution to the history of Western India during the Mutinies which has yet, in a popular form, been made public."—*Athenæum.*

"Few men more competent than himself to speak authoritatively concerning Indian affairs."—*Standard.*

EDUCATIONAL COURSE OF SECULAR SCHOOL BOOKS FOR INDIA. Edited by **J. S. Laurie,** of the Inner Temple, Barrister-at-Law; formerly H.M. Inspector of Schools, England; Assistant Royal Commissioner, Ireland; Special Commissioner, African Settlements; Director of Public Instruction, Ceylon.

"These valuable little works will prove of real service to many of our readers, especially to those who intend entering the

Civil Service of India." — *Civil Service Gazette.*

EXTRACT FROM PROSPECTUS.

The Editor has undertaken to frame for India,—what he has been eminently successful in doing for England and her colonies,—a series of educational works, which he hopes will prove as suitable for the peculiar wants of the country as they will be consistent with the leading idea above alluded to. Like all beginnings, his present instalments are necessarily somewhat meagre and elementary; but he only

awaits official and public approval to complete, within a comparatively brief period, his contemplated plan of a specific and fairly comprehensive series of works in the various leading vernaculars of the Indian continent. Meanwhile, those on his general catalogue may be found suitable, in their present form, for use in the Anglo-vernacular and English schools of India.

The following Works are now ready:—

	s. d.		s. d.
THE FIRST HINDUSTANI READER, stiff linen wrapper .	0 6	GEOGRAPHY OF INDIA, with Maps and Historical Appendix,	
Ditto ditto strongly bound in cloth .	0 9	tracing the growth of the British	
THE SECOND HINDUSTANI READER, stiff linen wrapper .	0 6	Empire in Hindustan. 128 pp.	
Ditto ditto strongly bound in cloth .	0 9	Cloth.	1 6

In the Press.

ELEMENTARY GEOGRAPHY OF INDIA.

FACTS AND FEATURES OF INDIAN HISTORY, in a series of alternating Reading Lessons and Memory Exercises.

EXCHANGE TABLES OF STERLING AND INDIAN RUPEE CURRENCY, UPON A NEW AND EXTENDED SYSTEM, embracing Values from One Farthing to One Hundred Thousand Pounds, and at rates progressing, in Sixteenths of a Penny, from 1s. 9d. to 2s. 3d. per Rupee. By **Donald Fraser,** Accountant to the British Indian Steam Navigation Co., Limited. Royal 8vo. 10s. 6d.

"The calculations must have entailed great labour on the author, but the work is one which we fancy must become a standard one in all business houses which

have dealings with any country where the rupee and the English pound are standard coins of currency."—*Inverness Courier.*

BOOKS FOR THE YOUNG AND FOR LENDING LIBRARIES.

———◆———

PHANTASMION. A Fairy Romance. A new Edition. By **Sara Coleridge.** With an Introductory Preface by the **Right Hon.** Lord Coleridge of Ottery S. Mary. In 1 vol., crown 8vo. Price 7s. 6d.
[In preparation.

CASSY. A New Story, by **Hesba Stretton.** Square Crown 8vo, Illustrated, uniform with "Lost Gip." Price 1s. 6d. *[In the press.*

THE KING'S SERVANTS. By **Hesba Stretton,** Author of "Lost Gip." Square crown 8vo, uniform with "Lost Gip." 8 Illustrations. Price 1s. 6d.

Part I.—Faithful in Little. Part II.—Unfaithful. Part III.—Faithful in Much.

"The language is beautifully simple, the stories are touchingly told."—*Watchman.*
"Told in Hesba Stretton's tenderest style."—*Graphic.*

"A cleverly told story . . . The local colouring and the simple thought and language of the better class of poor are well preserved."—*Guardian.*

LOST GIP. By **Hesba Stretton,** Author of "Little Meg," "Alone in London." Square crown 8vo. Six Illustrations. Price 1s. 6d.

** *A HANDSOMELY BOUND EDITION, WITH TWELVE ILLUSTRATIONS, PRICE HALF-A-CROWN.*

"Thoroughly enlists the sympathies of the reader."—*Church Review.*
"Full of tender touches."—*Nonconform.*

"An exquisitely touching little story." *Church Herald.*

DADDY'S PET. By **Mrs. Ellen Ross (Nelsie Brook).** Square crown 8vo, uniform with "Lost Gip." 6 Illustrations. Price 1s.

"We have been more than pleased with this simple bit of writing."—*Christian World.*

"Full of deep feeling and true and noble sentiment."—*Brighton Gazette.*

SEEKING HIS FORTUNE, AND OTHER STORIES. Crown 8vo. Four Illustrations. Price 3s. 6d.

CONTENTS.—Seeking his Fortune.—Oluf and Stephanoff.—What's in a Name?—Contrast.—Onesta.

"Plain, straightforward stories, told in the precise, detailed manner which we are sure young people like."—*Spectator.*
"Romantic, entertaining, and decidedly inculcate a sound and generous moral.

We can answer for it that this volume will find favour with those for whom it is written, and that the sisters will like it quite as well as the brothers."—*Athenæum.*

———

THREE WORKS BY MARTHA FARQUHARSON.

Each Story is independent and complete in itself. They are published in uniform size and price, and are elegantly bound and illustrated.

I. **ELSIE DINSMORE.** Crown 8vo. 3*s.* 6*d.*

II. **ELSIE'S GIRLHOOD.** Crown 8vo. 3*s.* 6*d.*

III. **ELSIE'S HOLIDAYS AT ROSELANDS.** Crown 8vo. 3*s.* 6*d.*

THE AFRICAN CRUISER. A Midshipman's Adventures on the West Coast. A Book for Boys. By **S. Whitchurch Sadler, R.N.**, Author of "Marshall Vavasour." Illustrations. Crown 8vo. 3*s.* 6*d.*

"A capital story of youthful adventure. . . . Sea-loving boys will find few pleasanter gift books this season than 'The African Cruiser.'"—*Hour.*

"Sea yarns have always been in favour with boys, but this, written in a brisk style by a thorough sailor, is crammed full of adventures."—*Times.*

"A book of adventures told in a style at once lively and elegant . . . . Just now, when the Ashantee war is attracting more than usual attention to the coast of Africa, such volumes as the 'Cruiser' will be eagerly read."—*Edinburgh Review.*

"A first-rate book for boys." — *John Bull.*

THE LITTLE WONDER-HORN. By **Jean Ingelow.** A Second Series of "*Stories told to a Child.*" Fifteen Illustrations. Cloth, gilt. 3*s.* 6*d.*

"Full of fresh and vigorous fancy: it is worthy of the author of some of the best of our modern verse."—*Standard.*

"We like all the contents of the 'Little Wonder-Horn' very much."—*Athenæum.*

"We recommend it with confidence."—*Pall Mall Gazette.*

Second Edition.

BRAVE MEN'S FOOTSTEPS. A Book of Example and Anecdote for Young People. By the Editor of "**Men who have Risen.**" With Four Illustrations. By **C. Doyle.** 3*s.* 6*d.*

'The little volume is precisely of the stamp to win the favour of those who, in choosing a gift for a boy, would consult his moral development as well as his temporary pleasure."—*Daily Telegraph.*

"A readable and instructive volume."—*Examiner.*

"No more welcome book for the school-boy could be imagined."—*Birmingham Daily Gazette.*

Second Edition.

PLUCKY FELLOWS. A Book for Boys. By **Stephen J. Mac Kenna.** With Six Illustrations. Crown 8vo. Price 3*s.* 6*d.*

"This is one of the very best 'Books for Boys' which have been issued this year."—*Morning Advertiser.*

"A thorough book for boys . . . written

throughout in a manly straightforward manner that is sure to win the hearts of the children for whom it is intended."—*London Society.*

Second Edition.

GUTTA-PERCHA WILLIE, THE WORKING GENIUS. By George Macdonald. With Illustrations by Arthur Hughes. Crown 8vo. 3*s.* 6*d.*

"An amusing and instructive book."—*Yorkshire Post.*
"One of those charming books for which the author is so well known."—*Edinburgh Daily Review.*

"The cleverest child we know assures us she has read this story through five times. Mr. Macdonald will, we are convinced, accept that verdict upon his little work as final."—*Spectator.*

THE TRAVELLING MENAGERIE. By Charles Camden, Author of "Hoity Toity." Illustrated by J. Mahoney. Crown 8vo. 3*s.* 6*d.*

"A capital little book . . . . deserves a wide circulation among our boys and girls."—*Hour.*

"A very attractive story." — *Public Opinion.*

New Edition.

THE DESERT PASTOR, JEAN JAROUSSEAU. Translated from the French of Eugene Pelletan. By Colonel E. P. De L'Hoste. In fcap. 8vo, with an Engraved Frontispiece. Price 3*s.* 6*d.*

"There is a poetical simplicity and picturesqueness ; the noblest heroism ; unpretentious religion ; pure love, and the spectacle of a household brought up in the fear of the Lord. . . . ."—*Illustrated London News.*

"This charming specimen of Eugène Pelletan's tender grace, humour, and high-toned morality."—*Notes and Queries.*
"A touching record of the struggles in the cause of religious liberty of a real man."—*Graphic.*

THE DESERTED SHIP. A Real Story of the Atlantic. By Cupples Howe, Master Mariner. Illustrated by Townley Green. Crown 8vo. 3*s.* 6*d.*

"Curious adventures with bears, seals, and other Arctic animals, and with scarcely more human Esquimaux, form the mass of

material with which the story deals, and will much interest boys who have a spice of romance in their composition."—*Courant.*

HOITY TOITY, THE GOOD LITTLE FELLOW. By Charles Camden. Illustrated. Crown 8vo. 3*s.* 6*d.*

"Young folks may gather a good deal of wisdom from the story, which is written in an amusing and attractive style."—*Courant.*
"Relates very pleasantly the history of

a charming little fellow who meddles always with a kindly disposition with other people's affairs and helps them to do right. There are many shrewd lessons to be picked up in this clever little story."—*Public Opinion.*

AT SCHOOL WITH AN OLD DRAGOON. By **Stephen J. Mac Kenna**. Crown 8vo. 5*s.* With Six Illustrations.

" Consisting almost entirely of startling stories of military adventure . . . Boys will find them sufficiently exciting reading."—*Times.*

" These yarns give some very spirited and interesting descriptions of soldiering in various parts of the world."—*Spectator.*

" Mr. MacKenna's former work, ' Plucky Fellows,' is already a general favourite, and those who read the stories of the Old Dragoon will find that he has still plenty of materials at hand for pleasant tales, and has lost none of his power in telling them well."—*Standard.*

" Full of adventure of the most stirring kind."—*Scotsman.*

" A book of genuine military adventures, written in such a manner as must captivate the hearts of all who are fond of this kind of narrative."—*Brighton Gazette.*

FANTASTIC STORIES. Translated from the German of **Richard Leander**, by **Paulina B. Granville**. Crown 8vo. Eight full-page Illustrations, by **M. E. Fraser Tytler**. Price 5*s.*

" Short, quaint, and as they are fitly called fantastic, they deal with all manner of subjects."—*Guardian.*

" ' Fantastic' is certainly the right epithet to apply to some of these strange tales."—*Examiner.*

" One of the most delightful books which for some time has come under our notice . . Singularly beautiful, and perfectly enjoyable by young and old."—*Glasgow Herald.*

" A book of fancy tales and fairy imaginings of a very attractive character." —*Brighton Gazette.*

Third Edition.

STORIES IN PRECIOUS STONES. By **Helen Zimmern**. With Six Illustrations. Crown 8vo. 5*s.*

" A pretty little book which fanciful young persons will appreciate, and which will remind its readers of many a legend, and many an imaginary virtue attached to the gems they are so fond of wearing."—*Post.*

" A series of pretty tales which are half fantastic, half natural, and pleasantly quaint, as befits stories intended for the young."—*Daily Telegraph.*

THE GREAT DUTCH ADMIRALS. By **Jacob de Liefde**. Crown 8vo. Illustrated. Price 5*s.*

" A really good book."—*Standard.*

" May be recommended as a wholesome present for boys. They will find in it numerous tales of adventure."—*Athenæum.*

" Thoroughly interesting and inspiriting."—*Public Opinion.*

" A really excellent book."—*Spectator.*

LAYS OF A KNIGHT ERRANT IN MANY LANDS. By **Major-General Sir Vincent Eyre, C.B., G.C.S.I.**, etc. 6 Illustrations. Square crown 8vo. Six Illustrations. Price 7*s.* 6*d.*

Pharaoh Land.
Home Land.

Wonder Land.
Rhine Land.

WORKS BY ALFRED TENNYSON, D.C.L.

POET LAUREATE.

	PRICE s. d.
POEMS. Small 8vo	9 0
MAUD AND OTHER POEMS. Small 8vo	5 0
THE PRINCESS. Small 8vo	5 0
IDYLLS OF THE KING. Small 8vo	7 0
,, ,, Collected. Small 8vo . .	12 0
ENOCH ARDEN, &c. Small 8vo	6 0
THE HOLY GRAIL, AND OTHER POEMS. Small 8vo .	7 0
GARETH AND LYNETTE. Small 8vo	5 0
SELECTIONS FROM THE ABOVE WORKS. Square 8vo, cloth extra	5 0
SONGS FROM THE ABOVE WORKS. Square 8vo, cloth extra	5 0
IN MEMORIAM. Small 8vo	6 0
LIBRARY EDITION OF MR. TENNYSON'S WORKS. 6 vols. Post 8vo	10 6
POCKET VOLUME EDITION OF MR. TENNYSON'S WORKS. 10 vols., in neat case	45 0
,, gilt edges	50 0
THE WINDOW: OR, THE SONGS OF THE WRENS. A Series of Songs by ALFRED TENNYSON, with Music by ARTHUR SULLIVAN. 4to, cloth, gilt extra	21 0

65, Cornhill; & 12, Paternoster Row, London.

POETRY.

LYRICS OF LOVE, Selected and arranged from Shakspeare to Tennyson, by **W. Davenport Adams.** Fcap. 8vo, price 3s. 6d.

"A most careful and charming compilation, stands altogether apart from previous collections on several grounds. We cannot too highly commend this work, delightful in its contents and so pretty in its outward adornings."—*Standard.*

"Carefully selected and elegantly got up. . . . Mr. Davenport Adams has exer-

cised great taste in the selections which he has made, and has laid under contribution all the best English authors. It is particularly rich in poems from living writers; but other favourites, whose writings have stood the test of time, are by no means overlooked."—*John Bull.*

WILLIAM CULLEN BRYANT'S POEMS. Red-line Edition. Handsomely bound. With Illustrations and Portrait of the Author. Price 7s. 6d. A Cheaper Edition is also published. Price 3s. 6d.

These are the only complete English Editions sanctioned by the Author.

ENGLISH SONNETS. Collected and Arranged by **John Dennis.** Small crown 8vo. Elegantly bound, price 3s. 6d.

"An exquisite selection, a selection which every lover of poetry will consult again and again with delight. The notes are very useful. . . . The volume is one for which

English literature owes Mr. Dennis the heartiest thanks."—*Spectator.*

"Mr. Dennis has shown great judgment in this selection."—*Saturday Review.*

HOME-SONGS FOR QUIET HOURS. By the **Rev. Canon R. H. Baynes,** Editor of "English Lyrics" and "Lyra Anglicana." Handsomely printed and bound, price 3s. 6d.

THE DISCIPLES. A New Poem. By **Harriet Eleanor Hamilton King.** Crown 8vo. 7s. 6d.

ASPROMONTE, AND OTHER POEMS. Second Edition, cloth, 4s. 6d.

"The volume is anonymous, but there is no reason for the author to be ashamed of it. The 'Poems of Italy' are evidently inspired by genuine enthusiasm in the cause espoused; and one of them, 'The

Execution of Felice Orsini,' has much poetic merit, the event celebrated being told with dramatic force."—*Athenæum.*

"The verse is fluent and free."—*Spectator.*

SONGS FOR MUSIC. By **Four Friends.** Square crown 8vo, price 5s.

CONTAINING SONGS BY

Reginald A. Gatty.   Stephen H. Gatty.
Greville J. Chester.   Juliana H. Ewing.

"A charming gift-book, which will be very popular with lovers of poetry."—*John Bull.*

ROBERT BUCHANAN, THE POETICAL AND PROSE WORKS OF. Collected Edition, in 5 Vols. Vol. I. contains.—"Ballads and Romances;" "Ballads and Poems of Life," and a Portrait of the Author. [*Is now ready.*

Vol. II.—"Ballads and Poems of Life;" "Allegories and Sonnets."

Vol. III.—"Cruiskeen Sonnets;" "Book of Orm;" "Political Mystics."

The Contents of the remaining Volumes will be duly announced.

POETRY—*continued.*

HOLY FOOTSTEPS. A VOLUME OF SACRED HYMNS AND POEMS. Crown 8vo. [*Shortly.*

THOUGHTS IN VERSE. Small crown 8vo. Price 1s. 6d.

This is a Collection of Verses expressive of religious feeling, written from a Theistic stand-point.

COSMOS. A Poem. Small crown 8vo. Price 3s. 6d.

SUBJECT.—Nature in the Past and in the Present.—Man in the Past and in the Present.—The Future.

NARCISSUS AND OTHER POEMS. By E. Carpenter. Small crown 8vo. Price 5s.

"Displays considerable poetic force."— *Queen.*

A TALE OF THE SEA, SONNETS, AND OTHER POEMS. By James Howell. Crown 8vo, cloth, 5s.

"Mr. Howell has a keen perception of the beauties of nature, and a just appreciation of the charities of life. . . . Mr. Howell's book deserves, and will probably receive, a warm reception."—*Pall Mall Gazette.*

IMITATIONS FROM THE GERMAN OF SPITTA AND TERSTEGEN. By Lady Durand. Crown 8vo. 4s.

"An acceptable addition to the religious poetry of the day."—*Courant.*

"A charming little volume. . . . Will be a very valuable assistance to peaceful, meditative souls."—*Church Herald.*

VIGNETTES IN RHYME. Collected Verses. By Austin Dobson. Crown 8vo. Price 5s.

"Clever, clear-cut, and careful."—*Athenæum.*

"We were hardly prepared for the touches of genuine beauty which adorn so many of these little poems."—*Spectator.*

"As a writer of Vers de Société Mr. Dobson is almost, if not quite, unrivalled." —*Examiner.*

"Lively, innocent, elegant in expression, and graceful in fancy."—*Morning Post.*

ON VIOL AND FLUTE. A New Volume of Poems, by Edmund W. Gosse. With a Frontispiece by W. B. Scott. Crown 8vo. Price 5s.

"A careful perusal of his verses will show that he is a poet. . . . His song has the grateful, murmuring sound which reminds one of the softness and deliciousness of summer time. . . . There is much that is good in the volume."—*Spectator.*

METRICAL TRANSLATIONS FROM THE GREEK AND LATIN POETS, AND OTHER POEMS. By R. B. Boswell, M.A. Oxon. Crown 8vo, price 5s.

EASTERN LEGENDS AND STORIES IN ENGLISH VERSE. By Lieutenant Norton Powlett, Royal Artillery. Crown 8vo. 5s.

"Have we at length found a successor to Thomas Ingoldsby? We are almost inclined to hope so after reading 'Eastern Legends.' There is a rollicking sense of fun about the stories, joined to marvellous power of rhyming, and plenty of swing, which irresistibly reminds us of our old favourite."—*Graphic.*

EDITH, OR, LOVE AND LIFE IN CHESHIRE. By T. Ashe, Author of the "Sorrows of Hypsipyle," etc. Sewed. Price 6d.

"A really fine poem, full of tender, subtle touches of feeling."—*Manchester News.*

"Pregnant from beginning to end with the results of careful observation and imaginative power."—*Chester Chronicle.*

THE GALLERY OF PIGEONS, AND OTHER POEMS. By Theo. Marzials. Crown 8vo. 4s. 6d.

"A conceit abounding in prettiness."— *Examiner.*

"Contains as clear evidence as a book can contain that its composition was a source of keen and legitimate enjoyment. The rush of fresh, sparkling fancies is too rapid, too sustained, too abundant, not to be spontaneous."—*Academy.*

THE INN OF STRANGE MEETINGS, AND OTHER POEMS. By Mortimer Collins. Crown 8vo. 5s.

"Abounding in quiet humour, in bright fancy, in sweetness and melody of expression, and, at times, in the tenderest touches of pathos."—*Graphic.*

"Mr. Collins has an undercurrent of chivalry and romance beneath the trifling vein of good-humoured banter which is the special characteristic of his verse."— *Athenæum.*

EROS AGONISTES. By E. B. D. Crown 8vo. 3s. 6d.

"The author of these verses has written a very touching story of the human heart in the story he tells with such pathos and power, of an affection cherished so long and so secretly. . . . It is not the least merit of these pages that they are everywhere illumined with moral and religious sentiment suggested, not paraded, of the brightest, purest character."— *Standard.*

POETRY—*continued.*

CALDERON'S DRAMAS.
Translated from the Spanish. By Denis
Florence MacCarthy. 10s. ●

"In the volume now before us, each
play is rendered in the very number of
lines and half-lines of the original. Every
variation of metre, every change of vowels,
is followed and reproduced. Yet in such
rigid fetters the lambent verse flows with
an ease, spirit, and music perfectly natural,
liberal, and harmonious."—*Spectator.*
"It is impossible to speak too highly of
this beautiful work."—*Month.*

SONGS FOR SAILORS. By Dr. W. C.
Bennett. Dedicated by Special Request
to H. R. H. the Duke of Edinburgh.
Crown 8vo. 3s. 6d. With Steel Portrait
and Illustrations.
An Edition in Illustrated paper Covers,
Price 1s.

WALLED IN, AND OTHER POEMS.
By the Rev. Henry J. Bulkeley. Crown
8vo. 5s.

"A remarkable book of genuine poetry."
—*Evening Standard.*
"Genuine power displayed." — *Examiner.*
". . . . . . Poetical feeling is manifest
here, and the diction of the poem is unim-
peachable."—*Pall Mall Gazette.*

SONGS OF LIFE AND DEATH. By
John Payne, Author of "Intaglios,"
"Sonnets," "The Masque of Shadows,"
etc. Crown 8vo. 5s.

"The art of ballad-writing has long been
lost in England, and Mr. Payne may claim
to be its restorer. It is a perfect delight to
meet with such a ballad as 'May Margaret'
in the present volume." — *Westminster
Review.*

A NEW VOLUME OF SONNETS. By
the Rev. C. Tennyson Turner. Crown
8vo. 4s. 6d.

"Mr. Turner is a genuine poet; his song
is sweet and pure, beautiful in expression,
and often subtle in thought."—*Pall Mall
Gazette.*
"The dominant charm of all these sonnets
is the pervading presence of the writer's
personality, never obtruded but always
impalpably diffused. The light of a devout,
gentle, and kindly spirit, a delicate and
graceful fancy, a keen intelligence irradiates
these thoughts."—*Contemporary Review.*

GOETHE'S FAUST. A New Translation
in Rime. By the Rev. C. Kegan Paul.
Crown 8vo. 6s.

"His translation is the most minute
accurate that has yet been produced. . . .
—*Examiner.*
". . . and his translation is as well suited
to convey its meaning to English readers
as any we have yet seen."—*Edinburgh
Daily Review.*
"Mr. Paul is a zealous and a faithful
interpreter."—*Saturday Review.*

**THE DREAM AND THE DEED, AND
OTHER POEMS.** By Patrick Scott,
Author of "Footpaths between Two
Worlds," etc. Fcap. 8vo, cloth, 5s.

'A bitter and able satire on the vice
and follies of the day, literary, social, and
political."—*Standard.*
"Shows real poetic power coupled with
evidences of satirical energy."—*Edinburgh
Daily Review.*

SONGS OF TWO WORLDS. By a
New Writer. Fcap. 8vo, cloth, 5s.
Second Edition.

"These poems will assuredly take high
rank among the class to which they belong."
—*British Quarterly Review, April 1st.*
". . . the promise of a fine poet."—*Spectator, February 17th.*
"No extracts could do justice to the
exquisite tones, the felicitous phrasing and
delicately wrought harmonies of some of
these poems." — *Nonconformist, March
27th.*
"A purity and delicacy of feeling like
morning air."—*Graphic, March 16th.*

**THE LEGENDS OF ST. PATRICK
AND OTHER POEMS.** By Aubrey
de Vere. Crown 8vo. 5s.

"Mr. De Vere's versification in his
earlier poems is characterised by great
sweetness and simplicity. He is master of
his instrument, and rarely offends the ear
with false notes. We can promise the
patient and thoughtful reader much
pleasure in the perusal of this volume."—
Pall Mall Gazette.
"We have but space to commend the
varied structure of his verse, the careful-
ness of his grammar, and his excellent
English."—*Saturday Review.*

FICTION.

—✦—

BEATRICE AYLMER AND OTHER TALES. By the Author of " Brampton Rectory." 1 vol. Crown 8vo. [*Preparing.*

JUDITH GWYNNE. By Lisle Carr. In 3 vols. Crown 8vo, cloth.

TOO LATE. By Mrs. Newman. 2 vols. Crown 8vo. [*Just out.*

LADY MORETOUN'S DAUGHTER. By Mrs. Eiloart. In 3 vols. Crown 8vo, cloth.

MARGARET AND ELIZABETH. A Story of the Sea. By Katherine Saunders, Author of " Gideon's Rock," &c. In 1 vol. Cloth, crown 8vo.

" Simply yet powerfully told. . . . This opening picture is so exquisitely drawn as to be a fit introduction to a story of such simple pathos and power. . . . A very beautiful story closes as it began, in a tender and touching picture of homely happiness." —*Pall Mall Gazette.*

" The story is told in fine and well-polished phrases." —*Daily News.*

" A successful contrast to the mass of fictitious rubbish it is our duty to peruse." —*Athenæum.*

MR. CARINGTON. A Tale of Love and Conspiracy. By Robert Turner Cotton. In 3 vols. Cloth, crown 8vo.

" Brilliant and ingenious. . . . Will certainly find and please many readers. . . . as amusing as he is naughty." —*Standard.*
" Clever and worth reading. . . His heroes and heroines think, speak, and act like English gentlemen and ladies." —*Echo.*
The writer is a man of remarkable and unique power." —*Hour.*
" A novel in so many ways good, as in a fresh and elastic diction, stout unconventionality, and happy boldness of conception and execution. His novels, though free spoken, will be some of the healthiest of our day." —*Examiner.*

TWO GIRLS. By Frederick Wedmore, Author of " A Snapt Gold Ring." In 2 vols. Cloth, crown 8vo. [*Just out.*

" A carefully-written novel of character, contrasting the two heroines of one love tale, an English lady and a French actress Cicely is charming ; the introductory description of her is a good specimen of the well-balanced sketches in which the author shines." —*Athenæum.*

HEATHERGATE. In 2 vols. Crown 8vo, cloth. A Story of Scottish Life and Character by a new Author.

" Its merit lies in the marked antithesis of strongly developed characters, in different ranks of life, and resembling each other in nothing but their marked nationality." —*Athenæum.*
" Worth reading for its pictures of Scottish life and character in the early years of this century." —*Graphic.*
" The plot is woven with touching ingenuity. . . . The descriptions of nature deserve praise for their simple beauty and delicacy of touch. . . . Many will read and be interested in the book." —*Hour.*

THE QUEEN'S SHILLING. By Captain Arthur Griffiths, Author of " Peccavi." 2 vols.

" . . . . A very lively and agreeable novel." —*Vanity Fair.*
" ' The Queen's Shilling ' is a capital story, far more interesting than the meagre sketch we have given of the fortunes of the hero and heroine can suggest. Every scene, character, and incident of the book are so life-like that they seem drawn from life direct." —*Pall Mall Gazette.*

MIRANDA. A Midsummer Madness. By Mortimer Collins. 3 vols.
" There is not a dull page in the whole three volumes." —*Standard.*
" The work of a man who is at once a thinker and a poet." —*Hour.*

SQUIRE SILCHESTER'S WHIM. By Mortimer Collins, Author of " Marquis and Merchant," " The Princess Clarice," &c. Crown 8vo. 3 vols.
" We think it the best (story) Mr. Collins has yet written. Full of incident and adventure." —*Pall Mall Gazette.*
" Decidedly the best novel from the pen of Mr. Mortimer Collins that we have yet come across." —*Graphic.*
" So clever, so irritating, and so charming a story." —*Standard.*

FICTION—*continued.*

WHAT 'TIS TO LOVE. By the Author of " Flora Adair," " The Value of Fosterstown." 3 vols.

THE PRINCESS CLARICE. A Story of 1871. By Mortimer Collins. 2 vols. Crown 8vo.

"Mr. Collins has produced a readable book, amusingly characteristic. . . . ."—*Athenæum.*
"Very readable and amusing. We would especially give an honourable mention to Mr. Collins's '*vers de société,*' the writing of which has almost become a lost art."—*Pall Mall Gazette.*
"A bright, fresh, and original book."—*Standard.*

REGINALD BRAMBLE. A Cynic of the 19th Century. An Autobiography. 1 vol.
"There is plenty of vivacity in Mr. Bramble's narrative."—*Athenæum.*
"Written in a lively and readable style."—*Hour.*
"The skill of the author in the delineation of the supposed chronicler, and the preservation of his natural character, is beyond praise."—*Morning Post.*

EFFIE'S GAME; How SHE LOST AND HOW SHE WON. By Cecil Clayton. 2 vols.
"Well written. The characters move, and act, and, above all, talk like human beings, and we have liked reading about them."—*Spectator.*

CHESTERLEIGH. By Ansley Conyers. 3 vols. Crown 8vo.
"We have gained much enjoyment from the book."—*Spectator.*
"Will suit the hosts of readers of the higher class of romantic fiction."—*Morning Advertiser.*

BRESSANT. A Romance. By Julian Hawthorne. 2 vols. Crown 8vo.
"The son's work we venture to say is worthy of the sire. . . . The story as it stands is one of the most powerful with which we are acquainted."—*Times.*
"Pretty certain of meeting in this country a grateful and appreciative reception."—*Athenæum.*
"Mr. Julian Hawthorne is endowed with a large share of his father's peculiar genius."—*Pall Mall Gazette.*
"Enough to make us hopeful that we shall once more have reason to rejoice whenever we hear that a new work is coming out written by one who bears the honoured name of Hawthorne."—*Saturday Review.*

HONOR BLAKE: THE STORY OF A PLAIN WOMAN. By Mrs. Keating, Author of "English Homes in India," &c. 2 vols. Crown 8vo.
"One of the best novels we have met with for some time."—*Morning Post.*
"A story which must do good to all, young and old, who read it."—*Daily News.*

OFF THE SKELLIGS. By Jean Ingelow. (Her First Romance.) Crown 8vo. In 4 vols.
"Clever and sparkling."—*Standard.*
"We read each succeeding volume with increasing interest, going almost to the point of wishing there was a fifth."—*Athenæum.*
"The novel as a whole is a remarkable one, because it is uncompromisingly true to life."—*Daily News.*

SEETA. By Colonel Meadows Taylor, Author of "Tara," "Ralph Darnell," &c. Crown 8vo. 3 vols.
"The story is well told, native life is admirably described, and the petty intrigues of native rulers, and their hatred of the English, mingled with fear lest the latter should eventually prove the victors, are cleverly depicted."—*Athenæum.*
"We cannot speak too highly of Colonel Meadows Taylor's book. . . . We would recommend all novel-readers to purchase it at the earliest opportunity."—*John Bull.*
"Thoroughly interesting and enjoyable reading."—*Examiner.*

HESTER MORLEY'S PROMISE. By Hesba Stretton. 3 vols.
"'Hester Morley's Promise' is much better than the average novel of the day; it has much more claim to critical consideration as a piece of literary work,—not mere mechanism. The pictures of a narrow society—narrow of soul and intellect—in which the book abounds, are very clever."—*Spectator.*
"Its charm lies not so much, perhaps, in any special excellence in character, drawing, or construction—though all the characters stand out clearly and are well sustained, and the interest of the story never flags—as in general tone and colouring."—*Observer.*

FICTION—*continued.*

THE DOCTOR'S DILEMMA. By Hesba Stretton, Author of "Little Meg," &c. &c. Crown 8vo. 3 vols.

"A fascinating story which scarcely flags in interest from the first page to the last. It is all story; every page contributes something to the result."—*British Quarterly Review.*

THE ROMANTIC ANNALS OF A NAVAL FAMILY. By Mrs. Arthur Traherne. Crown 8vo. 10s. 6d.

"A very readable and interesting book." —*United Service Gazette,* June 28, 1873.

"Some interesting letters are introduced; amongst others, several from the late King William IV."— *Spectator.*

"Well and pleasantly told. There are also some capital descriptions of English country life in the last century, presenting a vivid picture of England before the introduction of railways, and the busy life accompanying them."—*Evening Standard.*

THE SPINSTERS OF BLATCH-INGTON. By Mar. Travers. 2 vols. Crown 8vo.

"A pretty story. Deserving of a favourable reception."—*Graphic.*

"A book of more than average merits, worth reading."—*Examiner.*

A GOOD MATCH. By Amelia Perrier, Author of "Mea Culpa." 2 vols.

"Racy and lively."—*Athenæum.*

"As pleasant and readable a novel as we have seen this season."—*Examiner.*

"This clever and amusing novel."—*Pall Mall Gazette.*

"Agreeably written."—*Public Opinion.*

THOMASINA. By the Author of "Dorothy," "De Cressy," &c. 2 vols. Crown 8vo.

"A finished and delicate cabinet picture; no line is without its purpose, but all contribute to the unity of the work."—*Athenæum.*

"For the delicacies of character-drawing, for play of incident, and for finish of style, we must refer our readers to the story itself."—*Daily News.*

"This undeniably pleasing story."— *Pall Mall Gazette.*

VANESSA. By the Author of "Thomasina." 2 vols. Crown 8vo. [*Shortly.*

JOHANNES OLAF. By E. de Wille. Translated by F. E. Bunnett. Crown 8vo. 3 vols.

"The art of description is fully exhibited; perception of character and capacity for delineating it are obvious; while there is great breadth and comprehensiveness in the plan of the story."—*Morning Post.*

THE STORY OF SIR EDWARD'S WIFE. By Hamilton Marshall, Author of "For Very Life." 1 vol. Crown 8vo.

"A quiet, graceful little story."—*Spectator.*

"There are many clever conceits in it. . . . Mr. Hamilton Marshall can tell a story closely and pleasantly."—*Pall Mall Gazette.*

LINKED AT LAST. By F. E. Bunnett. 1 vol. Crown 8vo.

"'Linked at Last' contains so much of pretty description, natural incident, and delicate portraiture, that the reader who once takes it up will not be inclined to relinquish it without concluding the volume." —*Morning Post.*

"A very charming story." — *John Bull.*

PERPLEXITY. By Sydney Mostyn. 3 vols. Crown 8vo.

"Shows much lucidity—much power of portraiture."—*Examiner.*

"Written with very considerable power, great cleverness, and sustained interest." —*Standard.*

"The literary workmanship is good, and the story forcibly and graphically told."— *Daily News.*

MEMOIRS OF MRS. LÆTITIA BOOTHBY. By William Clark Russell, Author of "The Book of Authors." Crown 8vo. 7s. 6d.

"Clever and ingenious." — *Saturday Review.*

"One of the most delightful books I have read for a very long while. . . . Thoroughly entertaining from the first page to the last."—*Judy.*

"Very clever book."—*Guardian.*

CRUEL AS THE GRAVE. By the Countess Von Bothmer. 3 vols. Crown 8vo.

"*Jealousy is cruel as the Grave.*"

"An interesting, though somewhat tragic story."—*Athenæum.*

"An agreeable, unaffected, and eminently readable novel."—*Daily News.*

Thirty-Second Edition.

GINX'S BABY; His BIRTH AND OTHER MISFORTUNES. By Edward Jenkins. Crown 8vo. Price 2s.

FICTION—*continued.*

Fourteenth Thousand.

LITTLE HODGE. A Christmas Country Carol. By **Edward Jenkins**, Author of "Ginx's Baby," &c. Illustrated. Crown 8vo. 5*s.*

A Cheap Edition in paper covers, price 1*s.*

"Wise and humorous, but yet most pathetic."—*Nonconformist.*

"The pathos of some of the passages is extremely touching."—*Manchester Examiner.*

Sixth Edition.

LORD BANTAM. By **Edward Jenkins**, Author of "Ginx's Baby." Crown 8vo. Price 2*s.* 6*d.*

LUCHMEE AND DILLOO. A Story of West Indian Life. By **Edward Jenkins**, Author of "Ginx's Baby," "Little Hodge," &c. 2 vols. Demy 8vo. Illustrated. [*Preparing.*

HER TITLE OF HONOUR. By **Holme Lee.** Second Edition. 1 vol. Crown 8vo.

"With the interest of a pathetic story is united the value of a definite and high purpose."—*Spectator.*

"A most exquisitely written story."—*Literary Churchman.*

THE TASMANIAN LILY. By **James Bonwick.** Crown 8vo. Illustrated. Price 5*s.*

"The characters of the story are capitally conceived, and are full of those touches which give them a natural appearance."—*Public Opinion.*

"An interesting and useful work."—*Hour.*

MIKE HOWE, THE BUSHRANGER OF VAN DIEMEN'S LAND. By **James Bonwick**, Author of "The Tasmanian Lily," &c. Crown 8vo. With a Frontispiece.

"He illustrates the career of the bushranger half a century ago; and this he does in a highly creditable manner; his delineations of life in the bush are, to say the least, exquisite, and his representations of character are very marked."—*Edinburgh Courant.*

Second Edition.

SEPTIMIUS. A Romance. By **Nathaniel Hawthorne**, Author of "The Scarlet Letter," "Transformation," &c. 1 vol. Crown 8vo, cloth, extra gilt. 9*s.*

The *Athenæum* says that "the book is full of Hawthorne's most characteristic writing."

"One of the best examples of Hawthorne's writing; every page is impressed with his peculiar view of thought, conveyed in his own familiar way."—*Post.*

PANDURANG HARI; or, MEMOIRS OF A HINDOO. A Tale of Mahratta Life sixty years ago. With a Preface, by **Sir H. Bartle E. Frere, G.C.S.I.,** &c. 2 vols. Crown 8vo. Price 21*s.*

"There is a quaintness and simplicity in the roguery of the hero that makes his life as attractive as that of Guzman d'Alfarache or Gil Blas, and so we advise our readers not to be dismayed at the length of Pandurang Hari, but to read it resolutely through. If they do this they cannot, we think, fail to be both amused and interested."—*Times.*

HERMANN AGHA. An Eastern Narrative. By **W. Gifford Palgrave**, Author of "Travels in Central Arabia," &c. 2 vols. Crown 8vo, cloth, extra gilt. 18*s.*

"Reads like a tale of life, with all its incidents. The young will take to it for its love portions, the older for its descriptions, some in this day for its Arab philosophy."—*Athenæum.*

"There is a positive fragrance as of newly-mown hay about it, as compared with the artificially perfumed passions which are detailed to us with such gusto by our ordinary novel-writers in their endless volumes."—*Observer.*

GIDEON'S ROCK, and other Stories. By **Katherine Saunders.** In 1 vol. Crown 8vo.

CONTENTS.—Gideon's Rock.—Old Matthew's Puzzle.—Gentle Jack.—Uncle Ned.—The Retired Apothecary.

JOAN MERRYWEATHER, and other Stories. By **Katherine Saunders.** In 1 vol. Crown 8vo.

CONTENTS.—The Haunted Crust.—The Flower-Girl.—Joan Merryweather.—The Watchman's Story.—An Old Letter.

COL. MEADOWS TAYLOR'S INDIAN TALES.

THE CONFESSIONS OF A THUG

Is now ready, and is the Volume of A New and Cheaper Edition, in 1 vol. each, Illustrated, price 6*s.* It will be followed by "TARA" (now in the press) "RALPH DARNELL," and "TIPPOO SULTAN."

THEOLOGICAL.

THE CHURCH AND THE EMPIRES. Historical Periods, by **Henry W. Wilberforce,** preceded by a Memoir of the Author by J. H. Newman, D.D.   1 vol.   Post 8vo.   [*Preparing.*

THE HIGHER LIFE. A New Volume by the **Rev. J. Baldwin Brown,** Author of " The Soul's Exodus," etc.   1 vol.   Crown 8vo.
                                                        [*Preparing.*

HARTHAM CONFERENCES; OR DISCUSSIONS UPON SOME OF THE RELIGIOUS TOPICS OF THE DAY. By the **Rev. F. W. Kingsford, M.A.,** Vicar of S. Thomas's, Stamford Hill ; late Chaplain H. E. I. C. (Bengal Presidency).   " Audi alteram partem." Crown 8vo.   3s. 6d.

STUDIES IN MODERN PROBLEMS. A Series of Essays by various Writers.   Edited by the **Rev. Orby Shipley, M.A.**

A Single Copy sent post free for 7d.   .   .   .   .
The Series of 12 Numbers sent post free for 7s., or for 7s. 6d. if 13 } *if prepaid.*
Additional Copies sent at proportionate rates.   .   .   .   .

ORDER OF ISSUE.

SACRAMENTAL CONFESSION.
                                A. H. WARD, B.A.
ABOLITION OF THE 39 ARTICLES.
                                NICHOLAS POCOCK, M.A.
THE SANCTITY OF MARRIAGE,
                                JOHN WALTER LEA, B.A.
CREATION AND MODERN SCIENCE.
                                GEORGE GREENWOOD, M.A.

RETREATS FOR PERSONS LIVING IN THE WORLD.
                                T. T. CARTER, M.A.
CATHOLIC AND PROTESTANT.
                                EDWARD L. BLENKINSOPP, M.A.
THE BISHOPS ON CONFESSION.
                                THE EDITOR.

UNTIL THE DAY DAWN. Four Advent Lectures delivered in the Episcopal Chapel, Milverton, Warwickshire, on the Sunday evenings during Advent, 1870.   By the **Rev. Marmaduke E. Browne.**   Crown 8vo. Price 2s. 6d.

"Four really original and stirring sermons."—*John Bull.*

A SCOTCH COMMUNION SUNDAY. To which are added Certain Discourses from a University City.   Second Edition.   By **A. K. H. B.,** Author of "The Recreations of a Country Parson."   Crown 8vo.   2nd Ed. Price 5s.

"Short of an actual attendance on the services, we know of nothing which will so enable us to understand their true character when conducted in their best form."— *Queen.*
"Some discourses are added, which are couched in language of rare power."— *John Bull.*

"Exceedingly ˜fresh and readable."— *Glasgow News.*
"We commend this volume as full of interest to all our readers.   It is written with much ability and good feeling, with excellent taste and marvellous tact."— *Church Herald.*

CHURCH THOUGHT AND CHURCH WORK. Edited by the **Rev. Chas. Anderson, M.A.,** Editor of " Words and Works in a London Parish."   Demy 8vo.   Pp. 250.   7s. 6d.   Containing Articles by the Rev. J. LL. DAVIES, J. M. CAPES, HARRY JONES, BROOKE LAMBERT, A. J. ROSS, Professor CHEETHAM, the EDITOR, and others.

THEOLOGICAL—*continued.*

WORDS AND WORKS IN A LONDON PARISH. Edited by the **Rev. Charles Anderson, M.A.** Demy 8vo. 6s.

"It has an interest of its own for not a few minds, to whom the question 'Is the National Church worth preserving as such, and if so how best increase its vital power?' is of deep and grave importance.' —*Spectator.*

EVERY DAY A PORTION : Adapted from the Bible and the Prayer Book, for the Private Devotions of those living in Widowhood. Collected and Edited by the **Lady Mary Vyner.** Square crown 8vo, printed on good paper, elegantly bound. Price 5s.

"Now she that is a widow indeed, and desolate, trusteth in God."

ESSAYS ON RELIGION AND LITERATURE. By Various Writers. Edited by the **Most Reverend Archbishop Manning.** Demy 8vo. 10s. 6d.

CONTENTS :—The Philosophy of Christianity.— Mystical Elements of Religion.— Controversy with the Agnostics.—A Reasoning Thought.—Darwinism brought to Book.—Mr. Mill on Liberty of the Press.— Christianity in relation to Society.—The Religious Condition of Germany. —The Philosophy of Bacon.—Catholic Laymen and Scholastic Philosophy.

WHY AM I A CHRISTIAN? By **Viscount Stratford de Redcliffe, P.C., K.G., G.C.B.** Crown 8vo. 3s. Third Edition.

"Has a peculiar interest, as exhibiting the convictions of an earnest, intelligent, and practical man."—*Contemporary Review.*

THEOLOGY AND MORALITY. Being Essays by the **Rev. J. Llewellyn Davies.** 1 vol. 8vo. Price 7s. 6d.

"There is a good deal that is well worth reading."—*Church Times.*
"The position taken up by Mr. Llewellyn Davies is well worth a careful survey on the part of philosophical students, for it represents the closest approximation of any theological system yet formulated to the religion of philosophy . . . We have not space to do more with regard to the social essays of the work before us, than to testify to the kindliness of spirit, sobriety, and earnest thought by which they are uniformly characterised."—*Examiner.*

THE RECONCILIATION OF RELIGION AND SCIENCE. Being Essays by the **Rev. T. W. Fowle, M.A.** 1 vol., 8vo. 10s. 6d.

"A book which requires and deserves the respectful attention of all reflecting Churchmen. It is earnest, reverent, thoughtful, and courageous. . . . There is scarcely a page in the book which is not equally worthy of a thoughtful pause."—*Literary Churchman.*

HYMNS AND VERSES, Original and Translated. By the **Rev. Henry Downton.** Small crown 8vo, 3s. 6d.

"It is a rare gift and very precious, and we heartily commend this, its fruits, to the pious in all denominations." — *Church Opinion.*
"Considerable force and beauty characterise some of these verses."—*Watchman.*
"Mr. Downton's 'Hymns and Verses' are worthy of all praise." — *English Churchman.*
"Will, we do not doubt, be welcome as a permanent possession to those for whom they have been composed or to whom they have been originally addressed."—*Church Herald.*

THEOLOGICAL—*continued.*

MISSIONARY ENTERPRISE IN THE EAST. By the **Rev. Richard Collins.** Illustrated. Crown 8vo. 6s.

"A very graphic story told in lucid, simple, and modest style." — *English Churchman.*

"A readable and very interesting volume."—*Church Review.*

"It is a real pleasure to read an honest book on Missionary work, every word of which shows the writer to be a man of large heart, far-seeing views, and liberal cultivation, and such a book we have now before us."—*Mission Life.*

"We may judge from our own experience, no one who takes up this charming little volume will lay it down again till he has got to the last word."—*John Bull.*

THE ETERNAL LIFE. Being Fourteen Sermons. By the **Rev. Jas. Noble Bennie, M.A.** Crown 8vo. 6s.

"We recommend these sermons as wholesome Sunday reading."—*English Churchman.*

"Very chaste and pure in style."— *Courant.*

"The whole volume is replete with matter for thought and study."—*John Bull.*

"Mr. Bennie preaches earnestly and well."—*Literary Churchman.*

THE REALM OF TRUTH. By **Miss E. T. Carne.** Crown 8vo. 5s. 6d.

"A singularly calm, thoughtful, and philosophical inquiry into what Truth is, and what its authority."—*Leeds Mercury.*

"It tells the world what it does not like to hear, but what it cannot be told too often,

that Truth is something stronger and more enduring than our little doings, and speakings, and actings." — *Literary Churchman.*

LIFE: Conferences delivered at Toulouse. By the **Rev. Père Lacordaire.** Crown 8vo. 6s.

"Let the serious reader cast his eye upon any single page in this volume, and he will find there words which will arrest his attention and give him a desire to know more of the teachings of this worthy follower of the saintly St. Dominick."—*Morning Post.*

"The book is worth studying as an evidence of the way in which an able man may be crippled by theological chains."—*Examiner.*

"The discourses are simple, natural, and unaffectedly eloquent."—*Public Opinion.*

Second Edition.

CATHOLICISM AND THE VATICAN. With a Narrative of the Old Catholic Congress at Munich. By **J. Lowry Whittle, A.M.**, Trin. Coll., Dublin. Crown 8vo. 4s. 6d.

"We may cordially recommend his book to all who wish to follow the course of the Old Catholic movement." — *Saturday Review.*

SIX PRIVY COUNCIL JUDGMENTS — 1850-1872. Annotated by **W. G. Brooke, M.A.**, Barrister-at-Law. Crown 8vo. 9s.

"The volume is a valuable record of cases forming precedents for the future."— *Athenæum.*

"A very timely and important publication. It brings into one view the great judgments of the last twenty years, which will constitute the unwritten law of the English Establishment." — *British Quarterly Review.*

THE MOST COMPLETE HYMN BOOK PUBLISHED.

HYMNS FOR THE CHURCH AND HOME. Selected and Edited by the **Rev. W. Fleming Stevenson,** Author of "Praying and Working."

The Hymn-book consists of Three Parts:—I. For Public Worship.—II. For Family and Private Worship.—III. For Children; and contains Biographical Notices of nearly 300 Hymn-writers, with Notes upon their Hymns.

** Published in various forms and prices, the latter ranging from 8d. to 6s. Lists and full particulars will be furnished on application to the Publisher.

THEOLOGICAL—*continued.*

WORKS BY THE REV. H. R. HAWEIS, M.A.

Sixth Edition.

THOUGHTS FOR THE TIMES. By the **Rev. H. R. Haweis, M.A.,** "Author of Music and Morals," etc. Crown 8vo. 7s. 6d.

"Bears marks of much originality of thought and individuality of expression."— *Pall Mall Gazette.*

"Mr. Haweis writes not only fearlessly,

but with remarkable freshness and vigour. In all that he says we perceive a transparent honesty and singleness of purpose.' —*Saturday Review.*

SPEECH IN SEASON. A New Volume of Sermons. By the **Rev. H. R. Haweis.** Crown 8vo, uniform with "Thoughts for the Times."

[*Preparing.*

UNSECTARIAN FAMILY PRAYERS for Morning and Evening for a Week with short selected passages from the Bible. By the **Rev. H. R. Haweis, M.A.** Square Crown 8vo. [*Preparing.*

WORKS BY REV. C. J. VAUGHAN D.D.

FORGET THINE OWN PEOPLE. An Appeal for Missions. Small Crown 8vo. Price 3s. 6d. [*In the Press.*

WORDS OF HOPE FROM THE PULPIT OF THE TEMPLE CHURCH. Crown 8vo. Price 5s.

Third Edition.

THE YOUNG LIFE EQUIPPING IT-SELF FOR GOD'S SERVICE. Being Four Sermons Preached before the University of Cambridge in November, 1872. Crown 8vo. Price 3s. 6d.

"Has all the writer's characteristics of devotedness, purity, and high moral tone."—*London Quarterly Review.*

"As earnest, eloquent, and as liberal as everything else that he writes."—*Examiner.*

WORKS BY THE REV. G. S. DREW, M.A.,
VICAR OF TRINITY, LAMBETH.

Second Edition.

SCRIPTURE LANDS IN CONNECTION WITH THEIR HISTORY. Bevelled Boards, 8vo. Price 10s. 6d.

"Mr. Drew has invented a new method of illustrating Scripture history — from observation of the countries. Instead of narrating his travels, and referring from time to time to the facts of sacred history belonging to the different countries, he writes an outline history of the Hebrew nation from Abraham downwards, with special reference to the various points in which the geography illustrates the history. . . He is very successful in picturing to his readers the scenes before his own mind."—*Saturday Review.*

Second Edition.

NAZARETH : ITS LIFE AND LES-SONS. Second Edition. In small 8vo, cloth. Price 5s.

"We have read the volume with great interest. It is at once succinct and sug-

gestive, reverent and ingenious, observant of small details, and yet not forgetful of great principles."—*British Quarterly Review.*

"A very reverent attempt to elicit and develope Scripture intimations respecting our Lord's thirty years' sojourn at Nazareth. The author has wrought well at the unworked mine, and has produced a very valuable series of Scripture lessons, which will be found both profitable and singularly interesting."—*Guardian*

THE DIVINE KINGDOM ON EARTH AS IT IS IN HEAVEN. In demy 8vo, bound in cloth. Price 10s. 6d.

"Thoughtful and eloquent. . . . Full of original thinking admirably expressed." —*British Quarterly Review.*

"Entirely valuable and satisfactory. . . . . . . There is no living divine to whom the authorship would not be a credit." —*Literary Churchman.*

WORKS OF THE LATE REV. F. W. ROBERTSON.

NEW AND CHEAPER EDITIONS.

SERMONS.

Vol. I. Small crown 8vo. Price 3s. 6d.
Vol. II. Small crown 8vo. Price 3s. 6d.
Vol. III. Small crown 8vo. Price 3s. 6d.
Vol. IV. Small crown 8vo. Price 3s. 6d.

EXPOSITORY LECTURES ON ST. PAUL'S EPISTLE TO THE CORINTHIANS. Small crown 8vo. 5s.

AN ANALYSIS OF MR. TENNYSON'S "IN MEMORIAM." (Dedicated by permission to the Poet-Laureate.) Fcap. 8vo. 2s.

THE EDUCATION OF THE HUMAN RACE. Translated from the German of Gotthold Ephraim Lessing. Fcap. 8vo. 2s. 6d.

LECTURES AND ADDRESSES, WITH OTHER LITERARY REMAINS. A New Edition. With Introduction by the Rev. Stopford A. Brooke, M.A. In One Vol. Uniform with the Sermons. Price 5s.   [*Preparing.*

A LECTURE ON FRED. W. ROBERTSON, M.A. By the Rev. F. A. Noble. Delivered before the Young Men's Christian Association of Pittsburgh, U.S. 1s. 6d

WORKS BY THE REV. STOPFORD A. BROOKE, M.A.

Chaplain in Ordinary to Her Majesty the Queen.

THE LATE REV. F. W. ROBERTSON, M.A., LIFE AND LETTERS OF. Edited by Stopford Brooke, M.A.

I. In 2 vols., uniform with the Sermons. Price 7s. 6d.

II. Library Edition, in demy 8vo, with Two Steel Portraits. Price 12s.

III. A Popular Edition, in 1 vol. 6s.

THEOLOGY IN THE ENGLISH POETS. Being Lectures delivered by the Rev. Stopford A. Brooke.
[*Preparing.*

Seventh Edition.

CHRIST IN MODERN LIFE. Sermons Preached in St. James's Chapel, York Street, London. Crown 8vo. 7s. 6d.

"Nobly fearless and singularly strong. . . . carries our admiration throughout." —*British Quarterly Review.*

Second Edition.
FREEDOM IN THE CHURCH OF ENGLAND. Six Sermons suggested by the Voysey Judgment. In 1 vol. Crown 8vo, cloth. 3s. 6d.

"A very fair statement of the views in respect to freedom of thought held by the liberal party in the Church of England."— *Blackwood's Magazine.*

"Interesting and readable, and characterised by great clearness of thought, frankness of statement, and moderation of tone."—*Church Opinion.*

Seventh Edition.
SERMONS Preached in St. James's Chapel, York Street, London. Crown 8vo. 6s.

"No one who reads these sermons will wonder that Mr. Brooke is a great power in London, that his chapel is thronged, and his followers large and enthusiastic. They are fiery, energetic, impetuous sermons, rich with the treasures of a cultivated imagination."—*Guardian.*

THE LIFE AND WORK OF FREDERICK DENISON MAURICE: A Memorial Sermon. Crown 8vo, sewed. 1s.

THE CORNHILL LIBRARY OF FICTION.

3s. 6d. per Volume.

IT is intended in this Series to produce books of such merit that readers will care to preserve them on their shelves. They are well printed on good paper, handsomely bound, with a Frontispiece, and are sold at the moderate price of 3s. 6d. each.

A FIGHT FOR LIFE. By Moy Thomas.

ROBIN GRAY. By Charles Gibbon.

"Pure in sentiment, well written, and cleverly constructed."—*British Quarterly Review.*
"A pretty tale, prettily told."—*Athenæum.*

"A novel of tender and pathetic interest."—*Globe.*
"An unassuming, characteristic, and entertaining novel."—*John Bull.*

KITTY. By Miss M. Betham-Edwards.

"Lively and clever . . . There is a certain dash in every description; the dialogue is bright and sparkling."—*Athenæum.*

"Very pleasant and amusing."—*Globe.*
"A charming novel."—*John Bull.*

HIRELL. By John Saunders.

"A powerful novel . . . a tale written by a poet."—*Spectator.*
"A novel of extraordinary merit."—*Morning Post.*

"We have nothing but words of praise to offer for its style and composition."—*Examiner.*

ONE OF TWO. By J. Hain Friswell.

"Told with spirit . . . the plot is skilfully made."—*Spectator.*

"Admirably narrated, and intensely interesting."—*Public Opinion.*

READY MONEY MORTIBOY. A Matter-of-Fact Story.

"There is not a dull page in the whole story."—*Standard.*
"A very interesting and uncommon story."—*Vanity Fair.*

"One of the most remarkable novels which has appeared of late."—*Pall Mall Gazette.*

GOD'S PROVIDENCE HOUSE. By Mrs. G. L. Banks.

"Far above the run of common three-volume novels, evincing much literary power in not a few graphic descriptions of manners and local customs. . . . A genuine sketch."—*Spectator.*

"Possesses the merit of care, industry, and local knowledge."—*Athenæum.*
"Wonderfully readable. The style is very simple and natural."—*Morning Post.*

FOR LACK OF GOLD. By Charles Gibbon.

"A powerfully written nervous story."—*Athenæum.*
"A piece of very genuine workmanship."—*British Quarterly Review.*
"There are few recent novels more powerful and engrossing."—*Examiner.*

ABEL DRAKE'S WIFE. By John Saunders.

"A striking book, clever, interesting, and original. We have seldom met with a book so thoroughly true to life, so deeply

interesting in its detail, and so touching in its simple pathos."—*Athenæum.*

THE HOUSE OF RABY. By Mrs. G. Hooper.

OTHER STANDARD NOVELS TO FOLLOW.